ALSO BY ALEX BERENSON

Nonfiction

The Number

Lost in Kandahar

The Prince of Beers

Tell Your Children

Fiction

JOHN WELLS SERIES

The Faithful Spy

The Ghost War

The Silent Man

The Midnight House

The Secret Soldier

The Shadow Patrol

The Night Ranger

The Counterfeit Agent

Twelve Days

The Wolves

The Prisoner

The Deceivers

THE
POWER
COUPLE

ALEX
BERENSON

SIMON & SCHUSTER
New York London Toronto Sydney New Delhi

Simon & Schuster
1230 Avenue of the Americas
New York, NY 10020

First Simon & Schuster hardcover edition February 2021

SIMON & SCHUSTER and colophon are registered
trademarks of Simon & Schuster, Inc.

For information about special discounts for bulk purchases,
please contact Simon & Schuster Special Sales at 1-866-506-1949
or business@simonandschuster.com.

The Simon & Schuster Speakers Bureau can bring authors to
your live event. For more information or to book an event, contact
the Simon & Schuster Speakers Bureau at 1-866-248-3049
or visit our website at www.simonspeakers.com.

Interior design by Kyle Kabel

Manufactured in the United States of America

1   3   5   7   9   10   8   6   4   2

Library of Congress Cataloging-in-Publication Data
Names: Berenson, Alex, author.
Title: The power couple : a novel / Alex Berenson.
Description: First Simon & Schuster hardcover edition. | New York :
Simon & Schuster, 2021. |
Identifiers: LCCN 2020018866 (print) | LCCN 2020018867 (ebook) |
ISBN 9781982103699 (hardcover) | ISBN 9781982103705 (paperback) |
ISBN 9781982103712 (ebook)
Subjects: GSAFD: Romantic suspense fiction.
Classification: LCC PS3602.E75146 P69 2021 (print) | LCC PS3602.E75146 (ebook) |
DDC 813/.6—dc23
LC record available at https://lccn.loc.gov/2020018866
LC ebook record available at https://lccn.loc.gov/2020018867

ISBN 978-1-9821-0369-9
ISBN 978-1-9821-0371-2 (ebook)

For Percy

Prologue

Marriage is a mirror.

Your spouse, the first person you see when you open your eyes. The last you touch as you slip into bed. The person who knows you better than anyone else. Who shares your public joys and private sorrows. Who beds you and you alone. Who makes children with you and builds those children into adults.

How it's meant to be, anyway. The deal you've made. Both of you.

Call your spouse your best friend, if you must. Your partner. Really your spouse is your *reflection*. That face, always there. That body, reaching when you do. Inescapable. A comfort mostly, a burden sometimes. Haven't we all dreamed of different faces, different bodies? Taller, fitter, darker, lighter, more beautiful in a hundred different ways?

But we have our own, and that's enough. It has to be.

Nothing lasts forever. Time cuts, the wounds barely visible at first, then obvious. Bellies sag. Gray hairs pop. Skin loses its glow. Muscles soften. Still you're *you*. You'll always be you.

So you think. So you tell yourself.

Then one day you look in the mirror. And you can't recognize yourself.

You can't recognize *anything*.

PROLOGUE

o   o

To have and to hold, from this day forward, for better, for worse, for richer, for poorer, in sickness and in health, to love and to cherish, till death do us part.

This is the story of how I broke my vows. Broke that mirror.

Don't judge me until you've finished.

I

KIRA AND REBECCA

(NOW)

1

Barcelona, Spain

Have fun! See you at midnight like we agreed! XXX Mom

Kira Unsworth swiped left, stung the red delete box. Goodbye. She didn't remember *agreeing*. She remembered Rebecca saying *Midnight, okay?*

Not okay. Not even close. Even if Jacques didn't show . . . and Jacques *was* going to show . . . she wasn't Cinderella and she wasn't going to be home at midnight. Not in Barcelona. People came from all over to party here, the ultimate late-night city.

She could say the time difference had confused her, though Mom wouldn't bite. *Did it confuse your phone too?* Rebecca could smell fibs from ten feet away. *You do remember your dear old mother works for the FBI.* Trying to sound like she was joking, though they both knew she wasn't. The words a challenge: *Don't even try it.*

Mostly Kira didn't. She'd learned the best lies were the ones she didn't have to tell. Tonight she would play it cool, no excuses. *I'm nineteen, I'm not a baby, come on.*

Dad would be fine as long as she made it back by one. Maybe even a little later. Good ol' Bri, part of him still wanted to *be* nineteen. With his microbrews and Nirvana T-shirts.

3

Even Becks would lighten up once Kira got back to their Airbnb. She knew midnight was ridiculous.

Reediculous, Kira mouthed at the girl in the mirror behind the bar. The room around her was long and dark and stuffed with torn leather couches and paintings of long-gone Europeans that had been covered in graffiti and sliced up. The net effect was a castle post–zombie apocalypse. But with better music. MGMT shading into Twenty One Pilots shading into Fleet Foxes. Even the occasional band Kira didn't know, and she knew just about everything. She loved new music. She loved music, period. The bar was called The Mansion—lots of Barcelona bars had English names—and was supposed to be one of the coolest places in the city. Though it was still mostly empty.

Kira should have been intimidated to be here alone. She was, a little. But she felt more confident than she'd expected. Probably because she already knew she was meeting someone.

She was drinking sangria from a battered copper cup. Dark and sweet and it didn't seem to have much kick, but she felt soft after one drink. She tipped the dregs into her mouth and set the cup down. The bartender slid over. He had wide dark eyes, nice arms poking out from his black T-shirt.

"One more?" Everyone in Europe insisted on talking to her in English. Of course not too many Spaniards had blue eyes. But couldn't she pass for German? Swedish? They all knew she was American before she opened her mouth.

"Stella, *por favor*." She didn't want to be drunk when Jacques got here.

"Try the Estrella, it's local. Better."

She nodded. The bartender turned around, leaned over the mini-fridge. He rummaged around a little longer than he needed to, made sure she had time to check out his cute butt—in his cute black jeans. At last he pulled a brown bottle, popped the top with a flourish.

"First time in Barcelona?"

"First *night* in Barcelona. Where is everyone?"

"Only ten forty-five. You'll see. Okay, first night, the cerveza, you don't pay." He tapped his chest.

4

"Thank you."

He winked, *American girls are good for business*. She sipped her beer, washing the sticky sangria from her mouth. Nice to be in a country where she could drink legally, no fake IDs, no frat basements. Civilized.

Her phone buzzed. A text from a number starting with thirty-three. The country code for France, as she'd just learned. Jacques. Though she hadn't put his name in her phone. He'd have to earn that.

See you soon

Here, she typed, then deleted it. She didn't want to seem too eager. Though she was.

o   o

Jacques was a graduate student at the Sorbonne. Kira had met him the night before, in Paris. She and her brother, Tony, were at this café on the Place de la République, this big square where French students hung out. Tony had dragged her there. Tony was seventeen. Tony was tall and skinny. Tony was . . . a dork. The classic Tony story: A week into ninth grade a bee flew into a Coke he was drinking, stung his mouth. The next day he came to school with his mouth swollen and grotesque, his lower lip the size of a tire. He looked like a washed-up model who'd cheaped out on plastic surgery. *Why did everybody make fun of me*, he said that night in Kira's room, *I didn't want to drink a bee*. Kira could only shake her head. She'd never even had acne.

Worse, Tony desperately wanted to escape loser prison. Kira knew the effort would only make matters worse. Despite her advice, he'd even worn his hair in a ponytail for a while in tenth grade. He was still living that one down. Maybe he could start fresh in college.

Poor Tony. Kira looked out for him, truly, but she could only do so much. The worst part, he was funny and smart and *nice*. She wasn't saying so because she was his sister. He was. And he was going to be handsome once he grew into his face and gained about twenty pounds.

A couple of her friends had said so. *Wait until he's twenty-five, we'll all be sorry we missed out.*

A forecast that hardly helped him now.

Anyway, Tony had wanted to go to this Place de la République. *Where the students protest*, he told Kira.

Kira had no idea what French students might have to protest. Paris looked pretty good to her. But she was glad Tony made her go. Because afterward they stopped in this café for a *bière pression* or whatever, and in walked tall, dark, and yummy. In general French dudes were good-looking, but they came off as too stylish for her taste. Even though it was July they hardly sweated. Kira didn't want to worry that the guy she was with had better hair than she did.

Not this guy. His hair was cut close to his head like he didn't want to have to think about it. His stubble didn't look planned. It looked like he'd forgotten to shave that morning. He was big, broad-shouldered. He looked like a Marine. A French Marine. When he caught her looking at him he didn't play it cool and pretend he hadn't noticed. He tilted his head, stared back. Then smiled.

Thirty seconds later he was at their table. Her table. Tony might as well have been invisible.

"What's your name?" In English, of course.

"Kira."

He extended his hand, the gesture oddly endearing. He had big hands, gorgeous long fingers. "Kira. I'm Jacques. What's your favorite thing in Paris so far?"

The question was blunt enough to flummox her. The Louvre? The Eiffel Tower? She didn't want to sound like a tourist. Dumb, she *was* a tourist. "Kind of unfair, don't you think?"

"How so?"

"Run it on an American girl to throw her, and you've got some cool answer ready."

"Swear I've never asked before."

"Ever been to America, Jacques?"

"Maybe."

"If I came up to you on your third day in New York and I said what's your favorite thing—"

"The subways. Not like our little Métro, with the tickets and the air puffs. Steel submarines that never stop running."

Not a bad answer. "Well I'm from D.C., and our subway sucks."

"We're actually from Maryland," Tony said.

"This is my brother, Tony."

"Hi-oh."

"Hi-oh," Jacques returned. Like Tony was a parrot that had spoken for the first time and needed reassurance.

"Tony was just going outside to see the protests." She felt guilty for getting rid of him, but only a little. Having him watch her flirt would embarrass him and throw her off her game. Besides, they'd been hanging out nonstop for three straight days.

"Ahh, the protests. I forget what they're protesting this time."

"Universal basic income," Tony said.

As he stood up, he spilled his beer, sending a bubbly river Jacques's way.

Jacques grabbed a napkin more quickly than Kira thought was possible and mopped the beer before it could soak him.

"Sorry."

"It's okay." Jacques seemed unflustered, and Kira liked him all the more. "I'll take care of it."

o   o

They watched him go.

"Your brother," Jacques said.

"He's a good kid."

He nodded. She could feel them deciding as a pair not to mention Tony again.

"That was amazing."

"What?"

"Your reflexes. With the beer."

"Oh." He didn't seem to know what to say.

"Have you decided your favorite thing yet?"

Really, her favorite thing so far had been the women here, the way they dressed and walked and held themselves. The way they ate and smoked. They all looked so *confident*, even if they weren't pretty, even if they weren't young. They were stylish without even trying. Unlike her mother. It wasn't that Rebecca wasn't successful. But she never made anything look *easy*.

Kira wasn't going to explain any of this to Jacques. "Let's say I like keeping my options open."

He smiled. One of his top teeth had a tiny crack. "That how it is? French boy, good story for your friends?"

"Dumb American girl? Fresh meat?"

o o

She'd grown used to standing around kegs in dirty basements, yelling over the music. *That new Kanye song sucks*, or *Yeah, I know pre-med is a ton of studying but if I get in doctors have it made*. The conversation was juvenile, just something to get out of the way before they fooled around. She felt different with this guy. More grown-up. Like she'd enjoy hanging out with him even if all they did was talk.

"So what brings you to Paris?"

"My parents' twentieth anniversary. They decided to take us to Europe."

"My parents got divorced when I was eight."

"I thought mine might. There was like five years when they hardly spoke . . ."

He stared steadily at her with his gray-green eyes.

"Don't know why I'm telling you this, it's not something I talk about."

"Because you'll never see me again and my parents, they stunk too."

"Don't be so sure."

"Don't be sure my parents stunk? I am *quite* sure, Kira."

She liked the sound of her name in his mouth. "That we'll never see each other again."

He closed his eyes, opened them again. "Now we have."

Cheesy but good.

o   o

He told her he was twenty-six, studying for a PhD in economics.

"You don't look like any of the grad students I know."

"A personal trainer too."

"Full service for middle-aged Paris ladies?"

"It's mostly men. And, too bad, some of them think like you."

"I'll bet." She expected him to smile. Instead he frowned.

"My job is to provide motivation for people who want to lose weight, be healthy. Make sure they stretch, do the exercises properly. Why must I deal with being pinched by some husband?"

He looked so serious, so offended, so *French*, she couldn't help but laugh. "Poor baby."

He touched a finger to her lips. *"Ferme ta bouche, mademoiselle."* But he was smiling.

o   o

Tony proved he wasn't completely clueless by giving them almost an hour before he came back. "Kira, we promised we'd be back by twelve thirty. The hotel's way on the other side of town."

"Paris isn't that big."

"It's pretty big."

"Five minutes?"

He walked outside again.

She and Jacques stared comfortably at each other across the table. A smile played over his lips.

"Tomorrow I take you to the best place in the whole city."

"Your apartment, right?"

He shook his head like she'd disappointed him. "Canal Saint-Martin. It's a beautiful walk. You'll see." He reached across the table, squeezed her hand. A flame of pleasure lit her arm.

"Can't. I'm sorry."

"You have zee *boyfriend* at home?" He put on a ridiculous accent. To hide his disappointment, she thought. "You have zee *promise ring*. For zee *chastity*."

"We're going to Barcelona."

"Stay. Take a train on Sunday."

"If you knew my parents—"

"Then I will come to you. Tomorrow night."

"That's silly." *Shut up, shut up*, she told herself. *Don't blow it.*

"Americans, you have no idea what romance is. Romance, it's seeing a beautiful girl and knowing that if you have to get on a train to see her again, no problem."

"We know what romance is. We just don't have time for it."

"Exactly. Besides, I love Barcelona. All those Catalan girls." He winked. Not too many guys could pull off a wink, but he could. "Tomorrow then? Unless you don't want me to."

She knew what her mom would say: *He seems pretty aggressive, K.*

"It's just a drink. Maybe dancing. Give me your number. I'll text you in the morning."

So she did. He stood, leaned across the table. Kissed her once, lightly, and ran his fingers down her cheek. Then he was gone. She watched him walk out with what she knew was a silly dazed smile.

o   o

He didn't make her suffer. He texted before breakfast. They arranged to meet here, The Mansion, at 11 p.m. She told Tony but swore him to secrecy. She didn't want her parents to know. Rebecca would insist on hearing everything about Jacques. And she wouldn't be happy with what Kira told her. *Twenty-six is too old, K. Did you tell him you were nineteen?* No, she was keeping this date from Mom.

A lie she didn't have to tell.

Ten fifty-two, her phone said now. Kira ran early, she was Rebecca's daughter that way. *Build in a few extra minutes, you won't be stressed. A little edge but every edge matters.* Another of Mom's annoyingly accurate life lessons. She should write a book. *The Seven Habits of Highly Effective FBI Agents.*

Kira took a pull of the Estrella, felt the room blur a little more. She wasn't a huge drinker. But she liked the temporary softening in her *edge*, yes. Her mom had drilled the lesson, *Life is tough, especially for a woman, you can never stop paying attention . . .*

Mmph. Rebecca was usually right, but that didn't make the constant prodding any easier. She might as well be here if they were going to talk in Kira's head all night. Maybe they should try it. Hang out for a few hours. Would Becks chill, flirt with this bartender? Did she have any game? Kira had never known her mom to flirt, though she'd seen pictures from back in the day that suggested the possibility.

She took another swallow of the beer. She didn't have to worry about drinking and driving, anyway. This bar was a max twenty-minute walk from the apartment they'd rented. Three bedrooms and two bathrooms in this cool old building up in Eixample, not too far from La Rambla.

o o

She'd made sure to give Tony the bedroom next to her parents. The trip was their twentieth-anniversary present to each other, no doubt they'd be enjoying each other's company. So to speak. Lucky for Tony, he was a heavy sleeper. Kira looked at herself in the mirror, remembering the only time she'd caught her parents truly going at it.

She was in a strange mood tonight. Maybe drunker than she thought. She rarely let herself have this memory. It shamed her.

She was a sophomore in high school, a month short of sixteen. The middle of the night, and she woke up famished. She was in her not-eating phase. Five nine, almost five ten, Kira was, aiming for one hundred twenty pounds. The target seemed reasonable enough, the numbers drumming in her head. Five nine one two zero, the zip code of the promised land. If she lined them up a whole world would open for her. *Beverly Hills, that's where I want to be . . .*

She never went full anorexic, she and her skinny-ass friends liked to joke, *You never go full anorexic,* the line stolen, repurposed, from *Tropic Thunder.* No, you starve yourself just enough so everyone says how good you look. You turn the boys' heads and the girls' too. Not so much that you can count your ribs. Not all of them, anyway. *Good anorexia,* they called it.

But good anorexia was a balancing act. And Kira tipped far enough the whole world treated her differently that fall. Like she was a crystal; Baccarat, shiny, precious, easily shattered. She watched her parents watching her at breakfast and dinner, dancing around the *issue.* They snuck looks at her plate, asked if she wanted more yogurt or carrots. They never knew what to say. Looking back, Kira had to admit that watching Becks—sure-footed Rebecca—turn wobbly and tongue-tied had been part of the appeal. Cruel and selfish in retrospect. Maybe even at the time.

Lucky her, even if she didn't think so back then, she liked to eat too much to starve herself. She never went below one-two-two, maybe one-two-one on the digital scale she bought. And she was past all that now. She hadn't even needed to *see someone*—a phrase that Mrs. Daye, her kindly physics teacher, tossed out after she nearly fell over one morning—to get her head on straight.

She just decided she was tired of being hungry. She wanted to be strong. She wanted to play soccer without worrying she was going to collapse. She was about one hundred thirty-eight now, one-three-nine, though she tried not to weigh herself too often. When the numbers lined up in her head she swiped them left.

But on that fine December night, morning, whatever 3 a.m. was, her parents and brother asleep, she'd woken up hungry. That month was the worst of it, her lowest point. She'd always *liked* eating at Thanksgiving and Christmas, not just the turkey but the desserts, all those carbs and gooey fillings.

She snapped awake with one thought, the leftover pumpkin pie, creamy and sweet. She stepped out of bed. Every light in the house was off, her dad liked a completely dark house. She'd learned how to move in the black. She heard Tony snoring in his bedroom on the other side of the wall and behind it a murmur she didn't recognize.

Until she opened the door and stepped into the hall.

And realized Becks and Bri were most certainly not asleep. What she had stumbled on was not the nonsense all parents got on with from time to time, *Go to sleep kids, Mom and Dad need a little time together*. No. Rebecca was moaning, low and wordless and involuntary. Like she wanted to catch her breath and couldn't. Like something inside her was breaking loose and taking her with it.

Kira was a virgin back then. She'd spent the fall playing around with a cute senior named Jared. He was gentle, never pushed her. She was just realizing he might be gay. She didn't care. One strange part of not eating: though she got more male attention than before, she was less interested. And her friends who'd had sex said things like *I'm glad it's over, It didn't hurt that much, It was fine fun actually*. Though Leigh—the soccer goalie, who had more experience than the others—had refused to say much, just, *Oh, you'll see*, her eyes stunned and quiet. Kira hadn't understood why. Now she did.

Because what she heard in that hallway was not *fine fun actually* but something she hadn't known existed, a pleasure she had thought was a fantasy that YouPorn proffered to horny boys.

She stood frozen, feet locked to the hallway carpet. Suddenly her mother *groaned*, a long low sound. Kira couldn't imagine what could make Becks make that noise. Couldn't imagine, though she knew. Whatever her father was doing or saying she couldn't hear, a minor blessing.

She sidled back to her bedroom, shut the door firmly.

Though now that she knew what was happening she couldn't help but hear. It went on another fourteen minutes, she clocked it. And who knew how long before? She was almost proud of them; they were both over forty.

By the time she fell asleep, she knew she'd never think about sex the same way again. Not now that she knew what it could be. She dumped Jared that afternoon. Maybe she wasn't ready to lose her virginity, but she was done hanging out with a guy who was more interested in his fellow baseball players than her. She started eating again too—she remembered a couple months later seeing her parents grin as she insisted her father fire up the grill on a cold February night and barbeque a steak.

In fact, Kira saw now what she never had before. That night had marked the beginning of the end of her anorexic episode. You couldn't have the pleasures of the flesh if you were a skeleton.

Great talk, Kira.

Kira Unsworth, nineteen, five foot nine inches tall, majoring in who-knows-what at Tufts University. Volunteer at Boston Children's, and not in a half-assed way: She never missed a week. She made the kids forget themselves for a little while. Secret reader of romance novels, the old Harlequin ones. Bit of a smart-ass.

She wasn't perfect. She'd spent a month flirting with a pretty lesbian in her Introduction to Women's, Gender, and Sexuality Studies class just to see how it felt. When the girl finally tried to kiss her, Kira had said, *Oh, no, I'm straight,* like the girl couldn't possibly have thought otherwise. She'd dumped her last boyfriend by text. He'd deserved it.

She was okay, really. Not the worst.

Ten fifty-nine.

Right on time Jacques showed up.

With a girl.

2

Rebecca and Brian and Tony found the wide stone apartment building just where they'd left it on Carrer de València. Twelve twenty-three a.m.

No Kira.

No shock, either. Rebecca had expected Kira would want to prove her independence by running late. She'd be back soon enough. Or maybe she'd text, *Promise 1*.

Rebecca didn't love the idea of a nineteen-year-old girl out alone in a foreign city. But Barcelona was safe—safer than Boston—and Kira had insisted she wanted a few hours to herself. She was cool-headed for her age, trustworthy. She had survived her first year at Tufts without much damage, one cheating boyfriend and one stolen jacket notwithstanding. She was the one her friends texted when they found themselves stumbling out of the party with the quarterback and his two best friends: *find me plz they say its cool idk . . .*

Rebecca couldn't imagine being the mother of a quote-unquote difficult teenager. The easy ones were difficult enough.

Still, she was faintly disappointed Kira wasn't waiting. She'd imagined maybe they'd go for a drink, leave Bri and Tony at the apartment. She should have said so before dinner. But she'd worried Kira might give her a half-pitying *Mom, you're way too old for these places* look.

The foolish pride of the fortysomething woman.

o o

She walked hand in hand with Brian up the sweeping marble staircase to their second-floor apartment. "A Grand Apartment," the listing had promised: a living room with twelve-foot ceilings, a crystal chandelier, a Juliet balcony, and yes, a grand piano. Four hundred sixty euros a night. But they said they wouldn't worry about money on this trip. Rebecca said, anyway. *Let's do it right. I'm budgeting a thousand dollars for every year we've been married*, she had told Brian.

Twenty K? His nostrils twitched the way they had in the lean years. *Bet you'll have no problem spending it.*

She hadn't.

The big problem with the apartment: no air-conditioning. After fifteen years in Birmingham and Houston and Washington, three cities where ice-cold air was practically an entitlement, Rebecca wondered how she would sleep. No wonder the Spanish stayed up so late.

Still, she liked Barcelona better than Paris, which felt like a theme park. All those Americans and Brazilians and Chinese shuffling around Notre Dame, hoovering up skirts at the Galeries Lafayette, *We're not so different, we all love to shop.* Someone needed to create a Disney World–style app to beat the lines, *optimize the experience.* She should tell Brian.

Barcelona had tons of tourists too. Still, it felt a little more real. And the Gaudí architecture was fascinating. Buildings that seemed to be melting. Maybe they were. Maybe *she* was. She mopped the sweat from her forehead, flopped on the couch, kicked off her low black heels, stretched out her legs. Still good. Legs were the last to go. Ask any coroner. *Based on her calves she might be as young as twenty-five, but her neck proves she's forty-three.* Forensics!

She was buzzed, she realized. If not flat drunk. Besides the pitcher of sangria the three of them had shared, she and Brian had split a bottle of wine. She hadn't had this much to drink in a long time.

Maybe since that last dinner with Todd Taylor.

All at once she could see his face. His hazel eyes and creased tan skin. She shoved the memory down. In the garbage. Where it belonged. Especially at this moment.

o   o

"Wine?" Brian said. They'd bought two bottles at a convenience store. With fluorescent lights. Even in Barcelona not everything was cool.

"The white is cold, right?"

"Coldish."

"Rhymes with goldfish. Sold."

"Can I have a beer?" Tony said.

Rebecca: "No." Brian: "Yes."

Brian liked to be the cool one, make her play the villain.

"It's Barcelona."

She had a feeling she would hear that answer a lot on this trip. *It's Barcelona. It's Madrid. It's our anniversary.*

"You think he doesn't drink at home, Becks? Remember that morning, we picked him up—"

She remembered. Tony had texted, *I'm in Silver Spring please get me please.* When they arrived they found that someone had written I LUV DICK! AND BEES! in orange on his forehead. "AND BEES!" seemed especially cruel.

Tony. Let me wipe that off.

Wipe what off?

"He needs to learn to hold his booze," Brian said now.

"Okay, one beer. You pour it in a glass though and drink it like you're civilized."

"It's actually slower to drink it from the bottle."

"Quit while you're ahead, my number one son."

"Anyone see an opener?" Brian yelled from the kitchen.

She looked at the wine bottle. "It's a screw top."

"My favorite kind of top." Brian reappeared with three wineglasses.

"Dad!" Tony said.

Any sexual banter between them creeped Tony out. Rebecca supposed the reaction was normal. Kira had never seemed as bothered. Instead she looked at them with her cool blue eyes—Brian's eyes. A look that shut the jokes down in a hurry, as Kira no doubt intended.

Brian poured the wine, handed Tony the third glass. Tony raised his eyebrows, *Beer from a wineglass?*, but wisely kept his mouth shut. Brian sat beside her. "Cheers."

"I love you, husband." She did, too. Even if she'd forgotten for a while. A long while.

His eyes flashed. She wondered if he too was thinking about the years they'd spent wandering the marital desert. He kissed her lightly. "Here's to twenty years. And three months."

"And twenty more with these rug rats out of the house so we can do what we like." She put her glass to his harder than she had intended. The *clink* echoed off the high ceilings and wine slopped out.

"Glad I didn't splurge on the twelve-euro bottle." He nodded at the piano. "You should play."

"I'll be terrible."

Not true. She'd be excellent. She'd played growing up, lessons four times a week for eleven years. She was skilled enough to impress people who didn't know better, but also skilled enough to know how big a canyon lay between her and greatness. She played the piano. The true artists *felt* it, melded themselves to it.

In college she'd quit. Cold. She'd told herself playing was as effete and pretentious as every other part of her life at the time. Though she knew it wasn't, knew she'd earned her skill and she ought to protect it. Knew the real reason she quit was that she couldn't accept she wasn't good enough to get into Julliard. Brian was the one who'd sent her back to playing, and for that she would be forever grateful.

o   o

She slid across the polished wood floor in her stocking feet and sat at the piano.

"Remember this?" She hadn't played the Schubert in years but the notes came back effortlessly.

The sangria made her sloppy, and this piano hadn't been tuned in a while. No matter, she played with flair, half-drunk melodrama, raised her hands high, pounded the keys. Made sure the neighbors would hear and the cats on the street.

Then the Schubert was done and she slid into the Beethoven, lush and romantic. Now and again she turned her head toward Brian. He leaned against the wall and sipped his wine and watched with his unreadable smile, the one she'd loved until she hadn't and now did again.

When she finished he came to her, stood behind her. Put his hands on her shoulders and leaned over and kissed her.

"Bed," he murmured in her ear.

"Tony," she whispered back.

o   o

Across the room Tony stood from the couch like he'd heard his name.

"Mom. You know it's like one twenty."

She loved Tony more than anything, her only son, et cetera . . . but he seemed to have no idea that she and Brian were having a moment. He desperately needed a girlfriend, or just a girl friend.

"Yes, so?"

"Where's Kira?"

3

"Kira." Jacques kissed her cheek. "This is Lilly. Lilly, Kira."

Lilly was early twenties, brown eyes, with a long platinum-blond wig.

Kira's stomach knotted. Jacques had brought his *girlfriend*?

"My sister."

Now Kira saw the resemblance: the strong chin, the narrow mouth. "You didn't think . . ."

Tonight he was wearing a baseball cap with a big unbroken bill and a logo she didn't recognize. She didn't like the hat. It made him look like a bro. "I didn't bring my *brother*."

Lilly said something in French.

"I don't speak French."

Lilly smirked. "I said, American heartbreakers, better keep an eye on you."

That fast Kira couldn't stand this hipper-than-thou Paris chick. Lilly wore a black Violent Femmes T-shirt, purple velvet pants tucked into knee-high black boots, and a sneer. Jacques's eyes tracked between the two women as if he'd just realized his mistake.

"Let's have a drink."

Kira lifted her Estrella. "I'm okay."

The place was filling now, louder by the minute, the bartenders busy. They were stuck at the bar for a while before Jacques could order.

21

Kira had dressed for a date, an off-the-shoulder white peasant top, a black flowered skirt, mid-calf gladiator-style sandals for an edgy touch.

"Nice sandals."

Was Lilly being sarcastic? *Better to be polite*, Rebecca always said. *Be the higher mammal*. "Thanks."

"So popular in Paris two years ago."

At least now Kira didn't have to wonder.

The bartender handed Jacques a pitcher of sangria and three copper mugs. They squeezed around a circular table in the back. Lilly gabbed at Jacques in French. No doubt intentionally, knowing Kira couldn't understand. Kira didn't mind, she had to figure out her next move. She was torn between wanting to ditch them and making sure Lilly didn't win without a fight.

Jacques poured sangria. "To new friends. *Salud.*"

"First time in Europe, yes?" Lilly said.

Kira wished she could spin a fable about her globe-trotting youth. "*Oui.*"

"Here I thought you didn't speak French."

"You at the Sorbonne too, or do you spend all your time looking for velvet pants?"

"They don't sell these at Abercrombie." *Aber-crombie.*

During Kira's anorexic days she'd found she could be nasty. No surprise, hunger didn't improve her mood. Now that she lived on full rations she didn't usually play the mean girl.

Except on special occasions. Like tonight. She poked at Lilly's Violent Femmes T-shirt, just above the waist of the pants. As she'd expected they were a touch too tight, giving the French girl the hint of a muffin top. "Pro tip. Up a size next time."

Lilly muttered under her breath, stood up, and walked off.

"Why is she here?"

Jacques shrugged and an oddly helpless expression crossed his face. "I promise you she'll find a guy, she won't bother us."

"Hope she finds somebody soon, because I can't stay out all night."

"What time?"

"I turn into a pumpkin at one."

"One? That's barely one hour and a half."

"One thirty *maybe*. But you'll be here tomorrow, right?"

"Yes, but I have to go back in the afternoon. I have clients."

Easy come, easy go. What had seemed like true love barely twenty-four hours ago had turned into a one-night stand before they'd even properly kissed. Lilly's fault. Or maybe the baseball cap's. Either way, Kira wasn't sure how to undo it. More sangria, maybe. She raised her mug. "To Barcelona."

He smiled. She looked at his cracked tooth and nearly forgave him for his terrible sister. "Yes, Barca."

The bar was nearly full now, cool kids shouting in multiple languages. "They know how to have a good time."

"We're lucky, aren't we?" Jacques said abruptly.

"How so?" She hoped he wasn't going cheesy, *I'm so glad we found each other—*

"To be so privileged, live in peace, have the money to do what we like, all the knowledge in the world on a computer in our pockets, *bip bip boop—*"

"You are aware that's not how they sound—"

Lilly came back, poured herself a fresh cup of sangria. "I always feel better after a nice piss. How about you, Kira?"

Kira ignored her.

"What were you talking about, anyway?"

"The benefits of late capitalism," Jacques said.

"Oh yes, Americans never think about capitalism, do they? Early, late, or in the middle. It's just the foul water they drown in."

"Don't see you volunteering at the soup kitchen tonight, Lil." Kira sipped her sangria, promising herself this cup would be her last.

"It's not about volunteering, it's about a just society. So poor people don't depend on *charity* to survive." She spat the word like charity was the worst idea possible.

Kira flashed to Ayla, the seven-year-old she'd been visiting all spring at Boston Children's. A tiny girl with ringlets and big brown eyes.

Barring a miracle, leukemia would kill her. She didn't need a just society, she needed someone to hug her and paint her face like a tiger's.

Only someone who had never volunteered could dismiss the notion so airily. Kira was almost starting to enjoy Lilly in her awfulness.

Jacques said something in French. Lilly snapped back, stood, walked off again.

"I tell her I know what she's doing, it won't work—"

"Are you *sure* she's your sister?"

He laughed like the question had surprised him. "Unfortunately yes. Listen, I have an idea. Let's go to another place, called Helado—"

"Doesn't that mean ice cream?" She'd seen a sign on La Rambla.

"Frozen, yes. It has a dance floor. You like to dance?"

"Now and then." She loved to dance.

"Then yes, really great music, the best, I think." He waved to Lilly, *Come over—*

"Can't we just ditch her?"

"It's not worth it, trust me."

o   o

The lights outside hit Kira harder than she expected.

Lilly pulled a silver cigarette case from her purse. "Brother?"

Jacques shook his head. A small victory, anyway. Kira had only kissed a smoker twice. The sour acrid taste had made her vow never again.

"I'd ask you, Kira, but I know Americans *hate* to smoke, they want to live forever."

"You're gonna look great with a trach hole in your throat."

Jacques led them left and right, through the narrow streets of the Gothic Quarter, the old neighborhood east of La Rambla—the famous pedestrian boulevard—where the city's bars and clubs were concentrated. Kira thought they were headed toward the harbor, though she wasn't sure. No matter. She had her phone, as well as a city map. Rebecca always insisted Kira and Tony carry maps. *In case you lose your phone.* Though Kira couldn't imagine losing her phone. It was never more than a couple feet from her even when she slept.

Anyway, Jacques wasn't exactly leading them into some deserted alley. The streets grew more crowded as they walked, men and women clustering around tiny bar fronts, leaning out windows, drinking beer in the heat.

○   ○

After fifteen minutes or so they crossed a street that was two lanes wide, a superhighway by Gothic Quarter standards. Kira wasn't sure but she thought maybe they'd left the Quarter behind; these streets were just as narrow but not quite as busy.

"Five minutes," Jacques said.

Sure enough, after another five minutes, they came to a windowless three-story brick building. The thump of bass leaked through its walls. She couldn't have found this place on her own. The club had no sign, only a single red bulb in front of a black-painted door. A trim man in a blue T-shirt stood in front, a discreet bouncer.

The man said something to Jacques as they approached.

"Forty euros, twenty for me and ten each for you two." Jacques reached for his wallet. "Let me pay."

Normally Kira would have insisted on paying her own way, but she was still annoyed with Jacques for spoiling their date.

Behind the black door, a cashier sat in a glassed-in booth. Jacques handed over a fifty-euro note and then they were inside. Strobes flashed in the darkness, and an old-school Studio 54–style disco ball spun overhead. A twentysomething woman sat at the DJ station at the back of the dance floor, her hands constantly moving among two iPhones and three turntables. She reminded Kira of those multiarmed Indian statues from her Introduction to World Religions class, the *Whateversvada.* But the woman was fantastic; really good DJs found connections in the music that weren't obvious until they made them. They turned beats into waves, dancing into surfing. Endless summer. The Beastie Boys slid into some kind of African drumming into Cold

War Kids into the briefest cut of Adele, a transition that should never have worked, but it did, yes it did. Plus, the place had a fantastic sound system . . .: pure, clean, the music seemingly coming from everywhere without being overwhelming.

Kira wanted to put her arms up and *move*, open the gates to the rhythm flooding through her.

Or maybe she was just drunk. No matter. Jacques and Lilly turned for the bar, but she grabbed them both and led them to the floor and they danced, hips swaying, nothing mattered but *now*, and Lilly felt it too. She smiled, and Kira grinned back, recognizing a fellow traveler.

Finally, she didn't know how long, Jacques led her off. "Beer?"

"Yes, please."

Lilly stuck out her lower lip as they walked off, an exaggerated pout, *You're leaving me*, but even before they reached the bar, a Spanish guy took her hand and pulled her deeper onto the dance floor.

Kira wanted to pay for their beers, but Jacques insisted. "I owe you. I'm sorry, I know my sister wasn't what you expected."

She couldn't disagree. They found a couch in the corner. Jacques sat next to her and put an arm around her and they watched the dancers writhing in pleasure.

"What would aliens think, if they came down and saw this?" *Drunk question alert!*

"I think they would park their spaceship, yes?" Jacques said, "and join in."

"Intergalactic peace. Well, if me and your sister can get along"— she snuck a look at his watch. About one. *Ugh.* Kira hated to end this night now that they'd finally unlocked it. But she'd better text Becks, check in. She'd promise to be home by two. Two thirty, maybe. She knew she was pushing her luck, but how mad could they get?

She reached into her purse. Gone. Her phone was *gone*. No way. It must have fallen out somehow, this wasn't her usual purse. It was a little date-night black one, a snap instead of a zipper, and she'd over-stuffed it. Stupid. She checked again: three twenty-euro notes, credit card, driver's license—her passport was back at the apartment. Lipstick, mints, condoms. Three condoms. Might as well think positive. A rape whistle courtesy of the Tufts Women's Center and pepper spray courtesy of her mom, *If somebody grabs you, whistling won't cut it.*

No phone. She wondered if she should retrace her steps, but forget it, it was an iPhone, not even a year old, no way was anybody giving it back.

"Can I borrow your phone?" she asked Jacques.

He unlocked it, handed it over. She couldn't remember Rebecca's number for a minute, embarrassing. She always depended on her phone for it. Then she did, sent off a quick text, *Mom its K at helado dance club lost my fone home soon 2ish.*

Okay, not the greatest message but whatever. Now they knew where she was. She clicked Send, watched the text go through. She gave Jacques back his phone. "If she texts let me know."

Just then Lilly showed up, followed by her new dance partner. He was older and rougher than he'd looked from a distance. In his thirties, muscular going to fat. The strobe lights revealed his pitted skin.

Jacques stood and Lilly sat next to Kira on the couch. "This is Rodrigo."

"Hi, Rodrigo."

"He's got a present."

Rodrigo reached into his pocket, came out with a plastic bag. Inside, a glass vial, a tiny silver spoon, a bottle of nasal spray.

He unscrewed the vial, tilted it at them so they could see the white powder inside. His nails were painted black, Kira noticed.

Okayyy then. Kira shook her head, *No thank you.* She'd never even seen the stuff before.

"It's just cocaine," Lilly said.

"Oh, just cocaine." Kira figured coke was just as illegal in Spain as in the United States.

"It's fun."

"You first."

"I thought you'd never ask." Lilly took the vial, spooned out a little bump of white powder. She leaned forward, snorted, and the powder disappeared. *Poof.*

Lilly followed up with two quick hits of nasal spray, leaned back against the couch. "Oh, that's nice. Your turn."

This is where you leave. Kira heard Rebecca's voice in her head, clear and loud. *Get out of there, joke's over.* "Not for me." She waited for Lilly to say something snide.

But Lilly only grinned. "One hit and we'll dance, you'll see, dancing on coke is *the best*—"

"Like Adderall?" She'd taken Adderall a few times, mainly to help finish papers. She had to admit she liked the wide-awake sensation, feeling like she could see around corners. Though the day after, she felt gray and cold, a dementor camped out in her bedroom.

Poor girl's coke, one of her friends had said.

"Try and see."

Suddenly a snippet from this old Killers song was playing:

He doesn't look a thing like Jesus / But he talks like a gentleman / Like you imagined . . .

"When You Were Young," it was called.

Kira loved The Killers. First band she ever cared about. First concert she ever saw. Her drunken brain slid the pieces together: the song was a *sign,* she was in Barcelona, and young and nothing could touch her—

Don't, Rebecca warned, *don't*—

Kira took the spoon and vial from Lilly, dipped the spoon deep into the vial—

"Not so much, first time," Lilly said. She patted Kira's arm, *I'll be your spirit guide.*

Kira tapped the spoon against the top of the vial until most of the coke was gone. "Good?"

"Perfect."

Kira lifted the spoon to her nose, pushed her left nostril shut—

You don't even know these people—

And inhaled.

4

Where's Kira?

Rebecca had been so busy banging at the piano that she'd forgotten her daughter. She grabbed her phone, expecting a text.

Nope. She found herself looking at the usual lock-screen picture of her kids, Kira and Tony standing together, fireworks overhead, red, white, and blue strings across the night sky. Even during the bad years in D.C. Rebecca had insisted they spend Independence Day on the Mall, go in the early afternoon with a blanket and picnic basket. The tradition had taken hold. Rebecca could track their progress as a family by their faces. In this year's photo, only a couple of weeks before, the two wore big mock-goofy smiles and looked relaxed. Happy.

"Bri—"

Her husband was already holding his phone. "Nothing."

She looked to Tony. He shook his head.

"I'm sure she's fine," Brian said.

"Oh, you're *sure?*" Rebecca knew she should control her temper, but the alcohol was coursing through her and fifteen years at the bureau had taught her to hate meaningless reassurance.

Especially since Brian didn't know what she did.

"It's Barcelona. Not Beirut. And it's not like it's five a.m. Just getting started out there."

"She *always* texts."

Rebecca called Kira. The phone rang until it went to voice mail. "Tony, try her please?"

"Voice mail," Tony said.

Rebecca texted Kira: *K where are you? Call me now please.*

"Maybe she met a guy," Brian said. "Or is that what we're afraid of?"

"What was the bar she said she was going to?"

"The Mansion," Tony said. "Supposed to be cool."

Rebecca hesitated. She imagined Kira sitting in the corner of the bar, making out with some hot Spanish guy. Was she really going to be a helicopter parent? *Thwack-thwack-thwack, I'm not letting you out of my sight for more than an hour* . . . Kira was nineteen. Soldiers went to war at nineteen. People got married at nineteen.

"How about we give her until two and if she's not home by then we go over there and drag her out by her hair," Brian said. "Even in D.C. the bars don't close until two."

"Okay, two."

Brian sipped his wine, crisis averted.

"Umm . . ." Tony said.

Rebecca looked over. Her son had the unmistakable look of a teenager about to confess, sheepish and defiant at once. She hated when her kids kept secrets. Unreasonable, she knew. Teenagers were entitled to their own worlds. Pushing too hard only caused a backlash. Yet she couldn't help herself.

"You know something, Tony? Now would be a good time to share."

"Don't be *mad.*"

"We're not mad," Brian said. "We're listening."

Brian reassured. She too often slid into anger.

"She had a date tonight," Tony said. "I promised I wouldn't tell."

"We were with her all day," Rebecca said. "When did she make a *date?*"

"His name's Jacques. She met him last night in Paris."

Now she was genuinely confused.

"He wanted to hang with her up there. She told him we were leaving this morning. He said he'd come down to see her."

Rebecca closed the windows against the street noise. The room was instantly hotter, airless. She felt the sangria washing through her and made herself focus. "This guy yesterday, he was by himself?"

"Yeah. A grad student at the Sorbonne."

French grad students weren't Kira's type. Not as far as Rebecca knew. "What was he studying?" Like it mattered.

Tony shrugged.

"When *exactly* was this?" Brian said.

"Last night, this café on the Place de la République, the Toucan, I think it's called. We were sitting, he came in, like a minute later he was with us. I left, but they talked for an hour at least. She was totally into it." Tony spoke with the dull envy of a virgin who expected he'd be that way forever.

"And this guy, Jacques, he came down here to see her?"

"That's what she told me, that was the plan. He texted her this morning."

"Why didn't she *tell* me? Us?" Though Rebecca could already guess the answer.

"She said you'd freak. He's older, like twenty-six."

"Do you remember what he looked like?" Rebecca said.

"Short hair, almost like a military cut."

"Was it black?"

"I think brown. He was good-looking. Tall. Ripped. White. He didn't really look like a student. Kira said he was a personal trainer on the side."

At least Rebecca understood Kira's interest better. Tall and ripped was more her type.

"Did she say anything else?"

"Just that they were going to meet at that place at eleven."

Timing that meant Kira hadn't planned to come back here before one at the earliest.

"Do you know if she told him anything about us, about me? Like where I worked?"

"I told you, I left them alone, but I don't think you were a big part of the conversation, Mom."

"Can you give me and Dad a second?"

"Really?" Tony looked dismayed, no surprise.

"Really."

"Yeah whatever." He walked out.

o   o

"Did you notice anything weird in Paris?"

"The baguettes were stale that one place."

Brian had a habit of joking at the worst possible times. She told herself he deflected tension with humor. Though she wondered whether at his core he had some unmeltable male immaturity. Even after they were married and had kids, so many men worried more about fantasy football than becoming fully formed adults.

But she was only distracting herself from the conversation they had to have.

"I'm serious, Bri. Did you notice anything weird when we were there?"

"I don't know what you mean by 'weird.' "

Sometimes she feared marriage was nothing more than endless simultaneous gaslighting. *You're immature! No, you're crazy!*

"Because a month ago the agency"—the CIA—"passed us a tip that the Islamic State was looking to kidnap the family of an American diplomat or any USG personnel in Europe." The FBI loved acronyms; USG was standard shorthand for "United States government."

"How come you didn't tell me?"

"It wasn't actionable. Didn't mention a specific country. Plus, the story was they were looking for a kid, snatch-and-grab, maybe on the way to school. I didn't want to bother you with it."

Plus, she knew what he would have said: *Come on, Becks. The*

Islamic State barely exists anymore. If you changed your mind about the trip you don't need a fake terrorist plot.

"Okay, you got this tip."

"But that was the end of it, pretty much. No follow-up. I basically forgot. But the reason I mention it, yesterday in Paris, I swear I felt like somebody picked us up outside the hotel—"

"As in we had a *tail*?"

"Two. Male and female. I saw them on the Métro near the Arc de Triomphe and then at Sacré-Coeur. Then I thought maybe I saw the woman later."

"You didn't say anything."

"What was I supposed to say? Anyway, the guy I saw wasn't tall and had black hair. It can't have been the guy Kira met."

Now that she'd told him, the story sounded ridiculous to her own ears, the product of too much sangria. In the unlikely chance that this kidnapping plot was real, the original version made more sense. Grab a kid. She figured Brian would tell her to relax, finish her wine.

Instead he stood. "Come on. Let's check the bar."

She realized she'd *hoped* he would tell her to relax. "You sure?"

"Better safe than sorry. Hey, Tony . . ."

Tony popped into the room like he'd been listening in the hall. Maybe he had. Not that it mattered.

"We're gonna go find your sister," Brian said. "If she texts you, tell her to stay where she is and text us right away."

"And promise you won't go anywhere," Rebecca said. "*Promise.*"

"I promise. Is everything cool?"

"Kira's about to get grounded for the rest of her life," Brian said. "But it's fine."

"I'm sorry I didn't tell you—"

"It's *fine*, Tony."

The tension in Brian's voice suggested he feared otherwise.

o   o

As they left the apartment, she pulled out her phone—*nothing, ugh*—and found The Mansion on the map. "You think she's there."

"Of course she's there. Don't get too mad at her, Becks."

"Just a little mad." She saw neither of them wanted to consider the possibility that Kira had left the bar without telling them. Because Jacques might not be an Islamic terrorist, but he was still a *guy* . . .

5

Kira knew it wasn't cocaine as soon as it went up her nose.

She felt no acceleration. No rush. Only the sweetest pleasure imaginable, an orgasm, five, ten, her body loose and soft. Like staring into the sun. Only instead of blinding her the light made her so very warm.

What, she tried to say, but her mouth didn't work. She flopped back against the couch, her head dropped, tongue lolled.

She knew she should care but she couldn't think at all, the words melted into a silver sea. Her mind slid into neutral; she couldn't follow the strobes or the music, the lights and noise were a million miles away and in her fingertips all at once.

Someone grabbed her, arms under her, pulling her up.

No wait—

But she couldn't speak.

Anyway, it didn't matter. She wanted to feel like this forever.

Even *breathing* felt like too much work—she had to pull the air into her lungs, and she couldn't figure out how.

The hands held her and, unknowing, she moved through this place to another.

A long, dark hallway, a door open . . .

A car.

Inside it.

Her eyes closed and she knew she was going to die; the dark rose in her. She couldn't breathe at all; the air was thick as cotton.

She fell.

Into the black . . .

o   o

Her eyes sputtered open.

Her nose. Something jammed in her right nostril. Her head back. A puff of liquid spurted into her.

Her shoulders shuddered. Her head twitched. She opened her mouth to breathe again—

Another squirt of the spray and another.

The seconds passed and the ecstasy faded; her first thought, how badly she missed it. But slowly she came back to life, the pieces fit.

She was in a car. Moving. A city at night, barely visible through dark tinted glass.

Men on either side, squeezing her.

Her wrists cuffed together in her lap. A big hand on her right forearm, gripping it.

"She's coming to," the man on her left said. She knew his voice.

Barcelona. The club. Dancing.

The cocaine that wasn't cocaine.

And one final squirt up her nose. What was left of the pleasure fled her body. In its place, fear. Nothing made any sense. Maybe she'd fallen and hit her head. Maybe she was dreaming.

She didn't feel like she was dreaming. She tried to raise her arms. Jacques held them in place. She didn't speak. As long as she stayed quiet she could pretend nothing was real, nothing was happening.

o   o

"Kira. Nod if you can hear me."

She opened her mouth to scream, but the man on the other side put a hand over her lips.

Jacques jammed something into her belly. An electric pain stabbed her. She tried to writhe away but they were too strong, they held her as the fire coursed through.

Jacques lifted his hand. The agony ended. Tears jumped to Kira's eyes. The other man's hand stayed on her mouth. The strange smell of nail polish on his thick fingers. Rodrigo. The car turned left, picked up speed.

"Stun gun." Jacques's voice was flat, almost robotic. Nothing like the man she'd met in Paris. "Understand? Make a fist."

She tried to look at him, plead with her eyes. The palm over her mouth kept her still.

"Make a fist if you understand."

She squeezed her left hand into a fist. The tears kept coming. *Stop crying stop crying stop.* Her own voice, no one else's.

"You're ours now. Behave, you'll be fine. Don't, I'll hurt you. Make a fist if you understand."

She made a fist.

"That powder you snorted was heroin. A little fentanyl for kicks."

Now the pleasure made sense.

Sophomore year, soccer, she'd run full-out on a breakaway, tripped on a muddy patch, broken her left ankle and tibia. She had never known what pain meant until then. The orthopedist had prescribed her Oxycontin. *I'm only going to give you ten days, be careful with this stuff, what you hear is true.* The pills put her on a cloud. This stuff had sent her straight into space.

"We gave you naloxone as an antidote." Jacques sounded like a doctor now, not a graduate student. He was probably neither, she realized. She had no idea *what* he was. "We were gone from the club in less than a minute. No one noticed. If they did they would think you overdosed and we were getting you help. Happens all the time. Make a fist if you understand."

She made a fist. And thought of the text she'd sent her mom, her parents would be at Helado soon enough.

"My phone was rigged." As if he could read her mind. "The text you sent didn't go through. Your phone is gone. Even if your brother told your parents about The Mansion, they won't find it. Or you. Your parents have no idea where you are. No one does. Make a fist if you understand."

She looked for a hole in what he'd told her. Couldn't find one. She didn't make a fist this time. He didn't seem to care.

"This car, the doors are locked. If you scream we'll punish you. We've done this before. Make a fist if you understand."

She hesitated, made a fist.

"Good. No screaming. Rodrigo—"

Jacques nodded, and Rodrigo lifted his hand.

Immediately a scream rose in her.

She swallowed it down.

Her first test, her first decision. They were still in the city. If she screamed loud enough maybe someone would hear. But probably not. Jacques and Rodrigo were far stronger than she was. She couldn't fight her way out. *Be good. Do what they say. Watch and wait.*

"Why?"

The only word she could manage.

"*Pourquoi?* Only an American would ask. For money, of course. Why else?"

"*Money money money money,*" Lilly said from the front seat. "Bitcoin, gold, diamonds, pearls. Makes the world go round. An American should know that."

"Bitch," Kira said, before she could stop herself.

Jacques punched her in the stomach.

She gasped, bent over, desperate for air. In the front seat Lilly laughed.

o   o

Back when the Unsworths lived in Houston, Becks had helped out on a serial killer case the bureau investigated in South Texas. Kira was ten or eleven. Old enough to understand the snatches of conversations she overheard.

The Border Bandit, the killer was called. A cute name, a not-cute-at-all case. He stuck mainly to undocumented immigrants and first-generation Mexican Americans. No one put the murders together until a rancher's plane in Dimmit County crashed practically on top of a grave where he'd left three new victims. All with bullets in their skulls, all raped. The local cops asked the FBI for help.

Her parents hadn't been good at the time. The case had made them worse. It had pulled Rebecca out of the house. Maybe made her hate men a little. Brian had been angry, too. *You want to spend weekends working for free.*

He's killing women. For fun. Cool with that, Bri?

Maybe don't talk about it in front of the kids.

Maybe Brian was right, Rebecca should have tried to keep Kira innocent. But later, Kira realized Rebecca wanted her to know, women really did disappear. Defenseless women. Mexican girls crossing the desert to work at chicken plants. Runaways selling themselves, meeting truckers at gas stations in the night. Some vanished for years before anyone even noticed.

They weren't always poor. Sometimes they were middle-class secretaries who'd gotten pregnant by a married boyfriend who hated kids as much as child support. Who went out for runs and never came back. Those women were reported missing right away. Volunteers trampled forests for them. But their bodies never turned up. The suspects had carefully concocted alibis the police couldn't shake. Eventually everyone except the victims' families forgot.

Years later, Kira had asked Rebecca about the Border Bandit case. *No joy,* Rebecca said. The FBI never found a plausible suspect, never even figured out how many victims he had. Eventually the murders ended. Maybe because the killer had gone to prison for some unrelated crime. Or died. Or maybe he'd moved to a new state, started a new spree. Serial killers rarely woke up one morning and said, *Hey, this is wrong, better stop.*

○   ○

A single thought: *I'm going to die.*

Jacques would kill her. Or sell her to someone who would. A super-rich psychopath who had decided he wanted something different, something fun, an American girl.

The idea seemed impossible. But here she was, vanishing into the night, Barcelona falling away as they came to a more American-looking stretch of road, strip malls on either side. The airport was around here somewhere, she thought. Minute by minute, mile by mile, she was leaving her mother and father and brother behind.

Then what? Would they take her to the coast? Throw her onto a yacht?

No. She couldn't think that way. Rebecca and Brian would be looking for her even now. They'd wonder why she hadn't texted. They *knew* her, knew disappearing wasn't her style. They wouldn't waste time. Rebecca was a senior FBI counterintelligence officer. She'd get the whole United States government on the case. These idiots would find out they'd kidnapped the wrong dumb American girl.

But Kira better try to make her own luck, too.

If it ever gets rough, Rebecca had told her a couple of years before, the last time Kira asked about the Bandit, *don't show him any mercy. Because he sure AF won't show you any.*

Kira would have plenty of time to be terrified. Beg for pity. Right now she needed to *think.*

6

At 1:50 a.m., the line outside The Mansion was a United Nations of the cool. Tall Nordic women, a stick-thin girl with blue-black skin, a Japanese couple in matching white silk shirts. Even a few Spaniards.

At the front, a man in a black T-shirt guarded the wooden front doors.

"Excuse me," Rebecca said.

"Line starts there."

His English was unaccented American, mid-Atlantic. Maybe they'd caught a break. "You from D.C. too?"

"I'm a citizen of humanity."

You're an idiot. "We're looking for our daughter, she's not answering her phone—"

"Probably just can't hear it."

"Please, I'll leave my driver's license if you like."

"Line starts there." He gave Rebecca a *you are dismissed* look.

Pissant. Rebecca reached into her purse for her FBI badge, then stopped. In the United States, flashing it would have gotten them in, no questions asked. A century of branding had given the three letters an almost magic power. Rebecca doubted they carried the same weight here. They might even put the guy's back up.

Step two: *lying.* "She has diabetes. She sent this weird text, it didn't make sense, we just want to be sure she's not passed out in a bathroom stall."

"For real?"

"We're not here to harsh your mellow," Brian said.

"Harsh my *what?*" The guy smirked, nothing funnier than old people saying uncool things. As Brian had known, Rebecca thought. "Okay, ten minutes. Give me your licenses."

o   o

Inside, the place looked like a tornado of hipness had hit it. A make-out session at the bar. Three shirtless boys dancing on a table. A confident beat backed a reedy voice: *So let's set the world on fiiiiire / We can burn briiiiiighter than the sun . . .* The song had been in a Super Bowl commercial a few years back, Rebecca remembered. *Taco Bell.* Old people dancing crazily.

The place was fifty feet deep, twenty feet wide, a second smaller room at the back.

"I'll go back," she said to Brian. "You stay here." *Clear the room, box the target.*

The FBI agent in her calculating. But her motherly sixth sense already told her Kira was gone. If she'd ever been here. Cologne and perfume mingled with sweat and beer. Girls sat on boys' laps, boys whispered in girls' ears, all swimming in the endless present. Rebecca wanted to be twenty again.

But the feeling passed even more quickly than it came. If she'd been here *with* Kira she could have afforded sentiment, nostalgia, even jealousy. Not now. Now she wished she could send all the revelers home, clear the room to see Kira more easily.

She swiveled her head left and right. SIPDE: Scan Identify Predict Decide Execute. Another bureau acronym. Her fingers brushed her hip for her Glock. A reflex. But it was back home. She missed it. Even FBI agents couldn't bring weapons to Europe without diplomatic bags. Uncle Ned had told her when she joined the bureau, *You'll be surprised how used to it you get. After a while it's like it's part of you.* As usual, he was right.

Rebecca stepped into the back room, saw Kira's head, her honey-brown hair.

No. As the woman turned, Rebecca saw she was ten years older than Kira.

The bathroom next. Rebecca pushed by the women waiting outside, ignoring their complaints. Two stall doors swung open simultaneously, revealing women who weren't Kira. The third stall, the one in the corner, stayed shut until Rebecca rapped on it.

"Kira?"

"*Uno momento!*" a female voice said. Not Kira. Rebecca turned and left.

She worked her way carefully back through the bar. Just to be sure. Because as soon as she reached the front door, she would no longer be able to avoid the fact that her nineteen-year-old daughter was missing in a foreign city after meeting a man she'd known barely a day.

Forget the strange couple she'd seen in Paris; forget the terrorist chatter. Kira wasn't the type to vanish that way. She just *wasn't.* Rebecca *knew* her daughter.

But then didn't parents always think they knew their kids?

Brian stood at the front door, scanning the room. They shook their heads simultaneously.

"Okay, find the manager, someone senior has to be here on a night like this," she said. This bar would make thousands of euros tonight. Someone had to make sure the employees didn't steal too much. In fact—

She looked at the ceiling. Yep, the place had a bubble camera behind the bar, another over the door. She pointed to the cameras and Brian nodded. They pushed to the bar. A couple of kids gave them rough looks, but Brian shook his head and something in the set of his jaw must have warned them off.

The bartenders were less accommodating, avoiding eye contact. *If I just keep my head down, I'll be safe from the oldsters.* After a minute Rebecca had waited long enough. "Grab one."

The next time a bartender walked by Brian locked a hand around his wrist, reeled him close.

"We need the manager," Rebecca said.

"He's busy." The guy tugged his arm but Brian held fast. "Let go."

"Get him," Brian said.

"Fine. I'll text him. His office is upstairs. There's a door by the bathroom, locked."

o   o

When the door to the stairs swung open, Rebecca expected a rock star, hollow-cheeked and coke-twitchy. This guy looked more like an accountant, khakis and rimless glasses. He led them upstairs to a white-walled, air-conditioned office. A cabinet stocked with energy drinks sat against one wall. The sounds of the bar were muffled in a way that suggested music-studio-level soundproofing. She didn't see video screens or laptops, much less a safe. Those must be in the inner office.

"You have problem?" Decent English, not great. The question was directed to Brian. Rebecca answered.

"Kira—our daughter—came here to meet a guy. Now she's missing."

"Okay."

"She's nineteen. She was by herself."

"Nineteen, legal to drink in Spain. And other things."

"The guy's older."

"How much?"

Twenty-six wasn't going to impress him. "Obviously you run a tight ship, but things happen—"

"I don't understand."

"Drinks get drugged. Incidents. You have cameras. All we want to do is get a look at the guy. See how they interacted."

The guy didn't deny the surveillance. "Maybe she doesn't want you to know. Why don't you go downstairs, have a cerveza. See if she comes back."

Rebecca stared at the guy and he stared back. She felt her temper rising, the fury unexpected. After fifteen years in the bureau, she'd grown used to the power of her badge. Maybe too used to it. The people she talked to might lie to her, but they *never* disrespected her. "She said she'd be back by midnight." Close enough to true.

"Then she must be busy."

"Just take a look," Brian said. "Please." His voice cool, collected. His face a mask. Open anger wasn't his style. During the bad years he'd retreated into himself, gibed at Rebecca so subtly that at times she wondered if she was imagining his feelings. *Just tell me what you're thinking*, she'd said more than once.

Now she appreciated his calm.

"Show me her picture."

Rebecca tilted her phone to him.

"We close at four," he said. "If I have a chance, I'll look before then. Give me your numbers."

o   o

Downstairs Rebecca took one last survey, confirming what she already knew. Kira was gone. The bar seemed actively malign to her now, its excitement cloaking a deeper chaos. A flytrap.

Outside, they collected their licenses from the bouncer. "Not here?"

"No." Rebecca showed him Kira's picture. "Remember her?"

"Tall, right? She came early."

"Did you see her leave?"

"I'm more focused on who's coming in. Good luck." He turned to the line.

Rebecca reached for him but Brian tugged her away. "That's the one place we know she *isn't*."

He was right. They found a quiet doorway down the block. "The cops"—Rebecca, thinking out loud—"they'll blow us off." "At least until tomorrow."

○   ○

Tomorrow. She couldn't imagine Kira would be gone tomorrow. In fact, some part of her wanted to believe Kira would beat them back to the apartment. She was nineteen, after all. So very young. Rebecca had made plenty of mistakes at nineteen. The one she regretted most, even twenty-five years later: Sophomore year, getting on a motorcycle after a house party maybe five miles from campus. The guy who owned it lived in the house. They'd talked for a while and then made out for a while. Nothing serious.

When the keg kicked, Rebecca realized she'd said goodbye to all her friends, waved away their protests, *It's fine, see you tomorrow.* She had no way home. *I'll take you on my bike,* the guy said.

Your bicycle?

My motorcycle. He seemed obscurely offended.

She didn't know how many beers she'd had. Four, five, maybe, in those big red cups. Light beer. Who got drunk on light beer? She was merely tipsy. Mere-lee tip-see. *You're cool to drive? Ride?*

Oh yeah, I've had like one beer. Which wasn't true. She'd seen him have three. Or four.

Rebecca had never ridden on a motorcycle before. Her mother would have been aghast—that was the fifty-cent word that came to her that night, *aghast*—at the thought. And as soon as she thought it she knew she would agree.

The bike was a big rumbling old Harley. Neither of them wore helmets. Connecticut didn't have helmet laws for adults, surprising for a northeastern nanny state but true. *A brain bucket?* the guy said. *Forget it. Just hold on tight.*

He brought her home in one piece. Didn't even try to take her inside. A gentleman, or maybe he had a girlfriend. His name was

Jake, or Nate, or Dave—even at the time Rebecca hadn't known. Four letters, ended in an *e*, all she could remember when she woke up the next morning, her head in a vise and her stomach doing backflips. *Never again*, she told herself.

Not the motorcycle, she had to admit she liked the motorcycle, its unavoidable carnality. The way she'd spread her legs around his waist, the thrum of the engine. If dancing was a vertical expression of a horizontal desire, riding a motorcycle was sex backward. But riding drunk, with a guy she'd just met, stupid stupid stupid.

One pleasure at a time.

So yeah, Rebecca understood, nineteen was not exactly the age of wisdom. She understood more than Kira thought. She understood something else, too. It was her fault, not Kira's, that Kira hadn't trusted her enough to tell her about this guy. Because probably Kira would be fine, probably she'd escape this mistake just like Rebecca had slid off that Harley without a scratch.

But if Kira didn't . . . Rebecca would blame herself, now and forever.

o   o

"Becks," Brian said, bringing her back to the sticky Spanish night. "You okay?"

Not even close. "We split up. Show her picture to every bouncer in the Gothic Quarter. You work back toward the apartment, check on Tony. I'll go the other way."

"You sure?"

"Cover twice the ground."

He nodded. "Meet back here around four? We can talk to the Mansion manager?"

The question bothered her, though she wasn't sure why. "Sure."

They mapped the blocks. Brian wrapped his arms tightly around her. "After we find her, we're gonna take her to the vet to get her chipped."

"I like it." She extracted herself from his arms. "Go."

He went. She watched him turn a corner and disappear into the Gothic Quarter before she realized why his *meet back here around four* comment had bothered her. He hadn't said, *Unless we find her first.* He'd just assumed they wouldn't.

7

Somewhere in Spain

Frigid air poured out of the car's vents. Kira found herself shivering, a high-frequency shaking that set her handcuffs rattling. Jacques and Rodrigo didn't seem to mind. She didn't understand the point of the air-conditioning.

Maybe she was overthinking. Maybe there was no point.

So much she didn't understand.

Panic real as water poured down her throat. For the second time this night she couldn't breathe. But now she felt no opiate pleasure, only a desperate need to escape.

Impossible. She lowered her head, made herself see the stun gun Jacques held. Two choices. Scream and be punished. Or close her eyes and *think*. She didn't feel drunk anymore, the fear had overwhelmed the alcohol. Maybe the spray they'd put up her nose had helped too. She didn't know how that stuff worked. Still, reality kept sliding away from her. She wanted to tell herself she was dreaming.

She rubbed her wrists in the handcuffs. These men had hurt her already. They would hurt her more. Pretending she was dreaming wouldn't stop them.

Pretending she was dreaming was the same as giving up.

o   o

She couldn't count on her parents. Or the police. Or anyone. She'd better figure out how to save herself.

The biggest panic of her old life, her life BK, *before kidnapping,* had been the SAT, the college admissions exam. Her first practice test was dismal. The second was worse. Rebecca's advice came down to *study study study some more.* Casual reassurance, not Mom's strong suit. Kira could feel her eating disorder creeping back as the test approached. *Forget college, I'll get skinny enough to model.*

One night, the exam still weeks away, Brian came into her room. Kira was staring miserably at a book of practice tests. Without a word he grabbed it and tore it in half along the spine, a long lovely *rippp.*

Dad! She was half-thrilled, half-offended. Half Bri and half Becks.

She'd seen her father's impulsive streak before. If *impulsive* was the word. Most memorably August before tenth grade. A family trip west. Fly to Denver, drive to Las Vegas. But Rebecca only got to Salt Lake before she had to fly back to D.C. Some crisis in some investigation. There was always some crisis in some investigation. So, she wasn't around for when they headed south from Salt Lake, the mountains to the left, the desert to the right.

They'd been on the interstate for an hour when Brian said, "This is boring, let's check out the sand."

They wound up on a two-lane road that knifed through the ugliest land Kira had ever seen. Scrubby bushes, brown sand, rocks that seemed to melt in the sun. Waves of superheated air shimmered off the asphalt. The emptiness made judging distance difficult. Not another car or truck in sight, much less a building.

NO SERVICES NEXT 70 MILES, white letters warned on a blue sign. CHECK FUEL.

"That was boring?" Tony said. "What's this?"

"One hundred and eleven degrees," Brian said. "A rattlesnake speedway in the Utah desert."

He turned on the radio and it spun endlessly. "Searching for signs of terrestrial life."

"Clever. Can we go back to the highway, Dad?" Tony was more like Becks, who would surely have considered this road a waste of time. All downside, no upside.

"Let's see what this brand-spanking-new Hyundai Santa Fe can do. Two-point-four liters, yee-hah." Staccato like he was talking to himself, not them.

He pulled the steering wheel left and put them in the center of the road so the double yellow line split the SUV in half.

"This can't be a good idea," Tony said.

"Once in a lifetime, here or the Autobahn."

The engine roared, and they accelerated, eighty-five, ninety, ninety-five—

A warning chime rang—

One hundred. The Hyundai shook and Kira watched Brian tighten his grip on the wheel.

"This isn't funny, Dad," Tony said.

"We're fine." Brian's voice sounded unnaturally calm.

One hundred and four. Tony tapped her arm. "Say something. He listens to you."

But no, she didn't want to say anything. She remembered when she was five six seven, how her dad held her hands in his and whipped her around and Mom yelled but he just grinned and spun her faster—

One hundred and seven. The air howled hurricane-loud.

The Hyundai went over a bump in the road. On the landing they caught air and pushed right. If they had been in their lane they would have edged off the asphalt.

The jolt snapped Kira out of her reverie:

"Dad, please!"

Brian exhaled and the car slowed, one hundred, ninety-five, ninety, the shaking stopped.

He looked over his shoulder at them. "Got a little excited."

His blue eyes scared Kira. Flat and empty as the flame from the Bunsen burners in chemistry class. Like the speed was all that counted.

Brian blinked and the look was gone.

Forty minutes later he pulled over at a convenience store, the first they'd seen since the interstate. "Sorry. Thought it would be fun. Anybody want anything?"

He left them in the car.

"That was weird," Tony said.

Kira knew *weird* was standing in for a bunch of words they didn't want to say. *Crazy. Terrifying.* Though she couldn't help remembering how calm she had felt until the end. "I guess."

"We should tell Mom."

And yet Kira *couldn't*. Even the idea seemed like a betrayal. "Yeah, no, I don't think so. She'd freak. Anyway, what would we say? Dad drove really fast for like a minute and nothing happened?"

And without another word they agreed not to talk about it.

o　　　o

But yeah. Dad had a rough streak, even if he tucked it away most of the time.

And as Kira sat cross-legged on her bed that night and watched him tearing up the SAT prep guide, pulling out pages, ripping them lengthwise, she knew she was seeing it.

"NSA, the programs are incredibly complex. To handle them we simplify, go step-by-step. Each question on its own. Pare away the wrong answers. You'll get there. It's just words and graphs and drawings. You're smart, you'll be fine."

The strange part, he was *right*. She stopped freaking out after he explained it that way. Not that she wasn't still nervous, but her fear went to a manageable place.

She just had to try the same trick now.

o　　　o

She closed her eyes. Start at the beginning. *Why her?*

Jacques must have targeted her. Planned to kidnap her soon as he saw her in Paris. Or even before. Maybe he'd known she was going to Barcelona the next day. Hard to believe. Yet he and his buddies had taken her *here*, not in Paris. He'd led her away from safety. He'd made her phone disappear. He'd taken her from The Mansion to Helado.

She could see now how carefully they had set her up. Lilly was the key. *He's with his sister, yeah she's a jerk but it's more proof he's safe.* Then Lilly picked up Rodrigo. Suddenly Kira was with three strangers, not just one. Lilly even did the so-called cocaine first and hit herself with the antidote to reverse its effects. Then she made sure Kira took the right amount, didn't overdose.

Everything made sense now, right down to Lilly's wig. So no one would know what she really looked like.

They must have a place to hide her, too. Whoever was driving this car hadn't asked Jacques where to go. He'd steered them straight out of Barcelona. Kira was pretty sure they were moving into the center of Spain. She'd seen a sign for Madrid. *Barcelona on the beach, Madrid in the middle,* Tony had said on the train down from Paris. *Don't you know anything about Spain?*

Okay.

Go with the idea Jacques had targeted her. *Why her?* Okay, he said for the money. Maybe so. But if not . . . she was nobody. Tony was nobody. Her dad was a coder for the National Security Agency along with about a thousand other guys. But her mom . . . her mom wasn't nobody. Rebecca Unsworth ran the Russia counterintelligence desk at the Federal Bureau of Investigation.

At least in Washington, D.C., Rebecca was the real deal. Especially these days.

How big? Kira wasn't totally sure. Becks talked to the FBI director. She'd even briefed the president. Would spies target Kira to get to her mother? Could they think Kira knew something important, some password? Could they be that crazy?

The other possibility was that Jacques had picked her at random. Say he cruised around Paris, looking for young female tourists. Kira had been with Tony last night. But she had gotten rid of him fast. Jacques would figure she would be by herself when she met him again.

But how had he pulled off the kidnapping in Barcelona when they'd met in *Paris*? Okay, maybe he went back and forth. Two huge party cities, American tourists on their Rick Steves trips. Maybe this was Jacques's game: Find a girl in one city, kidnap her somewhere else. The police wouldn't connect anything.

So was he part of a gang? Maybe. Did Europe even have big gangs? The mafia, right? But she was pretty sure Jacques wasn't Italian. Maybe he freelanced. Called his buddies if he found a target. In fact . . . maybe she was wrong about what he had in mind. He hadn't said anything about *selling* her. Maybe he just wanted to ransom her back to her parents.

Or maybe *not*. They'd gone to a lot of trouble already. Maybe Jacques already had a *buyer*, someone who'd pay for a tall American—

That fear snapped her eyes open. Beside her Jacques stared out his window. She wondered if she should just reach between the front seats, grab at the steering wheel with her cuffed hands, try to take them off the highway before they could take her wherever they were taking her.

Lilly turned, looked at Kira. Like she could read Kira's mind.

Kira sat back. Waited. *Think.* Thinking keeps the fear away. Should she say something about her mom, try to convince Jacques he'd screwed up? *Everybody makes mistakes. The whole FBI is going to be up your ass in about twelve hours.*

But she had a feeling Jacques wouldn't care.

o   o

The driver stayed in the right lane, drove steady, not too fast. The countryside was mostly bare, scattered houses in the darkness. Not the Utah desert, but emptier than she'd expected. She thought of Europe as all cities. Obviously not.

She felt Jacques tense beside her, and in the rearview mirror she saw blue flashing lights that could only be police.

Even faster than she'd thought.

Jacques reached up, put painful hollows in her cheeks with his thumb and forefinger. "They stop us, you say *nothing*."

He tucked the stun gun under the driver's seat, came out with a pistol. "Understand, Kira?"

"I understand." She didn't pray much, but she was praying now, *Please God, let them pull us over.* She'd take her chances.

The lights brightened. Kira could see now there were two sets. Two police cars, they *couldn't* have shown up randomly.

The driver said something in French.

The headlights closed in until they flooded the sedan even through its tinted windows. Kira thought of the strobes at Helado—

Hit your sirens, pull us over, be the good guys—

Jacques squeezed her hands tight in her lap so she couldn't show them her cuffs. The first police car drew even. She just had time enough to glimpse the officer in the front passenger seat looking them over before the car pulled away. *No. Oh come on.*

The second sedan passed without even slowing. The cruelest joke yet. "Please." Even as the word left her lips she knew she shouldn't have spoken.

Jacques gave the sedans a fingertip wave as they disappeared. "*Please?*" He touched the pistol to her temple, its muzzle cool against her skin. She made herself keep her eyes open.

"Beg."

No. He wasn't going to shoot her, not after going to so much trouble to take her. "No."

He pulled the pistol back, held it sideways in front of her so it pointed at Rodrigo's window. Its silver muzzle glinted in the dim interior light. "Walther. Semiauto. Do you know how it works?"

o   o

She knew. One side effect of having an FBI agent for a mother. The week after Kira's eighteenth birthday, Rebecca brought her to Quantico for target practice. *You don't have to hit a quarter from a hundred feet, but we have a firearm in the house. You should be able to use it.*

I've seen movies. It's just a gun.

Not a gun, Kira. Use the right word. Firearm, pistol.

Just like Becks to insist on the terminology. *Whatever. Pull the trigger,* boom.

Don't be dumb, Kira. How to load it, swap out the magazine, clear it if it jams, fire it. It's like a car, it can be dangerous or it can save your life.

It's nothing like a car, Mom.

Yet discovering her mother trusted her enough to put a pistol in her hands felt good. She stopped arguing.

Rebecca's first lesson: *Never point it at anyone unless you're willing to pull the trigger. Which means, never point it at anyone who isn't a threat. Not even if you've checked it and are sure it's unloaded. Never.*

o   o

Too bad Jacques hadn't had her mom as a firearm-safety teacher. He pressed the pistol into her ribs. "I said, do you know how it works?"

She shook her head. No point in giving away too much.

"It's called a double-action pistol. That means once it's loaded, I fire just by squeezing the trigger. I pull it halfway to cock it, then the rest of the way to shoot it."

He twisted forward to look at her face. He was *enjoying* himself, she saw. He wanted to feel her fear.

His finger tightened around the trigger, millimeter by millimeter, until the pistol gave a tiny metal *click.* "It's cocked now—"

"*Please.*" She had never been so afraid. She hadn't imagined she *could* be so afraid. "I'm sorry."

She didn't even know what she was apologizing for. Being alive.

On her other side, Rodrigo stirred. "Jacques—"

Jacques leaned forward.

The two men stared at each other and then Kira felt Jacques pull the pistol away.

"I think he likes you," Jacques said. He grinned as he decocked the pistol and shoved it away.

o   o

Grab it. Just grab it. Her hands were cuffed in front of her, not behind. She had a chance. She might be able to reach it. She couldn't shoot all four of them. But she should be able to get at least one shot off. Maybe through the back of the driver's seat. Or toward Jacques. What then? Maybe they'd freak out and let her go. Maybe the Walther was the only gun in the car.

Jacques cocked his head, smirked at her. She had the eerie feeling he'd shown her the pistol hoping to tempt her into going for it.

Anyway, she wasn't sure she had the guts to do anything if she *did* get it.

She'd better be sure.

Still. It was so close.

The driver turned on the radio. Kira had the mad fantasy she'd hear a bulletin, *If anyone has seen an American girl.* Instead, the car filled with crappy Spanish pop she never would have put up with if she'd had her own songs. Oh the irony, ha ha. She'd had an iPhone since she was twelve. She'd never had to listen to music she didn't like, never had to wait for the next day's paper for news.

She was never out of touch, either. Her friends expected they could reach her whenever they wanted, and vice versa. Not replying when a friend texted was just rude. At least a *K* or a *busy hit you l8r*.

Her parents, too. They might not expect her to text in two seconds. But if they called she'd better pick up or they'd freak pretty soon. Not just Becks. Her friends' parents, too. They'd all bought into the same fantasy, grown-ups and kids, *We're safe as long as we're in touch.*

She'd learned better tonight. The phone wasn't safety. It was the illusion of safety.

"Five minutes," Jacques said to Kira.

To what? She saw the mystery was part of the game for him, another way to play with her, wind her up.

o　　　o

Ahead, an exit. They pulled off down a short ramp that ended at a stop sign: ALTO. Turned left, beneath the overpass that supported the highway. A tall white van waited, pulled over, hazard lights blinking. The cargo compartment windowless.

A man stood beside it, his cigarette flaring in the dark. He flung it away, pulled open the back doors.

NFW. Not a van with no windows. They might as well make her wear a sign that said I AM GOING TO BE MURDERED.

The pistol. She leaned forward, tried to see how far down Jacques might have put it, how she could reach it. Jacques was big, his legs were in the way. But he'd have to get out before she did.

"Sit up." Jacques pushed her against the seat.

Distract him, say something, anything.

"The cuffs. They're hurting."

Lilly handed Jacques a black bag, thick mesh.

Jacques eyed Kira as he opened the bag. His face was eager. He *wanted* her to reach up with her cuffed hands and grab for it. He *wanted* her desperation.

A terrible thought came to her. What if Jacques had no plans to ransom her? What if he was just playing with her? What if he'd taken her for himself and would use her until there was nothing left?

"Don't scream."

Then she could think of nothing else but her voice tearing through the night—

But she said nothing, nothing at all.

And then the bag came down and the darkness with it.

8

Barcelona

Three forty-nine a.m. Rebecca's mood was as dark as the Gothic Quarter's grimy streets.

The Barri Gòtic, as locals call it, is a rectangle-shaped district that angles northeast from Barcelona's waterfront. The famous pedestrian street La Rambla divides it from the seedy but gentrifying neighborhood of El Raval to the west. Together the Quarter and El Raval are only about a half-mile wide, a mile long, but they hold hundreds of places to eat and drink.

After she and Brian split, Rebecca worked her way south to the waterfront. Then she doubled back to the Plaça Reial, an open square just off La Rambla. The plaza was the center of Barcelona's tourist nightlife, a block from The Mansion. The walking sobered her up. She noted every stop she'd made on her phone.

In two hours she showed Kira's picture to forty-three people, mostly bartenders. Bouncers were a better bet. They were paid to stop trouble before it started, so they had to keep their eyes open. But many bars in the Quarter were too small to have bouncers.

In any case, Rebecca came up empty forty-two-and-a-half times. At a bar called Ginger, on the eastern edge of the Quarter, a bouncer said maybe he'd seen Kira walk by. Maybe. *With someone?* Two people, a man and a woman. *Two?* Yes, two.

Didn't totally make sense but he seemed sincere. Rebecca offered him twenty euros. He waved the money off, a fact that made her think he was telling the truth, he wasn't in it for the money. He took her number and promised to call her if he remembered more.

Of course, many of the people she'd tried to ask had simply ignored her. No doubt they saw her as an overprotective American chasing a teenager who hadn't even been missing a whole night.

After a while Rebecca hated them all. Had she ever been this besotted with herself, immune to everything but her own pleasure? The answer had to be yes, but that didn't make seeing these golden children any easier. The streets blurred, and Rebecca began to wonder whether she was in purgatory, condemned to chase her missing daughter endlessly.

Though that wouldn't be purgatory, would it?

After three, slightly earlier than she'd expected, the streets calmed. Smaller bars shut their doors. The partiers still out split into two main categories.

The drunks hung out in groups of six or eight, mostly guys, loud and sloppy. They slap-fought as they drifted toward La Rambla. Lots of yelling in English. *Kill you brah, how can you say Durant is better than Kawhi.*

Rebecca worried about the women with them. But they weren't her problem tonight. And she couldn't imagine her daughter with them. Kira had a weakness for frat boys, sure. But her type was more Ralph Lauren than *Animal House*. She wasn't a huge drinker, either. She'd seen Tony's awful nights.

The cokeheads were still up, too. Though they were less of a nuisance. They hung in groups of two or three, sniffling and blinking under the weak streetlights. They were Spanish and French and Italian, divided almost evenly between men and women. Rebecca could see how their Eurotrash glamour might have seduced Kira. Under normal circumstances, she would have been less than happy to see her daughter with them. Tonight, she wouldn't have minded. *We'll talk about this later, 'kay?*

But what Rebecca wanted was irrelevant. Kira was nowhere. Not with the drunks, not with the cocaine cowboys, not with the Irish bachelorette party Rebecca had seen marching down the sidewalk wearing foot-long rubber penises for necklaces.

She must still be with Jacques. If she'd left him, she would have called or texted. Even if she'd lost her phone, she could have borrowed someone else's. Maybe she was too busy with Jacques to give them a heads-up. But why wouldn't she at least tell Tony where she was?

The other scenarios ranged from bad to worse. Kira was drunk and lost, despite the map Rebecca insisted she carry. She was stumbling around the less pleasant parts of El Raval, near the harbor. She'd been hit by a car, taken to a hospital. She'd been mugged, robbed, left unconscious.

Worst of all, she *was* with Jacques, but not voluntarily.

The bureau rarely involved itself in standard crimes-against-persons cases. *The FBI doesn't get its hands dirty*, local cops said. They weren't entirely wrong. So Rebecca had never faced the raw moments of victim notification, telling family members their loved ones had been killed.

But in Texas, years before, she'd gotten into a serial killer case. The Border Bandit. Some deaths had initially been classified as accidental, undocumented immigrants who'd died from exposure or animal attacks. But the Texas Rangers ultimately linked the killer to almost two dozen victims, maybe more; evidence showed the perp had worked the Mexican side of the border too. Rebecca interviewed their parents and siblings. Sometimes they turned tight-lipped. She wondered if she was too hard-edged, too northeastern, for them. Now, even with Kira not really *gone*, no police department in the world would take a report at this point, Rebecca understood as she never had before why those mothers and fathers had hated talking.

Her phone buzzed, and she reached for it, *Kira*—

Nope. Brian, *At Mansion. You close?* She wanted to scream. After *three hours*. How would she feel after three days, three weeks?

o   o

She saw her husband standing, arms folded, outside The Mansion. He was scanning the street as though if he just looked hard enough he'd see Kira. Rebecca tried to ignore the ugly thought, *I'd trade you for her. In a second.* Traitorous, but no doubt he felt the same. Your spouse rented you. Your kids owned you.

"I keep thinking I'm going to turn a corner and there she'll be."

"How's Tony?"

"Quietly freaking. He wanted to come but I told him no, stay there in case she comes back. He's blaming himself for not telling us."

Yet another reason to find Kira, like they needed one.

"Becks? We're gonna find her."

She almost snapped at him, something nasty like, *Glad we cleared that up.* Instead she hugged him, felt his strength. The only person in the world who loved Kira as much as she did. "Come on, let's see if the manager shows us the video on his own or I have to choke him out."

o   o

The Mansion was mostly empty, three guys finishing beers at the bar. The music was still playing, turned down, a song old enough for Rebecca to remember from two decades before. *I know who I want to take me home, take me hoooome. . .* "Closing Time." Semisonic. The more things changed . . .

The bartenders were already sorting glasses for the next night. Despite its end-of-the-world look the place ran smoothly. The professionalism might help them. The manager wouldn't want them angry.

They waited as the music stopped and the bouncers shooed the last stumbling kids into the night. A minute later, the door to the stairs swung open. "You didn't find her? Okay, come up with me. There's something . . ."

The inner office was windowless, with a steel desk, a laptop open. A fifty-inch TV screen played live feeds from four surveillance cameras, one behind the bar, one on each side of the front door, and the last a wide shot of the main room.

"Good footage," Rebecca said.

"We made three million euros last year. A problem, someone stealing, we want to know." He clicked on his laptop until the big screen on the wall lit up with a color feed from a camera behind the bar. The time stamp indicated 22:18:30. Ten eighteen p.m. Kira sat at the bar, alone, eyeing herself in the mirror, a copper mug in front of her. She looked confident. Happy.

Rebecca wanted to warn her daughter, *Beware, beware*—

"There she is. As you said. You can watch it all, but I tell you, she came her by herself, ordered a sangria from the bartender. She drank it, then a beer. She talked a little to the bartender, no one else. Waiting for someone. You see we weren't too crowded when she first came, then we fill up."

He clicked on the laptop and the screen jumped ahead, one frame for each half minute.

The manager stopped the fast-forward, went to normal speed.

22:59:22. A man made his way through the thickening crowd to Kira. Tall, broad-shouldered, mid- to late twenties, wearing a baseball cap with an oversized brim that did a good job hiding his face from the camera. Kira smiled at him. They'd have to check with Tony, get a screen grab, but this guy had to be Jacques.

The guy kissed her cheek. Then he stepped back and introduced Kira to a woman behind him. The woman was his age, pretty in a big-chinned TV news anchorwoman way. She wore a platinum-blond wig that flopped over her forehead. Kira forced a smile and the three talked.

A man and a woman. As the bouncer at Ginger had said.

"You see, this woman was with him," the manager said unnecessarily.

Yeah, and why? Jacques had been alone when he met Kira in Paris. To Kira, the woman's arrival had been annoying but hardly alarming. Now it seemed sinister. As did the fact that both Jacques and the woman both had worn headgear to help hide their features.

"Sound?" Brian said.

"Too much background, too loud." The manager paused the video. "Okay, I tell you, they talk, order sangria. Then to the back of the bar, off this camera. You want to watch regular speed or fast?"

"Regular," Rebecca said.

The manager turned the footage back on and they watched in silence. Kira and the woman held themselves in a way that suggested they had taken an instant dislike to one another. Finally, the bartender brought Jacques a pitcher of sangria. He paid and the three walked off-camera.

"So, I warn you, only one camera watches the whole room. Where they were sitting, you barely see them. I looked at it quickly. You can see the girl with the wig get up from the table, come back, get up. Nothing else happens, and then, a bit before midnight, they leave. All three."

He pulled up a video from the camera mounted over the front door. 11:56:30. Kira and Jacques and the woman walked out together; both Jacques and the woman had their heads ducked in a way that obscured their faces. Then they disappeared. Into the night.

"They don't come back."

Rebecca felt as if she'd been in the bar, a ghost, impotent, useless, watching her daughter disappear. "Have you seen either of them before?"

"Never." The manager shook his head for emphasis. "You see, he pays cash, no card."

Rebecca scribbled down her and Brian's email addresses. "Can you send us a screen shot from when they met? And from when they walked out?"

"Of course."

"If she's still not back in the morning we'll want the whole video. Thank you for all of this."

"*De nada.* I'm sure you'll find her. Probably she just drank too much, she's passed out."

o   o

They hurried in silence up La Rambla and the broad boulevards of Eixample. Rebecca found herself wondering if they would return to an empty apartment, if someone had grabbed Tony while they were looking for Kira.

But Tony was just where they'd left him.

"You didn't find her?"

"We have a picture from the bar." She handed him her phone, with the screen shot.

"Yeah, that's Jacques."

"What about the girl? The one with the wig?"

"What about her?"

"Was she with Jacques last night?"

Tony tilted the phone in his hands, squinted at the screen. "I've never seen her."

"Anywhere in the café?"

"No. I'd remember." He pushed her phone back at her, as if holding it might make him an accessory. "You think this is serious."

"We don't know," Brian said.

"Then why didn't she *text*—" Tony raised his arm and suddenly punched himself in the head, the *smack* of knuckles on bone echoing under the living room's high ceiling. He yelped in pain.

Rebecca sat beside him, hugged him. His body was shaking. He hadn't laid off the punch, hadn't pulled it at the end. If Kira was a mature nineteen, Tony was a young seventeen.

"I *knew* the guy was messed up somehow."

"We're gonna find her," Brian said. "Let's all get a little sleep. If she's still not back in the morning we'll talk to the police."

"You want to *sleep*, Dad?"

"Come on, Tony," Rebecca said. She wondered if she'd have to lead him to his bedroom like he was a child. But he pushed himself up, disappeared into the hall.

o   o

After they heard the door to Tony's bedroom slam shut, she flopped on the couch. "You think the NSA can get a facial match?" From the pictures.

"Possible, but the hat's a problem."

"Twenty-five billion dollars a year well spent."

"What about tomorrow?"

"I think if we haven't heard anything by noon, we need to go to the cops." They'd have an in, an FBI agent who lived here and worked with the local cops, mostly on terror cases. The threat of Islamist terror was very real in Spain. In 2017, a truck attack on La Rambla had killed fifteen people and injured 150 more. The Spanish were generally happy to trade information with the FBI.

The bureau called its liaison officers "legal attachés," inevitably shortened to "Legats." The Legat here was Rob Wilkerson, a twelve-year vet who'd worked on the Joint Terrorism Task Force in New York before moving here. Rebecca didn't doubt Wilkerson would help. The bureau looked after its own.

"Okay." Brian reached down, swung his arms under her legs and back, grunted as he picked her up.

Surprising her with his strength, his raw male stink, sweat, maybe a cigarette. Had he smoked while he was walking the streets? She appreciated what he was trying to do, distract her for a few seconds. It didn't work, the voice in her head yelled *Kira's missing*, but at least he'd tried.

He carried her into the master bedroom, with its big four-poster bed. When they'd first brought their suitcases into the room, the bed had seemed charming, sexy. She'd imagined making love to Brian in it, biting her lip so Tony wouldn't hear. Now the idea repelled her.

Brian lowered her to the bed and she slid away from him, hoping he would understand that she didn't want to be touched. He flopped down beside her, rested a hand on her shoulder, pulled it away. *Good.*

She lay beside him and stared at the ceiling until sleep somehow took her.

9

Somewhere in Spain

Kira stood on a raft, brown water all around her, swirling and foul. She didn't belong here. She wasn't even wearing a bathing suit, only jeans and a sweater, both dry. Sweat puddling underneath. The raft shook, tossing her toward the edge.

She fell off, opened her eyes—

To darkness. She willed herself to see. Couldn't. The panic came then, worse than before. She'd gone blind, *where was she?*

Everything came back as the van slowed. She tried to sit up, pushing herself against the side wall. Anything to be a little less helpless.

The van stopped.

o   o

She reminded herself of a trick she'd used during her anorexic days. *Count down by sevens from one hundred, ninety-three, eighty-six, seventy-nine . . .* She hadn't been this conscious of her body, herself as a physical being, since then.

Forty-four, thirty-seven . . . Get to two and start again. Vary the cycle, add eight or multiply by three or divide by two. Give her mind something to do. The trick worked. She could feel them waiting for her to beg, or say anything. She stayed quiet.

She heard the back doors open. A hand touched her shoulder.

"Kira." Jacques's voice, gentler. Some part of her couldn't help but feel relief, at least she knew him —

She didn't know him.

He edged up the hood, and she could see. The van's back doors were open. It was parked inside what looked like a garage. The garage door was closed, and she couldn't see any light between the door and the floor. Probably it was still dark outside. She couldn't have slept long.

Jacques took her hand, led her out. Again this strange chivalry.

She could hear Becks in her head. *Pay attention. Every detail counts.* She paid attention. The garage had a new concrete floor. It was empty aside from cases of water and a half dozen red plastic gas tanks lined up against the back wall. The lights in the ceiling sockets were the spirals of compact fluorescents. Like the house had been built recently. But the vibe here was weirdly prepper, down to the blue emergency light on the back wall.

Jacques offered her a water bottle. She hesitated, then thought: he'd already kidnapped her, why would he drug her again? She took it and drank deep.

"Slow," Jacques said.

Too late; whether from the drug or the antidote, her stomach was queasy. She sputtered back the water. Lilly laughed.

Kira drank again, kept the water down. She nodded at the bottles. "Guess I'll be here awhile."

"We'll see."

"Or maybe I'm not the only girl you kidnapped this week?"

He tilted his head, an expression she already recognized: *playtime is over.* "Let me show you where you're staying." He grabbed her and pulled her along, his fingers digging into her arm.

o o

Into the house, up a staircase, down a hallway.

"You can let me go. Just dump me on the road. I don't know where we are, don't know anything about you . . ."

Her voice faded; she could imagine how stupid she sounded.

The hallway ended at an open door, a narrow rectangular room, the size of a walk-in closet. It had a square of plywood nailed to the far wall. To cover a window, Kira figured.

Two water bottles rested on a blanket in the corner.

"This way you don't get in any trouble." Jacques whipped his arm forward, slung her against the far wall.

Her head banged the edge of the plywood. She yelped, slid down. Her butt hit the ground, and she turned, looked at him. He watched her like she was a science experiment, his face grave and neutral.

"You're bleeding."

She touched a finger to her forehead. It came back wet.

"Get some sleep." He stepped out, closed the door. A deadbolt snapped shut.

At least he'd left the light on.

Then it went out, too. And she was alone in the dark.

His footsteps receded down the hall. She let herself cry then, silently. After a while she stopped. The bleeding stopped too, though her forehead ached, dull and tender. She was sure she'd be black and blue later in the day. Maybe they'd have to discount her. Or maybe the buyer liked his ladies a little banged up.

She took inventory. Good news: she wasn't dead, wasn't seriously injured. Bad news: Everything else. She was exhausted, fat-tongued, hungover from the drugs they'd used on her. Hungover and hating herself. She'd always been good. She knew the rules. Don't go out by yourself. Don't take a drink from someone you don't know. Don't leave without telling your friends. Remember that guys have higher tolerances and don't try to match them. Always use a car service. Most of all, trust your judgment. If he seems sketchy just get a number, you can always see him again.

Smart Kira. Careful Kira.
Kidnapped Kira.

o　　　o

New Kira. She felt herself changing. Even now.

When you grow up in a house where your parents don't like each other, you grow up attuned to disturbance. She needed to put that vision to work. Jacques wasn't a robot, even if he seemed like one. He'd make mistakes. If she could find them, she could use them.

She was more dangerous than they thought. All those self-defense courses Becks had made her take. *Guys are going to want you. Some won't like it if you say no.* Kira had thought it was Rebecca's way of trying to frighten her about men.

She'd let them think she was beaten. Not completely beaten, not right away, they wouldn't trust that. Mouthy but useless. Yes, better.

Stay strong. She'd stay strong. She'd beat them. *Promise?* Promise.

Then an awful little voice in her head: *The women the Border Bandit took, they probably thought the same thing.*

In some tiny rational corner of her mind she knew she was dizzy and weak and maybe had a concussion. She knew the fear wouldn't last. But for now it ruled her. She usually felt closer to her dad than her mom. But with her own thoughts pressing her into the abyss she turned to Becks and not Bri. Lie down with her eyes squeezed shut and her hands pressing on her ears and one thought: *Save me, Mommy. Mommy save me.*

10

Barcelona

Rebecca lay in bed as the day brightened. Beside her Brian snored lightly.

How could he *sleep*? She hated him for sleeping. She'd barely dozed. Though she knew he was right—they'd look crazy if they went to the cops at 7 a.m. He always played this role in their marriage, in their lives, their family. She got stressed, he played cool, *Take it easy, Becks.*

Only it wasn't easy, was it? And for a long time she'd thought his laid-back attitude had been nothing but an excuse for simple laziness. Until he proved her wrong—and made her wonder if she was a fool for ever having doubted him.

Rebecca rose, padded into the kitchen. Every time she looked at the apartment she noticed new details: the ornate corner moldings, the perfect cabinetry. The owners had taken great care with this place. The Unsworths had been lucky to get it. Lucky, lucky. They were lucky people. Now their luck had run out all at once.

She poured herself a glass of water, drank it as the streets outside slowly woke. The world wouldn't notice if Kira Unsworth vanished. No, that wasn't entirely true. Kira was a pretty girl, and the world noticed when bad things happened to pretty white girls. Nancy Grace would run a special on her, *Thirty-eight days since Kira Unsworth disappeared in Spain and police are no closer to finding her. Can we be sure her parents had nothing to do with her vanishing act?*

An ocean filled with fake tears. Grief manufactured for ratings. The thought made Rebecca grind her teeth—

Footsteps.

On the staircase outside, slow and heavy, the footsteps of a drunk woman coming home after a long night.

She'd been wrong. She'd overreacted. She was a fool. Kira had lost her phone, lost track of time, gone home with the French guy.

The steps came off the stairs, toward the apartment's front door.

Rebecca would wrap Kira up like a boa constrictor and drag her inside and yell at her, *Don't do that again. Do you know how worried we were?*

She pulled open the front door. "Kira—"

Found herself looking at a tall woman, late twenties, a yellow T-shirt streaked with sweat from dancing. The woman gave her a dazed drunk smile. Rebecca felt irrational anger, *How could you do this to me? How could you pretend to be my daughter?*

"Excuse me?"

"Yes?"

"You were out? Dancing?"

"*Ja*, the Opium Club. By the beach. DJ Kush, great DJ."

"Is it still open?"

"No. It closes, I think, at . . . six. Or seven." She slumped against the wall, winding down like a toy with low batteries.

Rebecca hadn't realized other places in the city would be open later than the Gothic Quarter bars. Some cop she was. *So stupid.* She should have been checking the clubs.

Still, the knowledge made her feel a little better. It was just possible Kira had lost her phone dancing, or couldn't hear it because of the noise, or had drunkenly decided to teach Rebecca a lesson. Unlikely but possible. Besides, finding Kira in a club with a thousand kids dancing would have been a long shot.

No, best to wait for the afternoon for the clubs. They would have lots of surveillance cams.

"Good night," the blond-haired woman said. She grinned drunkenly. "Or morning."

Rebecca wanted to fire more questions: *Did you see a tall American girl with some French guy who calls himself Jacques?* Useless. She closed the door, no goodbye.

○   ○

Back in the bedroom Brian slept curled up like he didn't want Rebecca or anyone else to touch him. A thin sheet covered him. She knew what he was wearing underneath, tight black Calvin Klein boxer briefs, his favorites. He'd always been proud of his body. Not without reason. Even when she hadn't *liked* him, she'd always been attracted to him. Suddenly she found herself on the path that had brought them here.

As if she could unravel the mystery of where Kira had gone by prowling the corridors of her history.

Or maybe she just wanted to distract herself. Anyway, she let the past take her . . .

II

REBECCA

(THEN AND NOW)

11

Charlottesville, Virginia

On their second date, Rebecca told Brian how she had played the piano, what it meant to her.

They were at a Japanese restaurant. She was a second-year law student at the University of Virginia. He was a freelance Web developer. This was the nineties. She hardly knew what the Web was. She had opened her first email account the year before, through the law school.

"You good?"

"I'm not bad."

He smiled. He was tall, blue eyes, dark blond hair, a nose that looked like it had been broken in a bar fight. His smile was crooked too, a badly hung picture. Higher to the right. She was tall as well, long black hair, eyes so brown they too were almost black, muscular legs, and small, high breasts. She already knew they'd make a striking couple. Looks-wise, anyway.

"Why'd you quit?"

"I don't know."

"Lying. So you don't play at all?"

Something else she liked: His boldness, his willingness to challenge her before they had done anything more than kiss. The fact he was right didn't hurt. "Even if I wanted to, and I *don't*, I don't know where to find a piano."

He didn't mention it again.

But two dates later he picked her up in his old Ford F-150, dark green, tinted windows, rust drooping from the quarter panels. He made a left, a right, and they were heading north on 601, out of Charlottesville.

"Is this the right way?" She was almost sure the multiplex was the other direction.

He didn't answer.

"Where are you taking me?"

"It's a surprise." His tone was flat, affectless. Her stomach tightened. How much did she know about Brian? Not much. He wasn't a student. She'd never seen his apartment, wasn't even sure exactly where he lived. They'd met in a bar. He had a mysterious backpack between his legs. And this truck was the rapiest vehicle imaginable short of a camper van.

Her uncle Ned was a cop in Boston, she'd heard too many terrible stories. Had she told *anyone* where she was going?

"Relax, 'kay?"

After a few minutes, he made a hard right onto a narrow road that ran east past farmhouses and a trailer park screened by a hedge. Not even 6 p.m., but the sun was disappearing over the hills behind them. She couldn't decide how scared to be. She had pepper spray in her purse, police-grade, a gift from Ned. She told herself if Brian turned onto a back road she would use it.

A couple miles on, a sign proclaimed the entrance to the JEFFERSON HOME FOR THE AGED AND INFIRM. To her surprise Brian swung the pickup into it, revealing a run-down three-story brick building. Beige Buicks filled the parking lot. Rebecca felt embarrassed at her nervousness. Whatever he had in mind tonight didn't end with her being fed through a woodchipper.

Though she still didn't know what he *did* have in mind.

"This your way of telling me you want us to grow old together? One day, Rebecca, we will fill our diapers here, as our children fail to visit . . ."

He grabbed his backpack, came around, opened her door. "Come on, they're waiting."

"Don't tell me your grandparents are in there or something."

She followed him through the front doors. As the smell of disinfectant hit her, she saw a black grand piano in the center of the lobby. Maybe forty women and men sat in folding chairs around it.

Up close she saw that the piano was a Steinway. A Model B, vintage, the paint scuffed but otherwise in great shape, the soundboard perfect. Worth she didn't even know how much. Lots.

An unexpected fear rose in her as she walked around the Steinway. Five years. What if she couldn't? What if she embarrassed herself?

Brian whistled, long and piercing. All the conversations in the lobby stopped at once.

"Please welcome Rebecca Kelly," Brian said. "America's favorite pianist." He winked her way and clapped. The oldsters followed uncertainly.

Oh why not? The Jefferson Home wasn't exactly Carnegie Hall. She could mangle Billy Joel and they'd be happy to have her. *Sing us a song you're the piano lady . . .*

He held out the backpack. "I brought music if you need it—"

She shook her head.

He nodded like he wasn't surprised she could play from memory. She took off her jacket, pushed up her sleeves, sat down, stared at the keys. Cracked her knuckles. Flexed her fingers. Scooted the bench close.

She started with Schubert's Sonata in D Major, a showy but technically simple crowd-pleaser, making sure she hadn't forgotten how to play. The piano sounded like it had just been tuned, which surprised her until it didn't. Brian must have brought in a tuner. He'd found her a Steinway . . . and had it *tuned* before he brought her to it. He'd brought music.

Gonna marry this guy. She'd never thought that about anyone before. The words were so surprising that she almost missed a note. *Focus.*

After the Schubert, Bach, the Italian Concerto, another crowd-pleaser, nice and slow, with chances to experiment. Then Beethoven, the Moonlight Sonata, always a winner.

The Steinway was fantastic. And so was she. Maybe the low stakes relaxed her. Maybe the years off had allowed her to understand her technique in a way she couldn't when she was practicing all the time. Whatever the reason, she grew stronger as the minutes passed, her hands loosening, quickening. She wished her last teacher, who toward the end had told her, *Rebecca, playing like you do is supposed to be fun, I wish I could see you smile*, had been there to watch.

Halfway through the Beethoven her hands weakened. She'd forgotten how much stamina these pieces required. She would quit while she was ahead. She quickly ended, turned to the oldsters.

She'd assumed half of them would be asleep. Wrong. They were enraptured, leaning forward in their seats. A woman cried, the tears cutting runnels through her heavy mascara. A man simply *stared*, his jaw open wide, revealing his empty mouth.

She'd forgotten how much power music could have.

Brian stood against the wall by the front desk, smiling. He gave her a silent thumbs-up and tears stung her eyes. Embarrassing. But he had given this joy back to her, he had seen what she couldn't.

She stood, bowed formally to the crowd like she really was at Carnegie Hall. "Thank you." They clapped, uncertainly at first, then steadily—

Then a *thump* echoed from the back row and a woman shouted "Gordon!" in a high, frightened voice.

Brian got to him before Rebecca. "Call 911!"

The man was heavy, maybe seventy-five, his thin gray hair was combed across the top of his speckled head.

He had landed on his side. Brian snaked an arm under him, put him on his back.

"Sir! Gordon! Can you hear me?"

Nothing. Brian touched two fingers to the man's neck, then reached down and slapped his face. The man's fleshy jowls jiggled.

Otherwise he didn't blink, didn't stir. "Oh God," the woman said. Rebecca was pretty sure he was dead. She'd never been this close to a newly dead person before.

The man wore a white button-down shirt with a greasy stained collar. Brian tore it open, revealing flabby breasts covered with white hair. Brian didn't seem fazed. He put his fingers in the man's mouth, tugged open his lower jaw. Two quick breaths, *puff puff*, the strange intimacy of CPR. Then pressed down on the man's chest with interlaced fingers, began compressions, counting aloud, *One two three four five* . . .

"My husband," the woman beside Rebecca said. She was among the younger residents, early sixties maybe, and wore shocking-red lipstick that had skidded onto her teeth.

"I'm so sorry." Rebecca reached to hug her.

"Don't touch me." The woman stepped back. "He's dead and *you killed him.*" The woman's brown eyes bulged. She clawed at Rebecca, a skeletal hand topped with red fingernails. "Witch." Screaming now. "Witch! WITCH!"

Rebecca staggered back as a staff member finally reached them. "Mrs. Hendricks, *please—*"

o   o

His name was Gordon Hendricks, they found out a half hour later in the manager's office. He was seventy-four and had worked in the UVA maintenance department for thirty-five years.

"A smoker, two previous heart attacks, a coronary waiting to happen," the manager told them. The screaming woman was his wife, Delilah, who was suffering from early-onset dementia. "She's flat-out crazy."

"I'm so sorry," Rebecca said. "Is she going to be okay?"

"She should be. I hope you know it wasn't your fault. They loved you. In fact, if that hadn't happened we'd probably ask you to come back every month."

"You still can," Brian said. "Free up some rooms."

"We take the death of any resident very seriously," the manager said.

"Too soon?"

The manager didn't smile. Rebecca didn't think what Brian had said was very funny either.

o   o

They walked back through the lobby, empty now, the chairs gone. A guy in a blue uniform mopped the floor where Gordon had collapsed.

Outside the parking lot lights glared down.

"Strumming my pain with his fingers," Brian murmured. "Singing my life with his words . . ."

Rebecca knew the lyrics. Everyone did. They'd been inescapable for almost a year. Lauryn Hill and the Fugees, a remake of Roberta Flack's "Killing Me Softly with His Song." She couldn't believe he was same man who had gone to the trouble to find her a piano to play. "He *just* died, Brian. He's still *warm*."

"You want to cry about it? Or laugh."

"Are those my only choices? Jesus, what's wrong with you." She stopped midstride, stared at him.

He nodded, then blinked. The humanity seemed to come back to his eyes. "Sorry."

She followed him silently to the truck. Inside the cab, he put the key in the ignition but didn't turn it.

"I am sorry. I mean it."

"How did you learn how to do that?" She needed to talk about something besides his ghoulishness.

"CPR, you mean? My dad was a medic—"

"Really?"

"Yeah, in the army, served in Vietnam. He taught me the basics when I was like twelve. Practically the only good thing he ever did for me. When I was eighteen I got my EMT training. I was thinking about becoming a paramedic, too."

The longest speech he'd given her in four dates. Maybe he was trying to forget his ghoulishness too. "What's the difference?"

"As a tech you can't do much more than CPR, oxygen mask. Paramedics can intubate, use needles." He looked over at her, tried a smile. "Not that any of it would have done Gordon much good. He was dead before he hit the floor. I would have needed Jesus training, that's like eight months plus a saint has to recommend you."

She laughed a little, the tension easing out of her.

"Before the Internet stuff I worked overnights as a tech. I guess, I don't want to make an excuse, but see enough ODs, car accidents, your skin gets thick."

He turned the ignition, and they were quiet as he steered the pickup out of the parking lot.

o   o

"So was this the worst date ever?" he said a few minutes later. "Or the best?"

"I'm trying to figure that out too." She'd married him and divorced him in barely two hours.

"I have to tell you one thing, though. You are a fantastic piano player."

A flush reddened her cheeks. "Stop."

"I'm serious. I mean, I don't know much about it, but you are *great*."

At 601 he signaled to turn left, back toward Charlottesville.

"Other way," she said. "I want a beer somewhere I'm guaranteed not to see anyone from school."

He swept the steering wheel right and the pickup rumbled north. She could already feel herself forgiving him, deciding that his fearless reaction when Gordon collapsed and his odd coldness afterward were inseparable.

The Virginia fields were dark, but she saw a big black horse silhouetted against the white light of an open barn door. She thought of the Steinway, how he'd found it and brought her to it.

o   o

They spent that night together, and the next, and the next.

Now they were curled up on her couch, and he was explaining the Internet.

"It's the future. I'm telling you."

"How is buying books on your computer changing anyone's life?"

"Instant communication with anyone, anywhere? That doesn't sound like a big deal?"

"You mean like a telephone?"

They were sitting on her couch, eating chocolate-chip pancakes and scrambled eggs with cheese. Saturday night. They'd said they were going to a movie. Then they'd started fooling around. Leaving the apartment had seemed like too much trouble. He'd said, *Let me cook.* Breakfast for dinner. His range was limited, but what he did make was perfect. He baked, too: blueberry muffins, warm and crumbly and tangy. He'd worked as a short-order cook for a few months up in Seattle, he said. *Cooks never starve. I can walk into a diner anywhere and get hired in ten minutes. Those places always need people.*

He was so different from the men she met in school. They thought smart was all that mattered, didn't care if they couldn't change their oil. Even the ones who could, who knew how to use their hands—the Virginia bros who spent weekends hunting, the Connecticut boys who built their own bookcases—weren't actually tough. They were hobbyists.

Not Brian. He was a survivor. He'd paid his bills a half dozen ways, from driving cabs to working as a landscaper—*a fancy way to say mowing lawns*, he'd said. Now he was a computer programmer who made "Web pages" for the Internet.

"Telephone?" he said now. "Tell me you're joking. Pretty soon you'll get music and movies and television this way. Right on your computer."

"It takes two minutes to see the picture."

"The connections aren't fast enough yet. But they will be."

"People aren't going to watch *television* on their computers, Bri."

"Why not?" He sounded genuinely surprised.

"They just aren't. Computers are for work."

"You'll see."

If he'd been one of her classmates, this certainty would have infuriated her. But they weren't talking about some case they'd both studied. She couldn't pretend she knew anything about the Internet. He was looking at a future she had never even tried to imagine.

She already felt how well they meshed. Not that they agreed on everything. He didn't care much about her friends or her family. Then again he wasn't close to his own parents. When she'd asked about them he mumbled, *My mom's long gone. My dad and I don't talk much, he's such an asshole.* She'd tried to press him a little, gently. But he shut down.

Yet. During the day, she found herself wishing she could talk to him after every class. They spent most nights together now, though he never pushed her. If she told him she would be studying late and couldn't see him he never minded. *Do your thing, I'll be here.*

And the *sex.* She wanted to tell her friends, but then again she didn't want to jinx it. Like if she talked about it too much she risked losing it.

"Bri?" *I love you.* But she couldn't say the words, she'd never said them to any guy. "I love you."

No. Not so soon, out of nowhere. She probably had scrambled eggs between her teeth, it wasn't like they'd been together for years.

He leaned over, kissed her, open-mouthed, slow and gentle. He tasted of Tabasco sauce. He laced his fingers through her hair.

"Love you too, Becks."

His blue eyes shimmered and for the first time in her life she found herself thinking, *Nothing else, let the world stop, I don't mind.*

"Never said that to anyone before," he said.

She traced a finger down his cheek. "I do. All the time."

Outside she heard Charlottesville on a Saturday night, boys yelling, girls hooting, glass breaking. *I'll never have to hit another bar. No more dates. I've made my choice. It's all good.*

o   o

They didn't have to discuss anything more.

She didn't tell her parents, not right away. But Eve, her mother, must have sniffed out what was happening, even from five states away. Two weeks after *I love you*, she caught Rebecca in her apartment: "I'm in D.C. for a conference this weekend, I'll come see you. Brunch."

"That's crazy, Mom. It's like three hundred miles."

"No it isn't. And we've barely spoken this semester. Whenever I call, you don't answer or you're busy—"

"Law school, Mom."

"Big kiss, see you Sunday."

o   o

She told Brian. "It makes me nervous."

"Your mom's coming. So what? You embarrassed about me?" Brian grinned like the idea was impossible. Then his grin winked off. "Wow, you are."

"I'm *not*." She wasn't, not exactly. But she wasn't sure what her parents would make of Brian. They were snobby enough to dislike the fact he hadn't gone to college. Eve was a documentary filmmaker who taught at Boston University and Pete an English professor at Northeastern and a very minor poet—was there any other kind?

They were decent and loving. But they were also pretentious Massachusetts intellectuals, and predictably hypocritical about money. They'd always lived above their salaries and depended on Eve's father, Jerome, to make up the difference. Jerome had made a couple million bucks in the seventies inventing the first commercially usable insulin pump. Over the years he'd quote-unquote helped Eve and Pete out, first buying a house for them in Cambridge, then paying for college for Rebecca and her sisters.

Rebecca didn't want to explain any of this to Brian, not yet. Maybe not ever. Discovering that your parents were fallible was one of the most unpleasant parts of growing up. It had been for her, anyway. Maybe Brian had known all along.

But the impulse to keep her parents away ran deeper than that. She didn't want to let anyone inside the world she and Brian had created. Not even her family. She didn't want her mom to ask if Brian wanted kids. *You need to make sure you two have the same expectations. Someone like him, from a different background, he might not want what you do.*

Different background. Ugh.

"I just want to keep you mine for a while." True, or true enough, anyway.

He wasn't ready to let her off. "You think I don't clean up nice. Maybe I better sleep at my place for a few days. Wouldn't want to scandalize dear old mom."

His tone bothered her. *Cold.* So cold, so fast. Like he was arguing over a parking spot with an annoying neighbor. Could he cut her off this easily?

"I promise this stresses me out more than you—" She heard the wheedling in her voice and hated it.

"Fine. But in that case, I'll meet your mom here. Let's not pretend I'm not practically living here."

She laid a hand on his shoulder. Her touch seemed to do the trick. He relaxed, sighed.

"I'm sorry, Becks. People looking down on me, it pisses me off."

"Eve's gonna love you. I promise."

o   o

And she did.

Brian was the best version of himself that Sunday, charming and polite without trying too hard. He and her mother wound up talking about novels that Becks hadn't read, early twentieth-century fiction, Upton Sinclair and John O'Hara, all the worthy books she'd missed in her headlong pre-law rush. *I had a lot of long bus trips*, Brian said.

He explained the Internet to her mom without being condescending. He listened to the mildly embarrassing stories she told about teenage Rebecca, *She almost failed her driving test, not that she couldn't drive, she was just so stressed about it—*

Becks was stressed? No way.

Rebecca could feel Eve settle in as the afternoon passed. "I really have to go," she said around five.

"Sure you won't stay for dinner?" Brian asked.

"Bri's a great cook."

"He *cooks* too?"

"Just this and that, not like I know what I'm doing."

"Come on, Rebecca, walk me to my car."

o   o

Rebecca came back to the apartment expecting to find Brian excited. Instead he sat on the couch, staring morosely at the television. She knelt in front of him, rested her hands on his legs. His eyes were flat, exhausted.

"What's wrong, babe?"

He ignored her.

"Brian. What is it?" Her confusion was real. "She loved you, Bri, you know she did. You know what she said? He's a keeper." She had actually said, *He's a keeper, don't blow it.* Thanks, Mom.

He didn't speak.

"Come on, Bri?"

"I wish I had a family like yours."

o   o

He went to a knee as they were picnicking in the Blue Ridge Mountains. Her surprise was genuine. They'd been together just five months. Her surprise and her pleasure. *Yes,* she said, *yes yes yes.* The day was perfect, a bright blue May afternoon, finals just over. On Monday she'd start her internship with Poynter Stone, a corporate law firm based in Philly. She was near the top of her class. She could have wound up at a high-end New York firm. But Poynter suited her because of its criminal defense practice. Even before she started law school she'd seen the degree as a means to an end.

By the end of her sophomore year at Wesleyan, she'd grown sick of the intellectual pretension around her. Worst of all was the way the kids talked about cops. *Criminals with badges.* Her uncle Ned, her dad's brother, was a Boston police sergeant. He wouldn't even take a free cup of coffee.

She decided to do something about it. At Thanksgiving break junior year, she told Ned she wanted to join the Boston police.

"Wesleyan to the BPD?" Ned was fleshy and strong, shaped like a keg, with oven-mitt hands. He looked her up and down, appraising her. "You're serious, huh? Let's go to Drakes."

He seemed grim, but the invitation thrilled her. She'd heard him talk about Drakes. Cop bar at the edge of Roxbury, where he worked. District B-2, worst neighborhood in Boston.

He wound through the city's streets like he was on autopilot. She tried to talk, but he turned up the radio. Late November in Massachusetts meant loooong nights. Only 7 p.m., but the sun seemed to have been gone forever. A freezing rain coated the windows.

He parked outside a two-story concrete building with a single reinforced window. No sign.

Inside, a dingy room reeking of smoke. Two jukeboxes, neither plugged in. A television playing *Wheel of Fortune.* Everyone in the place looked like Ned; they all had the same bulk in their shoulders and arms.

"New girlfriend, Neddie?" the bartender asked. "Little old for ya."

"My niece."

"Niece, sure, right."

"Nah, true."

Ned's accent was thicker here than at her house.

"Rebecca goes to Wesleyan. She wants to be a cop."

"Yeah?" one guy said to her. He was kinda cute, black hair, thirty or so. "Joking, yeah?"

"No."

"Fucking idiot."

"Thinks she's gonna toss her college degree," Ned said. "So she can do some good. I thought we should enlighten her about the realities of law enforcement in *underserved communities*."

He brought her to a booth. For a solid hour cops came over to tell her horror stories. Getting domestic violence calls from cockroach-infested apartments until the calls turned into murders. Fourteen-year-old girls pimped by their boyfriends, sold to a dozen guys a night. Fifteen-year-old boys shooting each other in the head for the chance to sell a couple hundred dollars of crack. Menageries straight from hell, dead cats and half-starved pit bulls. On and on, each tale worse than the next. In the early nineties, Boston had plenty of senseless violence to go 'round.

Even worse than the stories was the way the cops told them, flat and affectless, but with a hint of showmanship. Like they were numb to the horror, yet almost proud of it.

Rebecca barely spoke. She sipped her beer until it was flat and warm. Finally, even Ned seemed to have had enough. He waved them off, went to the bar, came back with two big shots. He lifted his glass.

"To Boston's finest."

The whiskey burned her throat. He didn't even blink.

"Half the guys in here are alcoholics. Maybe two-thirds."

"You're not."

"You'd be surprised how much I drink. Don't be a cop, Rebecca."

"I get it."

"Thought I might have to do this to my boys"—Ned had three sons—"but they just want to go to business school. Marry blondes, live in Cohasset, play golf. God bless 'em." He grabbed her hand. "Not that I think you can't do it. I mean, the street, it helps if you can ring somebody's bell, but the girls find ways around that."

"The girls. The female cops, you mean?"

He nodded. "It's everything else. All those cop shows get it wrong. We don't *solve* anything. We're san workers. Clean up after people who are too stupid, too bored, too mean, to do anything but hurt other people. And the bureaucracy, the crap lieutenants who decide they don't like you and find a hundred different ways to mess up your life—"

"It can't be *that* bad. You do it."

"I don't have a choice, Rebecca, I didn't go to *Wesleyan*. And guess what? The guys in here? They're the good ones. Not the ones too scared to be out there, or the freaks who've gone all the way over and get off on it. They're drinking because *they still care*."

He went back to the bar, left her alone. Occasionally the black-haired cop looked over his shoulder and smirked. Ned came back with four more shots, little ones, the liquor inside yellow and dangerous looking.

"Te-kee-la." He rattled two home, quick, slamming down the empty glasses. "Don't forget the guys on the take, we all know them, the smear sticks to everyone. But nobody busts them, nobody says a word. Because anyone who sees what we see is on one side of the line, and everybody else, they're on the other. Even the DAs."

Ned didn't usually talk this much. Now she knew why. She felt like he'd slapped her.

"Asshole."

"You do this, go in with your eyes open. That's all." He pushed a shot of tequila at her, grabbed the last one himself. "I have a solution." He raised his glass. "Drink, I'll tell you."

She'd known him her whole life and not seen him this way before, not ever, the alcohol in charge of him. The view unsettled her. She raised the glass, unwillingly. They drank. The tequila burned.

"Three words."

"I'm listening."

But he said nothing, went back to the bar, came back with two pints of beer and another shot of whiskey.

"You going to be okay to drive?"

"Good girl." He slid his keys to her.

"Three words, you said."

"FBI."

She'd always been under the impression Ned hated the FBI. "I'm not sure that's three words."

"College girl. How about this? Stupid fuckin' FBI. That three? Not in Boston, they suck here, protecting half the Irish mob, too dumb to figure out they're getting played. But over the years a couple of our best boyos have gone to the *federales*. They make cases, understand? They pick and choose, they have the time and money and toys."

"I thought you didn't like them."

" 'Cause I'm jealous. 'Cause you need a college degree, plus, to get in. They love lawyers, the feds. 'Cause you wear a suit and go after guys who deserve it. Not some chick who smoked rock laced with PCP and drowned her babies like kittens."

She remembered that case. She'd been in eighth grade.

Ned slumped in the booth. "First on the scene. Lisa Grant was her name. Sitting on the couch. Leaning forward, watching *General Hospital*. Didn't even move when I came in. Just nodded at the bathroom. I take a look, come out, I say, *You do this, ma'am?* Always give 'em a sir, a ma'am, they love that. Respect. Know what young Miss Grant said to me?"

Rebecca tried to imagine. Couldn't.

"Suck your dick for rock. Officer." Ned lifted the shot glass to his mouth. "It's the *officer* that always gets me. She wanted me to know she knew who I was. All I could do not to pick her up and put her in the bathtub along with the kids, but I kept myself steady, I wanted to be sure we didn't blow the case. Only she didn't even get life, she had some do-good defense lawyer talking about her *circumstances*, her *history of abuse*. Be out when she's sixty. Sometimes in the middle of the night I promise myself if I'm still around then I'll find her, put three in her. One for each kid. Dare 'em to arrest me in my wheelchair. You want to do some good, go nuts. Just not the BPD."

She drove home alone, left Ned at Drakes. *I don't want your dad to see me like this. Someone'll drop me off, get the car tomorrow.*

The next morning she dragged herself to the library to read about applying to the FBI. She had one advantage, she was good at languages. She was nearly fluent in Spanish and had some Russian too. But she could see that law school was a sure ticket in. Ned was right, the bureau liked lawyers.

Junior year at Wesleyan she worked as hard as she'd ever had, straight As across the board. She spent every spare hour practicing on the LSAT. The logic puzzles didn't agree with her, but eventually she cracked them. She wound up at the University of Virginia, one of the best.

Columbia had let her in too, but UVA was offering a partial scholarship, which she wanted. She knew she'd have to take out loans. Her parents wouldn't be paying, and Jerome didn't like lawyers. Even with the scholarship and working summers, she would graduate law school fifty thousand in the hole.

o   o

She told Brian about the FBI the day after Eve left. Her parents were the only other people she'd told at that point. They hadn't exactly been positive. *You know it's a paramilitary organization, right?* her dad had said. *I have a hard time seeing you there.* Her mom made the inevitable *Silence of the Lambs* joke, the movie had come out a couple of years before. *Like Clarice Starling, only your shoes aren't cheap.*

She didn't even try to tell anyone at law school. Her classmates were mainly worried about which firms paid the most. *You hear Cravath just went to eighty-six K for first years?* The few who did want to be in public service came at it from the left, environmental defense or death penalty appeals. Rebecca couldn't forget the way Ned had spat *do-good defense lawyer* like a curse. She kept her plans to herself.

But she figured Brian would understand.

"Sure it's what you want?" he said when she finished.

She nodded.

"Then it's good enough for me. How's it work? You go straight after you graduate?"

Not exactly. She explained her plan. She would work for a big firm for two or three years, pay down her law school debt so it wasn't hanging over her head when she became an agent. Getting into the bureau was a tough, multistage process. Long multiple-choice exams, interviews, a fitness exam, and a background check. If they took her, she'd train at Quantico for several months. Then they could send her anywhere in the country for her first post.

"You're okay carrying a gun?"

The idea of wearing a weapon made her nervous. Ned had promised her she'd get used to it. *It's a tool. Probably you'll never need it. But if you do you'll be glad to have it.*

"I better be."

He ran a hand down her back, let it rest on her hip. They were in bed together; no surprise, they were always in bed together. "Becks?"

"Yeah?"

"I don't mean to jump ahead, but what's it mean for kids? Do you even want them?"

Oh. The question thrilled and frightened her at once. "I want kids, yes."

"But you're going to have to wait a while."

Could she tell him? Were they ready to be this grown-up?

"In a perfect world I think I'd have them before the bureau. Being a pregnant FBI agent, it seems weird."

Also, big law firms tended to have good maternity leave policies. The unspoken quid pro quo was that female associates who wanted a chance at partner would make up the hours, work twice as hard later. But Rebecca had no interest in making partner. She could use the system to her advantage, take the paid leave twice and then get out. A cynical move, she had to admit. But ultimately it would help at the bureau.

He was quiet. She wondered if the talk of kids had scared him off. "Cool," he finally said.

She punched him, harder than she'd intended. "Cool? That's all?"

"That's all. You have a plan, I like it, I'll roll with it."

She couldn't let the unspoken contrast rest. "And you don't. Have a plan."

"I don't. Can *you* roll with that?"

She thought about her classmates, looking for the summer internship that would lead to the associate offer that would put them on a partnership track. Maybe she was wrong. Maybe she was being a snob in reverse. But she didn't want one of those men. Nothing was more boring than intensity without imagination.

o   o

They went to Philly for the internship, came back for third year. Still he wouldn't talk about his family. He deflected her every time she tried to ask. She started to wonder if his dad was even *alive*. Then, October, the phone rang.

"Hello?"

A gravelly voice, a smoker's voice, an old man's voice. "Bri there?"

"He'll be back shortly." He was out for a run.

"This Rebecca?"

She wondered how this stranger knew her name. "Who's this?"

"It's his dad." Pause. "Jerry." As if he might have another dad. "Could you tell him I said hello?"

"Of course, Mr. Unsworth, my pleasure. Will I ever get to meet you?"

"That's up to my son." Then he was gone.

Somehow she waited until Brian showered and dried himself off before jumping him with the call.

"My dad? You talk to him?"

"Not really, no. It sounded like he wanted to talk to you."

"Forget it, Becks."

"Why won't you talk about him? Or to him?"

He laughed, hollow and bitter. His face reminded her of the way he'd looked in the nursing home after Gordon Hendricks died.

"Maybe he was fine before he went to Vietnam, I don't know, I wasn't alive, but he came back with a drinking problem and a heroin solution, that's who he's been ever since. He gets clean, but you can never trust him."

"But if you tried to forgive him—not for him, for you."

"For *me*? He's got nothing for me. Most selfish person I ever met. You don't get it. Everyone you know is basically decent."

"Brian. I'm on your side."

He'd turned away from her, letting her know the conversation was over.

Again his coldness unnerved her. Yet some part of her respected him for his unwillingness to compromise his own anger.

Wow. She must really be in love.

o   o

They married not even a year later, spring break of her third year. Nothing fancy. A quick wedding in Boston, dinner with her family. Her idea more than Brian's, a way to handle the fact that his family wouldn't be there. Her friend Jane officiated, a quasi-civil ceremony. Rebecca didn't care. Her mom was Jewish and her dad Catholic. They both regarded religion more as an inconvenience than anything else.

As for the wedding itself, she'd already gone to enough friends' weddings to be over them. She didn't have the time or energy to pick the right band, the right venue, the right dress. They would have had to do it on the cheap, too, because her parents didn't have fifty thousand dollars lying around, and Brian certainly couldn't ask his dad. Grandpa Jerome was giving her ten thousand dollars as a wedding present. *Only one rule, Becks, you have to spend it, can't put it against your law school loans.* For ten grand they could have a lousy wedding or a great honeymoon.

Okay, sure, some part of her wouldn't have minded walking down the aisle in a perfect white dress. Having her dad give her away. The vision was manufactured, what she'd been sold her whole life. But she couldn't deny it held a certain surface appeal.

She asked Brian what he thought, but he was no help. She had begun to see that he considered displays of emotion—even private displays—contrived. Almost shameful. His vision of masculinity came straight out of a John Ford Western. Tight-lipped, straight-backed. Of course, that attitude was what had helped attract her to him in the first place. But sometimes she wished he'd tell her how he felt.

"We can do it however you like," he said.

"Maybe a chance to get all your friends together." In the year they'd been together, she'd met only one of his friends, a squirrelly guy named Jimmy who'd slept on their couch for a couple of days before vanishing. Afterward, Rebecca realized he'd filched the money from her purse. Brian hadn't even looked surprised when she told him.

"Not exactly the fancy wedding type, my friends."

"So whatever I want."

"I don't care about the wedding, Becks. I care about the girl."

That fast everything was fine.

o   o

They went for the perfect honeymoon instead of the lousy wedding. They spent Jerome's money on a five-star trip to St. Barts. A thousand bucks a day for ten days, endless blue skies, a suite with an ocean view. They swam, they snorkeled, they sailed a catamaran. They rode scooters. They drank. They watched sunsets.

Two weeks before, Rebecca had gone to her gyno, had her IUD taken out. She felt almost giddy as the doctor put it in a plastic bag and handed it to her. Her own fertility, returned.

Why not? We're getting married. Becks and Bri 4-ever.

She was pregnant by the time they flew home.

12

Birmingham, Alabama

"Mommy!"

The quivering voice cut through her sleep. She'd been dreaming about Draymond Sullivan. She could still see his face, pouchy and fleshy, corruption incarnate.

So much easier when the criminals looked like criminals—

"*Mommy!*"

Urgent now. Rebecca jolted up, *Kira, was something wrong—*

"Happy Birthday!" Thumping footsteps. Kira wasn't a dainty girl. Good for her. She ran into the bedroom, holding a giant cupcake with a candle. Behind her Brian and Tony followed.

Happy birthday? Had she forgotten her own birthday? Before she could stop herself: "Oh shit."

"Mommy you said sh—"

"No I didn't."

"We made you cupcakes!"

"Happy Birthday, Becks," Brian said. "Happy birthday to you."

Lately she'd noticed a touch of irony in the way her husband spoke to her. She heard it again now. Or maybe not. Maybe she was just sleep-deprived.

Brian and Kira sang birthday greetings as Tony squealed happily. *This is what matters, not Draymond Sullivan, the Boss of South Alabama.* For at least the next ten minutes.

Rebecca kissed Kira's perfect round cheeks. The cupcake was smeared with thick blue frosting.

"I put it on, Mommy."

"Thank you, baby."

The cupcake was good, fresh, the frosting even better, rich buttercream. Brian had added cupcakes to his repertoire since they'd moved to Birmingham. *Trying to be the best househusband I can be*, he said. That was definitely ironic, she thought.

"How is it?"

"Great." Still, she made herself stop after a couple of bites. *A minute on the lips* . . . For a while she'd thought she would never lose the weight she'd gained having Tony. Moving to Alabama had helped, perversely. All the barbeque and fried chicken. Every third person seemed morbidly obese, a walking advertisement for the virtues of sensible eating.

o   o

Breakfast waited in the kitchen. Scrambled eggs and fresh-brewed coffee. And a present, a white-and-silver device the size of a cigarette pack, with a little black-and-white screen.

"An iPod," Brian said. "It's a digital music player. I put some songs on there. I can help you download more."

"I know what an iPod is. I'm not a total loser." Though she wasn't quite sure about the downloading.

He nodded, *Of course you do.* She sipped her coffee, tried not to think of Draymond Sullivan's syrupy voice pouring out sweet nothings. He was probably the biggest real-estate developer in southern Alabama, and certainly the most corrupt. His name had come up in another bribery case, giving them just enough probable cause to put a wire on his phone.

As the junior agent in the office, Rebecca had to listen to the recordings. But she hadn't heard much worth transcribing. In this football-crazy state, his biggest sin had been saying he didn't think 'Bama could beat LSU. *Tigers gon' be tough this year.* Plus off-color cracks about his secretary's daughter Jenelle. Jenelle was sixteen.

Either Sullivan was clean—impossible—or he was too crafty to do anything over the phone. Either way, Rebecca was sick of his *sugars* and *honeys* and *sweeties.* No wonder the whole state could barely fit through a door.

"I should go in today." The day before a new batch of recordings had come in.

"It's your *birthday*, Mommy. And Saturday."

"The kids were looking forward to spending the day with you," Brian said.

"You *prommmised!*" Kira's voice rose to a wail.

Work would have to wait.

o   o

They'd come to Birmingham not even a year before, straight from Quantico. She'd entered the academy just after Tony turned one. In retrospect she wished she'd waited longer. FBI cadets lived at the training center five days a week, saw their families only on weekends. The kids couldn't live in the dorms at Quantico, so they'd stayed with Brian in Philly. She'd made the three-hour-plus drive back every Friday. Tony had taken her absences hard. He'd screamed when Sunday night arrived and she packed her bag.

But by the end, he just watched her go, no tears at all, stony and calm.

Stony and calm was worse.

But the training was over now, they were back together. The kids seemed to have forgiven her, though mornings like this made her realize that they hadn't entirely. Those months of absence still clawed. She wished she could talk about her guilt with Brian, but the only time she'd tried he'd nodded and said, "I have this right? I'm supposed to feel bad that you spent four months at scout camp while I took care of the kids?"

Scout camp was clever, she had to admit. Plus . . . from any reasonable point of view . . . he was right. She just wished he could see she'd paid a price too.

o   o

She'd been near the top of her class from the beginning of training, so she'd known she was likely to have her pick of jobs. Agents rarely received New York or Washington for first assignments. Otherwise, the country was open. Brian had suggested somewhere in the West, ideally San Diego or Denver. He'd seemed surprised she wanted Birmingham.

"Alabama summers are even more miserable than this." A sultry Saturday night, Philly in August. They lived in a two-bedroom apartment in a row house east of Center City. The place was cheap and had been an easy walk to work for Rebecca, but in the summer even the walls seemed to sweat.

"I've always wondered about the South."

"Charlottesville's not the South?"

"The Deep South. Growing up, everybody I knew treated that part of the country like it barely had electricity. Hookworms and Confederates."

"Don't you think the FBI thing proved you aren't your mom? Now we have to move to Alabama?"

"Plus the cost of living is nothing down there, we can finish paying back my loans."

She had another reason, too. Word at Quantico was, small offices were best for first postings. Every new agent got thrown on scut work like background checks. But the little offices offered a better chance for a real role on cases. And the Birmingham office was known for being aggressive about probing Alabama's political corruption.

"Your job, your choice," Brian said.

Rebecca relaxed, knowing she'd won. "If you really don't want to—"

"No, it's fine, try something new."

Neither of them liked Philadelphia. The city was a tattier version of Boston, filled with the same pointless loathing for New York. And Brian had had a hard time finding work. Small businesses here didn't care much about the Internet. The big law firms and financial services companies downtown wanted their tech staffers to be full-time employees with college degrees. Brian was stuck in the middle. *I'd be better off somewhere people aren't so afraid of computers.* Thus his preference for the West Coast.

Though Brian hadn't had much chance to work anyway. Someone had to take care of the kids, and Rebecca's maternity leave for Kira had ended after four months. Then she worked sixty-hour weeks at Poynter. She'd been exhausted even before she got pregnant again. And Tony had been a difficult pregnancy. During her first trimester she'd thrown up so often that she tore blood vessels around her eyes, like a late-stage alcoholic. Morning sickness didn't begin to describe the feeling. She survived on Gatorade, crackers, and gummy vitamins. But she made up for all those missed meals later. By the time Tony mercifully emerged, she'd gained seventy-two pounds.

But who was counting, ha ha.

Four months later, she was back at work. Again. Sixty-hour weeks. Again. And when she wasn't, her life was changing diapers and shopping for store-brand groceries, saving a few bucks to pay down her loans. She tried not to think about her Wesleyan friends, who all seemed to hopscotch from Tokyo to Budapest before landing in Williamsburg to work as set designers. (How *they* paid the bills was a question everyone was too polite to ask, at least out loud.)

Rebecca knew that as far as misery went hers was mild. Her kids were healthy. She worked in an air-conditioned office, not a sweatshop. Even so, she couldn't escape the sense that she'd gotten old fast, that somehow she'd cheated herself.

But she'd chosen this path, no one had made her. And for her these years of pain had a point, an endgame. Quantico. The Federal Bureau of Investigation.

What about her lawfully wedded husband? What was the point for *him?* She didn't know whether Brian had understood what their lives would become after her graduation. She felt almost afraid to ask. Between her days writing memos and her nights breast-feeding, she didn't have the emotional energy for a conversation about their lives and roles. When Brian would have a chance to collect on the chits he was banking. If they even were chits. If he even wanted to collect. Maybe he was *happy* staying at home, hanging out with Kira and Tony. He doted on them, read to them, made them laugh, cooked them oatmeal for breakfast and tacos for lunch. He was a good dad.

And she wasn't exactly sitting around eating bonbons.

So when he agreed to Birmingham she didn't argue the point.

o   o

Now here they were. She had the job she'd aimed for her since that conversation with Ned. And the job was . . .

Awesome.

From the first she had loved the bureau. She loved its sense of mission and purpose. She loved being the last line of defense, making complicated cases that the local cops were too overwhelmed or politically compromised to bring. She loved the resources the FBI had. If she had a question about fingerprints or DNA sequencing, someone at headquarters or Quantico would have the answer. If no one did, criminologists and scientists were happy to help when she told them she was an agent. While her classmates from UVA wrote briefs about collateral estoppel, she listened to wires, pulled phone records, took long-lens surveillance photos. *I can't believe I get paid to do this stuff.*

Birmingham had been a smart choice, too. After September 11, the bureau's biggest offices had put hundreds of agents on al-Qaeda—

related investigations. In cities like New York, up to half the agents were now chasing counterterror leads. The impulse was understandable, but so far the work had mainly come up empty. Maybe al-Qaeda did have dozens of sleeper cells in the United States waiting for orders to wreak havoc. But the FBI hadn't found them.

But Alabama had relatively few Muslims, which meant the Birmingham office could focus on the work it had always done, with less interference than usual from D.C. Mid-career agents might worry they would be marginalized because they weren't doing counterterror work. But Rebecca would have plenty of time to work her way up and wait for the tides to shift. Sooner or later the bureau would return to its more traditional strengths, like public corruption and organized crime — especially if the counterterror investigations didn't go anywhere.

She especially liked the senior agent in the office, a fiftysomething Tennessean named Fred Smith. He reminded her a little of Ned, but with more gray hair and a southern accent. In the FBI, the agent who ran an office was known as the Special Agent in Charge — and the joke at Quantico was that some SACs lived up to the name. Not Smith.

On her first day, he'd told her, "This is my last posting. Don't have to worry about political stuff from me. I just want my agents to make cases. Let me show you the ropes, work hard, we'll get along." The speech sounded too good to be true. But Smith had turned out to mean every word.

Really, the only problem with the job was that she liked it too much. She could always do more work. Agents interviewed witnesses in teams, so that part of the job was nine to five. But she could always pull another property record, listen to another wire, practice her shooting. The phenomenon of new agents plunging into the job was common enough to have a name: "Hoover Fever."

But unlike a lot of those new agents, Rebecca had two little kids at home. And a husband.

She'd helped Brian find a twenty-hour-a-week job as an information technology administrator at the University of Alabama, working on the school's email system and fix other computer issues. The job wasn't exactly sexy. But it made him something more than a stay-at-home dad. She thought having a salary would be good for his self-esteem. As for what *he* thought, she wasn't sure.

Maybe she was to blame. The energy she had left over after work she focused on the kids. She hated the idea that they would think of Brian as their go-to parent. Right now her priorities, truly, were bureau/kids/Brian, and the race wasn't all that close.

About the only place they still clicked was in bed. After she had Tony, their sex life had dried up, but since they moved to Birmingham, it had come back. She enjoyed him as much as ever.

Okay, almost as much. Like all couples, they'd lost a bit from the spectacular *have-to-have-you* of the first few months. But the fact that the sex was still good reassured her. Their marriage couldn't really be in trouble if they could still connect that way. The house was still solid. They just needed to change the light bulbs. Caulk the windows. Stop deferring the marriage maintenance. But there wasn't anything *wrong*.

So, she spent her birthday weekend at home. She tried not to think of those hours as maintenance and instead to be *present* not just for Kira and Tony but for Brian too.

Then she went back to the office on Monday and found the break she needed in the Draymond Sullivan investigation.

On a call with "Denny"—Denard Thomas Quincy III, his banker and golf pal—Sullivan's mask had slipped. Not much, but enough to give her a peek. After the usual NASCAR and Hooters talk, Denny had gotten down to business.

About the sixty-five property, Dray—

Get that new off-ramp, perfect for a hotel.

Yeah huh?

Pick it up cheap, that wetland thing. Everyone worried about permits.

That gonna be a problem?

Not once I talk to Ray-Ray.

How much you think?

Don't know what you're talking about, Denny. Sullivan slammed down the phone.

Ray-Ray was—probably—Ralph Waller, the Montgomery County surveyor, another of the good ol' boys who ran the county.

Denny and Ray-Ray and Dray. The names sounded like a punch-line to a joke about a pig roast. But these men were canny enough to have skimmed and stolen for decades. Unless Rebecca was very much mistaken, Quincy III had just suggested Sullivan bribe Waller to remove a wetlands designation so that he could build a hotel, which had led Sullivan to end the call immediately, in case someone like her was listening.

She spent the morning finding out everything she could about the hotel project. After lunch she asked Smith for ten minutes. "Might have something on the Sullivan case."

"Okay, go."

But as soon as she finished playing the tape, he shook his head. "No."

"Denny literally says, 'How much.' "

"And Sullivan says, 'Don't know what you're talking about.' "

"Because he *knows.*" She was flummoxed. "If Sullivan didn't know—honestly didn't—he would *ask.* Denny, buddy, what are you talking about? That's how real conversations go."

"You forget what they learned you in law school, Rebecca? Doesn't matter what he knows, it matters what he *says,* and he denies knowledge clear as day. Forget about it. Chuck would laugh me out of his office." Chuck was Charles Wave, the US Attorney for the Northern District of Alabama. "Chuck likes to *win.*"

"This is by far the best thing I've heard. If it's not good enough, we're never gonna get close."

"Maybe not."

"What then?"

"You don't like this guy."

"I don't." The way he talked about Jenelle shouldn't matter, but it did. *Them cheerleaders. She can do a split on my face anytime she likes.*

"Enough to take a chance? Something's come up that could give us a way in. I normally wouldn't suggest it to anyone as green as you, but it looks like you can walk and chew gum too. The fact that we're up here and he's down there, it could play."

"Sir? I have no idea what you're talking about."

"In or out, Rebecca?"

There was only one answer to that question.

13

The FBI named its undercover operation against Draymond Sullivan GULFSTREAM. It was a sting, though the bureau preferred not to use that word anymore, to avoid giving defense lawyers the chance to claim agents had entrapped their clients. Rebecca was at its heart.

She played the role of Rachel Townsend. Rachel had grown up in Mystic, Connecticut. She liked to party more than study and quit high school a month into senior year. After two years in New York, she found work as a flight attendant on private jets. The job opened her eyes to the world of the super-rich, and she liked the view. At twenty-four, in Geneva, she quietly married Oleg Fedanov, a sixty-something Russian billionaire real estate developer. At twenty-eight, she even more quietly divorced him.

Now Rachel was back in the United States, rebooting her life in Alabama, where she knew no one. She had $12.7 million in the bank and a love of real estate she'd picked up from Fedanov, who had built apartment complexes all over Russia. She was street smart and aggressive, happy to cut not just a corner but an entire side if necessary.

Setting the cover took months. The private jet company, Velocity Air, was real and had helped the FBI before. Fedanov was also real, and really lived in Geneva. He owed the bureau a favor or five. He was a millionaire, not a billionaire. But an investigator would need

Kremlin-level contacts to know for sure. Swiss marriage and divorce records were secret. The Townsend family would vouch for Rachel, in the unlikely event anyone ever knocked on their door in Mystic. Of course, Rachel's high school didn't have a yearbook picture of her. She hadn't graduated.

In Birmingham, Rachel lived in one of the new apartment buildings downtown. It had a doorman, so no one could knock on her door without warning. And according to Rachel's cover, she traveled frequently to California and Europe, which gave her an excuse for not being there.

The story wasn't perfect—no cover was perfect—but it was solid. If Sullivan got close enough to crack it, the FBI should know in time.

o   o

The cover was only the beginning.

Next Rebecca, aka Rachel, had to find a way to get close to Sullivan, an impossible job without help from the inside. But the FBI had a cooperator, Kevin Boone. Boone was a senior vice president at BankAlabama with an unfortunate fondness for pictures of naked five-year-olds. Boone's vices didn't extend offline, as far as the bureau could tell, so he was a safe bet for a delayed sentencing. As safe as a guy who liked kiddie porn could be, anyway.

Boone had offered to testify against Sullivan. But Boone didn't have the details on Sullivan's schemes. Besides, a jury would never convict Sullivan on Boone's testimony alone, not once it knew the charges Boone faced. Jurors tended not to believe child pornographers.

Northern District of Alabama prosecutors were reluctant to make a deal with Boone, but Smith convinced them that Boone offered unique access to Draymond Sullivan. Sullivan and Boone had known each other twenty-five years. BankAlabama had financed several deals for Sullivan. If Boone vouched for Rachel Townsend, Sullivan would listen.

Finally, prosecutors agreed to allow Boone to plead guilty to a sealed indictment. He received no promise of a reduced sentence.

Instead, the government merely agreed to wait on his sentencing hearing as long as he was helpful on GULFSTREAM.

The sentencing delay made sense. If the guilty plea became public, Boone's value as a cooperator would vanish. Sullivan would figure Boone had flipped and suspect anyone Boone brought to him. Meanwhile, the delay gave Boone the strongest possible incentive to sell Rachel's story. If the operation went south and the FBI pulled the plug, Boone would find himself headed to the nearest US Penitentiary. Do not pass go, do not collect two hundred pictures.

From the start, Fred Smith made sure Boone knew he was responsible for Rebecca's safety. *Any of them good ol' boys even breathes on her, you will spend the rest of your life in prison. Won't be one of those fun prisons, neither. No administrative segregation no matter how much you beg. And I personally will tell BoP to make sure everybody knows what you're in for. You understand?*

Boone understood.

o   o

Thus, Rachel Townsend became a high-net-worth client of Bank-Alabama. Thus, Boone helped her buy a pair of fleabag apartment buildings in Clanton, halfway between Birmingham and Montgomery.

Draymond Sullivan, who liked government rent checks, had rolled up Section 8–eligible apartments in the area for years. Sullivan was interested in his new competition, especially when Boone told him she was "a hottie from New York." He invited her to coffee in Montgomery. "Nobody knows more about land down here than me. Let me help you out."

Rachel wore her lipstick a shade redder than Rebecca, her perfume a spritz heavier, her blouse unbuttoned lower. Low enough to persuade Draymond to talk to her breasts instead of her face, so the microphone in her bra could pick up his voice more clearly.

The microphone was black, fingertip-sized. A two-inch wire connected it to a memory chip smaller than a dime. Two days before, she had brought bras to the office so that Walter, a surveillance technician on loan from the Atlanta office, could sew tiny pockets into their fabric. "Better to use your own undergarments, you'll feel more comfortable." Walter was fussy, fiftyish, with a crew cut and a round stomach. *Undergarments* sounded exactly right coming from him. In another era he would have been called a confirmed bachelor.

"What if he searches me?"

Walter tucked the microphone and chip into the black cotton of her bra—and they vanished. Even Rebecca could hardly see them. "Why would he? It's not transmitting, just recording to the chip. So no signal, only current. Even professionals have a hard time spotting these."

o   o

Their first couple of meetings felt like duds to Rebecca. Sullivan didn't pay much attention to her body *or* her story. Mostly he talked about himself, his apartment buildings and strip malls and hotels. *I own half of Montgomery County, sugar.* He couldn't seem to decide whether to hit on her, buy property with her, both, or neither.

She wondered why Sullivan would make her a part of his criminal conspiracy at all. After all, he had sixty-five million dollars stashed in local banks, at least as much offshore. For bigger deals, he could raise hundreds of millions from his partners or borrow from BankAlabama. He hardly needed her.

But Boone assured her he was interested. *Lots of folks can give him money. Just none of 'em look like you.* A polite way of saying that if she expected to get close to Sullivan, she'd have to let him get close to her.

A move that would have been easier if she liked Sullivan even a little. But everything about him, from his drawl to his double chin to his boots—*boy down near Mobile makes 'em from gators he catches his own self*—turned her off. Some successful men seemed to take perverse pride in their own awfulness, the fact that they dominated despite being ugly in body and soul.

Or maybe Sullivan just had no idea how he came off.

She made sure she never hinted at her feelings. She didn't think Sullivan was the type to notice, anyway. Still, after five months she feared she'd failed. The bureau had spent hundreds of thousands of dollars putting together her cover, made itself the proud owner of two apartment buildings barely fit for human habitation. She had asked Fred Smith about renovating them, but he insisted she do nothing. *Nothing will blow your cover faster than fixing 'em up.*

If GULFSTREAM failed, her FBI career would be in trouble. Maybe she could move to Clanton, manage the properties. Smith told her not to worry. *These jobs have a rhythm; he's checking you out.*

◦ ◦

Sure enough, her phone—Rachel's phone—trilled a week later. "This my favorite stewardess?"

"Dray? What a pleasant surprise."

"Rattrap for sale. Down 206 pas' that Piggly Wiggly."

"News to me." Though it wasn't.

"You think the bank calls you 'fore me?"

"Shouldn't have told me, now I have to outbid you."

"Why fight when we can you-know-what?"

"No, what?"

"This way you learn from the best. Gotta get it done quick, though."

So Rachel Townsend and Draymond Sullivan became partners not even six months after they met. The deal was small, three million in all, six hundred thousand down, the rest borrowed. No laws broken, at least as far as Rachel could tell. Fred Smith assured her they were making progress. *He wants to see what kind of partner you are. Don't ask too many questions, let him lead.*

Rebecca didn't argue with Smith, but she didn't entirely agree. Sullivan mostly ignored women unless they were either old and useful to him, like his secretary, or young and pretty, like his secretary's daughter. Yet he liked showing off for Rachel Townsend. Maybe her expensive flashiness reminded him of himself. Rachel drove a new BMW M3, a bright red rocket, two doors and 330 horsepower. The car became a crucial prop, and something more. When she got behind the wheel in Birmingham, she was Rebecca, but by the time she pulled off the interstate in Montgomery, she was Rachel.

Sullivan rode with her once on their way to Clanton. On a flat stretch of 65 where the cops couldn't hide, she hit 110, swishing the BMW between tractor trailers.

"Trying to kill me?" he said.

"Pussy."

He looked hard at her. The M3 was cramped, even for average-sized adults. Sullivan stood six foot three and weighed close to three hundred pounds. She wondered if she'd gone too far. Instead he smiled.

"Even wonder why I don't hit on you, Rachel?"

"You do hit on me."

"Yeah, but I stop when you tell me, so it don't count."

"You respect me."

A line that set him laughing so hard his belly shook.

"We both earned it the hard way."

"You spent your twenties on your back for a Russian too?"

"My daddy sold Buicks. Good money. 'Cept he had a problem with dice. Huntsville was just big enough to have its own place to roll. By the time he was done, no more Buicks. No more house. No more daddy, day the sheriff slapped that eviction paper on our door he went upstairs and ate hisself a shotgun."

"I'm sorry, Draymond."

He flapped a hand, *Don't be*. "Worthless coward bastard. My momma said she'd get a job cleaning houses, only she couldn't clean worth a damn. Soon enough white people didn't come poorer than us. Worst part was it happened when I was eleven. Old enough to remember when things were better. Thank God I loved hitting folks in the mouth."

She waited, but he didn't explain.

"How's that?" she finally said.

"All my talking, never told you I played right guard at Auburn, three years? It all started there."

Something changed between them then. She could see the dirt-poor teenager he'd been. The vision gave her the empathy she needed to get close to him.

Close enough to destroy him.

o   o

That night, back in Birmingham, she told Brian what had happened. He knew her cover, of course. Officially, agents weren't supposed to tell their spouses about undercover operations. But the rule was impossible to enforce, and the bureau didn't try.

Anyway, she needed Brian's help. She carried a second phone for Sullivan's calls. The kids couldn't be around when she answered, so Brian sometimes had to hustle them away.

They were lying in bed. She always found herself hungry for sex after she went to Montgomery. She tried not to think about why. Tonight, the first time ever, Brian had begged off, but she'd insisted. She'd rolled on top of him, grabbed his hands, pinned him down. Taken her pleasure as he lay on his back hardly moving.

Now she repeated what Draymond had told her about his life, how underneath everything they were alike.

"No doubt. You like being Rachel, don't you?"

"I don't know."

"Sometimes I think you like being her better than being you." She didn't know if he was serious. And she was afraid to ask.

"What am I supposed to say to that?"

"You're supposed to say no." He laughed. And rolled onto his side.

o   o

Over the next couple of months, she fell into an odd limbo. She was effectively on hiatus at the bureau. She couldn't risk conducting interviews under her real name as an agent. Alabama was too small for her to be sure she wouldn't run across someone who knew Sullivan.

So she was reduced mostly to document work when she wasn't playing Rachel. And both she and Smith felt a little Rachel went a long way. She went to Montgomery twice a month at most.

She couldn't work out of the main office in Birmingham, either. Its address was publicly available, and Rachel Townsend had no reason to be there. Of course, Rebecca wasn't the first FBI agent to have this problem. Every field office maintained at least two backup locations close by, rented through shell companies which had no traceable connection with any federal agency. At least one had to be hidden from local law enforcement, too.

So, Rebecca spent most days alone in a three-room office that the bureau officially referred to as TCF–NA, True Compartmentalized Facility–North Alabama. The space was supposedly rented to Cortho-South, a medical billing company. No one looked twice at the cover. Birmingham was a center of the American medical-industrial complex.

She and Smith met every other week in Atlanta, two hours east, though they had protocols if she needed to talk more urgently. Every so often he let her join the kind of surveillance where the watchers spent shifts in vans and had no contact with the world. Boring jobs, but at least she could hang out with other agents.

Not being allowed to do regular bureau work did have one advantage. Her cover job was nine to five, so she spent more time at home. But though she *saw* more of her family, she felt disconnected from her own life. Rachel was glamorous, rich, exotic. Rebecca had two kids and a rented ranch house. Rachel had an M3. Rebecca had an Accord.

On top of the lies was the truth, the danger of an undercover operation, even one with white-collar targets. As long as her cover held, she should be fine. Violence wasn't part of day-to-day life for Sullivan and his friends. But Rebecca couldn't be sure how they would react if they discovered the FBI was targeting them.

The upshot was that Rebecca spent a lot of time thinking about Rachel. But Rachel never wondered about Rebecca, much less Kira, Tony, or Brian.

○   ○

Sullivan introduced her to his buddies. Every new contact meant more targets. But they were potential trip wires too. Just because Sullivan had bought her cover didn't mean everyone else would. *Let him do the work,* Smith told her. *Anybody seems too suspicious, back off, we've got plenty already.*

But she didn't know exactly what that surveillance had found. Smith wouldn't let her listen, and he briefed her only broadly. He wanted to cut the odds that she would blurt out something she shouldn't know.

Still, she figured that Smith would tell her if he thought arrests were close. At the least, he would warn her prosecutors were starting to lean on targets, *How can you help us? How can we help you?* She needed to be ready if Sullivan turned squirrelly.

The deals she'd seen firsthand had been clean. Mostly. A little Section 8 fraud, minor tax evasion, low-level skimming. Misdemeanors, basically. Nothing to justify GULFSTREAM's time and expense. Sullivan liked teasing her, hinting he was breaking the law without letting her see the details.

She needed to do more.

○   ○

He started to quote-unquote flirt with her harder. She let him.

"We gonna run away together, Rachel?"

"Ask your wife."

"Suzie don't care long as she goes to Buckhead, shops at Neiman's. Know how much that woman spends on clothes? Come on, have dinner with me. Up north if you like."

"You mean New York?"

"I mean Birmingham. New York, *please.*"

A week later he called her again, to tell her about a deal in Mobile.

"Land straight from the city. Double our money. Only my old friends get this one." The more corrupt and profitable the deal, the closer Sullivan held it.

"Double? For realsies?" *For realsies* was definitely Rachel, not Rebecca.

"You want in?"

"You know it, Dray."

"Then have dinner with me."

"One condition."

"I don't wear rubbers, sweetheart."

Rubbers? Who said *rubbers?* Sixty-five-year-old men, that's who. "I want to hear about the deal. Not the usual. I want to know how it really works."

"Better if you don't."

"Don't bullshit a bullshitter, Dray. No surprises. I'm in, I'm in all the way."

"In all the way. I like the sound of that."

"Bet you do."

o   o

Dinner was at Bottega, Birmingham's best Italian restaurant. She dressed conservatively, a knee-high black skirt and a simple black blouse, knowing Sullivan wouldn't need any encouragement. She figured he'd be handsy, but she wasn't worried. Smith had asked her if she wanted to have backup in the restaurant, but she'd laughed him off, *You think I can't handle Draymond after all this time?*

Now they sat side by side on a banquette at the back of the mezzanine, out of sight of prying eyes. She lived on the other side of the city, ten miles north. Still, doing anything in Birmingham brought an inevitable risk that someone who knew her as Rebecca might see her. Sullivan's desire for privacy was simpler and more priapic. He kept touching her, her hand and arm and knee.

The food at Bottega was good. Sullivan ordered course after course, lamb and rabbit and steak, eating like the hungry teenager he'd once been. He washed everything down with glasses of Johnnie Walker Blue. The scotch loosened his tongue, and he obligingly walked her through not just the Mobile deal but all his greatest hits, a laundry list of tax fraud, public corruption, kickbacks, and bribery.

"That sounds even more illegal than everything else," she said, after he told her how a South Alabama sheriff had lifted seven ounces of cocaine from an evidence locker for him. He'd passed it to a hospital executive deciding where to build a new surgery center.

Sullivan laughed like he'd never heard anything funnier. "More illegal!" *Haw-haw-haw, haw-haw-haw!* "It's all illegal, sweetheart, every last bit."

By this point Sullivan was five scotches in. Heavy pours. She was trying to keep him from a sixth. She worried that he would slur his words so badly the recording would become useless.

She almost felt sorry for him as he put his head in the noose that she and the bureau had so carefully knotted.

Then he tried to kiss her. She pulled away.

"Gimme kiss." He leaned over, put his gnarled right hand on her skirt, trying to push it up.

"No, Dray."

"You promised." *Promisssed. The Return of the King* had come out a few months before. She couldn't help thinking Dray sounded like Gollum. He was sitting to her left. She clamped her legs together but he leaned in, pressed his right hand between them until his hand was between her knees.

He twisted over, swiped his left hand at her breasts. She grabbed his wrist with both hands—she didn't think he would feel the mic but she couldn't take the chance. Then she felt her skirt riding higher as he shoved his right hand up her thighs.

"*Enough.*"

"I say the same. 'Nough teasing, Rachel."

His old-man sweat overwhelmed a peppery aftershave that belonged on a frat boy. He was not just heavy but stronger than she expected, stronger than she was, muscle under all that fat. His bulk blocked her, pressed her into the banquette. They were alone on the mezzanine. The meal had gone late as Sullivan brag-confessed, and the waiters and everyone else had disappeared.

She kept her legs clamped but he pushed his hand up farther. The skirt began to tear, a slow *rrrrrip*, the sound horrifying. She had pepper spray in her purse but she didn't know if she could reach it.

"Stop. Please."

For a moment he hesitated, nodded as if to apologize.

Then he kissed her, his lips thick and rubbery, his tongue like a cat pawing at a mouse hole, his breath sour with scotch. Bile rose in her throat. This couldn't be happening. Not *here*, a public space, a restaurant. But it was. Sullivan grunted, a low animal sound. His self-control evaporated all at once. He pushed the table back with his legs like an animal who needed room, sending dishes clattering.

If she didn't do something, he was going to *rape* her.

She jerked her arm up, the self-defense training from Quantico taking over, and slammed back his chin. He cursed and slipped back, giving her enough space to scream.

Sullivan pulled away as a waiter thumped up the stairs to the mezzanine. They sat side by side in silence, staring across the empty room. As if the dishes had fallen by themselves. He was panting, from arousal or pain she didn't know.

The waiter hurried over. "Everything okay, ma'am?"

She stood, unsteadily. She leaned back against the banquette, feeling its cool leather against her hands. Now that she had escaped, every sensation was magnified; she heard a fork clicking against a plate downstairs as if the diners were at the next table.

"Bathroom." She staggered away.

o   o

The bathroom was empty. She ran the faucet, waited for her breathing to steady. Rachel and Rebecca had both been wrong. Sullivan was a bad guy, he took what he wanted, what wasn't his. Why had she imagined he wouldn't do the same with her? She was nothing but a warm hole to him. She splashed water on her face, reapplied her lipstick, smoothed her skirt.

She hated Sullivan. But she hated herself a little too.

o   o

At Quantico they'd had training for talking to survivors of sexual assault. One afternoon only. Rape cases were mostly local, not FBI. *Survivors often blame themselves for what's happened, wonder if they encouraged their assailants. You should remind them that the victim — the survivor — is never to blame.*

Never? She'd known what she was doing, teasing Sullivan into talking—

No. Not her fault.

She dabbed her face with a napkin once more. Thought back to Ned and that night at Drakes. Now she had a law enforcement story all her own. *Haw-haw-haw.*

When she came back the plates were reset, a new glass of scotch for Sullivan. He smiled at her as though nothing had happened. "Feisty."

"You have no idea." She kept her voice steady.

"You want coffee? Or should we get out of here?"

She needed every ounce of self-control not to pepper-spray him until he gagged. Was he *joking*? For the first time she understood gaslighting; she wondered if she could trust her own memory. Only it wasn't memory, it was *still happening*, her heart thumping one hundred fifty beats a minute. She wondered if she could last through coffee with him, decided the answer didn't matter. He'd given her more than enough. In every way.

"I'm gonna go home." She paused. "Alone."

"See you soon, babe."

"You know it."

o   o

She had planned to sleep that night in Rachel's downtown condo. She didn't want to risk Sullivan following her home. But as she left Bottega she found herself almost automatically tracing the route that led to I-65 and her house. To husband and daughter and son.

She swung the M3 around. She didn't get to go home. Not tonight. What would she tell Brian about Sullivan? What would he do? What if he confronted Sullivan and destroyed the investigation? What if he *didn't*? What if he simply accepted that this man had attacked her? What if he blamed her?

Which would be worse?

No. She didn't want him to know.

When she took the job, she'd promised Brian, *No secrets. In this together.*

Turned out she'd lied.

o   o

The arrests came three months later.

Two bank CEOs, seven state legislators, three sheriffs, an Alabama Supreme Court justice, four mayors, eight developers, almost two dozen assessors and bureaucrats and local judges. Plus the one-and-only Draymond Sullivan. More than forty in all, a huge haul. Even Rebecca couldn't keep track of everyone. She'd gathered evidence directly on almost half the targets. The rest had been developed off her leads. Among the biggest corruption cases the bureau had made in decades.

Smith took her out to dinner the next night, just the two of them, nothing fancy, a barbeque place with wooden benches, paper plates, cold beer, and perfectly smoked ribs. He seemed subdued on the drive over. She didn't understand what was wrong, until he raised his Coke—he didn't drink.

"Congratulations, Rebecca. You did it."

"We did it."

"Gonna miss you."

She thought he must be retiring.

No. He walked her through what she'd been too focused on the case to see. She couldn't stay in Birmingham. The defendants would learn her real name during discovery. Odds were that no one would try to come after her. Doing so would be impossibly foolish. Most of them were looking at one to five years. Even Sullivan was looking at twelve, fifteen at most. They could have gone after him for sexual assault too, but Rebecca had insisted they keep what had happened at the dinner far from the indictment.

So she should be safe from retaliation. But the sheer number of defendants raised the risk. Only one had to be crazy enough to try. And these were privileged men who'd never considered they might go to prison.

"What about testifying? I'll have to be here for that."

"Everyone's gonna plead. Almost, anyway. Bet on it. Can't argue those recordings and already half of 'em have their lawyers asking about flipping. You have to come in, we'll fly you back. Old home week. But the sooner you get out of here the better."

She hadn't realized until this moment how much she liked Fred Smith. He was plainspoken and honorable. He had helped her through the most difficult moments of the investigation.

"What about Boone?" The cooperator.

"What about him?" Smith said.

"He kept his word. We couldn't have made this case without him."

"No way the US Attorney's Office lets him walk."

"He seemed genuinely remorseful." Boone struck her as a guy who might decide a one-way swim in the Gulf was preferable to the public humiliation of being known as a child molester.

"The guy did what he did. He had a lawyer, a good one, he made a deal. Don't forget those are real live girls in those pictures."

True enough.

"Let's talk about you," he said. "You can go wherever you want. D.C. will take you in a second. New York."

"But."

"But. I'd stay in the field for at least one more rotation. Land mines everywhere up there; you really want to understand how the bureau works before you go north. Anyway, you're too good right now to waste time in meetings."

"CI?" Counterintelligence seemed like a natural fit for her. She'd spent some of those hours in the CorthoSouth office practicing Russian.

"If you like. The big bosses are still so focused on CT though." Counterterror.

She could tell he had a specific office in mind. "Out with it, Fred."

o   o

She came home that night to find Brian in the garage, greasing the chain on his Ducati. He'd bought the bike used a month before. But it had needed fresh brake pads. Then the fuel line had clogged. He'd barely ridden it.

She knelt beside him, rubbed his back. "Kids okay?"

"Asleep." He reached up and pressed the starter and the engine roared to life. He leaned against the bike, striking a pose. "Come on, Becks, let's go."

"What if they wake up?"

"Just around the block." But he was already nodding, conceding defeat. He turned off the bike. "How was dinner?"

"Fine. Fred's a really good guy."

"Deputy Dawg? What's he want?"

She hated when Brian called Smith *Deputy Dawg*. "Remember a couple of months ago you said you'd had enough of Birmingham?"

"I'm not sure that's what I said."

It wasn't. What he'd said was, *We'd better get out of here, I'm starting to like it.*

"I get it, Becks. Your cover's blown, time to bounce."

"Busted." She smiled, hoping to lighten the mood.

"Bet you already have somewhere in mind. You put in for it yet?"

"Of course not. You know I couldn't—" She stopped herself. She'd been about to say, *I couldn't have done this without you*, but she had a feeling the words would only inflame him.

"Couldn't what?"

"Come on, take me around the block. I'm serious."

"First tell me where we're moving."

"It's not like that, Bri."

"No? So if I say I really want to go to LA next, that'll be cool?"

"Do you really want to go to LA?"

He turned on the bike, straddled it, rolled the throttle until the engine roared.

"Houston. Fred thinks I should go to Houston." She hopped on behind him, rested her hands lightly on his hips. "Now shut up and take me out before the kids wake up."

He did. And for a few minutes they were fine.

14

Houston

Buzzing at her feet. An angry hiss, as if an inch-high demon were stuck in her purse.

Her BlackBerry. Again.

Probably the office. She couldn't be sure. Because she couldn't see it. Because she'd left it in her purse so she wouldn't check it during dinner. Of course, if she'd really planned not to check it she would have left it at home.

She *should* have left it at home. She and Bri hadn't had a date night in months. Tough to make time for dates when she didn't get home until seven thirty on weeknights and spent every other weekend chasing a serial killer and maybe something else too in South Texas.

Now she sat across from Brian at a white-tablecloth sushi restaurant in River Oaks, Houston's fanciest neighborhood, surrounded by oil company executives and their second wives. She and her husband were sipping sake they didn't like and eating yellowtail rolls they couldn't afford.

Happy anniversary!

Because not going out together for six months meant overcorrecting when the big night arrived, trying too hard to prove everything was copacetic. Even though Rebecca *knew* the mistake she was making. Even though she could still remember when the perfect meal was fried eggs and hash browns and a kitchen counter on which to enjoy Brian's company.

Because those hash browns might not even have been that long ago—eleven years wasn't *that* long—but that couple no longer existed. Might as well have been Antony and Cleopatra, that's how dead they were. The days of push-the-plates-in-the-sink sex were gone and not coming back.

She and Brian needed to be a different couple, a grown-up couple. They needed to celebrate their anniversary properly. To find a new way to be together. Maybe the new way wasn't as much fun as the old way, but they needed to pretend it was, or else . . .

"You can look," Brian said. "It's okay."

"What?" She feigned surprise. Badly.

"I know you want to check, just go ahead."

o   o

She'd been intimidated when they arrived in Texas three years before. The Houston office had over three hundred agents, many more than Birmingham, investigating everything from money-laundering by Mexican cartels to big white-collar crime cases like Enron.

What Rebecca had pulled off in Birmingham didn't mean much here. And the office was *very* male. The bureau claimed almost a quarter of its agents were women. But that number was misleading. Human resources and other back-office jobs leaned female. Only a few women were frontline agents doing real investigative work.

For the first time Rebecca saw the bureau's casual sexism. It had been hidden at Quantico, because headquarters watched training so closely. In Birmingham, Fred Smith hadn't put up with it. But here male agents hung out after work at bars where the only women were cop groupies.

Smith had connected her with two agents he knew, but one rotated out a month after she arrived. The other had suffered a heart attack and retired. Quickly she felt like a cog in a big machine, jumped from case to case on the orders of her bosses. Whatever momentum she'd had from Birmingham was gone. She worried coming here had been a mistake.

It was Brian who gave her the answer.

"What about the US Attorney's Office? Bet it's not ninety percent guys."

He was right. From what she'd seen, at least one-third of the prosecutors in Houston were women.

"You've got a law degree, they'll like that. And maybe they're tired of dealing with all that testosterone coming out of Jester." T. C. Jester Drive, home of the bureau's main Houston office, although the bureau was moving to a new building off the Northwest Freeway.

"You think the way to get ahead is to ignore what my bosses want and beg the AUSAs for help?" The question came out more aggressively than she'd intended.

"I think if the prosecutors like you, it'll make your bosses happy, Becks. Have coffee with them. Help them out when you can."

"Extra work."

"Not usually a problem for you."

I'm not worried about me.

o   o

Brian was right. The prosecutors took to her. Within six months they were asking for her. Her immediate supervisor, a crusty Oklahoman, tried to complain, but *his* boss told him to stop yapping. *They like her, one less problem for me.* Rebecca had to admit, for a guy who had always bounced from job to job, Brian understood office politics.

But she was right, too. She paid the price with the kids for the late nights. Kira was in school now, and Tony kindergarten. Both were old enough to know she was shorting them. She had one ironclad rule. She reserved Sunday afternoons for family. But they needed more.

The second-worst part was that Brian barely seemed to care. She had steered him to a new job as a systems administrator at Conoco-Phillips, which would happily hire anyone with an FBI connection. When she asked him if he liked it, he said, "Installing and maintaining enterprise software, every boy's dream."

But they both knew he couldn't quit. They lived basically paycheck to paycheck. Working for the FBI was surprisingly expensive. The bureau expected its agents to dress professionally. Good women's clothes didn't come cheap. Rebecca was stuck buying five-hundred-dollar Theory suits. Plus, yes, she had one indulgence. She'd bought a 330i, the BMW one model down from the M3. It was a sedan, so she could haul the kids in it, though after one too many spills on the leather she tried to keep them in Brian's old Jeep Cherokee.

Should she have spent thirty-eight K on a car? Maybe not. But the M3 had spoiled her, and she did drive a lot. Everyone in Houston drove a lot.

Anyway, she was the primary earner, wasn't she? A *man* in her position would have bought himself a nice car and not felt guilty. She knew, because the FBI garage was filled with equally flashy vehicles. The feeling in the office seemed to be that a million-dollar house was impossible—and would make everyone wonder how you'd paid for it—but a thirty-five-thousand-dollar car was achievable.

She didn't just spend on herself, either. She wanted the kids to have nice clothes. Maybe because she felt guilty about not spending enough time with them. A predictable feeling, but its predictability didn't make it less real. Not to mention taxes, and babysitters, and trips back to Massachusetts to see her parents, and groceries, and making sure she picked up her share of the drinks when she went out with the AUSAs, and everything else—no, Brian couldn't quit. They needed the thirty-four thousand he made just to stay on top of the bills every month.

"So you don't like the job?" she said.

"Does it sound like I like the job?" He used the Socratic method with her a lot these days.

"I just want you to be happy, Bri."

"That what you want? For me to be happy?"

So often their conversations now slipped into the thrust-and-parry of a swordfight. Or maybe more accurately the cape-waving of a bull-fight. She wasn't sure who was the matador.

She wanted to scream at him. Maybe she should. Maybe a good screaming match would break the glass wall that was rising between them, a millimeter a day, slow and certain. She could still see him. He still looked the same. But she couldn't *reach* him. Even their sex life had withered. They weren't in a dead bed, not yet. But they rarely got together more than a couple of times a month. He'd wanted the lights off recently, another first. She wondered what porn star or model he was thinking about, because she knew it wasn't her.

She couldn't help but laugh. "Do you know how annoying you are these days? Professor Unsworth?" She looked over, hoping the joke had broken through. Not that she particularly cared. If the *second*-worst part of her dereliction of duties at home was that Brian hardly cared, the worst part was that she didn't either. Yes, she missed the kids. She wanted to do more for them, with them. But all her guilt didn't get her home a minute earlier.

Being an agent was still her dream job. Especially now that Brian's advice had put her career in Houston back on track. Maybe one day she'd get cynical, tired of the bureau. Not yet. Every morning she woke up in awe of her responsibility. She put criminals in prison.

And, yeah, she liked showing all the bureau's Jims and Johns that she could make cases better than they could, find the pressure points in interviews, the hidden bank accounts, the extra video camera that had the clear angle.

Anyway, if she and Bri were asking rhetorical questions, how about this one: What had he expected when they met? If she hadn't gone to a big law firm, she'd be a young partner at this point, working nights and weekends. Or she wouldn't have made partner, and she would have had to find another job at a smaller firm. Either way, they'd have more money, but she'd spend even less time at home.

Thing about rhetorical questions, they are mostly better off unasked. So she didn't. She poured herself into the bureau instead.

Most nights, Rebecca barely made it home in time to tuck in Tony, talk to Kira for a few minutes. By ten she was ready for bed herself. The schedule gave her an hour or two to spend with Brian. But she *needed* that time to decompress. To watch dumb television, *American Idol*, *The Bachelor*, whatever. Anything that would lock her mind in the off position.

Sometimes she wanted to tell him about her day. But she could rarely find the energy. His own work was so boring neither of them could pretend to care. When they wound up talking for more than a few minutes on weeknights, the subject was usually the kids.

Then she went to bed—alone—and woke by five forty-five to work out for an hour, get Kira and Tony dressed and pour their cereal. Having breakfast with them was the only way she could know she'd see them each day.

Meanwhile Bri hung in the kitchen past midnight, wearing headphones as he stared at his laptop. He claimed he was coding an app. But the couple of times she'd surprised him, he'd snapped down the screen so fast she figured he was watching porn. He'd been right about movies on the Internet, she had to admit.

He was right a lot of the time. In truth, he was probably smarter than she was. But if she had learned anything since college, it was that brains only went so far. Getting ahead meant grinding.

Only she wasn't sure Brian cared about getting ahead. Though the layer of irony that coated him meant she couldn't entirely tell. She understood. They were both Generation X. They had grown up with irony as their default setting. When they were teenagers, no cultural influence—at least for white kids—had been more important than Nirvana, its very name a thumb-in-the-eye joke. Brian had seen Nirvana *in Seattle*. He had his signed first-edition copy of *Microserfs*. If she tried, she could still connect with him that way. But trying no longer interested her much. The FBI wasn't a very ironic place. Solving crimes wasn't a very ironic job. For the most part she'd left irony behind.

Sometimes she feared she'd left her husband behind, too. Viewed in straightforward, brutal terms, the equation was simple. Her workday left her barely enough time to be a mother or a wife. Not both.

She saw what the job was doing to her family. She tried to back off. Truly. She stopped raising her hand for Saturday jobs. She read to Tony and listened to Kira.

○   ○

Then the Border Bandit showed up.

Rebecca hated everything about the case, starting with the cheesy nickname the media had given the perp. "Border Bandit" made him sound like a used-car salesman, not a psychopath who had murdered somewhere around twenty women in Texas and more in Mexico.

She hated the way the murders were caught in immigration politics—the women were nearly all either undocumented or first-generation arrivals. She hated the fact that the investigators couldn't even guess what the body count on the Mexican side might be. Corpses from the narco wars piled up in the desert so fast that the *federales* could barely make basic cases, much less help a transnational homicide investigation.

She hated the killer's effectiveness at covering his tracks. He'd left only the faintest traces of forensic evidence: a partial tire track at one murder site, a piece of rope at another. She hated that investigators had processed some crime scenes so poorly that they weren't even sure if the Bandit had killed his victims where they were found. She hated her sneaking feeling that the Bandit was a cop.

And she hated the way the bureau was stuck on the margins of the case. The FBI had become involved after the Texas Rangers asked for profiling help. But the Rangers wanted to keep control of the case, and they had the political juice to do so. In response, the Houston FBI office told agents they could work the case only as volunteers on days off. The political signal could not have been clearer. *We aren't responsible for an investigation that isn't ours. Enter at your own risk.*

But Todd Taylor, the director of the Ranger company in South Texas leading the investigation, came to Houston to ask for volunteers.

We all know that Austin wants us Rangers to run the investigation. Taylor didn't say anything about what *he* wanted, Rebecca noted. *But I look around this office, I see you have more agents than all the Rangers in Texas. I'd be a fool not to ask for help. Especially if you speak Spanish.* Outside a thunderclap hit, as if to punctuate his words. Then another and another. July in Houston meant end-of-days weather. *Can't promise any of us are going to be covered in glory. This case is tough. But I can tell you this. Guy's not gonna stop until we catch him. Reason I came up here.*

Rebecca found herself nodding.

Her vow to keep Sundays for the kids vanished. Every other weekend she drove to the border, three hundred fifty of the most boring miles anywhere. Even without stops, the trip took five hours. She ached to speed, of course, and she knew she could escape tickets if she showed her bureau identification. But getting pulled over inevitably cost more time than speeding saved. So she kept to a steady eighty-one, a pace that hardly counted as speeding on a Texas highway. She left before dawn Saturday morning, came home after dark Sundays. The schedule was ridiculous, exhausting. On Mondays she was a zombie. Even Tony noticed. *Mommy, are you okay? You look sickie.* One afternoon she realized that she hadn't seen Brian riding his motorcycle in a while. *You should go for a ride,* she said. *It's a nice day.* He looked at her strangely. *I sold it. Last month. So we could pay the credit card bill.*

Taylor's Ranger unit, Company D, was headquartered in Weslaco, a soupy, sleepy town a few miles from the Gulf. The bodies had been left in five different counties, as far away as two hundred miles northwest.

Taylor's Rangers and sheriffs' investigators were handling the more recent cases. He had asked the FBI agents for help with the earlier killings, starting by re-interviewing family members and friends. *Old-school detective work,* Taylor said. *No suspects, no DNA, not much forensics. Do this the hard way.* Which meant tracing connections between the victims, or at least patterns that might show them how the killer had found his targets.

The interviews took more out of Rebecca than she expected. Nothing was worse than having your daughter or sister murdered, except having her murdered and knowing years later that her killer hadn't been caught. Rebecca had doors slammed in her face. *Nobody's in jail because nobody cares,* one father told her. *She died, nobody cares.*

She found herself dreaming about crime scene photos, one in particular that showed a teenage girl with her hands pressed together in prayer. No one knew why the killer had placed her hands that way. No one knew her name. No one knew anything.

You need to stop, Brian said. *You can't solve this working two weekends a month. And you're not being fair to the kids.*

He was right. But she couldn't stop. She told herself the case badly needed a female perspective. The victims were women, but the investigators were men. Some victims appeared to have gone with the killer willingly. Maybe Rebecca could figure out how he'd managed that trick.

But after a while, she wondered if she was punishing herself to soothe some deeper guilt. Not just the guilt that she was alive and these women were dead. The guilt of pulling up in her cherry-red BMW outside rusted trailers. She might not be the perp, but she sure felt like a thief, stealing time and hope from these people. She poked at the holes the murderer had made in their lives.

Tell me everything you can remember about the most painful week of your life. By the way it'll probably be useless. And yeah, I'm the best hope you've got even though I'm only down here on weekends.

Going after Draymond Sullivan had been scary. But she'd felt like she was in a fair fight. Nothing about what was happening down here seemed fair.

o   o

She kept going. She grew to appreciate the otherness of the borderlands, the slums that lay not far from the gates of ten-thousand-acre ranches, the wide-legged way the men walked. Sometimes she had to remind herself that South Texas and Boston were part of the same country.

But her badge meant as much here as anywhere else. She didn't worry about working alone. She had her pistol, too. As Uncle Ned had predicted, it had grown to be a part of her.

She was more an archaeologist than a cop on this case. The Bandit had long since moved on to new victims. The biggest risk she faced was having her ego bruised.

Or losing her heart to Todd Taylor.

o   o

She didn't realize what was happening at first. But inch by inch her life turned inside out. The border weekends were what mattered. Two days on and twelve days off.

She always checked in at Company D on Saturday mornings, even if her interviews were a hundred miles north. She had a good excuse. She couldn't link to the Ranger computer system, so she had to visit the office physically to catch up on documents and forensics.

Taylor just so happened to be in the office every Saturday morning, reviewing the week's work. He had to work the case on the margins, too. The Ranger higher-ups in Austin wanted the case, but they didn't like it. The victims were an all-too-forgettable batch of Annas and Esmeraldas.

One fine Saturday morning in December, the unsparing heat finally gone for a couple of months, she didn't see Taylor's Silverado in the lot behind Company D's headquarters. Her heart wilted. *What am I doing here? Might as well just go home*, the words unexpected, and then—

Oh shit. She couldn't pretend she didn't know what she'd meant. Her disappointment had nothing to do with the work. She wanted to see Todd Taylor, with his cowboy slouch and piercing hazel eyes. She wanted him to nod her into his office and look her over the way he always did. He never said anything, and he never looked *too* long, just long enough to make her pulse pick up. She wanted to see him in a way she hadn't wanted to see a man in a while. Though in truth she knew next to nothing about Taylor, except that he didn't wear a wedding ring.

When the receptionist buzzed her into the secure area she was surprised to see Taylor in his office, cowboy boots perched on his desk, flipping through a file. Surprised and *relieved*.

"Where's your truck?"

"In the shop. What I get for changing the transmission fluid myself. How was the drive?"

And they were off. Not much had happened in the case in the last two weeks. In fact the Bandit had been quiet since the spring. One reason Rebecca suspected he was a cop—waiting to see if the investigation had picked up, if they were close. They weren't. Taylor had drawn up a list of everyone in the five-county region who had a murder or rape conviction, asked investigators to request they provide DNA samples and fingerprints. Of course, the state already had their prints and samples. Taylor was hoping to provoke them, see if anyone reacted.

"Could work," she said. Though she didn't think so.

"So, look, can I take you out to dinner tonight?"

Okay, *that* was unexpected. *What? Yes, no, please.* Suddenly she was conscious of what she was wearing, so juvenile but she couldn't help herself.

"I'm sorry, I didn't mean to be presumptuous. Just, you drive down here for free, spend weekends, I thought it was the least I could do."

"I'm in Zapata tonight."

"I can meet you up there, there's a barbeque place that's pretty good. If you like barbeque."

"Your wife won't mind?" *Smooth, Rebecca.*

"Doubt it. Seeing as we've been divorced five years."

o   o

Their affair began.

Not that they ever kissed. Much less had sex. But she *yearned* for him, and she knew he felt the same. On their dates—if *dates* was the word—they drank lightly, he sipped Shiner Bock and she allowed herself a single Bloody Mary, if one was on the menu. The drink's peppery tang went equally well with barbeque and Tex-Mex. They tried not to talk about the case, but her frustration boiled over.

"If the Rangers want it so bad how come they won't work it properly?"

"I know."

"Have you ever thought about resigning?"

He put his beer down and looked at her. "Easy for you to say."

"I don't like women getting killed and left for the coyotes. I know, call me crazy."

"You have some bite, don't you, Boston?"

"Now and then."

They rarely talked about their families, preserving the illusion of freedom. But eventually, he told her about his marriage. He'd grown up in Lubbock, gone to the University of Texas—the main campus, in Austin. Sophomore year he'd met the middle daughter of an old-money Texas oil family from Houston.

"She liked the idea of marrying a guy who had nothing to do with oil. I think she had the wrong idea about my job. And I didn't know what growing up with money like hers meant. Full-time staff in the house, mommy and daddy never saying no. She was nice, really, but she had no idea how entitled she was. She was great when I was in Garland—that's Dallas, basically. Then they moved me to El Paso. She didn't like El Paso. Anyway, when they told me I was coming here she said no way, it was her or Weslaco."

"And here you are." She wondered if he'd try to kiss her tonight. She wondered what she'd do if she did.

"Here I am." What might have been a smile crossed his face. "I shouldn't joke about it. Divorce stinks, and divorce with kids stinks worse, but she's a good mom and a good person and we didn't fight about custody. And she's decent about it; she lets me take my vacation with them, and I was always too into the job to be the dad I should have been. This way I don't resent them, I value the time I have with them."

Rebecca's stomach knotted. *Resent?* Did she resent Kira and Tony?

"You're looking at me like I'm the world's biggest jerk," Taylor said.

"Or maybe you're just being honest."

He coughed into his hand. "I should go," he said a few seconds later. "Long day ahead." She realized afterward that the word *honest* had triggered him, that he wasn't comfortable doing whatever it was they were doing.

She spent the entire drive home on Sunday doing what she'd sworn she'd never do, comparing Brian and Taylor. Taylor wasn't clever or ironic. He was dogged and quiet, genuinely furious that he had failed to catch the Bandit. He wasn't perfect. Sometimes he showed an unthinking acceptance of the disparities in wealth and power that cut through the borderlands like barbed wire. *I don't make the laws, I just catch people who break them.* On the other hand, Rebecca was sure if he did sniff out the Bandit he would follow the trail just as hard whether it ended in a slum or the King Ranch.

o   o

The next time she came to town he didn't ask her to dinner, and she couldn't help feeling like the whole trip had been a waste. The lack of progress on the Bandit didn't help. If the guy had left any patterns, she couldn't see them. He'd been quiet for almost a year now, too. Too long.

Back home Brian had gone mostly mute. He took the kids to school, cleaned the house. Like he was practicing for life without her. Only in the bedroom did he expose his feelings. He seemed to know he was losing her, because more and more often he turned savage, slapping and biting her, fucking her like she was a toy, until the pain turned into pleasure and the pleasure turned to orgasms and the orgasms turned back to pain. She didn't try to stop him. She didn't say *No, don't*—though sometimes she found her mind drifting, not so much to Todd Taylor but to the border itself, the unforgiving land that had swallowed those women.

Not then or ever did they talk about what she was doing, much less why.

She wondered what he knew, what he'd guessed. If she should even feel guilty.

o   o

Their tenth anniversary was coming. A Saturday, a Weslaco weekend. She would make the right choice. She would stay in Houston. She would have an anniversary dinner with her husband, the father of her children. Her life partner. She made a reservation for two at the sushi place that the *Chronicle* said was the best in town. And she told Brian, get ready, we're going out to dinner like husband and wife. *Alrighty then*, he said.

But even before they sat down, she knew she'd made a mistake. The place was wrong for them, too fancy, too expensive. The lights were low, the room was round and windowless. When the host whispered, "Reservation?" Brian whispered back, even more softly, "Yessss." Rebecca knew the pretension infuriated him. Maybe intimidated him too, though he'd never say so.

They fell back on the last refuge of the sinking couple, sneering at everyone else. The room had ripe targets, jowly sixty-year-old men and their thirty-year-old wives. The cattiness was no substitute for real intimacy. Suddenly she felt the void in her life, in their lives, of the way she'd thrown everything into the job.

"Brian." She reached across the table. "I'm sorry. I know I haven't been a good partner recently."

He pulled his hands away, leaned forward. He looked not sad or even angry but *eager*. Ready to pounce. "What does that mean, exactly?"

Don't do this. She couldn't play this game. Did he want her to confess? And to what, exactly? I had dinner a few times with the Ranger who runs the case? Because in reality she'd done nothing else.

Or, closer to the truth: *That I found someone who makes me feel the way you used to?*

And this: *I'm sorry you never found anything you like the way I like my job, but that's not my fault. Maybe we can try to make our lives more about you, but you have to ask.*

"It means I know I've spent a lot of weekends away. I know I care too much about this case." The safe answer. The true lie. "I can't stop thinking about it."

"Do you think you can solve it, Becks?"

He still called her Becks. Still used her nickname. A good sign, right? Except that being so desperate for hope in your marriage that you ticked off good signs was a bad, bad sign.

No. "I know I have to try."

"Uh-huh. Interesting people down there?"

She realized at that moment she wasn't cut out for an affair. If she felt this guilty without having *done* anything, what would she feel if she did?

They stared at each other over their yellowtail rolls. Until her purse buzzed.

o   o

"You can look," Brian said. "It's okay."

"What?" She feigned surprise. Badly.

"I know you want to check, just go ahead."

Don't. It's your anniversary—

She pulled out the BlackBerry. Not the office. Todd Taylor. *Call me. Please.*

"Sorry. The office. I have to call."

o   o

She stood beside the valet stand, where two Ferraris shared space with a Rolls. Quiet wealth was not the Houston way. "Todd? Everything okay?"

"You know it's been a month since we had dinner?" His voice was low, urgent, a tone she'd never heard. "I miss you, Rebecca."

"You must be bored down there." Her voice was light. False.

"Don't pretend you don't know."

She knew.

"Come down here. No—I'll come up."

A new life waiting. All she had to do was blow up the one she had. She thought of Brian, inside, alone, staring at an empty seat. Her children, waiting for her. Kira. Tony. "I need to think about this." Though she had her answer.

The dream had turned real and destroyed itself.

"I'll drive up tomorrow."

"Don't do that. *Don't.*"

A long pause.

"You sure?"

The night blurred and the headlights on the avenue streaked, and she realized she was crying.

She wiped her face and went back to her husband.

o   o

She went down to Weslaco one more time. As soon as she saw Taylor she knew she couldn't be part of the case. He was friendly and polite. They had nothing to say to each other, and much too much. Even in May, when border patrol officers stumbled across two more corpses, the Bandit's first victims in more than a year, she stayed away.

And a month later, when a counterintel job on the Russia desk opened up in D.C., she put up her hand and grabbed it.

15

In Washington the stakes were high. Rebecca had a safe in her office where she locked away files stamped TOP SECRET/SCI/NOFORN/ NOCON. She talked about SIGINT and HUMINT and ELINT in windowless conference rooms swept weekly for bugs. She met once a quarter with the CIA's Russia desk officers — mostly at Langley, the agency's way of pulling rank over the bureau.

Yet for a while she couldn't help feeling the job was more of a game than her work in Houston and Birmingham had ever been. Move and countermove. The Russians recruited army colonels who were angry they didn't have stars on their collars, blackmailed scientists with drug problems, caused trouble wherever they could. The FBI tried to limit the damage. In Moscow the CIA and the FSB played the same game in reverse.

She had arrived in D.C. at the right time. The terror threat was waning, while the American effort to improve relations with Russia had gone nowhere. In fact, the Kremlin was becoming more openly anti-Western. Her ability to speak Russian made up for her lack of espionage experience. Within months, she'd been anointed a rising star. For the first time she felt as though her career at the bureau was assured.

The pace at headquarters surprised her, too—not because it was harder than the field. The opposite. In Houston, even before she became involved in the Bandit case, she'd always worked several others simultaneously. If she finished one, another inevitably bubbled over. In Washington, Russians were her only target. They were professionals, and they worked that way, mostly nine to six, nights and weekends only on special targets. Plus the deputy assistant director who ran her unit discouraged his officers from helping other desks. *There's going to be times I need you quick. I don't want to have to pry you from some van outside a mosque when I do.* For the first time, Rebecca saw the bureau's Washington fiefdoms up close.

o o

She spent the extra time at home. She saw the kids nights and week-ends. She glimpsed what she'd lost by being so absent in Houston and Birmingham. Sometimes Kira and Tony and Brian seemed to be a single unit, with their own in-jokes that she didn't always catch. She tried not to let the three-against-one vibe bother her, and over time it faded.

As for Brian . . . she didn't know what to do about Brian. The more time she spent with the kids, the more she respected how he'd parented. Kira and Tony were smart, decent, and fundamentally happy.

Yet he was as directionless as ever. The gap between her success and his stillborn career had grown painful. *And they needed him to make some decent money.* Money was by far their biggest problem. Though she was making more than she ever had.

She'd gotten a promotion in Houston and—unusually—another soon after she arrived in Washington. Between those two and her annual seniority bumps and the cost-of-living allowance the bureau gave its D.C. agents, she made ninety-nine thousand her first year, about what they had earned together in Houston. And the FBI had gold-plated health insurance and a great pension plan, if she got that far.

So they weren't *poor*, not by any means. But the cost of housing around Washington meant ninety-nine K in D.C. was more like fifty in Texas. No joke. They didn't have a prayer of buying a house here, not anywhere that wasn't an hour-plus commute. They couldn't afford private school, so they needed a town with decent schools. After a frantic search, they found a rental in Chevy Chase. Thirty-five seventy-five a month, on a busy street, and not half as nice as their house in Houston.

The taxes were brutal, too. *Everything* seemed to cost more. Electricity, food, laundry—Rebecca didn't know why dry-cleaning a skirt cost twice as much in Maryland as Texas, but it did.

She tried to spend less. No new suits. She hung on to the 330, though she'd already put more than a hundred thousand miles on it. All those trips to the border. She had teased herself with a test-drive of a 335, the new model. She shouldn't have. It had 300 horsepower and tons of torque. Every so often she would drive by the dealership in Rockville just to torment herself.

Fine. She didn't have to have a BMW. But she didn't want Kira and Tony to feel like they were the only poor kids in a rich town. They needed clothes, new bikes, decent vacations.

Fact was, money mattered way more in Washington than Houston. Houston was fundamentally a middle-class place. River Oaks was rich and the east side was poor, especially down toward the refineries. But mostly the city just stretched on and on. The neighborhoods blended into each other. The schools were not-great-not-terrible. People just wanted to work and drive their trucks and play catch with their kids.

Not Washington. The most powerful person in the world lived in the middle of the city. The biggest business in the world—the US government—filled it. D.C. was filled with people who wanted power and money, money and power. They judged one another ruthlessly, by their jobs and cars and clothes. And the Unsworths were not keeping up.

During the first year in D.C., they fell into a twenty-grand hole. Rebecca started paying the minimum on credit cards, got the rent in the last day it was due. Luckily—though *luckily* wasn't the right word, she knew—her grandfather Jerome died, leaving her thirty thousand dollars, enough to square them up.

But she couldn't lie to herself, she only had one rich grandfather. That bequest was a one-time windfall. They needed to be careful about money. All the time.

Being careful about money all the time *sucked*.

o   o

Of course, the problem had a solution. Dear hubby could find a job that paid decently.

Only he wouldn't. Or maybe he couldn't. She wasn't sure anymore. He insisted he was looking, he seemed to be looking, but the months stretched on without an offer.

She stopped being polite. Every night after they put the kids to bed she pushed him to find a job.

"You're smart, you've got ConocoPhillips on your résumé—"

"All the coding work up here is classified. They want guys with more experience than me."

"You know I can help. If you'll let me."

He shook his head like she'd wounded his pride. And she guessed she understood. But they were way past wounded pride.

"I'll bet, a little push, you can get into the NSA."

He'd walk away, and she'd follow, trying not to lose her temper.

"You like living this way, Bri?"

"I'm trying, Becks. Just let me be."

Trying, sure. Sometimes he'd go downstairs. Sometimes he'd walk out the front door and she'd hear him drive off. Always quietly. He wasn't a door-slammer. Didn't raise his voice. If she started to yell he would silently nod at the children's bedrooms, put a finger to his lips, *Shh.* He was right, too, she knew. Tony and Kira were old enough to understand these fights.

She feared she was turning into a shrew. A pushy middle-aged wife. But they needed the money, and he *should* find a job. Wasn't like he was taking care of the kids. Between classes and after-school activities Kira and Tony were scheduled until six.

Maybe if she'd stopped asking, he'd come through.

Or maybe he'd just sit on his ass and watch the past-due notices come in.

○　　　○

She had no one to talk to about what was happening, either. She was too new in D.C. to be close to anyone. Though she'd made a few friends in Houston and Birmingham, she'd always known she was leaving, so she'd never tried too hard.

Her friends from high school and college were hardly part of her life these days. They viewed her choice to join the FBI as exotic and bizarre. *Must be so interesting,* they said. They weren't being sarcastic. They would have listened to her stories, if she'd shared. She didn't.

She told herself she kept her mouth shut because so much of what she did was confidential. But she had another reason. Somewhere along the way, she'd become a cop through and through. Like her uncle, she didn't think anyone outside could truly understand.

But Ned and his buddies didn't need to vent to civilians. They had each other. They had lived and worked in the same city their whole lives. She didn't have close friends inside the bureau. Partly because of the moves. And she couldn't show weakness to male agents. Most of all, she couldn't hint at problems in her marriage. She would be inviting any guy she told to caricature her as a ball-buster—or hit on her. With the possible exception of Fred Smith. He was retired now and every time she asked him how he was doing, he said, *Bored to death.* But she just couldn't see asking him for marriage advice.

She wanted desperately to talk to Ned. But Ned had suffered a stroke while she was in Houston. Too much whiskey, too many unsolved cases. He'd died quickly, a small mercy. She couldn't have imagined seeing him in some hospital bed, unable to speak.

She wasn't pitying herself. She'd put herself in this box. She should have been less stubborn, done more to keep her old friends close.

○   ○

Turned out she hadn't given Brian enough credit.

"Guess who's got two thumbs and a job in Fort Meade?" Home of the National Security Agency.

"Working for the man. How's that feel?"

"Like sixty-eight thousand a year, plus a 401(k), plus vacation. Full and productive member of society. Once they confirm I'm not a serial killer."

"They don't care if you're a serial killer as long as you're not a Chinese spy."

"Noted."

Of course, the background check would take six months to complete. Until then he'd be stuck on part-time unclassified work. But just knowing he had a job changed everything. For the first time since Houston, she felt safe financially. She even bought a couple of new outfits.

Sure enough, he completed the check, no red flags, and to the NSA he went. He didn't talk much about the job, but he seemed to like it. Then he took an internal exam and wound up at Tailored Access Operations—the NSA's most elite division, its hackers. A genuine accomplishment.

For the first time in she didn't know how long she was proud of him. Though even then her pride had irritation mixed in; she wondered why he hadn't managed to be more successful before.

Whatever their problems, they had never mentioned divorce. Not once, not in Houston, not in Washington. Maybe their marriage had never been *that* bad. Maybe after what he'd seen growing up, Brian believed divorce would cut the kids too deeply. Or maybe he was simply too passive-aggressive to suggest ending the marriage, while she was too worried about her work. Being divorced was no longer the kiss of career death it had once been at the bureau. But the FBI still preferred its agents to have a spouse, two kids, and a dog. She also couldn't help thinking how expensive divorce could be, how she might be on the hook for child support and alimony.

In other words, maybe they stuck together for the exact reasons their marriage had been crummy in the first place.

Rebecca wondered sometimes what might happen after Tony graduated high school. She would still be in her forties at that point. Just young enough to start again. She wasn't exactly ticking off the days on the wall prison-style, but she couldn't pretend the possibility didn't offer relief. Like watching the flight map on a turbulent plane ride, miles scrolling slowly by. *This won't last forever.*

o   o

Still, she didn't have much to complain about as she left her thirties behind and began the long march through middle age. Her job became more interesting as the Russians became more aggressive. Then a flaw in a CIA communications system exposed whole networks of the agency's spies in China and Iran. One by one they vanished. The dead spies were not Americans, but foreign nationals whom the CIA had recruited. So the agency could hide its failure from the public for years. But the episode taught Rebecca that espionage really was a life-and-death business. Like China and Iran, Russia would not hesitate to execute anyone it caught spying for the United States.

Brian's NSA pay ended their short-term money worries. Of course, a house was still out of reach and she wondered about how they'd pay for college. But on a week-to-week, month-to-month basis they were okay. She even traded in the 330i for the 335i.

She wondered about Todd Taylor, whether he'd found someone else. Sometimes when she closed her eyes she saw his. She sometimes dreamed about him, dreams that usually ended in disaster. Once they were line dancing and an earthquake hit. But she never called him.

Watching the kids become actual independent people was both terrifying and gratifying. Kira turned twelve and hit puberty and turned gorgeous and skinny and then too skinny. Tony found a couple of dorky friends and started to play Dungeons & Dragons, the old-fashioned version with the twenty-sided dice.

And then they got rich.

Thanks to Brian.

One day at dinner, apropos of nothing, he announced he'd sold his app.

He'd mentioned some gambling app a couple of months before, and even gone out to Las Vegas for it. She'd hadn't paid much attention, to be honest. She figured he'd earned the right to a trip to Vegas, and if he wanted to dress it up with a work excuse so be it.

But it turned out he wasn't exaggerating. He'd created an iPhone and Android app called Twenty-One. It charted the best possible plays in blackjack and other games. Simulated versions of the games themselves, too, and fantasy sports betting, all in a simple-to-use format. Then he'd linked the app to the phone's GPS so casinos could target ads and even message players directly. More than twenty thousand people had already downloaded it. A casino consulting firm in Nevada liked it and wanted it.

"Guess how much they paid."

What were apps worth? She had no idea. But it turned out the answer was two million dollars.

The money changed everything.

Even after taxes they had well over a million. They set aside a chunk for the kids' college funds, put most of the rest toward a house. He even bought her a used Steinway. He started working out four days a week. In a year he replaced ten pounds of fat with ten of muscle. She could see the sharp lines of his face, the edge in him that had drawn him to her. Okay, truth, he looked good.

Not to put too fine a point on it, she fell for him again.

She didn't think the change in her feelings was about the money, or even what the money could buy. Not exactly. The money was *proof.* Proof that Brian could be a partner. In their marriage, in their life. Proof he'd been working and not just watching porn all those years.

Proof that *she'd* been right about him, right to fall in love with him. She hadn't chosen a loser man-child. She'd chosen a genius coder who could create a multimillion-dollar app *in his spare time.* Maybe money couldn't buy happiness, but it made unhappiness easier to avoid. Even when Kira slipped into near anorexia Rebecca felt somehow if they didn't overreact the phase would pass. It did.

Her career took off, too—and again she had to give Brian some credit. As the FBI investigation into Russian election interference accelerated, he warned her to stay away. *Doesn't matter who wins, it's gonna be a mess, it's gonna get political. If you have a choice, stay out. Stick to traditional counterintelligence, nobody can argue about that.* She trusted his read. So while other agents asked to join the investigation, she stayed away.

He was right. After the election, the investigation turned toxic. Within a few months, everyone involved faced such severe blowback that the bureau had to sideline them. Meanwhile, the Russians had taken advantage. They'd become even bolder, opening new operations against the DoD, CIA, and big contractors. Rebecca's unit could hardly keep up.

Sometimes, she felt like she was back in Houston, working nights and weekends. Fortunately the kids were older now. They had their own lives. They knew the importance of what she was doing. She liked to think she was setting an example for Kira, thriving in the FBI.

o   o

Life was good. Good job, healthy kids, a house, a marriage that had survived turbulence and was growing as it entered its third decade. She decided they should celebrate their twentieth anniversary in style, take a summer trip to Europe. Nice hotels, fancy restaurants. When they were old they would look back and remember.

Instead here she was, staring at the ceiling as the morning heat began to rise. Wondering where her daughter had gone. She'd wanted to believe exhuming the past would give her the answer. But she couldn't imagine the Russians would be crazy enough to go after Kira to get at her. Even during the worst years of the Cold War the two sides had avoided targeting each other's agents, much less families.

Other possibilities were even more far-fetched. Had Draymond Sullivan decided to spend his golden years taking revenge? Had the Border Bandit followed her to Barcelona? Nothing made sense.

The kidnapping was random. Had to be.

It had to be. Unless it wasn't.

Her last thought as she fell back to sleep.

III

KIRA AND REBECCA

(NOW)

16

Barcelona

Somehow she slept.

When she woke, everything was fine, the smell of strong fresh coffee filled her nose and—

Kira was back. Must be, or else Bri wouldn't have wasted time making coffee. He would have woken Rebecca as soon as his eyes opened. Nine forty-eight already, her phone said.

She pushed herself from the bed, leapt, really, thumped against the wooden floor, half ran into the living room. Saw Tony slumped on the couch, staring at his phone, and knew.

"Nothing?"

He shook his head.

"You've called her?"

"Like twenty times."

She could almost see the panic rolling toward her, a tsunami, silent and huge and sweeping aside everything in its path. "Brian!" she yelled. She couldn't help herself.

He walked out of the kitchen, a mug of coffee in each hand. He was freshly showered and shaved, like they were due for another day of sightseeing. She hated him. Then she saw the way his hands were trembling and forgave him, a little.

"How could you let me sleep?"

"You needed it." He pushed a mug of coffee at her. Like she needed coffee. Like adrenaline wasn't pouring into her blood.

"What I need is to call our Legat here, set a meet with the Mossos."

"The Mossos?" Tony said. "Is that the Spanish police?"

Not exactly, she told him and Brian. Barcelona was the capital of Catalonia, the country's northeastern province, which had a tense relationship with the rest of Spain. People here spoke their own language, Catalan, in addition to Spanish. They wanted full independence. As a compromise, the Spanish government gave Catalonia some autonomy, including its own police force—the Mossos d'Esquadra, the Squad Lads. The Mossos now had almost twenty thousand officers and a multibillion-dollar budget. They operated independently of the national Spanish police agencies, the Guardia Civil and the Policía Nacional. All three had offices in Barcelona, but the Mossos took the lead in policing the city.

"Sounds complicated."

"A little bit. In a way it's more like the US than Europe, overlapping agencies. But it shouldn't matter. The Legat here will know everyone." She hoped. She looked at her phone. Nine fifty-eight. She'd wasted *ten minutes*. "Let me call him."

o   o

"Rob Wilkerson here."

Brisk and efficient. She liked him immediately.

"Rob. I don't think we've met, my name's Rebecca Unsworth, I work out of D.C., I'm in counterintel . . ." She explained the situation, including the man and woman she'd seen in Paris.

"I have to ask," he said, when she was done. She knew what was coming. "You're sure there's no way she just went home with this guy Jacques?"

"You have kids, Rob?"

"Two. Fourteen and sixteen."

"Good kids?"

"Pretty good."

"Then you know. I'm not saying it's impossible she would have spent the night with him. Not her style, but we're on vacation, maybe she decided to go for it. But she would have called or texted one of us. Her brother for sure. One hundred percent. If she lost her phone she would have borrowed his to let us know. If he said it was dead or wouldn't give it to her she wouldn't have liked that, she might have walked away right then and either way she would have found another phone before she went anywhere."

Rob went silent.

"It's how they are, Rob."

"True."

"She wasn't mad at us when she left, not trying to make a point—"

Rebecca stopped herself. She'd mostly beaten her old habit of arguing after she'd already won, but it came back sometimes when she was nervous.

"Maybe she's in a hospital, got hit by a car or something," Wilkerson said.

"She had her driver's license."

"She could have lost it. That case, if she's unconscious, they won't know who she is. And even if they have her name—Are you in an Airbnb?"

"Yes."

"So no hotel key, no way of knowing where she's staying. Could be they're waiting for her to wake up."

The thought of Kira alone, anonymous, in a hospital bed didn't make Rebecca happy. Though it was better than the alternatives.

"You called anyone in D.C. yet?"

"I wanted to go local first. It's four a.m. there anyway, not much they can do at this point."

"Okay, I'll call the Mossos. The headquarters is in Sabadell, that's a suburb. I'd rather not start there anyway, it's Sunday, nobody's around.

Stay local. After the Rambla attack I got to know the Mossos supe for the Old City. Christiano Camps, everyone calls him CC. He can be prickly, we got into it a month ago, but his guys know every building in the Quarter. I'll see if we can meet him at the station house, it's on Carrer Nou, I'll send you the time, the exact address—"

Wilkerson was protecting her without saying so, she saw. By keeping the request local rather than going to Mossos headquarters, he would save her from embarrassment if Kira turned up safe. Plus, the first step would be checking hospitals and drunk tanks and talking to the manager at The Mansion. They didn't need high-level cooperation for that.

"Rob? Thanks."

"Like the shark said to the lawyer, professional courtesy."

o   o

She showered, dressed decently. Neither Wilkerson nor the cops would take her seriously if she looked like she hadn't slept.

Then she and Brian and Tony walked down Passeig de Gràcia, the handsome, well-manicured boulevard that ran through the heart of Eixample. She hadn't realized until they came here that Barcelona was as rich as London or Paris. Luxury brands filled the storefronts. The air was fresh, a sea breeze cooling the city.

Around them clumps of tourists consulted guidebooks, debated which Gaudí mansion to see first, checked ticket availability for La Sagrada Família, the cathedral that had been rising for a hundred years. Their casual happiness infuriated Rebecca. *My daughter's missing, and you're snapping selfies.*

"We need to print fliers, tape them up," she said.

"Let's talk to the cops first."

Another forty-five minutes gone. They were meeting Wilkerson at 11:15 outside the Gran Teatre del Liceu, a famous opera house on La Rambla. From there they'd meet Camps at eleven thirty. With every minute the search radius widened, the trail grew colder.

She needed to forget that fact or she would go insane.

○   ○

Wilkerson stood out from the tourists and the grifters on La Rambla in his lightweight gray suit. He was tall and black, about her age, his only surprise feature was hair that was not quite an Afro but was certainly higher and more styled than he might have tried for at headquarters.

"Mrs. Unsworth. Mr. Unsworth."

"Call me Rebecca. This is Brian. And Tony, our son."

"Thanks so much for this," Brian said.

"Not a problem." He looked at Tony. "What do you think? Any chance your sister is still, you know, out with the guy?"

Tony shook his head gravely, a wordless answer that seemed to satisfy Wilkerson more than anything Rebecca had said.

"Let's go talk to CC."

○   ○

The Mossos station in El Raval was a tall concrete box that loomed over a narrow street a few blocks from the harbor, the most run-down section of the district. A small, trim man waited for them in the lobby. He wore a white guayabera and linen pants that didn't match the holstered pistol on his hip. He shook hands with all of them, including Tony. He looked Rebecca over carefully. Cop eyes were the same everywhere, not exactly unfriendly, but quiet and wary.

"Sorry to do this to you on a Sunday, CC."

"Yes, I missed church." Camps laughed. The Spanish apparently didn't take religion any more seriously than anyone else in Europe. "Please, this way."

The bookshelf in his office included a dozen stuffed donkeys.

"Why all the donkeys?" Tony said.

Rebecca was secretly glad he'd asked.

"For Catalonians the donkey has a special meaning," Camps said. "In Madrid they say the national animal is the bull. We prefer the donkey. The bull sticks out its horns and gets killed. The donkey is

159

smart and stubborn and does only what it likes. Tony, I think it's better if you wait outside, is that okay?"

Tony looked to Brian and then Rebecca. She didn't like the way this guy had made a parenting decision. But he was probably right, and she didn't want to get sideways with him. She nodded.

o   o

As soon as Tony closed the door, Camps's smile vanished.

"Your daughter is missing how long?" A distinct emphasis on the last two words.

"Since last night. It's not just that she's not here, it's that she's not texting, nothing."

"She's nineteen, yes? Any"—Camps hesitated, seemingly looking for the English word—"disabilities?"

"No."

"A healthy nineteen-year-old woman meets a young man in Paris, he comes to Barcelona to see her, she spends a night with him? You'll excuse me if I say it sounds almost romantic. Not how I expected to spend my Sunday."

"We know our daughter. She wouldn't disappear this way."

"Okay, look, let's consider this with logic." Again Camps stressed the last two words. "Two possibilities, yes. First, something bad happened at random to your daughter. I understand, the Gothic Quarter at night, it looks bad. Seedy men. The cannabis clubs. You should understand, tourists don't get hurt in Barcelona. Maybe you get pick-pocketed, lose your phone. Maybe you're foolish, you want coca, you go into an alley, men with knives take your wallet. But in all of Catalan last year, we didn't even have one murder a week. The whole province. No one here has guns except the police. The Spanish don't hurt tourists, and the Africans, they know we're watching, they know if they touch a foreigner we'll send them home. They don't want to go home. Look past the dirt, the graffito, you'll see women and kids out at 2200, 2300. It's safe here."

Yeah, you're so good that you let a terrorist drive a truck down La Rambla in 2017. But then Manhattan had experienced a similar attack not long afterward. Those were unstoppable. And arguing the point would hardly help her with Camps.

"Robert, am I telling the truth?" Camps said.

Wilkerson sighed, not wanting to be in the middle of this mess. "Lots of petty crime in the Quarter, CC. But I'd agree, violence is rare."

"I'm not saying my daughter was a random victim—"

"The other choice, that she was targeted. By a gang that steals pretty American girls from bars? To sell? You're a professional, Mrs. Unsworth, so I speak openly to you. This is a fantasy of the cinema. If this happens anywhere in Europe, one time, the whole world knows."

"This man came from Paris for her."

"Yes. And maybe she feels like she wants to turn off her phone. She's at university, yes? Doesn't live at home?"

"Yes."

"Does she text you every day?"

Rebecca shook her head.

"Maybe for one night on this trip she wanted to be by herself without her mother watching her. You leave here when?"

"Tuesday," she said.

"So she knows she has time."

"Awfully sure of yourself," Brian said.

"Because all the time, tourists come in, tell us someone has disappeared, tell us we have to look for them. A day later, we follow up, they say, oh, he was just lost, drunk. Maybe in the hospital."

Rebecca felt her heart hammering. She hadn't expected Camps to promise he would drop everything and set all his cops after Kira. But she hadn't expected this open skepticism. She very rarely played the gender card. But she wondered if Camps would have treated her differently if she were a man.

"Here's what we know," she said. "We don't have this guy's name, phone, email, any contact info. He met her barely thirty-six hours ago. Now she's gone. Maybe you don't have enough kidnappings, murders, to know what those look like, superintendent, but in the good ol' USA we do, so I'll tell you. They look like *this*."

"Come back tomorrow," Camps said. "Tomorrow morning." He nodded at the door, dismissed.

"That's your answer?"

Rob Wilkerson clapped his hands on the legs of his suit. "CC. No one's asking you to shut the Quarter. Just give her picture to your guys, call the hospitals for anyone who matches her description. Check the arrest logs. If the girl's really gone you know the blowback's gonna be huge. Americans think this city is safe. Let's keep it that way."

"Did you forget last month, Roberto—"

"Your beef with the Guardia has nothing to do with this."

"You remember next time, you talk to me first."

Wilkerson nodded.

"Fine," Camps finally said. "As a courtesy. The hospitals, the other stations, the morgue." He looked at Rebecca as he said the last word. "But if you hear from her, when you hear from her—"

"You'll be our first call."

o   o

"I'm sorry," Wilkerson said to her afterward, outside the station. Tony and Brian were on their way to a print shop to make fliers. Rebecca was headed to the clubs she hadn't hit the night before. "Last month I briefed the Spanish cops on some guys. One was hooked up with the independence movement, which I didn't know. That made him a friend of the Mossos. They thought they deserved the first call. Camps and I talked about it, I thought it was done but obviously he didn't agree."

Rebecca didn't know what to say. She hated this jurisdictional nonsense. She hated it even more now that it might be messing up a search for her own daughter.

"This gonna be a problem, Rob?"

"I don't think so. Now that he's taught me my lesson he'll do what he said. He's good. He'll have answers from the hospitals and everywhere else by this afternoon."

Rebecca wasn't as confident.

"We'll find her," Wilkerson said. "She's out there, Rebecca. Someone saw her. Someone remembers her. We'll trace her phone."

Yeah, right. Neither the Spanish cops nor the NSA would do anything to find her phone for at least another day. Then Rebecca realized what she should have hours before. Maybe they couldn't trace the phone yet, but they could at least track Kira's calls and texts. They didn't need any technological tricks, either. All they had to do was log into their AT&T account.

For the first time in her life she was glad she was stuck paying her daughter's phone bill.

17

Somewhere in Spain

Good news. Kira still had one bottle of water.

Bad news. They'd forgotten to feed her.

Good news. She wasn't hungry. Fear was a great appetite suppressant.

So maybe good news all around, *har-har*. The Kidnap Diet. Get locked in a closet, watch those pounds vanish.

She figured it had to be afternoon. A line of sunlight leaked white through the narrow crease where the plywood was nailed to the window frame. Plus, the room had gotten hot. Uncomfortably hot. Sweat dripped down her back. Now, faintly, she heard the garage door wind open, *chk-chk-chk*. A minute later, maybe, the van rolled off. Had they left her alone? She waited. Counted up to two hundred, slowly, by twos. Then down to one hundred. Had to be at least five minutes.

The house was silent.

Her chance. If not to escape, at least to feel her way around her new home. Maybe she'd find a trapdoor back to Barcelona.

First the door. Just in case they were setting her up. She went to it. Slowly. On the balls of her feet. Listening. Hearing nothing but the occasional faint rush of traffic. Unless it was the wind. How could she know? Nobody had ever told her she'd need to learn to track *noises*. She was a city girl. Okay, suburban but—

Focus.

She found the doorknob. Turned it. It moved freely under her hand. But when she pulled and pushed the deadbolt gripped it firmly in place.

Okay, no surprise. An unlocked door would have been a Powerball long shot. She paced her fingers around the edge of the doorframe, didn't find a weakness. Wasn't like she knew how to pick a lock anyway. She thought about trying to kick her way out. But Jacques had taken her shoes and the door felt sturdy. No give. Breaking her toes wouldn't do her much good.

She turned, let her eyes adjust to the ribbon of light beneath the plywood. Because of Brian's preference for a nightlight-free house, she was used to moving in the dark.

She went to the back wall, ran her fingers along the plywood, reached under its bottom lip and tugged—

A flare of pain exploded up her right index finger. A splinter lodged deep under the nail. She tugged out the shard of wood, bit her finger to stanch the bleeding. And keep from yelling. Screaming her lungs out felt like a last resort, and unlikely to do much good. Jacques had taken such care in setting this up. She couldn't believe he'd brought her anyplace where someone might be close enough to hear.

The pain tamped down. Breathe. One step at a time. Tugging at plywood wasn't the answer.

She ran her hands along the right-side wall. Hoping for an air vent, even a coat hook. Nope. But she did touch a wooden shelf above her head. For sweaters or whatever. She hadn't noticed it before. Of course, she hadn't had much time in here with the light on.

She pushed the shelf up. Tentatively at first, biting her lip against the pain in her finger. Then harder. It gave. A little. Like maybe she could tear the shelf off. A long wooden shelf wasn't exactly the ideal weapon, but it was *something*. Especially if she could hide in the corner and bash Jacques over the head with it. A pleasant thought.

But she didn't try to break it off yet. She didn't have a plan. She didn't want them to know she was probing for weaknesses. And maybe some part of her didn't want to move too fast. She needed hope. The more slowly she explored the longer the hope would last. She reached up, slid her hand along the top of the shelf. Maybe they'd left something up there—

Footsteps.

In the hallway. Soft and swift.

Had she been so focused on the shelf that she'd missed the van coming back?

Or had someone been here all along, setting her up?

She scrabbled against the back wall as the deadbolt slid back.

Rodrigo stood in the doorway. He flicked on the light and she was blinded. She put her hands up, an involuntary gesture, submission. Luckily her finger had stopped bleeding.

"*Buenos días,* Cara."

Kira, you prick.

He held a bottle of water in one hand, a ball in the other. He tossed her the ball and she grabbed at it.

An orange.

"Hungry." It wasn't a question.

"Where are the others?"

"You miss them?"

"I'm a people person." She looked at the orange. He was right. Now that she had food, hunger flooded her. She peeled it slowly, piled the rind neatly on the floor, made herself eat one slice at a time, the sweetest fruit she'd ever tasted.

She had the insane idea of offering him a piece. *He's not your friend.*

He seemed annoyed that she hadn't, though. He sat down across from her, almost touching her. He hadn't showered in a while. A sour scent came off his skin. His face was shiny with sweat. His eyes were twitchy. She thought maybe he was high. Coke? Adderall? Did people in Spain snort Adderall? Probably, why would they be different from anyone else?

"Did you like it?"

Mind your manners. "Yes. Thank you."

"I mean in the club. The drug. You looked like you liked it. Wanted more." He leered.

"Is that what you thought?" She couldn't help herself.

He seemed disappointed. Like *she* was the criminal and he was the innocent.

He leaned close and raked her cheek with his grubby black-polished fingers, hard enough to hurt. No warning.

She was almost glad for the pain because it flipped reality right-side up.

He reached behind his back—

Came out with a hood.

"You want it."

She shook her head, *No.*

"You do." He looked at it like it was precious, a gold mask. Then he seemed to lose interest in it, tucked it behind his back again.

The closet door was open. She could *see* the hallway. Beyond it, the stairs, the front door. Freedom. Maybe she could jump him, overpower him long enough to run. But even if she landed a punch or kick, she wouldn't keep him down. He was strong. Without a weapon she would need to put a thumb in his eyes or land a perfect shot on his neck, close to impossible.

A last resort.

She had lots of last resorts right now. Not so many good ones.

"What do you think of, Kira? I see in your eyes you've gone some-where."

She could give him this much. Keep him happy. "The beach."

He reached into his pocket, came out with a vial, held it up.

"I learned my lesson."

"No, this is the real one. Coca."

Yeah, I'll just get high and sit in this closet for a while. "Thanks, but no."

He shrugged: *Your loss.* He unscrewed the cap, tipped a tiny pile of while powder onto the back of his hand, leaned over and hoovered it up. Then blinked, rubbed his nose.

"Cocaine, you know what it's good for?"

She had a crawling fear of what he'd say next.

She made the mistake of looking at him. His eyes were feral now. The coke had lit them somehow. He wasn't joking. She needed to figure out exactly what to say.

Or he was going to rape her.

He reached for her—

"The stuff, what's it like?" Distract him.

He stopped. "It makes everything, I don't know—bright. You want some?"

What a sales pitch. "A little, sure."

He handed her the vial.

Her hand shook and she dropped it, sending the coke spilling on the floor. Not an accident, what she'd planned. She knew she risked angering him but she hoped she'd slow him down.

"Fuck." But he laughed.

"I'm an idiot."

"*Sí.* Idiot." Though he seemed weirdly cool about the coke. Maybe he had a pound in the sugar jar downstairs. Maybe they paid him in coke.

"I'm scared, Rodrigo." That much was true, at least. "Of everything." *I want you to keep me safe?* No, too much, too soon. "I can't trust anyone."

For a moment she thought maybe she'd reached him.

Then his eyes turned hard and covetous. He nodded to himself as though he'd decided something. He raised his hands to his mouth and blew on his fingertips, *puff, puff,* cleaning them somehow before he reached for her.

He grabbed her shoulder. He was *strong,* not gym strong, the casual strength of a guy who'd spent his life lifting boxes, digging ditches. Fighting.

"Rodrigo." That stupid, inescapable song from a few years back filled her mind, *I'm only one call away, I'll be there to save the day*—

Nobody was one call away. Not Superman or anybody else.

He didn't say anything, just pulled her toward him.

In the distance the garage door clicked up, the sound unmistakable.

He groaned. Kira understood. She'd made the same sound herself when she'd put a perfect ball on the net, a certain goal, only to have the goalie sweep it away at the last moment. *No way. That was mine. I was gonna score.*

He dug his fingers into her shoulder. "You don't say anything."

He grabbed the vial from the floor, stepped out, slammed the door, slapped the deadbolt in place. A moment later the light went out.

o   o

The chalk taste of fear in her mouth. She swallowed it. Now that she'd escaped, saved by the bell, she could try to laugh. *Afraid to get caught with your hand in the cookie jar, Rodrigo? Her* cookie jar, as it happened.

He was dangerous. But she could already see the chance he offered. He had come to her when the others were away.

He would come again. She needed to be ready.

She heard voices downstairs. Faintly. A man, a woman, another man. Jacques, Lilly, Rodrigo. Was it really just the three musketeers? She couldn't decide if she would be safer with someone else in charge.

She listened as hard as she could, but couldn't distinguish anything, not even the language. She decided to use the conversation as cover to check the room once more. Start with the shelf.

She stood on tiptoes, ran her hands along the top of the shelf. Nothing. The wood smooth, finished. Then, down in the corner, where the shelf met the front wall.

Metal. Ridged. A screw and then a smooth-finished *nail.* Maybe two and a half, three inches long. She imagined a carpenter finishing the doorframe, leaving these pieces behind. They'd rolled into the corner.

She poked it into her palm. It was sharp. Sharp enough to pierce skin, explode an eye. *Good.*

She left it where she'd found it. They hadn't noticed it yet. No reason they would now.

She checked the shelf once more, slowly. Touching every inch, especially where the wood met the wall.

In the back corner her fingers grazed what felt like a roll of electrical tape, a smooth tube a couple inches around. She could barely reach it; it was in the most awkward spot in the entire closet. She stood *en pointe*, silently thanking Becks for making her take ballet, got her fingers on the tape. Heard as much as felt something in the center of the roll.

She pulled the tape to the edge of the shelf, and the thing in the middle fell out. It thumped against the floor and she panicked. She had to find it. Whatever it was. She went on hands and knees like an oxy addict chasing her last pill.

There.

Smooth plastic, no larger than her thumb, a serrated metal wheel at the top—

A lighter. She flicked the wheel, pushed down the handle. A yellow flame spouted up. No more than two inches high.

A nail was dangerous. A flaming-hot nail was a *weapon.*

She let go. No reason to waste the butane—

She heard someone walking down the hall. Not Rodrigo, different steps. Lighter, surer. Jacques.

Shit.

She stood on tiptoe, pushed the lighter and the electrical tape back into the corner where she'd found them. Jacques reached for the door.

She sat, realizing Rodrigo had left the orange peel and the extra bottle of water. His problem, not hers.

The deadbolt snapped back. She willed her breathing to slow—

The light flicked on. Jacques stood in the doorway.

Don't look on the shelf, don't look in the corner. Don't.

"Kira. Been busy, I see."

171

18

Barcelona

Rebecca didn't like scrolling through Kira's phone records. She felt a little like she was reading a diary. But she had no choice. Back at the apartment, she logged into the Unsworth family account. Naturally she knew the password, didn't need to fumble for it. Naturally she'd brought her FBI-issued laptop on the trip, vacation or no. She could hear her daughter: *Always prepared, Mom, nothing ever gets past you*, somehow making the words sound like an accusation.

No surprise, Kira spent more time texting than calling. Like everyone else, she received a lot of robocalls—*the IRS has blocked your credit card, we can help*. Those all went to voice mail. Her outgoing calls were limited mainly to Rebecca, Brian, and other family members, fewer than a dozen numbers.

Her texting circle was far larger. Rebecca counted more than sixty recipients. A handful of numbers received most of the action. Rebecca knew three on sight; Kira's best friends from high school. She could guess at others. The 802 and 412 numbers probably belonged to Kira's first-year roommates, from Vermont and Pittsburgh. A 510 number showed up for a month, then abruptly vanished after a flurry of 3 a.m. texts. Kira had mentioned a boy from Oakland. A *trust-fund artist*, she'd said.

Others were mysteries. Brian and especially Tony might know some, but they were putting up posters on La Rambla. Without much discussion, she and Brian had decided that keeping Tony busy would be good for his mental health. And theirs. She hadn't heard anything yet from Rob Wilkerson, but she had to assume that CC had kept his word and was having Mossos officers check hospitals.

At the moment these records were her best lead. And by "best" she meant only.

Metadata, the NSA called these lists. Even without knowing exactly what the texts said, the pattern revealed plenty. They were spokes radiating from the hub that was Kira, thickening and thinning as friendships and romances came and went. If communication was life, metadata was its DNA.

The FBI and NSA used database software to comb these records for numbers known to belong to criminals or terrorists. Even then Rebecca liked to scan them herself to see if anything popped: A three-minute, 2 a.m. phone call to a number that otherwise only appeared in texts. A desperate attempt to reach a lover before an attack, maybe. A flurry of texts at the same time every day for a week, as a plan took shape.

Rebecca hoped to spot a similar anomaly in Kira's records. If nothing else, she wondered if Kira had been in contact with someone in Europe before the trip. If the kidnappers had targeted her, maybe they had laid the groundwork before she landed.

But Kira hadn't talked or texted with anyone in Europe before she'd arrived here. Not on her phone, anyway. Maybe she'd used another channel. An instant-messaging service like Kik or WhatsApp. Her Instagram account—*Kira7SUns*. Possibly Facebook, though she was more active on Instagram. Facebook was the choice of parents and other dinosaurs.

So the lack of texts didn't absolutely prove anything. But Rebecca had learned over the years that only the most careful perps avoided texting. It was the simplest, fastest way to communicate. And Kira wasn't a perp. She was a teenage girl with a thumbprint-locked phone her parents didn't touch. She had no reason to get fancy. The fact that she hadn't texted anyone in Europe strongly suggested she hadn't been in contact with anyone.

Until yesterday. When Kira had traded a half dozen texts with a French number, the 33 country code jumping out. The first came just after midnight. Rebecca didn't need to see it to know that it was the *This is me* initial connection from Jacques. Two more in the morning—presumably along the lines of *We still on?* Another in the afternoon: *Let's meet at 2300, 11 p.m. for you 'mericans.* And one final hit as the magic hour approached—*Can't wait! Wear your best kidnapping dress!*

Since then, nothing. Kira's phone had gone silent. The records showed dozens of incoming calls and texts from Rebecca, Brian, and Tony. Stray texts from friends back home. Nothing outbound. More proof Kira was gone. In the unlikely event that CC was right and Kira had decided to disappear, she would have told her friends. She would have told *someone*.

The 33 number had vanished, too. No incoming texts or calls from it today.

Still, Rebecca had a lead now, a French number to chase. And, lucky her, she and Brian had the juice at the National Security Agency to check it out immediately, especially since the number wasn't from the United States. The agency could move more aggressively against foreign targets. The Bill of Rights only protected Americans.

Rebecca doubted Jacques would still be carrying the phone he'd used with Kira. Hanging on to it would be an amateur mistake. But once it had the number, the NSA could track everyone he'd called and texted before the kidnapping. The best part of tracing metadata was that the threads never ended. The agency could widen the net until it had linked every phone number in the world to the original hit. A flow chart as big as Niagara Falls.

Of course, after three degrees of separation the importance of the connections diminished, but it didn't disappear. If Jacques turned out to be "only" four phone calls from a known Islamic State recruiter, the

NSA and even the CIA would pay far more attention. And no matter how careful he was, Jacques had to have left clues. Even if the phone was registered to someone else, he couldn't *use* it without connecting to a network and giving up his location. The NSA could always trace those details. The reason the Secret Service tried to keep presidents off cell phones was that using one without giving up compromising information was impossible.

○   ○

Rebecca liked the NSA much better than the CIA.

Working with Langley meant constant turf battles. But the NSA was its own empire and had enough to do without pretending to be the FBI too. It was happy to help the bureau, especially on investigations that targeted foreigners and wouldn't run into legal problems. Since her promotion, Rebecca had grown particularly tight with Jake Broadnik. He ran the NSA's efforts to stop espionage in the D.C. area. The job covered everything from old-school countermeasures like sweeping for bugs near the White House to attacking the encrypted messaging apps Russian intelligence officers used.

The technical details sailed past Rebecca, but she knew Broadnik was good at his job. She talked to him at least once a month, and they had coffee every so often. He was vegan, maybe 5'2" and 110 pounds soaking wet, with a shaved head and a wardrobe that consisted exclusively of chinos, white T-shirts, and blue Chuck Taylor sneakers. But underestimating him was a major mistake.

The NSA guys fell into two broad categories, Rebecca had learned. There were geek-cool coders who liked being able to hack on the government's dime. Brian fell in that camp, though he wasn't as into the actual coding as a lot of those guys.

Then there were the patriots who believed—not without reason— they were defending the United States on the front lines of twenty-first-century warfare. They took their jobs seriously. And no one was more serious than Broadnik. He had come to the agency a decade before straight out of Caltech. He wasn't married, didn't have kids, and worked nonstop. Rebecca had once sent him an email at 1 a.m. on a Saturday morning just to see how long he would take to respond. The answer came at 5:45 a.m. and began *Sorry it took me so long.*

She trusted Broadnik, too. He wouldn't break the rules for her, but he'd bend them. And if Kira did turn up in a hospital bed or a jail, he would never tell anyone she'd asked for help. Why she'd rather call him than ask Brian to go to the Tailored Access guys. Hard-core coders saw everything as a game. If and when they did decide to help, they'd never let Brian forget it.

Broadnik it was. Just picking up her phone to call him made her feel better.

o o

He picked up straightaway. "Rebecca Unsworth. Aren't you on vacation? Europe, right?"

"Europe, wrong." She didn't have the time or energy to sugarcoat. And Broadnik wouldn't care. "I need help." She walked him through what had happened.

"You believe he's non-US?" he said when she was done. "To a reasonable certainty."

The magic words, the ones that gave the NSA the authority it needed, no warrant required. "Yes. I'll put it in writing if you want."

"No need. So she went missing Friday night?"

"Last night."

"Not even a day."

Not you too. "I may not have a PhD, but I can count, Jake."

"You telling me everything?"

"Like *what?*" More sharply than she'd intended, proof how raw she was.

"I don't know, drugs?"

Drugs. She realized CC and even Rob Wilkerson must have wondered the same, *Maybe your little girl is just too high to pick up the phone.* The implication that Kira was on a bender—or, worse, that she was whoring herself to a skeezy French drug dealer—infuriated Rebecca.

"Guess again."

A pause, mercifully brief.

"I'll open a ticket. I'm gonna do it from campus to watch it myself." His way of protecting her. "Give me maybe half an hour, forty minutes."

She hadn't known Broadnik lived so close to Fort Meade. In fact, she had no idea where he lived. Their friendship was defined by work, she realized. It would evaporate if either of them switched jobs. It was a stereotypically *male* relationship, which didn't bother her in the least. One reason she'd succeeded in law enforcement, such a male-dominated field.

"Thanks, Jake."

She hung up.

Now what? Probably she should hit the big clubs next. Sunday or no, backpackers and tourists would be going out tonight. The clubs didn't fill up until late, but many had restaurants that served lunch and dinner. Their managers would be around by midafternoon to check guest lists, plan for the night.

But Rebecca wasn't counting on getting many answers from them, not unless she had the Mossos to help press them.

In the movies, the world was black and white. When detectives showed up and flashed their badges, everyone except the baddies answered their questions quickly and truthfully. In the real world most people looked out for themselves. They might not want innocent people to get hurt. But they wouldn't go out of their way to help, not when their paychecks were at risk. Nightlife was big business in Barcelona. At twenty euros a head just to get inside, plus drinks, food, and bottle service, a big club like Opium could gross millions of euros during the summer months. Employees would be told to refer questions to managers, who would know that they'd best tell the owners about anything tricky. And the owners had lawyers.

The indifference suddenly overwhelmed her. *Nobody cares. My girl is gone and nobody cares.* Rebecca leaned back against the perfect sofa, the perfect accessory for this perfect living room for their perfect vacation. The room was hot. Airless. She should open the windows. But she couldn't take the city's happy sounds.

She thought of Kira, the images flipping by like photos in an album, the first time she'd slept in her crib, her first day of school, the first time she'd ridden a bike, outside their house in Houston, Rebecca running alongside to protect her—

Though now she remembered it wasn't Kira's first time on a bike; she'd found out later that Kira had actually learned in a Kroger's parking lot with Brian.

How many other firsts had she missed? How many clues?

If she'd been a better mother, maybe Kira wouldn't have gone to this bar in secret. Maybe she could have been honest. Every night at the office, every weekend, they'd added up to this.

Some part of her knew she was punishing herself unfairly. Kira hadn't told Brian either. Anyway she was a *teenager*, every teenager kept secrets, it was practically a requirement. But the cold logic failed to comfort her—

The apartment door opened. She hadn't even heard the steps in the hall outside. Another failure. She stood quickly, as if her grief itself were illicit and needed hiding.

"Becks? You okay?"

Brian must have seen something in her face. She nodded. She didn't want to talk about her feelings. She was glad when he didn't press.

"Anything on the records?"

"Just the guy's number. It's French. The texts start early yesterday morning."

"Surprised he didn't block it."

"Kira would have thought that was weird. Maybe a deal breaker. Anyway, I just got off the phone with Jake Broadnik. He's running the number, says he'll have something soon."

Brian nodded. He knew Broadnik too, though they weren't close. The Tailored Access Operations guys kept to themselves.

"We put up like a hundred posters," Tony said. He pulled one from the plastic bag he was holding to show her. MISSING: KIRA UNSWORTH, 19, AMERICAN. REWARD FOR INFORMATION.

Two pictures: a face shot from high school graduation, Kira grinning, the sun shining from her eyes, and a full-body picture guaranteed to get noticed.

Rebecca's phone number and email address below. At the bottom, again: MISSING. REWARD IF FOUND.

"They're good," Rebecca said. "Did anything else strike you from Friday night, Tony? Anything weird, anything that didn't fit?"

"One thing—" Tony stopped. "I remember it hitting me on the Métro home. Maybe it's ridiculous."

"Nothing's ridiculous."

"Like his French was too perfect somehow. Like he was acting and wasn't French at all. If that even makes sense. I almost said something to Kira. He was too perfect. Then I figured she'd just tell me I was jealous, that's how you pick up girls if you're not a loser, Tony."

Which sounded like something Kira in a less-than-charitable mood might say.

"I should have warned her."

"Tony." She wrapped her arms around his skinny body. "You couldn't have known."

But he detached himself, pushed her away, stalked off to his bedroom.

Rebecca grabbed the posters and the tape. "I'm gonna go for a walk. Put some up."

"Becks—"

"I'll let you know as soon as I hear from Rob or Jake. Look at her phone records, see if anything pops."

o o

A few minutes later she stood in the Plaça de Catalunya, a giant concrete square at the north end of La Rambla. Double-decker buses and taxis rolled past. Tourists milled around an oddly sinister clown who wore pure white face paint and juggled four balls in endless loops. Rebecca swung her head side to side with a metronome's regularity, clocking the crowds. As if she could make Kira appear by staring hard enough.

Her phone buzzed. "Jake."

"This guy—well, judge for yourself." His voice had a strange edge.

Jake wasn't normally coy. He must have something he didn't want to tell her. "Go."

"The number's clean. Like spotless. It was lit up for the first time a month ago, in Paris. Up by Saint-Ouen, northern Paris, that big market up there, right?"

"Les Puces, right." The market had come up before in counter-terror investigations.

"So assume the phone was stolen and jailbroken and he bought it there." Jailbreaking a phone meant prying into the core software and modifying it so that it could run on any carrier and download apps that Apple or Google hadn't approved. Any decent hacker could do it. The phone might be glitchy but it would look normal.

"Sure," Rebecca said.

"Anyway. Your guy hooked the phone up to Orange S.A.; prepaid, there's no account, no credit card. Pure burner. But the phone was off. At least the mobile connection is off. Airplane mode, basically. Obviously, whoever has it could still use it through Wi-Fi to download apps, surf."

"Obviously."

"But understand, even that's a little bit dangerous for him. Every time he uses it, the phone's browser picks up cookies, and the more cookies get planted, the bigger the digital trace, even over Wi-Fi. Think of it this way: A specific phone's browser is trackable like a specific computer's; unless you have the skills to make sure it's generic, and that's not impossible, but it's trickier on a phone than a computer. Pretty easy to download Tor for a computer, not so much for a phone."

"So you have his browser, Jake? You can tell me what sites he visited?"

"No, he didn't use the phone enough. He only lit it up once. One call, to the Paris mayor's office—"

"*What?*"

"The main number, for less than a minute. Probably just to check the phone was working. Then nothing until the texts to Kira in Paris and then in Barcelona."

"Everything else was wireless?"

"Correct. On the regular networks the phone was only ever used to message your daughter's phone and that test call."

Rebecca saw why Broadnik was so amped. On the one hand, the phone was a dead end. Even the NSA couldn't trace links that didn't exist. On the other . . .

"No one uses a phone that way," she said.

"Correct. Can't even do a voice log."

For the last few years, the NSA had recorded most calls made over public networks, trillions in all. The agency had logged the voice of practically every human being, a fact it didn't advertise. An even bigger secret was the fact that its voice-recognition software could *compare* that library to new calls.

The software was close to perfect. To find matches it relied not just on pitch or intonation but on tiny differences in the length of gaps between words. Those were unique. As a result, the agency could determine with extraordinary confidence who had made a call, even if the person was calling from someone else's phone. Whoever Jacques was, the NSA almost certainly had a record of his voice. But if he hadn't *used* the phone, the agency couldn't match him.

So did Jacques know who she was, the resources she could call on? Or was he naturally careful? Clever or lucky. Lucky or clever. Either way, the next step would be going back to CC and Wilkerson. They'd have to pay attention.

"I'll check the sequentials too," Broadnik said. Meaning phone numbers close to the one Jacques had used. "If they were turned on at the same time, used in a similar pattern. Just in case they bought a bunch of SIM cards all at once. Wouldn't count on it though."

"Question. You think there's an app for a jailbroken phone that would let you simulate a message? So the phone would look like it had sent a message when it hadn't."

"Child's play. I mean, if there's not, I could write it in a day. It would be easier than coding a real messaging app, just a fake screen."

Thanks, Jake. Really glad to hear fooling my daughter was so easy.

But Rebecca would bet they'd solved the mystery of why Kira hadn't texted. Jacques had made her phone disappear and then when she'd asked to borrow his he'd agreed. *Go right ahead . . .*

"Thanks, Jake. I have to talk to the Spanish police."

"Want me to call the DGSI too?" The DGSI was the French equivalent of the FBI, the national law enforcement agency that handled counterterror and counterespionage.

"Not yet." Asking the French for help would be a whole new level of complexity, and Rebecca didn't see what it would add, at least for now. "But if you hear anything else—"

"Course."

o   o

On the way back to the apartment, her phone rang again. Rob Wilkerson.

"CC says they checked. No one matching her name or description in the hospitals or station houses. The coroner too. So that's good . . ."

Good, your daughter is still missing. "I have news too." She told Wilkerson what Broadnik had said.

"That'll get CC's attention."

"Enough to call in a couple detectives to come with me to the big clubs?"

"I think. I'll ask him to light up their informants too, see if anybody's heard anything."

"Can he pull video from Sants and the airport?" Barcelona Sants was the city's main train station.

Wilkerson hesitated.

"Unless you have some reason to believe she went through there I don't want to make that ask yet. The detectives, the snitches, CC can do that on his own. Tape from the transportation hubs is bigger. Even with the phone, realistically, it hasn't even been one day."

She wanted to argue, but Wilkerson was right.

"I'll call you after I've talked to him." Then he was gone. But she felt slightly better. The wheels were starting to turn.

o o

Step-by-step, her mood improved. So far, everything suggested Jacques was a pro. Thrill killers—even serial killers—were sloppier. And picked easier targets. Jacques had known from the start Kira was traveling with her parents. He would have expected they would search for her. If he'd wanted easier prey he could have found a woman traveling on her own.

The level of planning, along with the difficulty of the target, suggested that Jacques intended this job as a kidnapping rather than murder.

She hoped.

o o

At the apartment, she found Brian sitting on the couch.

"I know I should be putting up posters. Instead of sitting here just hoping she'll walk in."

She filled him on the calls from Broadnik and Wilkerson. "I'm gonna go to the clubs."

"I should come."

"Stay with Tony. He needs you."

"Becks." He sagged back. Suddenly he looked defeated. Old. She had *never* thought Brian looked old before. Even during the worst years of their marriage. Even when he had been sneaking into the basement with a bottle of bourbon, his face had never shown the stress. He'd picked up a few extra lines on his forehead, but his skin was still tight and he'd kept his hair. Now it seemed as if the years had hit him all at once, his jowls loose, his mouth slightly open.

He stood. His face changed again; tightened, toughened, the shift so decisive that for a moment she wondered if she'd imagined the weakness.

"You do the clubs if you think that makes sense. Tony and I will go to the train station, put these up" — he grabbed the posters — "the subways, the bus stops, walk the Gothic Quarter. We're not sitting here while she's out there."

She went to him. He put his arms around her, squeezed her almost hard enough to hurt, hard enough for her to feel how strong he was.

"We're gonna find her, Becks."

"Yeah, we are."

19

Somewhere in Spain

Alone again.

In the dark again.

Her life was a bad country song.

∘   ∘

Jacques had stood over her, nudged the orange peels and water bottle
with a booted foot.

"Rodrigo came?"

"No, I snuck out, got myself an orange. Then I decided I missed
it in here, so I came right back up and locked myself in."

He reached down, swept up the peels. Again she was struck by the
quickness and precision of his moves. Like the best instructors in her
karate classes. Personal trainer her ass. He had hand-to-hand combat
training. Too bad he hadn't mentioned it back in Paris.

"Clever girl." He nodded at the empty hallway. "He's not supposed
to bother you when we're not here."

*Because I'll be worth less if I get raped before I get sold? Because
you're jealous? Or just because you're a control freak?* She didn't much

care. As long as he stayed focused on her and didn't notice the lighter or the screw and nail.

"He didn't bother me. I like a man with the confidence to paint his nails." Probably talking too much, but she didn't care.

"Promise me you'll tell me if he tries anything like that again."

"Trouble in paradise, Jacques?"

"Don't be too clever."

He turned, pulled the door shut.

o   o

She counted to a thousand, slowly. She didn't cheat. *Four hundred and three . . . Four hundred and four . . .* A thousand didn't seem like a big number, not in a world filled with billionaires. But counting it took a while. *Eight hundred and five . . .* Lucky her, she had time. When she was done she stood, double-checked the shelf where she'd found the stuff, then the shelf on the other side. She didn't come up with anything else. She had the lighter, the nail, and the tape. Maybe a piece of wood if she was strong enough to tear the shelving off its hinges.

She had something else, too. The knowledge of trouble between Jacques and Rodrigo. Of course she couldn't ignore the chance they were only pretending, toying with her. She wouldn't put anything past Jacques. But Jacques's annoyance with Rodrigo had seemed real.

They could hand her off or move her to another safe house anytime. She couldn't wait too long to make her move. But she thought that for now she would be better off biding her time, figuring out how to take advantage of Rodrigo.

She sucked down the bottle of water, sat back, listened, waited. A sweet, dense smell seeped into the closet. *When the kidnapping's done, me and my boys love to chill with a fat blunt.*

o   o

After a while she realized she had to pee.

Badly.

Thanks, Rodrigo, for that extra water bottle. The need was not a gentle *I can hold this a while* itch but a heavy hot-stone pressure in her bladder. She tried to distract herself—*I'm thinking about kittens now, puppies and kittens, cute lil furballs*—but her body wouldn't take the bait.

Minute by minute, the stress worsened until it was nearly over-whelming. She didn't understand how a simple need could be such torture. Yet it was. Maybe because she knew she could relieve it in the simplest way possible.

But she didn't want to piss in here, to foul her nest.

She didn't want to beg for the bathroom, either. Humiliation atop humiliation. But she had no choice. She went to the door, knocked. Nothing. Downstairs the mumbled voices continued.

She knocked again. Hard this time, hard enough to rattle the heavy door on its hinges.

Finally she heard a slow tread on the steps. Rodrigo. She couldn't help wondering if he was taking his time on purpose. Like he knew what she wanted and liked making her suffer.

He pulled open the door. "Yes?"

Interesting. He hadn't pushed her away from the door or even told her to back off. She was standing, barely a step from him. If she'd had the lighter ready . . .

"I need the toilet."

He smirked. The weed had turned his eyes into a red-lined map of a country she didn't want to visit.

"*Uno o dos.*"

"Pee. Come on. Please."

He reached behind the door, came out with the hood. So they kept it on a hook out there. Another fact for the file.

She wasn't going to normalize wearing the hood. She shook her head.

He tapped his fingers to his lips. "*Un beso.*"

"A *kiss*?"

"*Sí, un beso.*"

Could she risk playing this game? What would happen the next time he had the house to himself?

"Jacques told me no."

"I don't see Jacques."

She shook her head. He raised his hands to her shoulders, pushed. She stumbled backward, barely stayed on her feet. He started to close the door.

"Okay. One kiss."

She put a hand to his cheek, pressed her lips to his, darted out her tongue. Flirty and light. Just a touch, enough to leave him wanting more before she pulled away. Didn't want to give him the wrong idea.

The *wrong idea*? Flirty and light? She ought to be clawing his face—

With Jacques and Lilly downstairs?

"That's all?" He leaned in again.

"For now." She kept her voice easy. "I really do have to pee."

He pointed down the hall, mock-courteous with his black-painted nails. Badly as she needed it, she made herself walk instead of run, checked out the hallway. Two closed doors. A plain wood floor. The bathroom door open a crack.

The smell of pot grew stronger. She could hear someone speaking *English* downstairs, the voice strangely familiar, "You're probably thinking, 'My boyfriend said this was a superhero movie but that guy in the suit just turned that other guy into a fucking kebab!' "

Great. They were watching *Deadpool*.

o   o

The bathroom was small, a plastic shower-tub, a cheap sink. Not too clean. A narrow frosted-glass window. Not exactly as impassible as the plywood in the closet, but enough to keep her from seeing out.

In a glass on the sink, three *razors*. Calling her name. She wondered if she was maybe a little stoned herself, she felt weirdly loose. They'd hotboxed her.

She started to close the door. Rodrigo put a hand on it.

"I watch."

"Forget it." She was serious, too. She'd yell for Jacques.

He looked around. His eyes stuck on the razors. "One minute." He closed the door.

She squatted down and pissed. Relief. Her stream mostly clear. Becks was big on making sure that one stayed hydrated, one's urine remained colorless. *Thanks Mom.* Through the window she heard the faint growl of a big truck moving fast. Not close, miles away. But still proof that this house was somewhere near a highway. Not in some empty valley in the mountains or a farmhouse ten miles from the nearest road.

The razors weren't even three feet away. But they were boy razors. Not leg-shaving disposables, certainly not straight blades. Multiple blades in a metal head. Even if Rodrigo didn't notice she'd taken one, she didn't see how she could pry the blade out.

Okay, best leave them.

What about a toothbrush? There were three in the water glass on the sink. If she taped the nail to the end of the brush, she'd have a real weapon. She reached for them—

"Almost done?" Rodrigo said from the hall.

She pulled back her arm. Not yet. He was paying too much attention. She knew she couldn't keep putting off the real risks. But for now waiting seemed like the best move. Gathering information, finding weaknesses.

The door swung open just as she covered herself. His eyes went straight to the sink, the razors.

"You took one."

"No." She didn't have to fake the tremor in her voice. Downstairs Deadpool merrily shot bad guys. "I promise."

Her fear seemed to please him. He stepped out of the bathroom and pointed at the closet, *Go, then.* Without a word she walked back to the closet. Hating herself. What progress had she actually made? Found a lighter she was afraid to use and a razor she was afraid to steal?

Worst of all, when she heard the deadbolt snap in place she felt not fear or anger but *relief.*

20

Barcelona

Rebecca knew the Mossos detective. Not personally, but the type. He was compact, no-nonsense, wearing a button-down blue shirt and neatly pressed khakis.

He stood next to Rob Wilkerson on the Passeig Marítim, where the city's narrow central beach met its fanciest nightclubs.

"Rebecca," Wilkerson said. "This is Ernesto Xili. Smartest cop in town."

"Smart enough to know that's a lie." His English was almost unaccented, with a hint of formality, as if he'd gone to boarding school somewhere. "Rob explained the situation. Do you have reason to think she came to Opium? Or any club?"

"I don't think they grabbed her right after they left The Mansion. She looked fine on the video. Either they stuffed her in a car while she was fighting or they hit her over the head in an alley or they softened her up somewhere else first. Told her they wanted to go to another bar or a club."

"This is speculation." His tone was even. Not accusatory.

"Yes. But I couldn't find anything in the Gothic Quarter. Kira loves to dance. Bring her to a club, spike her drink while she's dancing, she'd be easier to move."

Even as she outlined the possibility Rebecca wondered if Kira would leave her drink unguarded. Something didn't fit.

"Or she went in a car with them on her own."

"She would have texted first."

Though thanks to the possibility of a fake app, that logic no longer held. If Jacques had stolen Kira's phone and then let her use his, maybe she would have sent Rebecca or Tony the text and gotten into a car without being forced.

But Rebecca just didn't see it. Kira and Jacques and the unknown woman had left The Mansion before midnight. By Barcelona standards, the night had just been getting started. Kira would have wanted— expected, even—to stay out, not to go home with Jacques. Especially since nothing in their body language from the video at The Mansion suggested she was about to hook up with him. Which meant another club. And all these clubs were walking distance from The Mansion, especially on a nice summer night, the Mediterranean waves rippling against the beach. Kira would have wondered why Jacques insisted on driving. She was smart enough to know that getting into a car was inherently dangerous. Scream on the street, you could be almost sure someone would hear. Scream from a back seat, you could be almost sure no one would.

Under those circumstances, Kira wouldn't have just sent a text before getting in a car, she would have waited for an answer. Of course, Jacques could have anticipated that possibility and loaded a fake response onto his phone.

But what if Kira recognized the return message was off, it didn't sound like Becks or Tony? And the more she handled the phone, the more likely she would notice something was wrong with it. Jacques would want to keep her relaxed. Again, the best way to do that would be to take her to another bar or club.

Rebecca was prepared to explain all this to Xili, though she didn't particularly want to. Some detectives liked cases without obvious answers, pulling a suspect from thin air, Sherlock Holmes–style. *The butler. In the pantry. With an icicle that melted afterward.* They liked speculation, to borrow Xili's word.

Not Rebecca. She was methodical by nature. Give her a *target*, and no matter how hard finding evidence on him might be, she would. Cases like the Border Bandit's, cases she might never solve no matter how hard she worked—those bugged her even more than they did most cops.

Xili looked at her like he wanted to press the point, but he didn't. "Let's see what they have for us."

o   o

But they had nothing.

Not at Opium. Or Carpe Diem. Or Pacha. All high-end clubs clustered within a few hundred feet.

In each, the managers respected Xili, or his badge, enough to act polite. They promised to put up Kira's "Missing" poster in the back-of-the-house break rooms. They offered to let Rebecca check surveillance footage, a step—as they probably guessed—she didn't have time to take without hard evidence that Kira had come through their doors.

Meanwhile, the bouncers and bartenders glanced at Kira's picture long enough to seem interested before shaking their heads, *nope, never seen her, good luck, adios.* Rebecca believed them. But she also knew they'd wipe the question from their minds as soon as she left. They viewed this missing American girl as a chore, nothing else.

And after seeing the beachfront clubs, Rebecca couldn't help thinking they were *wrong* for a kidnap scheme. Not just because they weren't Kira's scene, too fancy and expensive and Eurotrashy. After all, Kira didn't know anything about Barcelona. She would have deferred to Jacques.

The more serious issue was that the big clubs presented practical problems for a would-be kidnapper. Kira and Jacques and his mysterious female friend had left The Mansion around midnight and would have needed a few minutes to reach their next stop. But after midnight these places all had lines. Skipping them meant putting a four-figure charge on a credit card for a VIP table with bottle service. The clubs noticed VIPs. Jacques wouldn't have wanted to be noticed. He wouldn't have wanted to stand on line either, and risk being remembered.

Plus, the big clubs were run like banks with million-watt sound systems. Cameras in every corner. Bouncers watching the dance floor. Alarms at every fire exit, so no one could sneak in without paying. They were crowded and loud, so Jacques could have spiked Kira's drink. But afterward he would have had to drag Kira out without anyone noticing she couldn't walk.

o   o

After two hours, they exhausted the beachfront. Xili drove them to Razzmatazz, in Poblenou, the city's old industrial district, northeast of the Gothic Quarter. Razzmatazz was more democratic, not as expensive as clubs like Opium, Xili said. More college students, fewer minor aristocrats.

"You know the scene."

"I've lived here my whole life," Xili said. "Razzmatazz, I remember when it opened, I was still in high school. Some others are even older. The first big one, Otto Zutz, my parents met there."

Rebecca couldn't think of anything similar back home. How could a nightclub, a place designed to make anyone over thirty feel hopelessly old, survive a generation? Her first year at Wesleyan she'd driven to New York to go to clubs like Limelight, places all the Manhattan kids knew and she'd only read about. An effort to be cool that was both desperate and half-hearted. In her heart Rebecca feared she was going mainly so she could tell herself later that she had. *Back in the day I partied in the East Village at 3 a.m.* One night she'd wound up at Save the Robots, a legendary after-hours joint; a cute skinny boy had offered her coke and she'd practically run away.

But Save the Robots and Limelight were long gone, turned into fancy gyms or boutiques selling thousand-dollar sweaters. New places had replaced them, and for all Rebecca knew, another generation of places had replaced those. The only fixture was Leonardo DiCaprio.

"Your parents?" she said. "Really?"

"In some ways the clubs capture Barcelona perfectly. The most modern city in Spain. But Spain isn't a very modern country." He turned right, stopped beside a huge building with a sign that screamed RAZZMATAZZ in giant capital letters. "Most nights it doesn't open until midnight, one a.m. But on Sundays they have evening shows."

Indeed, two bouncers stood outside, and as they walked up Rebecca could faintly hear a muffled sound check. But she already felt this place was wrong. It would have had even longer lines than the ocean-front clubs. It would skew younger too, and these days younger women were prone to protest if they saw a woman who seemed helpless and being moved without her consent. One noisy rape-crisis-center advocate would screw up everything for Jacques.

Plus, Razzmatazz was an even longer walk from the Gothic Quarter than the oceanfront clubs were. Maybe half an hour, which Rebecca guessed would be at the outer limits of what Kira would accept, even on a nice night, even with a guy she liked. She would have felt Rebecca's midnight deadline slipping away, would have realized she was going farther from the apartment in Eixample. After a few minutes walking, she would have wanted to pick a club and *dance*.

Speculation, speculation, speculation. Where, then? Or would they have to go back to the Gothic Quarter, start again, casing every bar? The idea made her cringe.

"Take this one," she said to Xili. "I need to think." Xili flashed his badge to the bouncers and disappeared inside, Wilkerson a step behind.

Somehow Rebecca had pictured Barcelona as a quaint town before she arrived. In reality it stretched for miles along the water, dense with apartment buildings, not much wasted space. The city had almost two million residents, its suburbs three million more. Plus, hundreds of thousands of tourists during the summer.

Rebecca believed Jacques *knew* this city, even if he wasn't from here. Knew where to bring Kira. A place that would lower her defenses. Where?

She sorted combinations until Xili and Wilkerson emerged from the club. She could tell they'd struck out again even before they spoke.

"Next Otto's," Xili said. "Then work our way down through Eixample."

"Let's stick closer to the Quarter, walking distance," Rebecca said. Her dissent seemed to surprise Xili. "You have an idea?"

"I don't know the place but I bet you do. Big enough to dance but smaller than these places. Maybe a more underground feel. No restaurants, no fancy website. Not so many cameras. Meant to intimidate outsiders a little. The place the locals go, and go late, so short lines at midnight."

"You think he's from Barcelona, this man?"

"No, but he knows the city. And I promise, if it doesn't work, we'll do it your way."

Xili drummed his fingers against the steering wheel. Finally, he nodded.

"Maybe I know a place. In Born-Ribera." The neighborhood between Poblenou and the Gothic Quarter. It had the same narrow medieval streets as the Quarter, but fewer bars, more fancy boutiques. "I don't think it's open now, but let's see if anyone's there."

Minutes later Xili turned into an alley behind a brick warehouse.

"This one opened last year but they keep it quiet. Changed the name already. I think they even put up bad reviews on TripAdvisor to scare away the tourists."

"What's it called?"

"Helado."

o   o

He led them around the building. The front door was locked. Xili rapped on it, hard and peremptory.

"Get lost," someone inside shouted in Spanish.

"*Policia!*"

A minute later the door opened, revealing a tall woman, her pupils dilated in a way that suggested opiates.

"Your name?"

"Flor. Yours?"

Xili flashed his badge. "I'm looking for a young woman who may have visited last night."

Rebecca held up a copy of the poster, and even before the woman said anything Rebecca saw the recognition in her drug-wounded eyes.

"We get a lot of people."

Xili glanced at Rebecca. She saw he'd picked up the flash too. He stepped closer to Flor, an old but effective cop trick, *I'm gonna violate your space, put you on the defensive.* "Is anyone else here?"

She shook her head.

Xili pointed at the camera watching the door. "You don't mind if we look at the video then?" He pushed by, wordlessly forcing Flor to decide, *Do I stop you or move along?*

She moved along.

o   o

The space inside held a sunken dance floor and a long bar. The room was nearly dark, a cathedral between services.

"Any other cameras?" Xili said.

"Just behind the bar."

"Show us."

Rebecca silently admired the way he'd taken control. Flor led them to an unmarked door beside the bar. The office was small and battered, nothing corporate, no energy drinks here. A baggie of grayish-white powder and a razor blade on the desk.

"Put it away," Xili said. "I don't care."

Flor stuffed the bag in her pocket.

"Show me the video."

The images were grainier than the ones at the other clubs, but they were good enough.

Twelve eighteen a.m. And Kira walked through the front door.

Wilkerson caught Rebecca's eye, nodded, *You were right.* And yet she felt neither surprise nor triumph. *Found you. Found you found you.* Only she hadn't. Not yet. In fact, seeing Kira this way was almost maddening. Jacques wore the big-billed baseball cap with the PARIS SAINT-GERMAIN logo she'd seen before to hide his eyes. The woman with them was clowning, hugging his back, in a way that obscured her face. Rebecca wanted to scream a warning at the screen, into the past, *Don't you get it, K?*

Xili stopped the playback, pointed to the screen. "Her. Do you remember her?"

"Not really."

If Flor cared, she was doing a good job hiding her feelings.

"We need to watch the video from inside too, talk to the bouncers. But first let's see when she left." Xili clicked Play on the video again.

"Better go faster," Flor said. "We didn't close until six a.m."

Trial and error showed that 8x fast-forward was the highest possible speed where they could be sure they wouldn't miss anyone walking out. Even at that setting, watching the feed took almost forty-five minutes.

But Kira never appeared again. Neither did the others. Not for a single frame. However they'd left this club, it wasn't through the front door.

"You have a fire exit?" Rebecca said.

"In back."

"It has an alarm?"

"Yes."

"Camera?"

"I told you, the only cameras are the front door and the bar."

"Let's see," Xili said.

o   o

The fire door had an alarm bar, as Flor had promised. But a wire hung from the cracked plastic housing that held the base of the bar.

Xili pressed it. No alarm. He pushed open the door, revealing the alley and his sedan.

"It was working," Flor said.

Rebecca stepped into the warm evening air. Nine p.m., but the sky was still more blue than black. The sweet smell of charcoal-grilled meat wafted from somewhere close.

Kill the alarm. Drug her, bring her out, put her in a car. No security cameras on the back door, no cameras in the alley. No one sees.

Except maybe someone had. A five-story gray stone apartment building overlooked the alley. Time for shoe-leather cop work, knocking on doors. Curtains covered most windows, but here and there the glass was uncovered.

"Detective. Rob."

She nodded at the windows.

"Think anyone was awake?"

"At one a.m.?" Xili said. "In Barcelona? *Everyone* was awake."

o   o

An hour later they had their answer.

Courtesy of a lady of a certain age who lived in an immaculate two-room apartment on the third floor. Unlike the club managers she was happy to talk. In fact she seemed thrilled to see Xili's badge. When Xili asked her name, she said, *Everyone calls me the Queen.*

The Queen was tiny, no more than five feet, her skin papery and pale, her hands trembling, Parkinsonian. But her eyes were awake. Rebecca sensed she'd be reliable. She led them to her bedroom. A plain wooden chair sat by the window that overlooked the alley. The back door to Helado was barely forty feet away.

She looked at Rebecca. "I want to talk to *her*. By myself."

"Yell if she gets rowdy," Xili said. He and Wilkerson walked out.

"I like to look," the Queen said. "The television gets boring. I see boys and girls in the back. Or boys, you know, with other boys."

"Does anyone see you?" Rebecca said in Spanish.

201

"I keep the light out."

"What about last night?"

The Queen turned out the lights, sat, stared at the empty alley. As if to reenact the moment.

"There was a dog. An ugly dog and I watched him catch a rat." She glanced at Rebecca. "This was around midnight. Is that what you meant?"

Let her have her fun, tease you, she'll get there.

"Anything else?"

"Later, a car came. Stopped by the door. Then two men came out of that door, with two girls. The men held one of them. Like she'd had too much drink."

Close now. "Do you remember, could she walk at all?"

"It looked to me, if they let her go she'd fall. Her head—" the Queen tilted her own head, rag-doll style.

So they'd drugged her. "Then?"

"They put her in the car, the back, and got in on each side. No talking. Quiet as mice. The other girl got into the front. Then they drove off. Only a few seconds. If I hadn't been watching I wouldn't have seen."

If I hadn't been watching I wouldn't have seen. Yogi Berra couldn't have said it better. "Do you remember the car?"

"Black."

"Small? Medium? Big?"

"Not so big, they were stuffed inside."

"Do you know what kind?"

"I don't know about cars," the Queen said primly. "Maybe a Toyota." *Maybe* meant definitely.

"Did anyone get out before they came?"

"No. The driver stayed inside. A man, but I couldn't see anything about him."

Rebecca handed her the poster of Kira.

The Queen held it in her shaking hands. "Yes, yes, her. The one they carried. Your daughter, yes?"

The Mossos should hire you. Now maybe the most important question of all.

"Do you know when this was?"

"Maybe after one, before one thirty. Does that help?"

Rebecca put her hands on the Queen's thin shoulders, felt the fluttering pulse beneath. "It might."

And by *it might* Rebecca meant *You have no idea how much.*

Because the Queen had given the Mossos what they needed to lock down the search. The alley didn't have cameras. But with the timing and the basic vehicle information, the police could look for cameras on the streets close to the alley.

A black sedan, most likely a Toyota, heading to the alley around 1 a.m., leaving a few minutes later.

A clear picture of the car and its passengers would be handy. But the license plate would be the real prize. They'd find it. Surveillance cameras were everywhere these days. They only needed one. And the plate would give them a whole new set of leads to chase.

21

Somewhere in Spain

The white glow where the plywood met the window frame was gone.

And the closet was as dark as anywhere Kira had ever been, a man-made cave, so lightless that the air around her was almost liquid. Black was not a color but a shade, with gradients. Kira hadn't known until now. Another lesson courtesy of Jacques and the gang.

Night. She'd been gone almost twenty-four hours. Her parents must be out of their minds. Tony would have told them about Jacques. No doubt they'd started searching. Probably Becks had even asked the FBI and Spanish cops for help. But they didn't have a name or a picture or any way of knowing where she'd gone.

Better not count on them showing up anytime soon.

Her friends were still in the house. She heard them now and then. But no one had come up to see her since her trip to the bathroom. Hunger and thirst were creeping up again. She remembered now, the ache carried a certain pleasure, the triumph of mind over body. Thirst, not so much. Her tongue was swollen, and she could taste her breath.

She closed her eyes and took herself to Boston Children's, a prison crueler than this one despite its clean white rooms. Thought of the last time she'd seen Ayla Lafan. She'd given Ayla a present, a T-shirt that said ALWAYS BE YOURSELF UNLESS YOU CAN BE A UNICORN.

Ayla stared at the shirt. "Are they real?" she finally said, in her soft high voice.

Kira had an answer ready. "They might be, A."

"But no one's ever seen one."

"No."

"They're not, are they? They're just not. They've never been and they never will be."

Words that forced on Kira a truth she tried to keep from herself. Ayla knew she was dying, and after so many trips to this place and so many friends lost probably knew *what* dying was. Her serenity didn't come from ignorance of the threat. If anything, Ayla wanted to spare her parents from their own fear.

Kira promised herself now that whatever happened she would be as tough as that little girl.

She drifted for a while . . .

Woke when the light snapped on.

o   o

She felt obscurely foolish. How come she hadn't heard the steps? How had she let someone surprise her when she was *in a locked room*? She rubbed the sleep from her eyes as the door swung open.

Jacques. No doubt he liked sneaking up here, scaring her even in her sleep. He had a folder tucked under his arm. He looked slightly goofy, like the graduate student he'd pretended to be.

"I need to ask some questions."

"Fuck off."

His face changed, and she knew she'd gone too far. He came at her in two steps, punched her. Just once, in the diaphragm, the blow placed perfectly and so fast she had no chance to avoid it.

His fist twisted her, left her gasping, drowning in the open air.

Finally her diaphragm unclenched, and she could breathe. She wiped the tears from her cheeks and stared up at him. She wanted to curse him again, tell him he didn't scare her. But he *did*. All those karate classes and she had no idea what violence really was, no idea what it was like to be hit by a man who wasn't holding back.

He opened the folder, held up her driver's license.

"Kira Unsworth. Not such a usual name."

He tucked the license back in the folder—such an organized kidnapper—and pulled out a piece of paper.

The Washington Post. She saw the newspaper's squiggly font, and she knew what was coming. "FBI Arrests Russian Agent in Maryland," Jacques read. "When we looked up your name, to see if we were lucky, you're a billionaire, this came up. Rebecca Unsworth, who supervised the investigation, said the FBI had received a tip about Kuznetsov several months ago." He handed her the paper.

She didn't see how lying would help. "My mom."

"Your mother is an FBI agent?"

"Way up in the bureau."

Jacques seemed pleased. "The US government will pay very much for you, I think."

"That's not how it works." Could he really be sophisticated enough to take her the way he had and naïve enough to think the FBI would hand him millions of dollars?

He shrugged. *We'll see.* He put away the *Post*, handed her one final piece of paper, the front page of a Spanish newspaper—*El País*—neatly folded.

"Stand up, hold this."

He pulled out his phone, took her picture. "Now give me mommy's email. And mobile. Daddy also."

She did.

"Are you rich?"

She wondered if she should ask him to define *rich*, but she didn't want to risk another punch.

"My parents both work for the federal government. Not super-rich."

"Any other money?"

Maybe he already knew, maybe he'd seen it on the Internet somewhere.

"My dad sold a phone app a while ago. Made a bunch of money." *Saved my parents' marriage. Without that stupid app maybe I wouldn't be here.*

Jacques smiled, the most real smile she'd seen from him. "This app—"

"It's called Twenty-One. Like blackjack, you know, for casinos."

"And how much did he get?"

"They never told me." A lie.

He squatted beside her, the greed flashing in his eyes. "Many millions, yes?"

What if he started to think her parents had ten or twenty million dollars hidden away? Better to tell the truth. "I think it was two million. Enough to buy a house."

"I thought they didn't tell you." A dangerous coldness in his voice.

"They didn't, but I overheard them once." Another lie, Brian had been proud of it.

"Spying on mommy and daddy."

"I *promise*, there's no way they have millions in the bank. We're not rich like that, we flew over in economy class, okay, premium economy—" She made herself stop.

You're talking too much, Kira. He's not your friend. He's not even some cop who pulled you over for speeding and will let you go if you flirt a minute. You're not going to convince him of anything, you're not going to make him like you, and if you try you may just make him mad. So hush. Don't speak unless spoken to.

"You don't know how much money your parents have?"

"No."

"But they love you. Their sweet little girl." He nudged her leg with his boot. "They would give all of it to get you back."

The question, statement, whatever it was, made her stomach hurt.

He walked to the door. Stopped. Looked her over, head-to-toe. "But, you know, part of me hopes they won't."

Even more than Rodrigo, Jacques made her feel dirty, made her want to take a long hot shower.

Then he was gone. The deadbolt slammed. The light dropped.

She wondered how much money he'd want. And what her parents would do to get it.

22

Barcelona

The Mossos had gone into high gear.

CC hadn't apologized for the way he'd acted earlier. He'd done something better. He'd called his boss, explained that an American girl had been kidnapped, a professional job. The Mossos needed to pull video footage to find the kidnap car, ask for help from Madrid and the French police too.

Surveillance cameras revealed an obvious candidate for the suspect car, a black Toyota Camry that came down Carrer de Trafalgar at 12:55 a.m. and then returned seventeen minutes later. No surprise, the Camry's back windows were heavily tinted. And the driver wore a hooded sweatshirt that shadowed his face. But the windows couldn't hide the fact that the Camry's back seat had been empty on its way to the alley behind Helado, full on the way back.

The windows couldn't hide the license plate, either. With it, the Mossos tracked the Camry along the Avinguda Diagonal, which ran to the ring road west of the city and the highways that connected Barcelona with France and the rest of Spain.

But the trail ended there.

The modern superhighway between Barcelona and Madrid, the AP-2, was a toll road with plenty of cameras. So was the AP-7, which ran from the French border through Barcelona and down Spain's east coast. But neither highway's cameras had captured the Camry.

Xili told Rebecca the vanishing act shouldn't surprise them. Most of Spain's older highways were not toll roads and did not have surveillance. The most notable was the A-2, an upgraded version of the old Route Nacional from Madrid to Barcelona.

The Camry itself also looked to be a dead end. Spain had a serious car theft problem. And based on its body type, this Camry had been built between 2006 and 2011. That model was notoriously easy to steal. The national stolen car database showed thousands of thefts of Camrys from those years.

Worse, the plates didn't belong to the car. They matched a Mini Cooper owned by a woman who lived north of Barcelona. She hadn't reported them stolen. The Mossos had already sent an officer to talk to her. But she wasn't home, and her car didn't seem to be around.

Rebecca suspected that the Mini's owner was on vacation, her car parked in an airport lot. Stealing a car from a garage was tricky. Gate cameras would catch every vehicle as it entered and left.

But stealing plates was easy. Find a car tucked in a corner. Preferably a small car tucked behind a bigger vehicle that hid it from cameras. Unscrew the plates. Toss them in your own car's trunk and drive out.

The combination of stolen plates and a stolen car meant that finding the Camry was going to be tough. The Mossos had put an advisory notice—what American police called a BOLO, be on the lookout—for the Camry into their system. Any officer who saw the car was supposed to pull it over.

But Rebecca already knew they weren't going to see it. It was in a garage somewhere. Or in a Madrid slum, unlocked, waiting to be stolen again. Or burned to its frame in some empty field. And if they did find it, it would be clean. No fingerprints, no clues. Because this guy Jacques didn't make mistakes.

○   ○

Sunday night rolled into Monday morning as the Mossos chased the Camry. All along, Brian and Tony were stuck at the apartment in Eixample. She called them every couple of hours with updates. Around midnight, she half-heartedly suggested they get some rest. "I'll sleep when you do," Brian said, almost angrily.

By 2 a.m., after the toll road searches came up empty, fatigue overwhelmed her. Yes, they'd made progress today. They'd put to rest any notion that Kira had disappeared on her own.

But they had no answers to the big questions: who Jacques really was, if he had targeted Kira for some specific reason, if he had any idea who Rebecca was, if he was hoping to ransom her back or pass her to someone else.

Not to mention the most crucial mystery of all, where Kira was now.

"I'll take you home," Xili said. "Sleep, we can meet around ten, figure out who to talk with in Madrid. The Guardia"—the Guardia Civil—"must have had cars on the A-2 last night, and they have cameras and plate readers. With luck that will tell us where they're headed."

"Sure."

She would call FBI headquarters, too. But she thought she should wait until Monday morning East Coast time—afternoon here. The Mossos seemed to be doing everything possible. She didn't see how extra pressure from the bureau would help.

This late on a Sunday night, even the Gothic Quarter was quiet, only a few drunks sputtering up La Rambla. Even Barcelona slept eventually. Neither Xili nor Rebecca spoke until he stopped outside her apartment.

"Thank you," she said. "For taking me seriously."

"Thank me after we find her."

"After we find her I'll buy you a ticket to Razzmatazz. Relive your glory days."

○   ○

She couldn't escape a crushing sense of failure. They were no closer to knowing where Kira might be. Normally Rebecca would have figured the kidnappers had gone to ground close by, somewhere near Barcelona. Moving a hostage was dangerous.

But nothing about this kidnapping was normal. Maybe Jacques had already smuggled her into North Africa. Or swung her north into France on her way to Eastern Europe.

Rebecca wondered more and more if the kidnapping was related to her job. She hadn't said much about the possibility to Xili. Getting the Mossos on board had been hard enough without conspiracy theories. But the degree of planning here suggested either high-level organized crime or a government-backed group.

Again, though, why would the Russians come after her this way? The risk of reprisal was too high. All this doomed speculation led back to the original theory. Maybe Jacques had just taken Kira randomly.

o   o

Brian was alone on the couch when she walked in. "Becks." They hugged and again she felt his strength, his solidity.

"Where's Tony?"

"Oh, he went out for coffee like an hour ago."

How could he be so calm. "Brian—"

He raised his hands. "I'm kidding. Bedroom, asleep."

He hadn't made a joke *that* terrible since that night in the nursing home. More than twenty years ago. *Plus ça change* . . . "Jesus, Brian."

"Sorry. Been a long night." Tony had been inconsolable, blaming himself, Brian said. "He's losing his mind."

o   o

Rebecca found Tony in his bedroom, sleeping badly, muttering in his dreams. She kissed his forehead lightly, not wanting to wake him, and went back to Brian. Who had moved to their bedroom.

"Tell me about the night," Brian said. "What you found."

"Can we do it in the morning?"

"She's my girl too."

He was right. So she told him—about Xili, the clubs, her revelation that Jacques must have taken Kira somewhere else. About Helado and Flor and the Queen.

"You did good."

"I did nothing. What if it's because of me, Bri? What if this really is some group that found my name in an article in the *Post* and somehow locked on to me—"

"Not a four-star general, not the director?"

"Those guys have security."

Brian shook his head. "I can't see it. There are hundreds of people further up the intel chain. Not that you're not important."

He was right again. She moved closer to him, felt him wrap his arms around her. She closed her eyes and began to drift within seconds. Brian was falling asleep too, his breathing settling, his grip on her easing.

"Gonna be okay, Becks." His voice a murmur. "I promise. . ." the words running down.

Summer on the Cape, and she stood at the top of Newcomb Hollow Beach, running down the dunes, the sand biting her heels—

Becks.

Dove for the relief of the cold gray ocean—

Tell.

Who said that? The surf rushed at her, a big wave, bigger than she'd expected—

Something—

And the water took her.

IV

BRIAN

(THEN AND NOW)

23

Charlottesville

Brian was taking it easy this winter.

No worries, he had eleven hundred bucks stuffed in the bottom of his duffel. Hadn't touched it since he came to Virginia. He paid the rent running pizzas on weekends, sometimes with a special side order for frat boys who needed a hookup. Not often, and nothing harder than pot or Addys. No coke, even if they asked. He didn't want a reputation. Didn't want the cops looking for him. But if he could pick up fifty bucks in five minutes selling pills he wasn't gonna say no.

Plus he could live on the cheap in this town. His rent was only four fifteen a month. A fourth-floor one bedroom, no elevator, mice in the walls. Sometimes they woke him up, *pitter-patter* behind his head. But the place was an easy walk to the bars on Main Street. Even had a round window that opened up to the hills west of town.

Brian liked Charlottesville. He had his laptop, his Nintendo, his *Introduction to C* manual. No more cold-enough-to-peel-skin midwestern winters, no more Seattle rain. And UVA deserved its rep as a party school. Especially during basketball season. When the games were done, the students poured out of the U Hall—the arena—and headed for the bars.

Of course, the grade A sorority sisters usually went straight to Frat Row. Even when they were at the bars, Brian didn't hit on them. Up north, rich coeds might slum once in a while. Down here the class system was set in stone. Fine. Let the nose-job girls chase their BMW-driving princes. Sixes and sevens were more his wheelhouse anyway.

Over the years, Bri had developed a clinical attitude toward the game. He played the odds, didn't take rejection personally, moved on if he wasn't feeling a vibe.

He'd figured out he had a type. Quiet outsiders. Girls majoring in philosophy who wanted to spend a year in Tokyo after graduation. He stayed away from real artists. Those women were too in love with themselves to pay attention to him—and if they did, they saw through his crap because they were just as full of it as he was.

He played instead to the middle-class romantics, the ones who convinced themselves that he had special insight into the human condition because he'd driven an ambulance. That he was a poet because he hadn't made it through his first year at Michigan State. They treated him with a seriousness he was pretty sure he didn't deserve, but that he could pull off for a night of drinking.

He tilted his head and listened—kinda—as they told him how they hated the conformity of college. He didn't have to push drinks on them. They got lit on their own, flushed with the excitement of talking to someone who wasn't majoring in business. Their cool-headed friends tried to get them to leave, tugged their wrists, whispered warnings loud enough for Brian to overhear, *You don't even know who this dude is, he's shady, too old for you, come on, let's go.* And the romantics shook their heads and stayed. Maybe they were genuinely into him, or the *idea* of him as a wanderer. Maybe they were just bored. Or drunk.

As for him?

He just wanted sex.

Brian was pretty much a realist, no illusions about the world or his place in it. He wasn't dumb, and spending so much time by himself had given him a chance to read a lot. But he couldn't stand doing any kind of intellectual work that didn't grab his attention right away. Same thing with manual labor. He was clever and good with his hands. He could learn most jobs in a hurry. But he couldn't make himself care enough to become great at any of them.

Jack of all trades, master of none.

What was true for work was doubly true for relationships. He was friendly to his neighbors, but he never got to know them past a *Hey, how are you.* He prized sensation over emotion. He'd tried practically every drug in existence. But if he felt himself wanting to use more than casually, he stopped. Stone-cold. Addiction was just a fancy word for *need.* More than anything in the world, he didn't want to need anything. Or anyone. Even getting too comfortable in any one town bothered him.

Mostly he wanted to float. His great weakness was laziness, he figured. The least of the seven deadlies. What was sloth compared to greed or wrath? No one killed anyone for the chance to sleep all afternoon. Still, it was on the list.

A realist, then. But in one way he was exceptional. In bed he was the opposite of lazy. He wanted to please, to *win,* to leave his conquests stunned by how hard and often they came. A performer with an audience of one. Grand passion was beyond him, but in a boozy one-night stand grand passion took second place to technique. And his technique was impeccable.

Besides, the girls he brought home were mostly comparing him to drunk nineteen-year-old boys who wanted to get off and pass out. The bar was low.

He didn't always succeed, of course. Sometimes the girls were too drunk. And occasionally, he came across a female version of himself, a woman who had seen every trick, knew his games.

But he usually sent his women home happy. Most seemed to know intuitively that they were one-night stands, that like any good magician Brian preferred a new audience every night. Though sometimes they weren't in on the joke. Back in Seattle he'd woken up to

Samantha—Susannah?—beating on his door. *You can't fuck me like that and then not call me,* she'd whimpered.

To which he'd said, *Why not?*

These days Brian defined himself by his prowess as a seducer. A cocksman, the word both archaic and strangely modern. If Charlottesville bored him, he could pack up, throw his bag in his truck. A day later, in a new bar in a new city, he'd have a solid chance of walking out with a woman on his arm. Without an expensive car to impress her or friends to laugh at his jokes. Pickups were a kind of alchemy. Only a fellow practitioner could truly appreciate the skill they required.

Two years before, he'd set a number for himself. One hundred. He wanted to bed—okay, fuck—an even hundred girls. And they had to be solid sixes and up. He reached the number on a cold January night in Charlottesville, a few flakes trickling from the gray sky.

o o

The next night he met Becks.

He was at the Fox 'n' Hound, one of Charlottesville's classier bars. Meaning its bouncers actually checked licenses. Brian usually avoided it. Nineteen-year-olds were his preferred targets. Like Matthew McConaughey had said in *Dazed and Confused*, his new favorite movie, *I get older, they stay the same age.* But that day he had built his first working website. He'd decided to reward himself with the Fox 'n' Hound's cheeseburger, voted Best in Charlottesville by the UVA student paper.

It wasn't even eight. The place was mostly empty. Soon as he walked in, he saw her, sitting with three friends in the corner. He knew right away she wasn't from Virginia. She was angular, a hint of hardness in her face. Not his usual type. But he liked the way she looked at him. The style here tended to hair flips and side glances. This one checked him out straight on. Fearless. Not the late-night courage alcohol brought, either. No booze shine in her eyes.

He parked himself on the short side of the bar, where he could keep an eye on her table. When she stood up he saw that she was tall, taller than he'd expected, and that her angularity extended to her body. She was skinny, narrow-hipped, almost flat-chested under her simple black T-shirt. Any local girl with tits that small would have insisted on a push-up bra.

She strode to the bar, positioned herself at the corner, three stools away.

Some guys hesitated in these moments, waited for a clear *go* signal. Not Brian. Waiting was weak. Anyway, the quicker he found out if he had a chance, the quicker he could move on if he didn't.

He edged off the stool, stepped toward her. "Hi."

She turned his way. Cool, appraising. Not pretending to be surprised at his interest. Some tall women seemed ashamed of their height. She held herself up confidently. Even if her face was a bit too planed to be beautiful, her nose too beaky.

"Hi."

"What are you having?"

"That's your opening, dude?"

He liked her even more for calling him on his line. "It's friendly and casual. Not too intrusive."

"You've thought this through."

"Not at all."

"Anyway, I haven't decided."

"I don't believe you. You know what you like."

She gave the tiniest shrug, *I don't care if you believe me or not.* She held his gaze and he surprised himself by looking away first.

"Scotch and soda," he said.

"You're overestimating me."

The bartender slid over. "Pitcher of Coors Light," she said. "And four cups. Please."

"Coors Light?"

"Is that a problem?"

"It wouldn't be my first choice."

Her lips twitched. A smile narrow and brief. Still, he couldn't help thinking of sunlight breaking through a heavy sky.

The bartender slid the pitcher across. "Sixteen, please."

She pushed a twenty over, left the change. Rich girl.

"When you're done choking that down come talk to me."

She stepped away from the bar, looked him over.

"You don't lack for confidence—" She lifted a hand, *What's your name?*

"Drink with me, I'll tell you."

"Bet it's extremely boring." Pause. "Your name, I mean."

"My name's exciting. I'm boring."

"Interesting sales pitch."

Brian let her have the last word and slipped back to his stool. Two cute chicks took the stools next to his. He ignored them. He didn't usually give up the initiative this way, but he sensed this tall girl might be worth the trouble. Not a girl. Not a chick. A woman who played back.

Every so often she peeked over. Brian couldn't read the look, didn't know if it meant, *Yes, I'm stuck here with my friends but I haven't forgotten you*, or, *Hey, creeper, still hanging around?* He made himself eat slowly. The burger was as delicious as promised. Medium-rare and just greasy enough. He finished his drink, ordered another. Vodka and grapefruit juice. A greyhound. His regular. Decent even with the cheapest vodka but harsh enough to discourage fast drinking.

An hour and a half drifted by. The room filled. One of her friends came up for a fresh pitcher. He finished the second greyhound, ordered one more, decided that when it was done he'd get gone. He had broken his own rules by hanging around like a lost puppy. *They like you or they don't, and if they don't, move on.* Plus the drinks here weren't cheap. Between them and the burger he was going to be out thirty-five bucks.

He was down to the ice in drink number three when she and her friends stood. He watched as they slithered between tables to the front door. *You kidding me?* Brian was a little drunker than he expected after three greyhounds. This bartender must pour with a heavy hand. She held the door for her friends. They walked out one by one. When they were gone she looked at him—and followed them out.

Dammit. He wasn't sure why he cared, but he did.

The door opened and back she came.

Lucky for him, the crowd was heavy. He had time to put his face together, lose the surprised look. She pushed her way into the corner.

"Sit." He gave up the stool. She hesitated, sat. Now she was looking up at him. A minor win.

"Time for your name."

"Brian."

"Rebecca." They shook hands, formally, ironically. "You lied. You said your name was exciting." She was a little drunk too, her eyes not as fierce as they'd been.

"In certain cultures."

"You thought I was gone." She had a Boston-type accent, he heard now. *Gahn.*

"I thought of nothing but my delicious burger." Thrust and parry, thrust and parry.

"Your kind needs to get taken down a notch."

"My kind?" But he thought of Amanda, zipping up her jacket and stumbling out of his apartment that morning. *Call me,* she'd said. Then, as she shut the door, *You're not going to call me, are you.* It wasn't a question.

"Think you're God's gift to the ladies."

The natural response would have been shocked denial. Instead he nodded, *What if I do? What if I am?*

"Can I buy you a drink?"

"Enough drinks. Let's go somewhere we can actually talk."

o   o

They found themselves in a tired all-night diner at the east end of Main Street. Not far from Brian's apartment, as it happened, though he'd already decided he wasn't going to mention that fact. The vents blew stale, warm air and the old-school jukeboxes at the tables were heavy on gospel.

"Think I can risk a cheeseburger?" she said.

He pulled a quarter from his pocket. "If you play 'Amazing Grace' first."

She went with the cheeseburger. He ordered a chocolate-and-vanilla shake. Because he wanted one and because he thought it would make him look a little softer, less of a player. Of course thinking that way proved that he was a player, but so be it.

She told him she was a law student, but she sounded almost embarrassed.

"You like it? Law school?"

"The last refuge of the boring upper middle class. I mean, that and med school, but at least doctors help people."

"When they're not playing grab-ass with the nurses."

"Somebody's a cynic."

"If you're not a cynic you're not paying attention."

He wondered if he'd gone too far, but she laughed.

She was from Massachusetts. Didn't know what to make of Virginia. "It's funny down here, especially for a woman. They don't want you to be too smart."

"Even in law school?"

"Especially in law school. Sometimes it's obvious. There's one professor, married, kids, big name. Three days after I got here I heard about him, the girl grapevine. Make sure his office door is open if you go in. Don't *ever ever* meet with him after hours or have a drink with him. Like, maybe he wouldn't actually *rape* you, but he'd definitely get handsy and hope for more."

"The girl grapevine? Is that a thing?"

"Definitely a thing. Not always bad, though."

Brian thought of the way he'd worked through half his apartment building in Seattle. "So one bad apple."

She laughed. "He wasn't the only one. Plus, these bow-tied lions of the South"—*liaaans of the Saawth,* she exaggerated the accent—"guys who were old twenty years ago, they think they're doing us a favor when they ask us the easy questions and give the men the tough ones. They think we're all here hoping to meet guys, get our Mrs. degrees."

"You're not?"

She slapped his hand, not quite playfully, a warning. "What about you? You like it?"

"Down here? I mean, it does feel different. Sometimes I think I'm not in on the joke, sometimes I think they're not."

"You really this polite, or is there some body-snatcher thing happening?"

"Exactly. Also, there's some weird black-white calculus going on all the time that only people born down here can follow. Like, they call the Civil War the War of—"

"Northern Aggression." Rebecca laughed. "I didn't believe it when I heard that the first time."

"They're not totally kidding when they say that."

"They're not kidding *at all*."

"Then again, it's beautiful and people do seem more relaxed."

"You mean the girls are easy."

"I didn't say that."

"You didn't have to. I see them in the bars, *Oh Trev, not another shot, Ahhm so drunk, Ah don't know what I'll do. What if my skirt just falls right off?*"

"Trev and Trip—"

"And Thurston."

"Come *on*."

"Truth, my class has a Thurston. Thurston Randall Jr. I swear. He's like Virginia gentry, he has the most perfect blond hair. Whenever I see him I think he belongs on a horse. In a Polo ad. In Massachusetts I'd be sure he was gay, but down here I don't think so. He's just *bred*."

"So you don't like it?"

"Yet in some weird way I do. Like you can complain everyone is so polite, but what's wrong with that? Boston, somebody knocks you over on the street and then yells, *F you, outta my way*. Folks in Southie will stab each other for the last chocolate frosted at Dunkin'."

"Southie?"

"South Boston. Yeah, everybody hates everybody in Boston."

o   o

The waitress, who was somewhere between middle-aged and *you really shouldn't spend so much time on your feet*, cleared out her plate. "Dessert?"

"Apple pie?" Rebecca said.

The waitress tilted her head, a slight but definite negation.

"Pecan?"

"Great choice. Coffee, hons?"

They nodded and she tottered off.

"Wonder what's wrong with the apple pie," Brian said.

"You caught that too."

"Oh yeah, she did not want you going near it."

They grinned at each other. *Hey, you're all right.*

When the bill came, she insisted on splitting it. Brian was smart enough not to argue. Or maybe not. He noticed the slightest hesitation when he agreed and she reached for her bag. Maybe living down here had gotten her used to freebies from the guys.

"Next time I'm paying," he said.

Which, honestly, was a little ridiculous. She must have way more money than he did. She was the one in law school. But whatever.

Still, they had a good night. Not just a good night, a nice night, and *nice* wasn't usually a word Brian used for his dates. He almost wanted to ask her back to his apartment. He made himself wait. Not because he was sure she would say no. Because he didn't want her to say yes. He *wanted* to have to work for this one. An unexpected feeling.

Instead he put his hands to her face, kissed her once, and asked for her number. She gave it to him but didn't ask for his—*If you want me, you'll have to call.*

o   o

For their second date they went to a hibachi restaurant. Brian had been there before. It was fun, watching the guys in the white hats toss the steak in the air, slice it when it hit the grill. Entertaining. He would have gone there more. But he'd learned the hard way that if you showed up at the same restaurant with too many different dates the waiters made cracks. Anyway, the place was busy. The guys behind the counter gave them the big bow and the *Hai!* greeting and clanked their knives.

Rebecca looked a little thrown.

"Ever done hibachi before?" he said.

"I'm more into sushi."

"Yeah?" He'd never tried sushi.

"I'm always kinda suspicious of restaurants where they give you a big show when you walk in. Like they're trying to distract you from the food."

"Never thought of it that way."

Those were the things you knew when you'd grown up going to lots of restaurants, he realized. He'd never been so conscious of class before. Not because Rebecca was super-rich, she wasn't. At least Brian didn't think so. But she had that combination of education and money that was more intimidating than money all by itself. He had a way easier time thinking about having a million dollars than going some-place like Harvard. The *Ivy League*. Rich was just about money. The other was about a whole way of looking at the world. Of being a snob without trying to be. He could see that Rebecca had that gift.

If *gift* was the word.

The knowledge of the gap between them intimidated him a little. Turned him on, too. Maybe he'd been looking for a woman like her without even knowing it.

Or maybe he was full of it and trying to psych himself up to pay eighty bucks for dinner when she'd basically told him the place sucked.

"You okay with this—"

"Of course, totally."

They sat side by side at the counter, watching the chefs slice and dice. Even before the food came they finished a beer and she loosened up. He got her talking about her family. She had a relationship with her parents that Brian couldn't even imagine. She talked about them like they were her friends. Not like they were perfect. She said they were ridiculous at times. Her mom thought documentary films actually mattered and her dad barely knew how to shovel snow, which was weird considering that his brother—her uncle Ned—was a cop, a genuine tough guy. But she *liked* them.

"You'd tell them if you had a problem? A real one."

"Of course. They'd probably give me terrible advice though. You wouldn't tell yours? Because they'd judge you?"

"Judge me, hah. Eff them." He saw her surprise. He'd been more honest than he'd meant to be. He tried to walk it back. "It's just, we don't have much in common."

He didn't want to think about his parents. He wanted to think about Rebecca. He leaned close, kissed her. No warning. She hesitated, then gave in, kissed back, open-lipped, soft. Their mouths gentle but his hand tight in her hair and her fingers digging into his arm.

Finally they broke off. Stared at each other, the restaurant disappearing into the ether.

"That was unexpected," she said, finally. She looked behind the counter, where the chefs had taken a break from cooking to check them out. "Gentlemen? Our food?"

"Hungry?"

"I've acquired an appetite, yes."

o   o

Toward the end of dinner Rebecca told him how she'd played the piano growing up, played a lot. More proof she'd grown up with money. But the way she talked about it she'd taken it seriously.

"Why'd you quit?"

"I don't know."

"Lying. So you don't play at all?"

"Even if I wanted to, and I *don't*, I don't know where to find a piano. I was good but I wasn't good enough, and then I got mad about it, and then I got mad at myself for being mad. Couldn't get out of my own way." She paused. "Have you ever *really* wanted anything?"

"Aside from right now?"

"I'm serious."

She kept making him think about his life. "Not off the top of my head. I don't know if that's good or bad."

"I don't either," she said. "But for me, the piano, you know all these guys who think they're gonna play pro basketball, but they're three inches too short or whatever, they're not good enough no matter how hard they work? There's just not enough spots for everyone. It was the first time in my life I realized I was gonna *die*, if that makes sense, that some things will or won't happen and it doesn't matter what you want. Know what I mean?"

That fast the memory broke through:

Pops kicking open the door to the bathroom, Mom on the floor, moaning, vomit trickling out of her, Brian trying to run inside until Dad backhanded him, hard enough to send him sprawling, *This is grown-up shit, little snoop, go wait in the kitchen—*

No. He didn't think about that day, any of those days. That boy was gone.

"Brian? I say something wrong?" He shook his head, shoved the memory away. Thought instead of the piano he'd seen delivering pizzas to that nursing home north of town, the Jefferson Home, a black baby grand. He wondered . . .

Persuading the place to let her play was easy. Of course, exaggerating her credentials didn't hurt. *Graduated from Julliard, you're lucky to be getting her . . .* Reaching into the bottom of his duffel for two hundred bucks to have the piano tuned was the clincher.

Why was he going to so much trouble? He didn't know. They hadn't had sex yet, but it seemed obvious they were headed that way. But he wanted to impress her. More, to surprise her.

And he did. Her tension as he drove them out of town annoyed him—did she really not trust him?—but he forgave her when he saw how she almost ran to the piano. And she brought it to *life*. He'd always thought classical music was boring. Not that day. He could see her, them, in a house with giant windows overlooking the ocean, her fingers lighting up a concert grand as he and their kids—for some reason, he imagined four of them, two boys and two girls—sat watching.

Man, I am falling for this chick.

Later he would wonder whether he'd fallen for *her* at all or the fantasy she represented, no linoleum floors, matching Porsches in the garage. But at the time, he found her intensity captivating.

Then, craziness. The oldster lurching off his chair, dead on the floor. Brian tried chest compressions, though he knew they were useless. Nothing was bringing this guy back. His heart was pancaked like a house in an earthquake.

Afterward, Brian felt his old EMT attitude kicking in, *Screw 'em if they can't take a joke, and death is the ultimate joke.* He knew he was saying all the wrong things, but he couldn't stop himself. By the time they left the manager's office Rebecca could hardly look at him.

Luckily, she decided to forgive him.

And they were off.

Within a couple of months they were spending most nights together. What could only be called a tidal wave of sex washed them away. It wasn't just that Rebecca was close to insatiable. Something about the way she lost herself made it possible for him not merely to perform but to *experience* her.

Without really thinking, much less consciously planning, they decided to get married. And quickly.

Even now, Brian didn't know if he'd been cynical or hopeful. Yeah, Rebecca had the money, the education, the prospects. He was marrying up. But he wanted to pull his weight too. And if her plans were more definite than his, so be it. Until now he'd let life carry him along more or less at random. Letting her choose his future for him was just another roll of the dice. He liked Becks. Cared about her. She was interesting. The FBI thing was cool. He couldn't exactly see her kicking down doors, but she was fierce. If she thought she could handle it, he wasn't gonna argue.

Did he love her? He didn't know what that word meant. He tried not to look too deeply inside himself, but when he did, he saw something missing—*stolen*—from him too many years ago to count. Becks was no dummy. She believed in him enough to marry him. That fact alone made him feel better about himself, made him think maybe he wasn't as broken as he thought. If she trusted him, who was he to argue?

So they went for it. And like a week later, Becks was preggers.

Which was honestly not what he was expecting. He should have, right? The way they went at it. But all those one-night stands, he'd never knocked anyone up. Sure, he'd been careful, but not *that* careful. He'd had a few accidents along the way. Maybe some part of him thought he couldn't.

Wrong.

When she called him into the bathroom, *Brian, you have to see this*, showed him the stick, he couldn't help himself, his first thought, *Oh shit*. But he looked at her, her eyes wide, overjoyed, her hand shaking a little with the excitement, and he knew that he couldn't even possibly suggest . . .

So he didn't.

o   o

They moved to Philly, found a row house east of Center City. Philly was rough, even downtown. Brian didn't mind. Fact was he liked the idea of protecting Becks and the baby. The man of the house. He'd been in a couple of fights over the years, held his own. He handled the house, the cooking. Becks studied for the bar exam and worked. Her belly got big. She wasn't one of those women who loved being pregnant or thought it was super sexy. Sometime during the second trimester their sex life went practically to zero, which came as a shock. Every morning Brian felt the pressure squeezing him a little more, five months, four months . . . He looked in the mirror and asked himself, *You ready for this? To be a father?* The answer that always came back was, *I don't know.*

Which he couldn't say to Becks. Because he could already see she *always* knew. Or if she didn't she didn't tell anyone, not even him. Maybe not even herself. He followed her lead, acted all practical. They went shopping for clothes, got the apartment ready. He didn't think she had any idea about his doubts. Becks was smart, but she wasn't super-intuitive. He saw why she liked law school, cases to memorize, rules to follow. Why she liked the FBI. Pick a side, white hat or black.

Even into the third trimester the firm didn't give her much of a break. Sometimes Brian thought they were working her harder, like they were pissed she'd tricked them into hiring her when she was pregnant. He worked freelance, building websites. Finding jobs was tough. He could code a decent-looking site, but he didn't like having to sell himself to some guy who owned a pizza place. He tried to psych himself up, tell him it was like walking into a bar and walking out with a girl. Only it wasn't.

Becks said, *What about a law firm, a bank?* He wasn't ready to go corporate. Besides, he came through with a couple of jobs a month, so it wasn't like he wasn't helping. And he figured once the baby came, her parents would help out. They'd *want* to, right? A new grandkid, the two of them just starting out?

But no. Her parents came for a week after Rebecca had the baby and then disappeared. Bought them a changing table and a car seat, sure. But didn't even leave fifty bucks to cover the takeout they ordered. Rebecca's dad giving him the fisheye the whole time. Brian had gotten along good with her mom from the get-go. Dad, not so much. He was always dropping not-so-subtle hints that Brian wasn't good enough for his darling Rebecca, asking when Brian planned to get a job full-time. Like he'd ever done an honest day's work in his life. Fucking poet.

Anyway, it didn't matter because they had Kira now. And to his everlasting surprise Brian loved that little girl from her first minute on the planet. Of course, taking care of her was as exhausting as everyone had told them. But he knew she needed him—that she couldn't survive without him. He'd never felt so *necessary* before, and for the first time in his life the thought of being needed came as a blessing, not a burden. Plus, the reality, he was more natural with her than Becks was. Funny, considering she was the one who'd wanted the baby.

Becks loved Kira, sure. She cuddled, breast-fed, changed diapers. She did all the right things, and she did them with her usual skill and efficiency. But Brian could tell she was itching to go back to the office. Not because she wanted to move up at the firm. She hadn't changed her plan to apply to the FBI. No, she just thought being a stay-at-home mom was a waste of her time. Even if she never quite said so.

Not Brian. He liked nothing more than to make Kira giggle, whisper foolishness in her ears, rock her to sleep while he made up nonsense rhymes. Even before Rebecca's leave officially ended, he was taking care of her most days, while Rebecca snuck back to the office to pick up memos to read at home.

Plus, yeah, they needed her salary. They both knew it. Even in his best month coding, he hadn't made half as much as she did.

"You work, I'll take care of Kira."

And the die was cast.

o   o

A nondenominational minister named Jane had officiated their wedding, one of those atheist northeastern ministers. Brian had never known they existed before he met Becks. *I don't believe in God, but I want to run a church.* Like, I hate food, but I'm gonna be a chef. Say what? But they were a real thing.

Anyway, Jane gave a little speech just before their vows. *Marriage can be a seesaw, one side rising as the other falls,* she said. *An endless tug-of-war, both of you fighting for control. Or it can be a partnership, a place where your happiness is his and his yours. A sacred space, a shaded grove. Live in the grove of happiness.*

Jane wasn't married, though. And, no surprise, Brian realized pretty quick she didn't have a clue. Their marriage wasn't a grove or a seesaw or a tug-of-war. It was . . . a bus ride, maybe? With Rebecca driving and Bri eight rows back. They didn't fight, but from the first they built their lives around her and her job. She made the money. She had the health insurance.

Brian didn't mind. Not at first, anyway. Rebecca took to being an agent. And Brian felt he got to live the job without having to put on a suit. She told him all about it, not just the cool parts but the bureaucracy too, the forms they filled out in triplicate, their old-school computer systems. Long after everyone else switched to email, the FBI still used *faxes* as a regular means of communication.

He liked Birmingham too. Practically no traffic, low cost of living, and cute UAB coeds for scenery. Even after Kira started going to pre-school, he had Tony. Goofball Tony. The kid walked into walls and insisted on taking two baths a day for exactly seven minutes each. He wasn't autistic. He made eye contact, he loved to be hugged. He was just weird. So be it. Brian was glad to hang out with him.

But sometime during their second year in Alabama, he realized he was turning into a *housewife*. And in Birmingham, men weren't supposed to be housewives. At the park where Brian took Tony to play, the moms gave him a wide berth. They never asked him to join their playdates. He found out why after a few weeks, when the cutest of them all—small and luscious, the opposite of his wife—sat down next to him on the bench that had somehow become his and his only.

Okay, he was turned on, he'd admit it. Their sex life had come back some now that the kids were a little older, sleeping through the night. But he could tell it would never be the same as it had been in those first few months. Becks was tired all the time. Besides, the old joke was true, just 'cause he liked Mexican food didn't mean he wanted tacos every meal for the rest of his life. This little piece of honey-dipped cornbread next to him . . .

"Nice to meet you." He put out a hand and she hesitated but then her Alabama manners took over. She had a boy who was maybe three, but she couldn't have been more than twenty-four. She wore a little gold cross between her perfect D cups. "I'm Brian."

"I'm Kaylee?" Women down here turned everything they said into a question. Even their names.

"Hi Kaylee."

"That your boy? Tony?" She nodded at Tony, who was sitting backward on a fire engine, cupping his hands around an invisible steering wheel instead of the real one in the front. Why? Who knew? Tony gotta Tony.

The question surprised Brian. Kaylee must have seen him bring Tony to the park dozens of times. "Of course."

"Like, *yours*?"

Finally the penny dropped. "You'd have to ask his mother, but I think so, yeah."

"You're not, you know"—she hesitated, finally came out with the word—"queer?"

Brian tried not to feel humiliated. So what if she thought he was gay? "Do I look *queer*, Kaylee?"

"Lil bit, not too much. But you can't always tell."

"Could you give me a percentage?"

She shook her head in a way that suggested the concept of percentages was foreign. "But are you?"

"Straight as a jaybird."

"Oh."

He didn't quite understand the disappointment in her voice.

"Was gonna ask if you wanted to bring your boy over to play with Karlin? They play good together."

Indeed, Karlin was giggling with psychopathic glee as he swung a pail at Tony's head.

"You still can."

"My husband said only if you're a queer. Otherwise no guys in the house."

Brian felt his temper rise. "He sounds confident in your relationship."

"Okay, sure." She stood, walked off, her heart-shaped ass taunting him with every step.

o   o

That night in bed he started to tell Rebecca the story. Then stopped. He had a sinking feeling the joke was on him. Anyway, Rebecca was crankier than usual.

"My mom's bugging me about coming up. They haven't seen the kids in like six months."

"They can come down."

"They came down last time, and the time before that."

"Drag the kids up there?" In truth, as both he and Becks knew, the real problem was that round-trip tickets from Birmingham to Boston ran five hundred bucks. Even if they drove to Atlanta they'd spend about three hundred each, and both kids needed seats now. Twelve, thirteen hundred bucks to see her crappy parents. And he knew better than to ask them to pay.

"You need to get a job, Bri."

He flashed to Kaylee's red lips. *That your boy?* A man who didn't have a job in Birmingham wasn't a man. Tony would be in pre-K next year, and then Brian would have no excuse at all.

Rebecca pulled a folded piece of paper from the bedside table, handed it over. A posting for a part-time job in the information technology department at the university. She was his guidance counselor now? Looking for work for him? But . . .

How could he argue? "Think they'll hire me?"

"Why not?"

That fast, he knew she'd already greased the skids. Talked to somebody. Easy enough for her. Down here they loved the bureau.

For the first time in their lives together, he hated her a little. But he took the job.

Truth was, he liked it better than he expected. The questions had obvious answers most of the time—*I can't send email, my computer is frozen, my dissertation is gone.* When they weren't, Brian had a knack for figuring out where problems lay, mostly in the intersection of hardware and software that different admins had added over the years.

What people who didn't work in information technology didn't understand was that although the theoretical core of modern computing was incredibly complex, the way the devices themselves fit together—or didn't—was simpler. Mechanics didn't need to understand the laws of thermodynamics to handle a grease gun. And Brian didn't need to know how to write code that could pass the Turing test to figure out why the English department's email system had gone down.

He kept that fact to himself. Most people thought computers were impossibly complicated and anyone who could handle them as a genius. Even Becks seemed to respect him more after he took the job, though she was so focused on this big case she was working that he couldn't really tell.

Becks and her case. Becks and the FBI. The bureau ate their lives day by day, night by night. Becks didn't have to stay up until 1 a.m. three nights a week reading backgrounders on the targets of her investigations. No one did. These were government jobs. Wasn't like she was putting in for overtime, either. When Brian asked why, she told him: ask for an extra buck, your FBI career was over. You were headed for a back-office job in human resources. The bureau had always considered working for it a privilege. Getting rich was not in the job description.

Fine. No overtime. But she didn't have to work seventy hours a week either. One week, he counted up the hours she worked at home: four Monday, three and a half Tuesday . . .

When he told her what he'd done, she wasn't happy. They were hanging out on the couch at the time. Brian was watching ESPN on mute, *Sunday Night Baseball*. She was poring over a manual on entrapment in undercover investigations, what was legal and what wasn't, how far you could go in stringing along the target.

She put down the manual, gave him the stare. The one she gave to anyone who cut her off in traffic. To the preschool teacher who told them Kira had pulled another girl's hair on the playground and then admitted that the other girl had yelled at Kira first. Her black eyes as flat as sunset in January with the snow already falling and a long night ahead.

Brian didn't know if she'd stared at him that way before she'd joined the FBI. Maybe she had, and he just hadn't noticed. Or maybe the bureau had brought out this righteous aggressiveness, or aggressive righteousness, whatever.

"Counting hours? I work twice as hard as every guy in the office. They know I'm married, they know I have kids; they're just looking for an excuse to put me on the mommy track."

"I thought you liked the SAC—"

"Yeah, but everybody else. I promise you. It won't be like this forever." She reached for him, stroked his face. "Come here, you. I'll let you make it up to me for giving me a hard time."

Thus the conversation ended.

But the next morning, as he thought about what she'd said, Brian knew she was lying. Both to him and herself. She would be working eleven-, twelve-, thirteen-hour days for years. Not just because she loved the job. Though she did. But because she wanted to *win*, and to win at a particularly male game.

Brian didn't feel jealous, not exactly. Sure, the bureau had plenty of good-looking guys. But Becks knew an office romance would blow up her career even faster than asking for overtime. She wasn't the cheating type. Too practical.

No, Rebecca wasn't cheating on him with any agent in particular. She was cheating on him with the job. The real cost to their relationship came in what they *didn't* do. They had no time to themselves, because when she was home she wanted to hang out with the kids. Brian understood. Honestly, she *should* hang out with the kids. Kira and Tony craved time with her.

So their marriage was an afterthought. Which didn't matter most of the time. Brian was comfortable alone. He'd spent years by himself. Back then he'd distracted himself with one-night stands. Today he had the kids. If weeks or a month passed when he and Becks didn't have a real conversation, hey, so be it.

But he couldn't escape the realization that if they weren't growing together, they were growing apart. Maybe it sounded all Oprah-y, but it was true. Marriage required compromise. A lot of compromise. Love wasn't enough. You had to *like* your spouse too, or the daily frictions of living together could be maddening.

She constantly left the lights on all over the house. A small thing, but it drove him nuts. She wasted money on clothes, then complained about their credit card bills. On the nights she did come home on time, she always wanted to take the kids to restaurants. She justified going out by saying he shouldn't have to cook, but he *liked* to cook.

He knew he did things that annoyed her too—beyond the big thing, the not making enough money thing. He cracked his knuckles constantly. He cooked mac and cheese too often. He let the kids watch TV more than she liked. Fine. Let her take care of them six days a week, see how often she turned on the television.

None of these complaints was a deal breaker. Even all together, they weren't deal breakers. They were more like slow leaks, rotting the marital walls from the inside out. If a storm came, a bad one, they'd regret not having done the maintenance.

But as long as he didn't think too hard, he could convince himself they were fine. And Becks was making the most of her career chances. She was deep into this undercover investigation. It dragged on for a while, but in the end she brought the case home. Mess with the Becks, die like the rest.

Brian sometimes wondered what had *really* happened at the dinner with Draymond Sullivan when everything clipped into place. When she came home the next morning she didn't say a word, just hung on to him like a shipwrecked sailor grabbing a raft.

Then they decided to move. She pretended to ask his opinion, but he knew as soon as she raised the issue he didn't have a choice. No matter that he and the kids liked Birmingham. Becks told him she had to go. The city was too dangerous after her work busting the Pablo Escobar of Alabama real estate.

He was almost sure the real reason she wanted to leave was because she thought she was too big for the Birmingham office now, needed to kick her career up a notch. He ought to be proud of her, but he couldn't help feeling he was turning into a supporting actor in the movie of her life. *Rebecca Unsworth, Crimefighter.* He was the spouse who shows up in a couple of scenes to humanize the lead character and then disappears until the end.

Worse, he wasn't sure Becks saw the movie any differently. Or that she cared.

o   o

Off to Houston they went.

There the rot started to break through.

Mainly because of money.

Rebecca and money.

They should have been able to live on her salary, with him doing the kind of half-time work he'd done in Alabama. Houston had plenty of universities that needed tech support.

But in Houston, Rebecca turned out to be a *spender* in a way he hadn't understood before. Maybe she hadn't either. She'd always made fun of her parents for the way they lived above their means, the way they'd let her grandfather subsidize them.

But now that she was into her thirties, the way Grandpa Jerome had paid for stuff didn't bother her as much. She made sure Brian knew how much she missed the trips to Jamaica, the vacations on Cape Cod.

Unfortunately, Jerome wasn't writing checks anymore. And so now, instead of asking him for help, Rebecca asked the friendly bankers at Wells Fargo. If she saw something she wanted, she bought it. Including a BMW. Worst of all, she didn't even tell him about the car until he saw it in the driveway.

"You're an FBI agent, not a stockbroker," he said that night, the kids asleep. They kept it together in front of the kids.

"No one says *stockbroker* anymore, Bri."

She had that tone in her voice he heard more and more. That superior tone. Ironic. Maybe she didn't even *know* she was doing it.

He waited for her to say more, to at least *justify* the Bimmer. *I'm in the car all the time, I got a great deal, we'll both drive it.* She didn't even bother. Because she didn't have to, right? She paid the bills. If she wanted to blow forty grand on a car she would.

"It's a sedan," she finally said. Throwing him a bone. "I can take the kids."

"No, it's cool."

During their first years together, Brian had found Rebecca's confusion about her class privilege endearing. She genuinely viewed her law school loans as a massive problem—when she had no other student loans to pay off and would be headed for a great job as an associate. She had no idea what it was like to be middle class, much less poor.

Now he had a darker view. The misunderstanding felt intentional, a way for Becks to get what she wanted without admitting her privilege. In fact, sometimes he felt he had to play along, to overestimate his own spending, just to hide the gap in their habits. Yeah, he took Tony to Rockets games in Houston a couple of times. But guess what? If you sat up high and didn't buy merch, you could get in and out for fifty bucks. Less than a pair of Rebecca's Lululemon pants.

Even so, he was afraid to call her on her bullshit. The subtext of any talk about the money she was spending would be *the money he wasn't making.* He worked in software, at a time when Silicon Valley was minting the greatest fortunes ever seen. So how come they weren't *rich*? At least rich enough for her to be able to buy a car without worrying?

o o

He didn't argue about the car. Instead he went to work for Conoco-Phillips. In Birmingham no one cared if he was five minutes late or wore sandals. He could at least pretend he hadn't turned into a total drone. Conoco wasn't a university. It was an oil company. It had a top-down, hop-to-it culture. But he didn't have a choice. Conoco paid better than an academic job would, and they needed the money.

Only good part was that his shift started early and ended by four. On the way home he could stop somewhere for a beer. After a while it was usually a beer and a couple of shots. Not more, though; he didn't want to be drunk when the kids got home from their after-school stuff. He usually picked places like Hooters. His hair was slowly walking back from his forehead, but he was still in solid shape. And he hadn't entirely lost his game. The waitresses liked him.

Still, he made sure to wear his ring. He wasn't ready to go past flirting. Not yet. He wasn't exactly sure why. Wasn't like he had any big moral problem with screwing someone else. If he did he could always think of that three-hundred-horsepower middle finger in their driveway.

But the kids were still too young, both in elementary school. Divorce messed kids up. As much as he'd hated seeing his parents fight, he'd hated bouncing between them even more. He'd told his mom once, *Just pick. I don't even care which of you gets me*—and he didn't, not really, his mom stank of cheap vodka every night and his dad walked around with the clenched rage of a guy waiting for a zombie attack—*Just pick.*

We both love you and want to spend time with you, she said.

He knew better. He was just something for his parents to fight over now that they couldn't scream in each other's faces. Sometimes he found himself fantasizing about them dying. At the same time, please. A head-on collision, her wasted and him speeding. Whatever. The more horrible the better. As long as they both bit it.

So he knew, his kids deserved better than divorce. Maybe when they were older. He knew something else, too: Becks would not give him a pass if she caught him with his pants down and a Hooters employee nearby. Hundred percent chance she'd kick him to the curb. And play the righteous victim, *Men are pigs.* She'd make sure that Kira knew, *Can't trust any of 'em, especially not dear old dad.*

Of course maybe he'd get away with it, Rebecca was busy. But he didn't feel like taking the chance. Fact was, he loved Kira and Tony in a way he couldn't have imagined possible before they'd arrived in the world. Watching them grow up, turn from babies into toddlers into real people who told jokes and practiced dunking on the adjustable hoop in the garage made him grin every day. He wanted to grin every day. He didn't want to be in some crappy half-time custody arrangement. He knew Becks would never agree to less, no matter that he did most of the work. That he was, truly, the better parent. She might even tell herself that the kids needed her more and fight for more. What would he do then? Try to convince a family court judge that the until-recently-unemployed dad was the better parent than the FBI agent wife?

Not a chance. Not in *Texas*. Probably not anywhere. Even the fact that the kids were closer to him than Becks would work against him somehow.

Plus, if he was being totally honest with himself, he wouldn't ever ask for alimony. He had some pride. Which meant he'd wind up working twice as hard and living in half as nice a house if Becks kicked him out.

So, fine, he split the difference. Stopped in Hooters for a couple of adult beverages and then went home to spend quality time with his laptop, take care of business. He checked out the hard-core stuff, gangbangs and bondage, it was all there, but in the end he was mostly into plain vanilla, the occasional threesome. *College Girls Get Wild.*

Maybe because it brought him back to his glory days. *They'll pass you by . . . in the wink of a young girl's eye . . .*

Screw Bruce Springsteen. Brian was way more into rap these days. Sublimating his rage with Eminem, especially. He'd turn the songs up until his windows shook. On the way to his job as a *Conoco sys admin.* The joke didn't escape him, but he couldn't do much about it. He was not so much trapped as triangulated. Sometimes he figured he should work harder, if he made more money he'd solve the puzzle. But a few thousand extra bucks a year wouldn't matter. It hadn't so far. Becks would just spend whatever he made. She couldn't help herself. Poor little rich girl. She had champagne taste and the worst part was that she didn't even know it. Every so often he'd realize she was wearing a pair of shoes he hadn't seen before, a new bag.

Expenses rise to meet income. One of the few smart things his dad had ever said.

As for sex, he still serviced Becks when she needed a tune-up, every two weeks or three case reports, whichever came first. Far as he could tell, she still enjoyed it. For him it was mostly muscle memory.

Basically, they had a fifties-style marriage. Hubby made the money and the decisions, wifey took care of the kids and rooted for hubby at work and dutifully provided sex when requested.

Totally traditional.

Except she was the husband and he was the wife.

o   o

His dislike of Houston only made matters worse. The city was too hot, too big, too flat, too churchy. Too Mexican *and* too white at the same time. Too many guns *and* too many cops. Too rich *and* too poor. Houston was a black Silverado that would not get off your bumper. It was humidity that never broke no matter how much rain came. It was the strange sour smell that the ground itself exhaled in the summer. It was driving down to the Gulf of Mexico to get away, ha-ha, and realizing the Gulf was just liquid Houston, a dull chemical soup that stretched on forever.

Maybe if he'd made some friends. But why bother? In a couple of years Rebecca would put her hand up for another office and away they'd go. When they weren't talking about Kira and Tony, their main topic was her career, so he knew enough to see she was turning into a star. Despite everything, he found himself proud of her. She'd sold him out, but at least she was getting full value. He figured they'd end up in Washington or New York, one of the real prestige jobs.

Then she started messing around at the border, chasing some serial killer who gave dirt naps to migrants. A crime that was in no way her job to solve. A crime that was *not her problem.* A crime that, as far as Brian could tell, no one at the FBI gave even a single crap about.

Before he even figured out what was happening, she'd turned it into a holy quest. Feminist nonsense. Brian was sorry about the migrants, but most murder victims were men. He didn't see Rebecca pitching in with the Houston cops to solve the cases piling up in the Third Ward, the gangbangers dropping each other. No, she preferred to chase a ghost.

Which was not just unfair to him and the kids, but stupid. For her to come home late because she was busting her butt on cases that might help her career, okay. He didn't love playing housewife, but he could deal. But he hated to see her wasting her time.

Even worse, she blew him off when he tried to talk to her about it. More proof she didn't respect him. Like he needed any.

Then he realized she had another reason for running down to the border. She had a hard-on for the guy at the border who was in charge of this totally useless investigation. Ranger Ten-Gallon Hat. Brian didn't know if she was actually having sex with this lawman, but she certainly liked his company. She'd slipped up a couple of times, talked about him in a way she never talked about any of her FBI buddies. How he "got it," he knew these weren't just a bunch of dead Mexicans. Not just what she said but the way she said it. Yeah, Brian knew.

And he was *pissed.* Because he had kept his side of the bargain, he hadn't banged any of those waitresses or the Conoco admins who looked his way. He could have. Some would have turned him down. But some would have said yes.

What gave her the right to cheat on him, or even think about it?

Only thing he knew was that he couldn't say a word to her. No way, no how. He would just embarrass himself. Boo-fucking-hoo. Whatever she wound up saying, he'd know what she thought, which was that he hadn't earned the right to question her. *Earned* being the key word.

So he let her take her shiny red rocket down to the border whenever she liked. But on the weekends she went down there, he put the kids to bed and went out. Not to Hooters anymore, either. Houston had its share of first-rate "gentlemen's" clubs—with oil at more than a hundred bucks a barrel in the last year of the Bush administration, the town was flush.

He never had sex, but he let them grind him until he came in his jeans. Never took more than two dances. He didn't know whether to be proud or embarrassed at the speed. *Well hello there*, the girls would say, leaning close, rolling on his crotch in their G-strings while he was still spurting. And *Good to the last drop*. And *Guess we don't need to go to the back room*. And, his favorite, from a blonde who reminded him of Birmingham Kaylee, *Ain't getting much at home, sweetie?*

Is it that obvious?

Mmm-hmm.

Maybe he was fooling himself but he thought the girls liked it, proof of their skill. He handed over an extra twenty when they were done. Money well spent.

o o

Then Rebecca's conscience hit her. Or the charms of Ranger Redneck wore off. Or, most likely, she realized she wasn't doing her career any favors, that she wasn't getting any extra credit from the bureau for wasting weekends. Becks was too practical to let a holy quest interfere with her climb up the FBI's ladder. Soon enough, she told him—no pretense of asking—that they were headed to D.C., she'd taken a job at headquarters.

"Counterintelligence."

"Being stupid? That's an official desk?"

She didn't smile. He couldn't remember the last time she smiled at a joke he'd made.

o o

The kids complained less than he expected about the move. They weren't into Houston either.

But D.C. . . . In Houston Rebecca had whined about not being able to spend the way she liked. But in D.C. they really couldn't live on her salary. Not anywhere that wasn't at least an hour-plus drive from the Hoover Building. Exurbs, the real estate agents called them. Like if you lived there you didn't even qualify for the suburbs anymore.

Of course, no law said FBI agents had a right to a fifteen-minute commute. The problem of their housing costs *did* have a solution, which was for them to move out to Germantown or Clarksburg, and for Rebecca to deal with the drive. But Rebecca insisted they be in one of the fancy close-in suburbs. For the schools, she said. Maybe. Or maybe Becks was just tired of driving. And of living in places where pickup trucks were more common than Volvo station wagons. You could take the girl out of Massachusetts . . .

Once again, what Rebecca wanted, Rebecca got. Instead of living in a town they could afford, they were stuck paying backbreaking rent for a dump in Chevy Chase. Stuck in a way Brian remembered from his childhood, when they had to choose which bills to pay and he dreaded the end of the month.

Worst of all, he knew what she was thinking. *If you'd just make decent money everything would be fine.*

She was wrong. They were way past that now, even if she wanted to pretend they weren't. But whatever. He figured it would be easier to get a job than deal with her disapproval. So he did. At the National Security Agency, no less. Turned out that his résumé looked better than he expected to the government. ConocoPhillips was the kind of place the NSA liked to hire from. The fact that his wife was a senior FBI agent didn't hurt either.

o   o

Then he caught a break. A break that changed his life even more than the night he'd walked into that bar in Charlottesville and met Becks.

The NSA did everything from operating spy satellites to protecting the fiber-optic cables that connected the White House with the Pentagon. It made the CIA look small.

But at the agency's heart was a group called Tailored Access Operations—the government's hackers. TAO was the computer equivalent of the military's Special Ops units. Its coders inserted malware into North Korean nuclear plants, hacked the phone of Iran's supreme leader. The Tailored Access guys could write code which would have gotten anyone else arrested. One famously nasty TAO bug called Carrie caused laptops to overheat and burn, even on sleep mode. The agency had used Carrie only twice, both times against North Korean nuclear scientists.

Tailored Access had barely two hundred coders, the elite of the elite. Brian's résumé was far too thin for the agency even to consider him as a hire. But the NSA knew that many of its engineers considered the chance to work for TAO a major job perk. Once a year, it offered an open competition, a twenty-four-hour chance to solve what the agency called a "theoretical targeting opportunity." Anyone who did was given the chance to join.

The official name for the challenge was the Annual Special Entry Program. It was more popularly known as "Ender's Game," from the famous Orson Scott Card novel. Despite the agency's insistence that the puzzles were theoretical, everyone assumed they were related to actual Tailored Access operations. They were next to impossible. One week after the contest, the agency announced how many winners it had had. The coders joked that in most years the number was binary—either 0 or 1.

Brian's first Ender's Game had come five months after he joined the NSA full-time. He was still learning the quirks of the place. But any coder could sign up, even one as new as he was. To avoid interfering with regular work, Tailored Access dropped the challenge at midnight on a Friday. Employees worked at their desks. They had access to their regular computers and the NSA's usual non-TAO software tools and databases. They had to work alone; teaming up resulted in immediate disqualification. Each year's instructions opened with a single line: *This is a problem, not a puzzle; answer accordingly.* The challenge followed.

Brian feared entering might annoy his new boss, a rickety NSA lifer named Jeff McNeil. *What, Mobile Support isn't good enough for you?* But McNeil encouraged him. "Rite of passage," he said. "The Coder Olympics. Sponsored by Red Bull."

Even then, Brian wasn't sure. Why waste a Saturday?

The entry deadline came two days before the contest. With a few hours still left to decide, he told Kira and Tony about it over breakfast. Nothing classified, just the outlines. Tony shoveled Raisin Bran in his mouth like an escaped prisoner. Kira picked at a clementine, one tiny slice at a time. Having a teenage girl meant never, never talking about food. At the counter, Becks was making coffee. Of course, she'd just bought a three-hundred-dollar brewer despite their financial crisis.

She really should have married some rich guy from law school.

"Sounds cool," Tony said. "You should do it."

"Not sure *cool* is exactly the word," Kira said. "But yeah."

"All right, maybe I will."

Becks grunted. He knew what that grunt meant.

"Doesn't Tony have a game Saturday?" she said. Without turning around, still fiddling with the Nespresso machine, like she was asking the air.

As if Tony was going to get off the bench for more than the league-required five-minute minimum. "You can take him. He'd like that." *For once you can be the parent who shows up.*

"If you think you have a chance, you should do it." *Which we both know you don't.*

At that moment he decided that nothing in the world would keep him from signing up.

○   ○

So it was that at midnight Friday, he found himself staring at his computer. No surprise, the challenge looked impossible. It involved a messaging system that an unnamed "Hostile Foreign Entity" used to communicate with its agents through the Internet. The encryption that protected the system was defined as a 1024-bit asymmetric key. A hundred messages were provided, strings of characters and numbers that the NSA had captured.

In theory, a chain of powerful computers working together for months might break the encryption. But Brian had no chance of writing the code necessary to attack the key directly. He had a basic understanding of encryption. He knew how the first cryptographers had developed public keys. He could explain the relative strength of asymmetric and symmetric systems. But he couldn't pretend to be an expert. Not at an agency that had PhDs who had literally written textbooks on the subject.

Anyway, he was sure that going straight at the problem would get him nowhere. The Tailored Access coders had no doubt tried that approach. Brian needed something else. If he couldn't decrypt the messages themselves, maybe he could find a pattern in the metadata, the headers and footers that surrounded them. Find a clue that the TAO guys could pursue, evidence he could think creatively.

Not the greatest idea, but it was all he had. Either that or go home, and he wasn't ready to go home. No way. He could already see the smirk Rebecca would give him.

He popped open a Red Bull and reconsidered the problem. The messages had been presented in apparently random order. He started by sorting them from oldest to newest, looking for a call-response pattern. Maybe they represented a single intelligence controller communicating with many agents at once. But he soon saw the messages had not been sent in any pattern, at least not one he could understand. Assuming the time stamps were accurate, they spanned almost two years.

Assuming . . . assuming. So much he didn't know. Like everyone else in the contest, he was operating with only a fraction of the information he would have had if he actually worked for Tailored Access. For example, the agency might have captured a hundred thousand suspicious messages and only provided these. Or these might be the entire data set.

Nor did he have any idea how the NSA had found the messages. They might have come off of the agency's standard Internet surveillance—which captured more or less all the data that came over the public Internet—and popped up as worth another look. On the other hand, the agency might have targeted a specific network. Or these messages might even have come off the hard drive of a single laptop that soldiers had captured in Afghanistan.

But in that case, Brian would have expected the messages to be roughly the same length. Working on corporate email systems had taught him that once people had a writing style, they stuck to it. Not these. Some were just a few characters or words. Others went on for several paragraphs. Brian decided it was more likely that they weren't from or to a single user, that the "Hostile Foreign Entity" the challenge referred to was an actual intelligence agency, not just a handful of terrorists.

A guess, but he had to start somewhere.

He tried again, dividing the messages by hours of the day. Maybe they were routed through specific Internet nodes at specific times. Again, he couldn't see any pattern. The drop points—the router addresses through which the messages had entered the Internet—had come from all over Central Asia and the Middle East.

Of course, skilled users could try to hide the real locations where they were connecting. But those methods left clues, such as transmission lags lasting a fraction of a second, that the NSA should have found. Brian saw no hints of those. He didn't understand. The obviousness of the drops cut against his first guess, that he was looking at an intelligence agency. If an agency was using this system to connect officers with frontline operatives, he would have expected security that extended past encryption, including falsified entry points.

Then again, maybe he just wasn't good enough to spot them. He put aside the messages and spent a couple of hours reading manuals on the agency's technical tricks for tracing message traffic. Nothing jumped out. By the time the sun rose he was exhausted. Though he was increasingly sure the message system wasn't particularly sophisticated. It looked like a commercial-grade instant messenger with encryption layered on top. But would a serious intelligence agency rely on an outside vendor for its messaging system?

Brian pulled papers from the agency's library about the potential holes created when encryption was added to preexisting message services. Software engineers called fixes like these bolt-ons. They were notoriously vulnerable to outside attack.

After some searching, he found a paper — *Secondary Encryption: Strengths and Vulnerabilities* — that addressed the issue. He downloaded it, promising on pain of his life, or at least the next five years, not to remove it from the agency in any form. It turned out to be thirty-three pages long, each paragraph more gruesomely difficult than the next: "*Assuming finite algorithmic variability, we find that random errors will rise at the square of . . .*" After two hours and three more Red Bulls, he had read twelve pages and understood maybe half.

He simply didn't have the training in core computational theory he needed to follow the logic here. He never would. The guys who wrote these papers were off the charts, and they'd spent their lives learning to think like computers and to make computers think like them.

Brian was just a mechanic.

He was also exhausted. He could have used a pick-me-up. Too bad he'd left his stash of Addys way back in the nineties.

He put his head on the desk and closed his eyes.

o   o

He wasn't sure how long he was out, but he woke up to a monsoon. He jumped out of his chair to find McNeil dumping a bottle of Poland Spring on his head.

"Dude."

"Lucky it's not Gatorade."

"Lucky I didn't deck you."

McNeil cackled. The guy was six feet tall, one hundred forty pounds, with a widow's peak that guaranteed him a spot as an extra in the next Addams Family movie. "How's it going?"

Brian shook his head, feeling the water drip down his back.

"I hear this one is even more impossible than usual. Half the guys have quit already. I'd offer you advice but I'm not allowed and it wouldn't help anyway." McNeil scooped up the paper that Brian had printed out. "This is some high-level shit. If I were you, I'd focus on beating the password protection, 1Gojihad1. 'Cause you've got about as much chance of figuring this out by midnight as learning Japanese."

"You're taking a little too much pleasure in this."

"We also serve who remotely shut down our masters' lost Crack-berries. I'll be glad to have you back on Monday." McNeil ostenta-tiously checked his watch. "Anyway, you have another eight hours and fifty-four minutes, so make me proud, son."

"Thanks. Don't you need to get back to your coffin and wait for dark?"

"Sick burn, Bri." McNeil saluted and left.

Brian gave him a minute before going to the bathroom to mop himself up. Staring at himself in the mirror he wondered what had happened to his life. He loved Kira and Tony, wouldn't have traded them for anything. Otherwise what else did he have? He still liked to think of himself as the cool rebel, the guy he'd been back in the nineties, the guy who'd once shared a bottle of Jack with Kurt Cobain.

In reality he was a tiny cog in the world's largest bureaucracy. He monitored software downloads for a living.

Oh well, whatever, never mind . . .

Might as well just go home. No shame in joining the quitters. Stop at a titty bar on the way, find a stripper willing to get up close and personal. He had a few more hours of furlough.

But he couldn't. Some part of him knew he was on the right track, that the mismatch of strong encryption and obvious entry points meant something. He also thought of something McNeil had said, *We also serve who remotely shut down . . .*

Despite its culture of secrecy, its internal surveillance, its constant reminders to be careful, the NSA faced a constant drip of lost phones and security breaches. After all, the agency's employees were only human. And sometimes they cut corners.

What if Brian was *right*? What if he was looking at a publicly available instant messaging system, nothing proprietary? Like AOL Instant Messenger but developed for a language other than English. Not many people knew how many different messaging systems had been developed over the years—maybe not even inside the agency. They sat on top of browsers, so coding them was straightforward, at least the ones that didn't have video. They could be optimized for different languages, different levels of user authentication and secrecy.

But the second- and third-tier systems faded away fast. If they didn't quickly build a big enough installed base to attract advertisers and sponsors, the developers stopped supporting them and they turned into relics. The tech industry had no place for losers, whether the TRS-80, the floppy disk, or AOL Instant Messenger.

Maybe the "Foreign Hostile Entity" had gone after one of those dying systems, repurposed it for its own use. After all, desktop computers were still the main way people outside the West connected to the Web. In developed countries, Internet connections were mostly mobile. Poorer countries still depended on hard lines.

Only a theory, but it made sense. And if it turned out to be right—

He might be able to figure out which system it was.

Back at his desk, he looked up the agency's files on instant messaging applications. They were solid on mobile messenger apps, thin otherwise. The agency had become so obsessed with smartphones that it no longer spent much time on browser-based services. A classic example of focusing on what was important to you rather than your enemy, Brian thought.

But as a matter of course, the agency did log every messenger application it found. The list totaled more than one hundred. Not good enough. To impress the guys at TAO, he needed more. They might like his theory. They might even use it. But they wouldn't hire him for coming up with it, not unless he figured out the specific app that the foreign entity had used.

Time for another guess. He eliminated all the apps from in the United States or Western Europe, or any that were too new. He focused on seven systems that dated from the early aughts, four in Russia and Eastern Europe, one in Turkey, one in Pakistan, and one in India. None had caught on.

He pulled the documentation the agency had recorded on the systems. Unfortunately, it was minimal. They had all been built off GPL or Freeware licenses, but the agency had spent almost no time looking at them. As far as Brian could tell, no one had even bothered to download copies of the original system software. A mistake. He wasted a few minutes throwing the names of the messengers at the agency's database querying system. But each request came back with tens of thousands of answers. He couldn't figure out a useful way to sort them. He tried to ignore the little digital clock on his computer, but he couldn't help himself; it was now 8:02 p.m. Less than four hours left.

He tried to find the apps on the Internet to install them on his computer, but they were all gone. The original websites for the developers were gone too. No surprise. Americans thought of technology companies as profitable giants like Apple. In reality, most tech companies, especially in places like India, were often not much more than a few twentysomethings in a room. They alternated between writing semi-legit code, dubious pop-up ads for penis enlargement pills, and outright hacks.

Even with the deadline looming, Brian decided to spend an hour documenting what he'd done. At least if he found something in the last few minutes, he could prove it hadn't been luck. The contest famously ended exactly on time. Coders had to file their work by midnight; TAO would not accept late submissions. *The rules don't have to be fair, they just have to be the rules*, the final paragraph of the challenge warned. *We don't want you wasting more than one day a year on this. (If you could have figured it out you'd already work for us.)*

But as Brian explained his steps, he couldn't help feeling like a fraud. Really all he'd done was guess, because he didn't have the skills to code a direct attack on the encryption—

Wait.

He'd looked for the companies. And they were gone. But he hadn't chased down the developers themselves. He'd forgotten—as the NSA sometimes seemed to—that programs didn't fall from the sky, that *people* had to write them. Maybe he could find traces of the coders.

Wasn't much, but he'd spent more than twenty-one hours on this stupid contest. Might as well finish strong. For once in his life he'd go to the limit.

He went back to the cached pages of the now-defunct developers, plugged the names on them he found into both the public Internet and the agency's database.

The name searches led everywhere and nowhere. The common ones pulled up hundreds of thousands of results, mostly in foreign languages. When Brian translated them, they were useless, random web pages for Moscow car dealerships or Bulgarian dating sites. The torrent of information on the Internet was its own best defense. He tried again, this time adding corporate names.

Again the results overwhelmed him. He could have wasted days looking through them. In pure desperation, he started to add search terms almost at random: *spying, espionage, secret, agency, encryption*—

There. The conference was called "Better Than Pretty Good Encryption." It had taken place at a Radisson in Jaipur, India, two years before.

"This two-day event will get you up to speed on the newest public key software!" A list of presentations was included. And—at the bottom, the lousy end-of-second-day slot—Brian found Vijay Patel, director of engineering at IRGG Services Limited, speaking about "Adding Public Encryption Layers to Instant Messaging Services."

Brian hadn't heard of IRGG Services. He searched for it along with Mumbai Communications Pvt Ltd, the company that had created the Indian instant messenger. Lucky him, the Indian software industry ran mostly in English. He found a two-line announcement on an Indian software blog: *IRGG Services has purchased Mumbai Communications, terms undisclosed.*

There. At last, a link between a third-tier messenger service and the encryption.

Eleven twenty-six. He couldn't risk missing the deadline. Still, he had to find out more about IRGG. He went back to the NSA's main database and found the very first hit for IRGG was a file called *Indian Army Software Suppliers*. A military application made perfect sense for a messaging service like this one, with decent but not top-rank encryption.

Brian looked everything over. Maybe he was wrong. Maybe he'd made some mistake so obvious that the Tailored Access guys would laugh at him and put up his submission as an example of what not to do. But if he had, he couldn't see it.

He wrote up what he'd found, included the links. And at 11:55 p.m. he sent it off.

o   o

He drove home that night as excited as he'd ever been. His mood didn't survive thirty seconds with Becks. Who was sitting on the couch by herself, watching *Saturday Night Live*.

"I did it, Becks."

"Did what?"

"Solved it."

"That's amazing." She couldn't have sounded less amazed if he'd told her he'd stopped on the way home to buy Cheerios. "When will you know for sure?" Her way of saying, *Yeah, right*.

"It was intense."

"I can smell that." She wrinkled her nose. "You should take a shower."

She was mad that he'd worked all day and not called, he saw. Did she have any idea what a hypocrite she was? Their entire marriage she'd worked this way, left him with the kids. He almost said something like, *I thought you'd be happy for me*, but screw it, he wasn't showing her any weakness. Let her sit there watching Kate McKinnon.

o   o

When he got in on Monday morning a short black guy was waiting at his desk.

"Brian Unsworth?"

"Guilty."

"Jim Reynolds. We need to talk."

The heat of Rebecca's disdain had evaporated whatever confidence Brian had felt. She was probably right. He couldn't have seen what no one else had.

"I mess up somehow?"

Reynolds didn't answer, just nodded, *Come with me.* He led Brian at race-walk speed down a fire staircase to a basement corridor that Brian hadn't known existed, swiped his badge to unlock a thick steel door. Down a hallway to a conference room, where a man and woman sat on one side of a table. On the other side, an empty chair, obviously meant for him.

Brian sat. Reynolds stayed standing.

"Can you walk us through your thought process on the challenge?"

Guess we won't be introducing ourselves. Brian hoped the truth didn't make him sound like an idiot. "I didn't see how I could beat the encryption directly. An end-around seemed like the best option."

"Did you have any outside help?" the woman asked.

"No." He shook his head for emphasis.

"Your boss came by." This from the guy.

"Only to dump water on me." Brian started to laugh, then stopped when no one else did. "Really."

"Someone from TAO tipped you," the woman said. Not a question this time.

"I don't even know anyone from TAO."

"You have ten minutes," Reynolds said. "Walk us through how you got from X to Y."

So Brian did. They listened, no questions. When he was done, Reynolds looked at him. "You'd be okay taking a polygraph to confirm this."

"This is getting weird." Though he knew the NSA loved the box. He'd already taken one before he was hired.

"Yes or no to the poly?"

"Yes, sure."

Reynolds looked at the other two. "Okay, you've met him. Any problems?"

They shook their heads.

"Okay," Reynolds said, and extended a hand. "Welcome to TAO. Assuming you pass the poly."

"Holy shit," Brian said.

o   o

Three days later Brian was officially part of Tailored Access. Over coffee, Reynolds explained the job, and why he'd hired Brian:

"We need some coders who think like you, who see cracks in the architecture, exploitable holes. I mean, a lot of the time it's not going to work, and I gotta warn you that some of the hard-core guys may not take you seriously. But it doesn't matter, we run a pretty open shop. I want you to feel free to ask questions. I've got enough tanks. I need some snipers. Make sense?"

"Sure does." What could be better than having the chance to think of himself as a sniper?

He didn't realize at the time that—like his marriage—his new job would never again be as good as it was in those early days. Be careful what you wish for.

o   o

But for a while all was well. Reynolds was as good as his word. The internal walls were low, and the coders encouraged to collaborate. Sure, some of the PhDs made clear they thought his Ender's Game win was a fluke. But so what? If he had to eat a little crap, so be it. He had plenty of experience with that at home.

And as for home . . . not much changed.

Sure, their money problems improved now that he was working, and he got a raise once he joined Tailored Access. They made progress on their credit card bills. But Brian couldn't see how they'd ever pay for college for the kids. Of course, he could live with them not going to college. Not his first choice, but he hadn't gone and his life had worked out. But he knew he couldn't even mention the possibility to Becks. She'd freak.

Worse, Becks still didn't treat him as an equal. Brian thought sometimes it was like she didn't *believe* he worked for Tailored Access.

What did she *want* from him? Now he had a real job, and she still didn't take him seriously. Maybe she was so used to thinking of him as her lovable loser husband that she couldn't look at him any other way.

Maybe she *liked* thinking about him that way, maybe she always had. But he was done trying to prove himself to his wife.

Now that he had a few bucks to spare, he started hitting the strip clubs again. He didn't like the ones in D.C. as much as Houston—those strippers had been the best part of living down there. But they did the trick, especially one club called the Peppermint, just inside the D.C.-Maryland border, about a half hour from Fort Meade. After the club he'd usually hit the gym on the way home. Gave him an excuse to take a shower.

He had no problem making sure Rebecca didn't find out. The kids had their own lives now. No one cared if he came home at six or eight. Plus he could always find an excuse, say he was having a beer after work. Not like Rebecca would check up on him. Maybe she didn't care, or maybe she was just busy. Anyway, if he was being honest with himself, he liked putting one over on her. The great FBI agent didn't even know what her husband was doing.

Though when the strippers offered to take him upstairs, the anything-goes rooms, he still said no. He couldn't explain why, but he supposed maybe his vows mattered to him more than he realized.

o   o

The thrill of being part of Tailored Access slowly faded. The NSA was pushing machine learning and artificial intelligence, letting the software do the work, at speeds humans couldn't comprehend. Writing those programs required an understanding of software theory Brian didn't have.

Funny part, no one seemed to notice. He wasn't a star, but he made himself useful on secondary projects, and every so often he had clever suggestions. Still, deep down, he felt like a fraud.

And he started to question the job itself. Sure, the stakes seemed high. Networks ran everything. The Internet was a new battlefield all its own, with skirmishes that moved across countries and nodes at the speed of light.

Still, it was all just *code*. A lot of NSA guys liked to think of themselves as soldiers. They tossed around the language of war a lot. But Brian figured none of them, including him, would have the stones for real war. The difference between him and the rest of them was that he knew it. If they made a mistake, someone else—on some front line somewhere—would pay the price long before they did.

He kept his opinions about the fake NSA machismo to himself. Not much percentage in talking about it.

o   o

The days went by. Rebecca laid off a little. Mainly they focused on the kids. Brian realized a strange truth: until it exploded, a lousy marriage could make for good parenting. Maybe he and Becks were competing to prove their worth to their children. Maybe, deep down, they hoped to save the marriage through the kids.

As he approached forty, Brian's life was objectively fine. He had a good job, healthy kids. Yet more and more he hated everything and everyone, except for Kira and Tony. No point in thinking about a divorce. Tony wasn't even a teenager, and Brian didn't plan to go anywhere at least until he'd graduated high school.

When he needed to psych himself up, he thought about the speech he'd give Rebecca after he filed the divorce papers. He used to play the same game with his father, imagining what he'd say at his funeral.

He wondered sometimes if Rebecca felt the same as he did. But from a practical point of view the marriage had worked for her. Rebecca was nothing if not practical, he thought. His practico-path wife.

o   o

Then it happened.

One Monday night at Planet Fitness, he noticed a woman reading a programming manual as she pedaled slowly on a recumbent. A female coder. He'd never seen her before. He would have remembered. Even at the NSA they were rare. She was skinny, small, with blond pixie hair and a tiny tattoo on her arm. Twenty-five or so. No wedding ring.

She looked up, caught him staring, smiled. A tiny smile, elven. He was about to take the bike next to hers when his courage deserted him. He chose a treadmill behind her instead and spent his workout watching her from behind. Lame and creepy. Back in the day he would have gone straight to her. Worst of all, he had something to talk about with her. She was reading more than working out, hardly moving the pedals as she paged through the manual. But as he decided to say hello, she finished, tossed her book in her bag, walked straight out. No shower.

He spent the next day waiting for his chance to go to the gym.

She wasn't there. He was furious with himself. Where had his game gone?

Then, Friday, he saw her. *Don't blow it.* He walked over, took the bike next to hers.

"I usually stick to something easy like Python when I'm exercising."

"You're a coder?" She sounded vaguely European to Brian, German maybe.

"Maybe."

"So, Mr. Maybe, can you walk me through this question of error correction?" She pushed the manual at him.

"I'll need something very important first."

"Yes?"

"Your name."

Eve. And they were off. They spent the next forty-five minutes chatting and pretending to work out. Brian liked her. She was younger than he'd realized, twenty-three, and shy. She was Finnish and had lived in Helsinki until she was nine. Then her dad took a job with Microsoft and they moved to Seattle.

"Do you miss Finland?"

"Not so much. The winters make everyone a bit crazy. And it's hard to understand if you're from this country what it's like to live in a place no one cares about. For a while we all thought Nokia was so important, the great mobile company, and then it stopped mattering, too."

"Honestly, I don't think I ever thought about Finland before Nokia. Or since. I probably shouldn't say that."

"No, it's fine."

Finally, she looked at her watch and stuffed her book in her gym bag.

"I have to go. I'm sorry."

"Will you be here Monday?"

"Will you?" She winked at him, the flirtiest gesture she'd made, though it was a little bit geeky, too. Again she ran out, no shower.

o   o

All weekend Brian felt like a kid waiting for his birthday, watching the clock. He had a feeling she'd be there Monday. And she was. She smiled when she saw him, patted the bike next to hers. The conversation picked up where it had left off. She'd spent the weekend at home working.

"Your boyfriend must have been bored." His old rule, better to ask fast, not waste time.

"No boyfriend. He moved to New York last year. Anyway, we weren't compatible in some ways."

Brian restrained himself from asking if she meant sex.

"How about you?"

"Married, but we're getting divorced." Not exactly a lie. More a matter of timing.

"Terrible. I'm sorry to hear that."

Her tone was neutral. Was she flirting, or just stating a fact?

"You think you know someone and you don't at all," she said.

"Or maybe you know them too well."

"That too."

He was looking forward to a long conversation but her phone beeped. "I have to go," she said. "I have a programming group in ten minutes."

"You won't have time to shower."

She leaned over. "Maybe I like being dirty," she said, under her breath so only he could hear.

Okay, she was definitely flirting. *Don't wuss out. Ask. In fact don't ask, just say it.* "Let's have lunch tomorrow."

"If you're sure your wife won't mind."

"I'm sure."

o   o

He met her at an overpriced Mexican place in Bethesda. They were early. The restaurant was nearly empty. They picked a booth in the back, ordered margaritas as soon as the waiter came by. She seemed to be having second thoughts.

"Have you ever done this before?"

"No." And he felt he was telling the truth. The strippers only wanted money. They weren't really *there*.

They sucked down the first margs even before the chips came, ordered another round. Twelve bucks a pop and strong. She relaxed.

"My parents are talking about going back to Finland. I tell them they're crazy."

"You have family there?"

"One brother, he's a lot older, never left. Let's not talk about my family, they wouldn't like my being here."

"What should we talk about?"

"C++."

"Exciting."

The drinks kept coming and Eve switched sides to sit beside Brian. He realized that without having to talk they had decided what would happen next. More than anything, he felt young, like his mojo had flown back in on the skinny shoulders of this Finnish girl.

When they walked out of the restaurant the sunlight stung his eyes.

"I can't drive," she said.

Fifty yards away a Marriott waited. They stumbled in hand in hand and after a short, awkward conversation with the clerk, *I know check-in is three but we need a room now, I'll pay for two nights if I have to*, he had the plastic key to Room 524.

"Are you okay with this?" Eve said.

"You have no idea how much. You?"

She squeezed his hand.

o   o

What came next surprised him. Because Eve turned out to be one of those quiet women who was someone very different behind the bedroom door. "See this." She pointed to a faded yellow bruise on her bicep. "This is what I like."

She wasn't the first woman he'd met who found pleasure in pain. "I get it."

"Yes? Really?"

In answer he picked her up and threw her onto the bed. He slapped and bit and put his hands around her neck and the more he pushed her the more she wanted. *Harder. More. Harder. Harder. Yes—*

By the time he finished he was exhausted, panting like he'd just finished a race. He pulled out at the last moment. She ran her hand down his cheek, the only bit of tenderness since they'd entered the room.

"I didn't know if you could do it."

"You're a totally different person in here."

She grinned, showing him her uneven Finnish teeth. "You like it?"

"Oh yes."

He rolled off, lay beside her. She went to the bathroom and he closed his eyes and dozed. He wondered if he'd feel guilty when he went home and realized, no, he wouldn't. He'd have dinner with Rebecca and the kids and think of nothing but this beautiful sliver of a woman.

He must have fallen asleep but then she was beside him again. She reached between his legs and began to stroke him.

"This time you hurt me. Really hurt me. I tell you to stop, you don't stop. I say no, you get rough."

A game he had never played before. It scared him a little. He wondered if it was the reason why her boyfriend had left. "Don't we need a safe word?"

"Hah."

"I'm serious."

"Okay fine. Avocado." She looked at him, those pale blue eyes. "Yes?"

She was still stroking him. Without stopping, she leaned in and bit his lip. Hard, no joke, and now he was the one who was bleeding.

"Oh you bitch."

"Then do it. Make me want it."

So he did. He held her down, shoved himself inside her. She kicked and snapped and whimpered.

After what seemed like a very long time but probably wasn't she dropped the pretense, stopped begging him to stop and instead pleaded for more. *Oh yes. Coming coming coming.* Soon he was too.

The strangest, most intense sexual experience of his life. One afternoon and he was ready to rob a bank for this woman. *She fucked my brains out* felt like a simple statement of fact.

"Next week? This time? This hotel?"

"Yes, please."

o   o

But when he turned up in the Marriott lobby a week later, she wasn't there.

That was the bad news.

The worse news came when a bulky man he'd never seen before said, "Brian?" and shoved a keycard into his hands—716—and walked away.

Maybe this was today's game. But he had a bad feeling.

The Marriott corridor was as bland as ever. He knocked on the door to 716. Nothing. He touched keycard to reader.

"Eve?" He pushed open the door.

No Eve. A man stood by the desk in the corner. Lights on. Curtains drawn. The smell of cigarette smoke, and Brian's first thought, he couldn't help himself, *Don't you know they fine you for that?*

"Come in," the man said. Tall, bald, brown eyes, heavy features. He looked Greek, maybe. He spoke like a man used to being obeyed.

The classic horror movie moment. *Don't go in there.*

Brian walked in.

"Put your phone on the desk."

"Why would I do that?"

"So you don't do anything stupid like trying to tape. Come on, do it."

Brian did, beside a laptop.

The man clicked the laptop's cursor. And a video began to play.

There she was. Begging Brian to stop.

Please don't, you're hurting me—

You love it, you know you do—

Mister, stop, you're hurting me—

Punching and kicking.

The man paused the video. "Big stud."

"It's not real." Brian's voice was surprisingly steady. *Who are you? Why do you have this?* Though he could already guess. "Watch it all, you'll see, we were playing."

"Three minutes long, it's all like this." He ran the video again.

Eve's screams crawled inside Brian. Sure enough the video ended with her still shouting *Please stop, it hurts.* The tape was so convincing that for a moment Brian wondered if he had actually raped her.

But everything about her and what had happened made sense now. All the loose ends that hadn't fit, that he'd chosen to ignore. He should have known. The NSA gave new hires special training about what were still sometimes called honeytraps. The agency knew very well many of its coders spent more time in front of screens than with the opposite sex. Brian didn't fall in that category.

Then again, he had his own issues with women, didn't he?

The man closed the screen. Extended his hand. Brian took it by reflex. "Feodor Irlov."

Brian saw no reason to pretend he didn't know what was happening. "With the SVR?" The Russian CIA.

"Very good. Some people confuse us with the FSB, but technically that's the FBI. I understand you know people there too." Irlov laughed, *heh-heh*, smarmy. "You are of great interest, Mr. Unsworth."

"It doesn't even make sense that she would have taped it."

"She was worried. The way you pressed drinks on her at the restaurant. She's very naïve."

"She said she was Finnish!"

Irlov shrugged, *I don't see your point.* "She will testify, you know. A young Russian woman who comes to the United States to work."

Suddenly Brian didn't know why he was arguing. Screw 'em all, the NSA, the FBI, the Tailored Access pukes, every last one of them. Including Becks. Especially Becks. Irlov thought he was *blackmailing*? Please. Brian's whole life was blackmail. His whole life had led him here, marrying Rebecca, lucking his way into a job where he felt like a loser every day.

Whatever offer Irlov made, Brian knew he was going to take it. At least the SVR thought he was worth setting up.

You want me to spy for you? When do I start?

"This tape isn't just a matter of your marriage or your job—"

"I get it. So what now."

Irlov looked confused. Brian recognized the feeling from long ago, those rare nights when after a single drink the girl had simply said, *Come on, let's go.* The game was supposed to be harder.

And Irlov was right. He *ought* to fight back. He was about to sell out his homeland.

But hell. The war was only virtual, right? Software. Video games, pretty much. Lines on a screen. They wouldn't ask him for the names of any agents. He didn't *know* any.

Irlov shook his head, *This is too easy.* "That's it? You don't insist on your rights?"

"What rights?"

Irlov gave him a slow, careful appraisal. "Easiest recruitment in history?" His nostrils flared. "Are you sure you're not Russian?"

I'm not anything, Brian thought. But he just stared at Irlov. Odd, now that he'd agreed, he felt every bit the man's equal.

"Good," Irlov said. "Then it goes away."

"In return?"

"You can imagine."

Brian could. The details of Tailored Access programs, and not just against Russia. The tricks the NSA used to protect its own computers. Maybe they'd even ask him to smuggle programs off the NSA campus.

He wondered how they'd found him, then knew—

"The Peppermint, right? Not too far from Fort Meade, somebody there watching for guys like me? Runs our plates against a reader you put near the agency. But you have to get a different girl, who cares what a stripper says."

"If you say so."

"I have to tell you, she's very good, Eve, whatever her name is. Do I get to see her again?" The most foolish thing he'd said. But he still wanted her.

"If you are very good, maybe."

"So no."

271

Irlov wrinkled his nose, *Don't be stupid.* "Of course no. It would only make problems. I must tell you. We know about your financial—concerns."

Brian didn't ask how. "Yes those."

"We can help."

"How's that? I inherit a million dollars from my deadbeat dad. My wife won't fall for that. Even NSA counterintel won't fall for that."

"Of course." Irlov pulled up a fresh screen on the laptop, filled with lines of code. "Don't you write apps like every other coder, the next *Angry Birds*?"

"Sometimes." Though not in years.

"Now, success." Irlov clicked a couple of keys and a sample app booted up, virtual cards fanning across a virtual blackjack table. "It's called Twenty-One. For gambling. Casino locations, payouts, what machines are running hot, all the games. For play money."

"I did that?"

"You did. Now you sell it."

"The money's clean?"

"What do you think, we wire from the Kremlin?" Irlov shook his head. "It comes through a consulting company run by a nice American. No vodka anywhere. Plus, why would anyone care? NSA doesn't care if you code on the side, nothing to do with the agency. You sold it, congratulations. Hard work pays off. Legal money. You even pay tax on it."

"The American dream."

"So how much?"

Irlov was eager to seal the deal. No surprise. The NSA had plenty of secrets, and Brian had access to the best. He considered. A million? A million was a nice round number.

He looked at the laptop that held his past and future. No going back. He might as well get *paid.*

"Two million dollars."

"Greedy." Irlov laughed.

"After taxes it's barely a million. Yes or no."

"For two million you tell us about your wife too."

Talk about getting even with Becks. Best part was that she'd *love* this money. "Done and done."

"Two million, then," Irlov said. "Half in six months, the rest next year."

"Six months?"

"Your wife has to see you working hard, yes? Writing the app, going to a conference—"

"She doesn't care."

"She's not stupid, she pays attention."

I didn't say she was stupid, I said she didn't care.

"NSA pays attention too. I give you the money now, it just goes to legal fees after they arrest you." Irlov closed the laptop. "Are you sure you don't want a few minutes to think about it—"

"I've been thinking about it my whole life."

o   o

Irlov encouraged him to show Rebecca bits of the app before he sold it so the deal wouldn't come as a surprise. But the first time he mentioned it, she sighed like he'd said he was going to invent an electric-powered jetpack. Somewhere along the way she had decided he was a loser, and even the Tailored Access job hadn't changed her mind. He didn't say anything else until he told her he was going to Vegas for a couple of days.

"You know the app? The casino thing?"

"Sure."

He waited for her to ask more, if she could look at it. She didn't. She pecked his cheek, turned out the light. She fell asleep almost instantly. Becks had always been a good sleeper. Absolute self-assurance was the best pillow.

He lay in the dark, listening to her breathe. Did he hate her?

He didn't, he decided. But he hated what she'd done to him.

o   o

He'd thought the Russians would take it slow with the debriefs. He was wrong. In their second meeting after the Marriott, Irlov asked him about the NSA effort to break into the Russian military Internet. One of TAO's crown jewels, a compartmentalized project called OAKLEAF. Brian hadn't seen much. Irlov wasn't pleased.

"Brian. We are honest with each other. In Bethesda, you say how much you want, I agree."

"You haven't paid me anything yet."

"You think, Feodor, he doesn't want to burn me, he won't ask anything hard. It's true, I want to protect you. But first I have to know you didn't go running to your bosses, *the Russians trapped me*—"

"Not my style."

Irlov nodded. "Yes, I agree. I don't think you have the patience to triple. Too many lies to keep straight. I'm your mistress, what's the point if you have to lie to the mistress? Enough lying to your wife, the mistress is for the truth."

Brian had never quite thought of it that way, but okay, sure.

"So, I tell you the truth," Irlov said. "I want to protect you, but I need to know you aren't playing with us."

"I'm not read in for OAKLEAF—"

"Okay, you tell me what you're working on."

"Right now we're trying to crack this bank in this Chinese city called Xiamen—we think there's a military satellite program for Iran the Chinese are funding through there—plus, there's a laser company there we're looking into—"

"Satellites and lasers. An offensive program? For Iran?"

"I don't see the output, you know that. Only the questions we're asking, the tools we're using."

Irlov nodded. "All right. And try finding out what you're doing about Google now that Snowden messed everything up for you, told everyone how much access you have there. Start with that."

"Two million dollars."

"Yes."

o   o

Brian still liked to cook after all these years. Rebecca was getting home in time to eat with the kids more often these days. Sometimes he wondered if she was planning a divorce, she wanted to be sure a judge wouldn't think of her as an absentee parent.

He decided dinner would be the place to tell everyone.

"I sold my app."

"What app?" Tony said.

"Your dad was writing something about Las Vegas," Rebecca said.

"Casinos, the casino industry. Guess how much they paid."

"I thought you were just watching porn all that time," Kira said.

"Hot young teens."

"Seriously, Dad, that is not funny," Tony said.

"How much?" Rebecca asked.

Eyes on the prize, that's my girl.

"Fifty thousand?" Kira said.

Brian lifted his thumbs.

"One hundred? Two hundred?"

"Two—"

"Two hundred thousand, Dad?" Tony said. "Not bad."

"Two *million*."

"Two million dollars?" Rebecca said. "For an app? Oh my God."

"Been downloaded twenty-one thousand times already." True. Nice trick from the Russians.

Rebecca came to him, hugged him, looked at him in a way she hadn't since—he couldn't even guess. Philly or maybe even Charlottesville. Her eyes proud and wanting, not the tired curdled lust of the last few years, *I want what you can do for me*, but the real thing, *I want you.*

She kissed him.

He almost laughed. All he'd needed to reclaim his manhood was two million dollars.

o   o

She didn't question the windfall. Why would she? Brian thought. She was Rebecca Unsworth, and good things happened to her. Over the next year, they paid off the bills, bought a house, put money away for the kids to go to college.

o   o

Stealing the NSA's secrets wasn't easy. After the Snowden fiasco, the agency had tightened its audit trails. Nobody walked out with USBs anymore. Brian had to do more sitting back and listening. He was good at it. Nobody thought he was a threat. He even caught up on OAKLEAF. Which was progressing in fits and starts. The Russians hadn't made breaking into their military Internet easy.

He saw Irlov and another Russian, Nikolai, the smartest programmer he'd ever met, every six weeks or so. Once in a while Nikolai helped him solve some minor technical problem so he'd look good at Tailored Access.

Actually, he kinda liked Irlov. Mostly they met in random parking lots and hotel rooms, but a couple of times the Russian had arranged for cooler stuff, like a Turkish bath in Philly. Old-school spy stuff, like Brian was a real secret agent. Irlov usually slipped him a few hundred bucks at the end of every meeting. Nothing huge, just enough to remind him that they were partners.

o   o

For the next couple of years everything was copacetic.

Until Brian, not for the first time, found himself hard done by. The two million was almost gone, and yeah, their life had improved. But he wanted more.

"Don't you think it's time for another app?"

"Even NSA might notice if you sell two apps no one uses."

"Money makes the world go round."

"Don't be greedy, Brian."

"Just ask the folks in Moscow, huh?"

A pause. "You're sure you want me to do this?"

"Yes."

o   o

Their next meeting was a month later, a strip-mall Chinese restaurant in those same Maryland exurbs where his wife had refused to live. The Taste of Beijing, molded plastic booths and pictures of the food behind the counter. The place empty at 2 p.m. Rebecca wouldn't have been caught dead in here. Funny part, the food was good. Brian had learned over the years, Rebecca's snobbery blinded her to certain simple pleasures.

"Anything on GALAPAGOS?" A Tailored Access project to infiltrate the wireless systems of the private yachts owned by Russian oligarchs and Saudi princes.

"Lots." Brian snacked on his sesame chicken. "Did you ask?"

He saw Irlov didn't even know what he meant. Then comprehension dawned. "About the money? Of course. There's no budget."

Irlov was obviously lying, annoying Brian more than if he'd just said no.

They went back to eating. Brian wasn't even sure why his back was up. Two million was real money. And Irlov might take care of him again eventually. If he played along.

But he didn't *want* to play along. No more begging for respect. Not with his wife. Not with this Russian.

"GALAPAGOS," Irlov said.

"I can't remember."

"Brian. The people I work for will not take this lightly."

Brian shrugged.

"Just work with me. Please. Give me some time."

Brian felt like he'd made his point, had Irlov moving the right way. Plus he wanted to think through, was he really going to push the Russians?

"GALAPAGOS, yes, we've made progress—"

○   ○

Two nights later he was lying with Rebecca, postcoital, spooning.

"You may not see much of me for a while," she said. "We think there's a new mole. High-level."

"Russian?"

"Why else would I care?"

"At CIA? That would be fun."

"It would. We're not sure yet. Maybe downtown . . ." The White House. "Could even be your shop. Whoever it is has great access."

Could even be your shop. Brian hoped she didn't notice the sudden uptick in his heartbeat.

○   ○

A month later the OAKLEAF team had an emergency call. It lasted four hours, ended with grim faces. Within a day the outlines of the disaster leaked to the rest of TAO. *A billion dollars gone. Total reboot.*

Like they knew we were coming.

He called Irlov, demanded an off-schedule meeting. Twenty-four hours later they were at a rest stop on 95 in Maryland. Cracked asphalt and pigeons and screaming kids. The ugliness suited Brian's mood.

"You're gonna burn me."

"What?"

"You just blew up a billion-dollar project. You could have been subtle about it, strung them along—" And then Brian realized. "But no, you wanted to stick it to them. You figure sooner or later it leaks, the *New York Times* runs the story, black eye for the NSA."

"I don't make those decisions."

"Gonna use me like a whore, you need to pay me like one. Where's my money?"

"I told you—"

"Yeah, you did. Don't be greedy. Or what? You'll out me? Please." After their last meeting Brian had read up on the history of American agents for the Russians. They often went dark for months or years. The Russians never gave them up. Why would they? Handing Brian over would just mean they could never use him again.

"Two million dollars. And not in some Swiss account. Money you could use."

"And look at what I gave you. It was a fair deal. It's over. Time for a new contract."

They were sitting in the back seat of Irlov's Honda Pilot. Not exactly a Lambo, but then Brian supposed he wasn't exactly James Bond. He reached for the door handle—

"No more treats until you do right."

"I tell you as a friend. Don't do this. The bill, it will be yours."

"Kill me. Who's gonna chirp about OAKLEAF then?"

"No one said anything about killing you, Brian."

"Glad to hear it."

Brian gave Irlov a quick two-fingers-to-the-forehead salute and stepped out. He felt about ten feet tall as he walked through the parking lot. Sooner or later they'd come back. What was a couple million dollars to the Kremlin?

o   o

The fall and winter passed with no word from Irlov. Not a threat, not a plea. Nothing. The spring too. Brian kept piling up information. He wanted to have a whole buffet for Irlov when they finally met again, let the SVR know what it had missed all those months.

After a year, Brian found himself growing nervous. He'd expected something, at least a flutter. Maybe he ought to contact the man himself. He still had the emergency codes.

But first they had this twentieth-anniversary trip to Europe.

o   o

Just as Irlov warned, the bill had come due. Higher than Brian had ever imagined.

As soon as Rebecca had mentioned the couple in Paris, he'd known. No way would Kira disappear on her own. She was too steady to go home with some random guy. If she did she would tell Tony. Maybe not Brian or Rebecca. But Tony. Tony was the family's goofy good-luck charm, the one who could always make them laugh even if he wasn't always in on the joke.

If Tony didn't know where she was, then she was *gone*.

Why? This operation was expensive and risky. Why not just pay Brian? But Irlov was making a point. Brian had insulted the man. He'd taken Russian money and walked.

Had he really thought the SVR would just *go away?* So stupid, so arrogant.

And they'd waited . . . and waited . . . and hit him in the most painful way possible.

Irlov had to know Kira and Tony were the only two people in the world he cared about. He'd bragged about Kira getting into Tufts, about Tony's first date. Meanwhile he'd joked about Rebecca—he'd once been late for a meeting because of a nasty accident on the Beltway and told Irlov, *Too bad it wasn't Becks.* Irlov had smirked. And listened. No doubt the Russians had a file on his motivations, his weaknesses. *Subject cares for his children, shows little interest in his wife.*

How had he deluded himself into believing these people were his partners?

o   o

He'd bought a burner two nights before, while he was casing the Gothic Quarter bars. He'd called and texted Irlov a dozen times. He'd even found a public phone and called the Russian Embassy in Washington directly, a huge operational mistake. "I need to talk to Feodor Irlov."

"Who?" a Russian woman said.

"Please—" But she'd already hung up.

The hours passed. Irlov didn't call. Or text. Or email. The man was letting him twist, making his point.

Meanwhile Rebecca raced from police station to club to apartment with her mad-dog efficiency. Brian wanted to tell her to stop, that she had no chance of finding Kira. But then he'd have to tell her the truth. A truth she'd never understand.

Because everything that had happened was *Rebecca's* fault. She was the one who'd taken away his manhood, who'd made him turn to the Russians.

Her fault. Not his.

Anyway, he believed Irlov would give him a chance to win Kira's freedom before the Russians did anything permanent. So he waited.

Now he couldn't wait any longer.

He lay beside Rebecca in bed in the apartment, Barcelona mostly quiet now, only an occasional distant shout. For once Rebecca was sleeping badly, grumbling and turning.

Maybe he could point Rebecca the right way without giving up his involvement. Maybe he should try Irlov again. Maybe—

No. He had to tell her. As soon as he did, everything would change. Someone senior would make a quiet call, *Let the girl go, she's not your problem.* The FBI director. Maybe even the president.

Kira would be safe. And Brian would spend the rest of his life in prison.

"Becks." A whisper. He would have to work his way up to it. "I have to tell you something—"

o　　　o

Beside him the burner buzzed.

A text, one line. *0630 AM*. Ten minutes. Brian pulled on a pair of jeans, a T-shirt, crept out of the room. Rebecca stirred but didn't wake.

He went down to the street. At six thirty exactly the phone buzzed. "Feodor?"

"A pleasure, a great, great pleasure to hear your voice," Irlov said. "And such a surprise."

"I'm so sorry."

"I don't understand."

Brian closed his eyes, tried to think of a clear blue sky. Anything to keep from screaming. Irlov wanted Brian to suffer. So Brian would suffer.

"My daughter, Kira—"

"Can you be more specific?"

Brian's composure cracked. "Fuck you—"

He was talking to no one. Irlov had hung up.

o   o

The phone slid out of his hands, bounced against the sidewalk. Lucky him, it was a cheap clamshell burner. His iPhone would have cracked.

He picked it up. Waited.

Finally it rang again.

"I don't enjoy being cursed at. If I hang up again it'll be the final time."

"Please. Do what you like to me, don't hurt her." Brian counted to ten, could take the dead air no longer. "I'm begging you."

"Why would I do anything to anyone as important as you, my friend?"

"Whatever you want. Never ask for money again."

"We're not *savages*, Brian. We keep our word. We like our friends to do the same."

"Just let her go."

"Assuming I know what you mean—"

"Please."

"I can't promise. Decisions have been made."

"But. Feodor. I don't understand. I mean this sincerely." Brian hoped he had the right tone, *I'm desperate but I'm still thoughtful, useful to you.* "If you hurt her. Doesn't your leverage disappear?"

"You seem to have forgotten, I understand, all this stress"—Irlov paused—"you have two children. Not one."

Brian found himself sitting on the sidewalk, his legs rubber. The phone at his side. He picked it up. Tried to call. Again. Again.

But Irlov was gone.

He stomped the burner until it was hardly recognizable as a phone, scattered the pieces.

o   o

Upstairs. Thank God. Rebecca was still asleep.

He had to tell her.

No. Not just because he'd spend the rest of his life in a cell. He had to give Irlov a chance. The man hadn't said no. He hadn't said yes, but he hadn't said no. Pressuring him might backfire.

He lay beside his wife, closed his eyes.

Suddenly he found himself in the back of an ambulance, a faceless paramedic putting a mask to his mouth, rattling over the rough road.

He didn't know how long he'd slept but his phone—his real phone, his iPhone—was buzzing. Rebecca's too.

A text from a blocked number.

A picture of Kira holding a Spanish newspaper. The text said only *Two million euros. Pay tonight. Tomorrow costs more.*

Rebecca sat up. "Brian?"

The moment of decision. But Brian had already decided.

Irlov had come through. Brian would keep his secrets to himself.

"She's alive."

V

KIRA AND REBECCA AND BRIAN

(NOW)

24

Somewhere in Spain

Kira was already growing used to being neither awake nor asleep, bobbing on the sea of her own semi-consciousness, fleeting Technicolor dreams.

Now the *snap* of the deadbolt pulled her back to the world. She saw Rodrigo's outline in the doorway, just enough gray light for her to distinguish him.

With the light still out, he stepped in and closed the door.

"Kira?" His voice slurred, accent stronger than before.

She had the fleeting hope he meant to free her. But she knew better. He stank of weed and booze. Something sweet. Sangria, maybe. He had to be wasted if he was coming for her with the others in the house.

"You know what Jacques said." No screaming. Persuade him to leave on his own.

"That *puta* just wants—"

Rodrigo broke off, leaving unanswered the question of what Jacques wanted.

"You'll get us in trouble, Rodrigo." Us. *I'm on your side. Buddies. Best friends, see?*

He stepped toward her. Put his hands on his hips as he considered his next move.

The light snapped on and she heard two quick steps. A pair of huge hands tethered themselves to Rodrigo's shoulders and flung him against the wall. Jacques. Before Rodrigo could recover Jacques put a shoulder into his chest. The two men thrashed, arms and legs and grunts. Kira stood. She wondered if she could edge past and run, reach the front door, maybe this was the moment—

But she didn't know who else was in the house.

Before she summoned the courage to move, Jacques had control. He wrapped his left arm around Rodrigo's head, punched low with the right hand, one two three four, the blows landing hard, their *smack* echoing through the closet. Jacques stepped away and Rodrigo sagged against the wall. His eyes were pure animal hatred, but his hands were low at his sides.

"Not for you." Jacques wasn't even breathing hard.

A trickle of drool spun from Rodrigo's mouth.

"Say it."

"Not for me." His voice a rasp.

"You think you sneak past me? You think I did this for you?" Jacques caught the Spaniard across the jaw with a right cross. So fast. Rodrigo's head whipped sideways, and he went to a knee.

"Next time I kill you." He turned to Kira. "And you, stop flirting. Egging him on."

Are you joking? But she kept herself from arguing. Let Rodrigo think she was encouraging him. Jacques was practically a cyborg. Rodrigo was the weak link. He was dumb and drugged—and he wanted her. Let him think the feeling was mutual.

"Tell her you're sorry," Jacques said.

"Sorry." Jacques pointed to the door and Rodrigo staggered out.

Just her and Jacques now. "This game you're playing. You won't like it if I leave him with you."

Her kidnapper, accusing *her* of playing games? And he was right.

Then he was gone. The deadbolt slammed into place. She tried to make herself feel better by imagining the nail, plunging it into Jacques's neck. Or Rodrigo's. The vision had no power. They were too big, too strong.

She needed a better weapon. But she had no idea what that might be, much less how to find it.

25

Sabadell, Barcelona

Noon.

The exterior of the headquarters of the Mossos d'Esquadra looked as new and glittery as the rest of Barcelona. But inside, the building was unmistakably a police station, bureaucracy with a coiled edge.

After the ransom demand hit their phones, Rebecca was smart enough not to say *I told you so.* She simply forwarded the picture to Wilkerson, let him wrangle the Spanish cops. She could imagine those conversations: *Mierda, meet fan. We flying in the whole bureau to find her, or do you plan to do your jobs?*

Now Rebecca and Brian sat with Wilkerson in a conference room on the top floor of Mossos headquarters. Across the table, three unsmiling fiftysomething men: Hector Barraza, the chief of the Mossos; Javier Garza, a colonel in the Grupo Especial de Operaciones, Spain's elite counterterror police; and Raul Fernandes, the deputy director general of the Interior Ministry. Fernandes had just come up from Madrid. He sat with arms folded, body language that suggested he'd rather be anywhere but here.

For the moment they had all tacitly agreed to ignore the ransom demand.

Instead Barraza walked them through the search. Marine patrols along the Mediterranean coast. Unannounced visits to the home of anyone in Catalonia who had ever been arrested for kidnapping. The promise to informants of what the Mossos called a "white card," a get-out-of-jail-free promise for any crime short of murder, in return for solid information on Kira's location. Added patrols on the roads near the Pyrenees, the mountains that separated Spain and France.

"Sea, air, and land. I promise you, if your daughter is still in Catalonia, we will find her."

Sea, air, and land. Rebecca itched to be out looking for Kira. But she'd be walking the streets of the Gothic Quarter for something to do. And the Mossos could track a hundred leads in the time it took her to find one, if they were properly motivated. After meeting Barraza, she believed they were. He was almost unhealthily skinny, with nicotine-stained fingers and deep-set eyes that didn't shy from contact. Some cops at his level were bureaucrats. Others were believers.

She pegged Barraza as a believer.

"Let me finish by saying, I understand the motives of the kidnappers remain" — Barraza hesitated — "opaque. To me, finding your daughter is the priority. Whether this is for money or it has a political element, we can sort that out when she is safe."

Rebecca wanted to argue. *Until we know who took her, how can we know where she is?* But Barraza had a point. Kidnappings weren't like other crimes. Normally, police only became involved *after* a crime. But kidnappings happened in real time. They didn't end until the victim was found, alive or not. Everyone in this room would happily give up arresting the kidnappers if doing so ensured Kira's safe return.

Maybe not *happily.*

"But who these people are must be connected to *where* they are," Brian said.

She tapped his arm, *No, Bri, this guy's on our side —*

"They've done everything possible to keep their identities from us. I don't suppose you have any ideas?"

The bluntness of the question seemed to throw Brian. "Don't you think I'd tell you if I did?"

"Of course. Raul—" Barraza nodded to Fernandes, the Interior Ministry deputy director general.

"Thank you." He ran his thumb along his strangely black mustache. "As you know, we only learned of the kidnapping this morning."

Great, Rebecca thought. *Ass-covering from the get-go. The opposite of Barraza.*

"We have increased highway patrols and asked our officers to be aware of young women who appear distressed."

Whereas normally, we'd just ignore them . . .

"We have also moved extra officers to Carabanchel." Carabanchel was a slum in southwestern Madrid. Phone records showed the kidnappers had sent the text with the ransom demand from there. "But we don't think your daughter is there. Mainly North Africans there. The photos from the bar suggest your daughter's kidnappers are European."

Rebecca found herself increasingly annoyed he wouldn't say Kira's name.

"They would stand out, and someone would give them up. Anyway, they knew we could trace the phone to there. They are careful, these ones. Why make the obvious mistake of sending a text from their own location?"

As much as Rebecca disliked the guy, he did have a point on Carabanchel. The phone was probably a dead end. It had vanished from the networks after the message was sent. No doubt it was already destroyed, the pieces scattered.

Further, Kira had been holding a paper from Sunday in the photo, so the picture could have been taken at any time Sunday. Then a kidnapper could have driven or taken a train to Madrid, sent the picture, and left.

As for the photo itself, Brian's NSA buddies had torn it apart, looking for geolocation tags or other information about the phone that had taken it. But whoever had sent it had expected that response. The text was actually a photo *of* a photo. The secondary picture had been taken in Carabanchel, without doubt on the now-trashed phone used to send the text. As long as the kidnappers didn't mind using a new phone for every new text, they could repeat that process indefinitely and frustrate the NSA.

The kidnappers had also been careful to make sure the photo itself would offer no clues. The wall behind Kira was covered with generic plywood. No light or electrical fixtures were visible, nothing that might narrow the location. The CIA and Special Forces taught their operatives to make subtle hand gestures if they had any idea where they were being held and who had them. Too bad Kira wasn't a CIA operative.

About all the NSA could say for certain was that the photo didn't appear to have been altered. Meaning Kira had been holding the paper. Meaning she was alive. Or had been yesterday, anyway.

o   o

Meanwhile, Fernandes was still talking. "As well as additional officers in Carabanchel, we are reviewing license plate readers for the Camry's plate. Examining records from similar cases. But primarily supporting our Catalan colleagues. Ready to respond to any request."

In other words, doing nothing. Rebecca understood the cool logic here, *This isn't our mess; the Catalans are so big on independence, let the Mossos deal with it.* Even so, she wished she could shave off the guy's Just For Men upper lip, make him spend a month with Barraza learning to be a real cop.

She didn't say a word, but Rob Wilkerson seemed to read her mind. He nodded at her, *I get it, let me handle this.*

"Thanks for that," he said, as smoothly as if Fernandes had promised house-to-house searches. "And this is Colonel Garza, from the Grupo Especial. I've had the pleasure of working with him, so I can tell you firsthand his men are superb."

"Thank you, Rob," Garza said. "As to new information, unfortunately, I do not have much. We focus on Islamists. Nothing suggests these are the people who took your daughter. Further, we have pen-etration into cells in Barcelona. We believe we would have heard of an operation this complex. We've gone back to our informants here and elsewhere, Madrid, Seville, to make sure they know the urgency."

Garza cleared his throat.

"In the meantime, we have put response teams here and in Madrid on what we call active standby. These are nine-person squads with tactical equipment. Access to helicopters with a fifteen-minute scram-ble. They can be almost anywhere in Spain in four hours."

"Thank you," Brian said. "Question."

Rebecca felt a flicker of irritation. Her business. He should let her take the lead.

"Have we decided what to do when the media calls? Those posters on La Rambla, it's only a matter of time."

"Perhaps better to take those posters down—" Barraza said.

"Oh, no bad publicity for Barcelona."

"Not at all. My officers do their jobs better if they don't have reporters chasing them. It may make the kidnappers nervous too. They're negotiating. They want ransom. I think we are all better off keeping this quiet for now."

They'd reached the crux of the meeting. Which had nothing to do with publicity. Or even what Barraza's officers were doing to find Kira.

"The ransom," Rebecca said. "I think we should pay it."

Fernandes jumped in before Barraza could answer. "That's your decision."

"You agree?"

"They haven't even offered you a way to say yes or no, much less make a counteroffer."

"Quibble over how much my daughter is worth?"

"Our daughter," Brian muttered.

"A counteroffer is standard," Fernandes said. "As I'm sure you know. Delay, give Hector's men a chance to do their jobs. Unless whoever has her explicitly threatens her. Which they haven't."

"Do these seem like the kind of people who negotiate?"

"Everyone negotiates."

Again, as much as she disliked Fernandes, he wasn't entirely wrong. They had no choice but to wait for another text to arrive. Rebecca wished the kidnappers had offered an email address or a Signal or Telegram account. But they weren't going to give the NSA a chance at their comms.

"What about you, Hector? What do you think?"

Barraza tapped his yellowed fingertips on the table. "These look like professionals. I think if you deliver the money, they keep the bargain."

"Colonel?"

Garza nodded. "It's a lot of money but not a crazy demand. Not a hundred million. Not impossible politically either, like the ones we see from the Islamic State, Spain must pull out of NATO."

"You have two million euros in cash?" Fernandes said.

"Of course not," Rebecca said. "But Spain does."

Fernandes shook his head, *No no no.*

"You've paid ransom before."

"For Spanish citizens. In special instances. Aid workers, doing their jobs in dangerous places. Helping the world. Not a girl who gets herself in a mess."

"You're blaming *Kira?*" Brian said.

"She didn't even first meet this man in Spain, we don't know if he's Spanish. He probably isn't."

"What if it's about *my* job?" Rebecca said.

"Let the FBI pay."

"You know we can't."

"Right. You have a rule, you don't negotiate with terrorists, you don't pay them. You want us to pay instead." Fernandes shrugged. "Anyway, this isn't Spain. It's Catalonia. Maybe we split it fifty-fifty. One million Madrid, one million Barcelona. What do you say, Hector?"

For the first time, Barraza seemed thrown. "This isn't a matter for the police. I can ask. But I think the mayor will see this as a national issue."

"Oh yes, when it's convenient for Catalonia, the problem is *national*—"

"You won't give us the money, I'll rob a bank," Rebecca said.

"Calm down," Fernandes said.

Two of the most enraging—and sexist—words in any language. *Relax, little lady, and let the men handle things.*

"Maybe there's a way," Rob Wilkerson said. His tone quieted them all.

Wilkerson explained. The Spanish government would *lend* two million euros to the Unsworths—today, in cash, in return for a promissory note. "An aid to the investigation. It probably will never be paid out. If it is, the Unsworths will pay it all back—"

"How long?" Fernandes said.

"Let's say ten years."

Brilliant. Wilkerson knew the Unsworths couldn't repay the loan. Not in ten years or a hundred. But if the money vanished and Kira didn't return, the Spanish government couldn't ask the Unsworths to repay it. Even if she returned, would Spain want to ruin a feel-good story and publicize the fact it had paid a ransom?

The "loan" would be a face-saving way for the Spanish government to give the Unsworths the money.

Fernandes pursed his lips like he'd swallowed a shot of Drano. "All right—"

That simple? But no.

"On two conditions. First, the United States government will guarantee the money." He twitched his lips under his mustache: *Turnabout is fair play.*

Wilkerson nodded. "That should be fine."

Rebecca knew Wilkerson didn't have the authority to agree. But she admired him for bluffing. *We can all argue about it in ten years.*

"You don't need to ask your bosses?" Fernandes said.

"No. The other condition?"

"Interest. It's a loan, yes? So interest on the two million. Three percent a year."

Fernandes's goal was obvious, to make the loan look as official as possible. Not for the Unsworths, but for the moment when Madrid told the FBI to repay the money.

And to be a prick.

"*Bendejo*," Brian muttered under his breath.

Not helping, though Rebecca understood.

"I am here as a courtesy." Fernandes pushed away from the table.

"You and I need to have a conversation in private," Rebecca said.

"I don't think so. I don't let the mother of a girl who's been kid-napped, possibly—"

"*Possibly?*"

"Has it not occurred to you that perhaps your daughter is a willing participant in her disappearance? Playing a game? With two million euros as the prize?"

Rebecca found herself stunned into silence. Only someone who had never met Kira could suggest the possibility. The practical problems were enormous. How had Kira found people to play the kidnappers? How had she decided she could trust them to split the ransom with her? Where had they gone? How had they arranged the phones and the car and everything else?

Worse, only a stone-cold psychopath would subject her family to such trauma.

"You must be joking. You think she would put us through this?"

Fernandes seemed to see he'd gone too far. "I meant only—"

"Or are you saying that I'm part of it too? Brian, the whole family."

Rebecca's fury was real. But she saw she had the edge, too. Time to pounce.

"Here's what we're going to do, Raul. You drop the nonsense now, the interest, the American guarantee"—get everything off the table while she had the chance—"all the bullshit, or I get on a plane back to D.C. and tell my bosses to pull cooperation on everything. I mean *everything*. No drugs, no CT. And next time your ambassador to Caracas makes the Venezuelans mad and they cut the embassy power and send a thousand paramilitaries over for a pool party and you come crawling to JSOC asking the Marines to save his ass, it'll be, sorry, three percent interest."

Like all good bureaucrats Fernandes knew when he was beaten. He nodded. "Sí, then. No interest, no guarantee. But we still need papers, and you and your husband need to sign."

"Our pleasure."

"Excellent," Wilkerson said, his best fake cheery voice. "Let's write it, sign it, get them to a bank so we have the money by the time the next text arrives. Doesn't matter anyway, because the Mossos are going to find her way before then."

"We'll do our best," Barraza said.

"We good then?" Wilkerson locking down the agreement like a good closer.

"Great," Rebecca said.

Fernandes didn't say a word.

26

Somewhere in Spain

The white light under the plywood was back. The room was an oven again. Another Spanish afternoon.

Which as far as Kira could tell meant it was Monday, the second full day since they'd taken her. Wasn't there a show about this? *The First 48*? If the detectives can't solve the case in forty-eight hours, they have no chance. Might as well burn the file.

But those were murders, right? And she was still alive. So good news.

o   o

Since the fight between Jacques and Rodrigo the house had been mostly quiet. A television played faintly downstairs, but they'd left her alone. She wondered if they'd made a ransom demand. If they thought Becks and Bri could pay millions of dollars they would be disappointed.

Anyway, how did they plan to escape with the money? Some untraceable cryptocurrency thing like Bitcoin? She wasn't even sure how Bitcoin worked. Plain old cash or diamonds?

Not her problem. No doubt Jacques had an idea on how to take the money and run. Assuming he really did plan to ransom her and not sell her to the highest bidder—

Steps along the hall. Rodrigo again, based on the heavy tread.

The deadbolt popped back, the door swung open.

Yep, Rodrigo. A plastic bag in his hand. He stood in the doorway and tossed it at her. Inside the bag, a bottle of water and a granola bar.

She wondered why Jacques had sent Rodrigo to deliver the water. Probably just to prove he could. *You go, and don't touch her.*

Rodrigo started to close the door.

"Wait, please. The toilet." And another shot at the razors. Though, truly, she did have to pee. "Please."

"She's downstairs. She can take you."

Kira had almost forgotten about Lilly. She hadn't been up here once, as if she had decided Kira wasn't worth her time. *Let the boys fight over your skanky American ass.*

"I don't trust her."

"You trust me?" But he waved his hand for her to get up.

She walked down the hall, looking for anything she might have missed the day before. Nothing.

Into the bathroom. "A shower would be nice."

"You don't want a shower."

He closed the door, leaving her to work out why: *Because it means we're going to give you to someone who wants you clean all over.*

"No razors," he said through the door.

So much for that plan. She pushed aside the grimy shower curtain. A bottle of shampoo and one of conditioner, Spanish, generic. A bar of pink soap. Useless.

On the sink. The razors. The toothbrushes. A tube of Licor del Polo, squeezed haphazardly. Becks would hate that. Becks rolled up toothpaste tubes neatly—

Focus.

Kira eased open the cabinet mirror. Two shelves. On the top, two pill bottles, empty. On the bottom, a dozen bottles of nail polish. In case Rodrigo wanted to freshen up.

And scattered in with them: three travel-size bottles of polish remover.

Acetone.

As good as lighter fluid. Put a flame to the stuff and up it went.

She grabbed a bottle of polish remover, closed the cabinet door.

She sat on the toilet and peed as she considered the bottle. It still had the plastic ring around its cap. Would they notice it was gone? Probably not. There were still two others. And they'd all been mixed in with the polish.

But what now? Obviously she couldn't carry it out.

"*Vamos,*" Rodrigo said.

"Just a second, *please.*"

One place she could hide it and be sure he wouldn't see. Back in the closet she could take it out—

What if the cap came off?

It wouldn't, it was sealed—

Fuel. She had to have it.

"I count ten," Rodrigo said.

She stuffed the bottle inside her. It wasn't huge but the shape was weird. She bit her lip so she wouldn't yell, pushed harder.

She stood up from the toilet, smoothed her skirt as the door swung open, leaned over to wash her hands.

"Too long," Rodrigo said.

"You're keeping me hydrated."

Rodrigo grabbed her shoulder as the bottle dug at her from the inside. Add nail polish remover to the long list of people and things that didn't belong in her vagina.

She stared herself down, *Don't you make a noise, don't even think about it.* Rodrigo was next to her, all tattoos and body odor. He looked at her side-eyed, like he knew something was wrong but couldn't figure out what.

Take a guess, big guy.

No, guess again.

"You can brush your teeth too."

Was he messing with her? Or did he just want her breath to be minty fresh the next time he tried to rape her? Sorry, Rodrigo, the space you want is already occupied. She carefully squeezed the toothpaste — Becks would be proud — gave herself a thorough brush. Rodrigo closed the door to the bathroom.

"I shouldn't say," he said. "But tomorrow we move you again. I don't know where."

She should have been frightened but she wasn't. Not with the lighter, not with the fuel.

"I want to see you." Her only play. Could she make him believe? "Alone. Tonight."

"What for?"

"Can you?"

Before she could reconsider, she put her hands to his face, kissed him. Not a peck this time, the real thing. *If you're gonna kiss him, make it good, make him like it.* She hadn't been this conscious of the mechanics of a kiss since her *first* kiss. His breath stank of weed but he wasn't a bad kisser. He didn't attack with his tongue, didn't bite her lip or do anything fancy, just opened his mouth and inhaled her. He grunted, the sound of a boy who had closed his eyes and swung and somehow sent the ball over the fence.

Nothing else. Let his imagination do the rest. She pulled back.

"Take me back. Before they notice."

o   o

Back in the dark she waited until his footsteps faded away. She lay on her back, eased out the bottle. She was tender but she didn't think she'd done any permanent damage. Anyway, now she had it. For a moment she panicked, what if it was a non-acetone brand? She unscrewed the cap, sniffed the liquid inside. Acetone for sure, every woman knew the smell.

Had Rodrigo believed her? Men were so unbelievably stupid about sex.

She put the acetone on the shelf with the lighter and nail. Though she didn't think she needed the nail anymore.

Now she had a weapon. Fire. The Daenerys Targaryen of kidnapped American chicks. Of course, it hadn't ended so great for Daenerys.

She'd have one chance. If she failed he'd surely kill her. Even his fear of Jacques wouldn't stop him. He'd strangle her, put his hands around her neck and choke her until her eyes bulged out—

No. She couldn't let fear paralyze her. They thought they'd broken her already. She had to prove them wrong.

Footsteps. The door swung open.

Jacques.

The worst of them. Though they were all the worst.

"Time for mommy and daddy to hear your voice."

27

Barcelona

Raul Fernandes hadn't had a chance.

Not that Brian liked the guy; he was a grade A asshole. The idea Kira would have staged her own kidnapping was beyond dumb. Still, Brian couldn't help but sympathize as he watched Becks tear Fernandes up. He had felt the Wrath of Rebecca himself too many times.

Of course, the fight over the money was stupid. Everyone knew they couldn't pay it back. But two million euros was two million euros.

Proprieties had to be observed when you took that much money from a foreign government.

As Brian had learned.

It was all a show. But the real show was happening in secret. The SVR was directing, with Brian as an audience of one.

Then why hadn't Irlov called again since this morning? The harder Brian tried to remember Irlov's exact words, the slipperier the conversation seemed. Irlov had never confirmed that the Russians had actually taken Kira, much less that they would give her back.

They had to have her, though. Nothing else made sense.

And the ransom demand had come so soon after the call. Like Irlov was proving he controlled the kidnappers even if he said he didn't. But why lie to Brian, then? And were the kidnappers planning to collect the money, or was the demand for show?

Too bad Brian couldn't run the possibilities by Becks. All those years in counterintel, she must have learned something about the Russians, how they worked. Brian wanted to buy another burner, call Irlov again. But he'd look even more desperate. All he could do now was wait. For Irlov. The kidnappers. Or both.

Then Barraza staring at him across the table, asking whether he knew anything. Sometimes cops had this weird radar with him. Like he gave off an *I'm a perp* vibe that they could feel even if they didn't know how.

The pressure made his head hurt. He cursed under his breath. To his surprise Becks reached over, squeezed his hand. Pretending to understand. Pretending this wasn't her fault. When the truth was even in here he'd felt her annoyance when he tried to talk. Let Special Agent Becks handle things. Same attitude as always. Same reason Kira was in this mess, if he came right down to it.

He squeezed her hand back.

"I'm gonna go check on Tony."

o   o

Outside the conference room, Tony sat in a blue plastic chair. Not texting, not looking at his phone. Just sitting, lips tight. Blaming himself. Bri felt for the kid. They trusted him enough to let him manage himself while they talked to the cops. Not enough to let him hear for himself what was happening.

Brian reached down, hugged him awkwardly.

"Almost done. We got the ransom money set up—"

"Really?" Tony sounded hopeful.

"The Spanish are gonna pay. Don't want to scare the tourists." Close enough to true. "And the Mossos guy, Hector, he told us everything they're doing, they're not messing around. Now we go to a bank to pick up the money."

"And wait for the people who have her"—he couldn't say *kidnappers*, poor kid—"to call us?"

"About right."

Tony nodded. "What's Mom think?"

"Ask her yourself." Try to help the kid, all he wants is mommy. "I mean, she'll be right out, let me see what's going on."

o   o

Back inside, the contracts were ready. Eight copies, four English and four Spanish. *Dos millones de euros . . . prometer pagar . . .* Fine, whatever. Brian signed them all.

Fernandes's phone buzzed. He had a rapid-fire Spanish conversation, hung up shaking his head.

"None of these banks have two million euros lying around. Even the Santander on Passeig de Gràcia says it only has half a million."

"Your central bank must have a branch here," Rebecca said.

"The Bank of Spain," Fernandes said. "We ask them, it will take all week."

"What about the casino?" Brian said.

o   o

Forty-five minutes later, the Unsworths and Fernandes stepped into an unmarked Mossos van. Two officers waited in the front seats, armed but no uniforms. Garza, the Special Operations colonel, had already left. *My men are ready*, his final words.

"Come on," Fernandes said. He had the tight-lipped look of a pool hustler who knew he'd been taken but couldn't figure out how. Brian knew the feeling.

They were quiet on the trip down to the waterfront. Even Becks seemed to have nothing to say. Brian wondered what his dearly beloved wife was thinking. She'd be blaming herself, no doubt, making the kidnapping all about her. He blamed her, too. For a change they agreed.

309

He wondered what she'd do if he told her the truth. But Becks wasn't the forgiving sort. He'd have to trust Irlov. At least the Russian knew what Brian was worth.

○　　○

A blond-haired man in a crisp blue suit waited for them in the Casino Barcelona garage. "Ken Harrington, director of security."

"You're Irish?" Brian couldn't help himself.

"Welcome to the modern EU. Free markets, free sangria, I think that's this year's slogan. Mr. Fernandes, may I see the letter we discussed?"

Fernandes handed Harrington an envelope. The letter inside guaranteed the government of Spain would repay the money within one week. Harrington scanned it, tucked it away.

"This way, please."

He led them to the employee entrance, spare and white-painted. The hallway ended in a no-nonsense steel door that reminded Brian of the NSA. Harrington put his badge to a wall sensor, led them into an anteroom watched over by a woman behind a plexiglass window.

"I probably don't need to say this, but please, no pictures." Harrington raised his badge to the window.

"*Cuánto?*" the woman said.

"*Cinco.*"

The lock buzzed. Harrington led them into another white-walled hallway, this one lined with cash carts and watched by two guards wearing pistols and bulletproof vests.

"I understand the security may seem severe," Harrington said. "But we move hundreds of millions of euros through here every year."

Near the end of the hallway yellow hospital gowns were stacked on a shelf. "Normally visitors wear gowns before entering a count room, but I'll make an exception. Please don't touch anything until I tell you. And I'd rather the boy wait here."

"No," Brian said. Tony had been alone too much today. "He'll be fine."

Harrington nodded. To Tony: "Hands to yourself, please, my son."

o   o

Harrington led them into a room whose walls were so white they almost glowed. Bubble cameras studded the corners. Digital safes were embedded in the walls. Two fiftyish women stood near the back of the room. They were identically dressed in hairnets, black pants, and black short-sleeved shirts. They stepped aside, revealing a table covered with inch-thick stacks of rubber-banded notes.

"Each note one hundred euros," Harrington said. "Two hundred notes per stack. One hundred stacks in all. One hundred times two hundred times one hundred. Two million. The Casino Barcelona has no interest in cheating the government of Spain but check them if you wish." He picked up a stack from the center, riffled it, showing them that each note was identical.

Brian had to admit, seeing so much cash aroused something primal in him, lit his blood. Maybe this was what other people meant when they talked about love. Most people worked their whole lives without ever seeing this much money. Here it was sitting on a table for him to take.

He stepped to the table to examine his temporary fortune. Compared to American bills, the European currency seemed fussy, almost fake. The notes were green and beige, a big blue-black 100 just off center. Bridges and archways decorated them. The Europeans couldn't pick historical figures to decorate their bills — one country's hero was another's villain.

He thumbed through a stack. All hundreds. He laid it down, tried another. Also perfect. Of course. As Harrington had said, the casino wasn't going to rip off the Interior Ministry.

"Looks fine," he said. He wanted to be in charge, at least for a moment.

Harrington pulled a soft green zippered bag from a basket beneath the table. "Good luck, then."

o   o

Twenty minutes later Brian, Rebecca, and Tony sat in CC's office at the El Raval Mossos station, the safest place they could find to keep the cash while they waited for instructions.

Fernandes was gone. At the casino, he'd taken pictures of the money with his phone. "Call if you hear anything." Then he'd left, barely saying goodbye.

"We should have gone upstairs, put it all on red," Brian said now. No one smiled.

"Double or nothing. Make an extra couple million." He could see the stacks doubling, multiplying, filling another bag and another.

"Shut up, Dad."

"Don't tell me to shut up, Tony."

"Or what? I'll get taken too and you'll talk about gambling the ransom?" Tony's voice was tight, angry.

"Tony," Rebecca said. "We're all stressed. Apologize."

"Sorry." The word a mutter. "I wish they wouldn't make us wait."

"She's okay," Brian said.

"How do you know?"

Because I know who took her, and I know why.

"Nobody goes to this much trouble to show off, Tony. This is about money. If these men didn't know who your mom was before, they've figured it out now. They'll know their best move is to get paid and go."

As if the kidnappers had been waiting for Brian to conjure them, his phone trilled with an incoming text. Rebecca's followed.

"I'm getting a Craigslist link," Rebecca said. "In New York."

"Mine's in Hong Kong." Brian clicked through, found nothing but a string of numbers and letters.

"I've got a link to a Dropbox account," Rebecca said. "Asking for a password."

"This must be it." Brian handed her his phone.

She copied the key into hers.

A single file. A voice recording.

"Mom. Dad. Tony. I miss you."

Kira's voice, unmistakable.

She stopped speaking for a moment, though the playback continued.

"I miss you," she said again. The words slow and careful. From a script, Brian thought. "I want to see you again. Please buy two first-class tickets on the 21:23, Barcelona to Madrid." The 9:23 p.m. train. Proof Kira was reading someone else's words. She would never say 21:23. "Tony stays in Barcelona. You travel without escorts. You carry the money in a soft-sided bag. You do not carry weapons. No tracker or dye packs in the bag. You will receive further instructions on the train."

Another pause.

"Follow these rules or you won't see me again." Her voice broke a little on the last words. "To accept this offer, send two male uniformed Mossos officers to walk three times around the Font de Canaletes"— she stumbled a bit over the Spanish—"at 1800 hours exactly. If you accept but do not yet have the cash, send two female Mossos officers. In that case you will have one more day. The price will be three million euros instead of two."

A pause, longer than the others, the silence grinding at them.

The timer on the file showed the recording had a few seconds left.

"If you do not accept—"

The recording ended.

They were silent as Rebecca tapped her phone. "That's it."

They played the message a second time, and a third. But Kira's words remained stubbornly scripted, her only message the one the kidnappers wanted to send.

"What's the Font de Canaletes?"

"A fountain near the top of the Rambla," CC said. "Always very crowded. No chance for decent surveillance. Why they chose it."

"Anyway, you better send two men. We're going to get on the train," Brian said.

"You're sure." CC looked at Rebecca, like Brian's opinion didn't count.

"Of course," Rebecca said.

"Then we need"—CC hesitated, looking for the word—"plain-clothes officers on the train too."

"You heard what she said."

"Hundreds of people on that train; our men are good, they won't know."

"Not worth it."

"I'm sorry, it's two million euros and there's danger for you too. If someone puts a pistol on you, takes the money, my men can see what's happening, protect you."

"Tony, you need to wait outside."

Tony walked out, slammed the door.

"I didn't want him to hear his, but let me be as clear as I can," Rebecca said. "I want her free, and if that means taking a bullet I'll do it. I'm sure Brian feels the same."

Brian nodded. Though he was really thinking, *Rebecca and her drama, Rebecca the avenging FBI agent, Rebecca the supermom* . . . The truth, yeah, she wanted Kira back, but she hated not being in control. She'd been antsy all day, she didn't like relying on these cops.

"No plainclothes," Rebecca said.

"All right."

Brian suspected CC would put the officers on the train anyway. "Tony," he yelled. "Come on back in."

Then he realized the kidnappers had made a mistake. Dropbox wasn't Telegram or Signal, a service designed to frustrate government monitoring, with uncrackable end-to-end encryption. It was an American company that had helped the NSA in the past. At the least, it should give them the IP address from which the message had been uploaded. If the message had been uploaded directly from a phone or iPad or other mobile device, the agency and the Spanish police might be able to find it fast.

Brian wondered if he should keep his mouth shut. Maybe Irlov would be angry if they found Kira on their own. But the Russian had made his point. "Becks—Dropbox—"

"They're a friend, right?"

So he didn't even get to tell her. He called the duty officer at Fort Meade, explained what they needed.

o   o

Fifteen minutes later they had an answer. Though not the one they wanted.

The IP address routed to a hardline network, not a mobile device. And the locations of hardline nodes were less precise than those belonging to mobiles. Mobile carriers needed to know the exact location of the devices they served. Hardline Internet networks were just big dumb highways with endless on- and off-ramps. A single node could serve a big neighborhood or a small city.

Nonetheless, the address provided a clue. It routed to central Zaragoza, a city of over seven hundred thousand people in northeastern Spain. Zaragoza lay almost exactly halfway between Madrid and Barcelona, and the 9:23 express from Barcelona to Madrid stopped there.

The kidnappers had been careful so far. Still, Brian doubted they would have driven too far from their base to upload this message. Most likely they were in Zaragoza, or close.

"Is there any practical way to narrow it?" Rebecca said when Brian finished the explanation. "If they did it at an Internet café, could the Zaragoza police go to the cafés with pictures of Jacques and the girl?"

"No way did they hang around."

"Maybe we could get a license plate from a car outside—"

"Zaragoza isn't part of Catalonia," CC said.

Meaning they would be asking Fernandes for help. So, they needed to keep the long shots to a minimum.

"Tell them we have a clue pointing to Zaragoza," Brian said. "Ask for police on the platform when the train pulls in. They'll do that."

"Still. They must be planning to take the money *before* they hand her over," Rebecca said.

"So we just hand two million euros to whoever asks and assume they keep their end, let us go?" Brian said.

"Do we have a choice?"

"I'm afraid they'll split you up," CC said. "Tell one of you, get off the train with the money, the other stays on, meets your daughter. Then you can't protect each other."

Brian and Rebecca didn't say a word.

28

Somewhere in Spain

Taping the message took longer than Kira expected. When Jacques gave her the script, she wondered if she could sneak in extra information, *Me and my three kidnappers, including one with black fingernails, who are not in Barcelona but still in Spain*, but he tapped her cheek and said, "Read it exactly."

Oh Jacques. Touchy, touchy.

They recorded in an upstairs bedroom. Scrupulously clean, the sheets tight over the mattress. No books, no clothes, no evidence of nationality or astrological sign or any human personality. So probably Jacques's. A blackout shade taped over the window. Rodrigo stood in a corner, eyes roving over her. She wasn't sure why Jacques had him here. Maybe an object lesson in what would happen to her if she didn't make the tape.

Jacques made her record the script several times. Finally he seemed satisfied. He saved the file onto a flash drive, murmured under his breath to Rodrigo, and handed it over. Rodrigo trotted out. A minute later she heard the distinctive thrum of a motorcycle engine.

"Want him to take you for a ride?"

She didn't bother answering.

"Hungry?" Jacques said. "I'm making panini."

Her stomach was tight. She didn't mind being hungry, but she wanted to stay strong and sharp.

Still, taking food from Jacques seemed like a bad idea. "It's all right."

"You think I'm going to drug you again? Why bother?"

"To move me more easily?"

"I don't need to drug you anymore. Maybe I just tell you, I kill you if you run."

Not this time. You move me, I'm going for it. Kill me if you want.

"Or, no, you don't listen, this time you plan to be brave. Okay, I tell you, we're taking you to your family. Mommy, daddy, Tony."

Rodrigo was her best bet for freedom, but Jacques was the one she wanted dead.

"But you decide you can't trust me, you still want to run. Then I tell you if you try to escape, I kill them. Start with Tony, you make fun but you like him, I think. The back of the head, he never even feels it." Jacques pointed a finger pistol at her, *gotcha*. "Would that work? Because that's what I'm saying, if you try to run, your family dies."

"Fuck you fuck you fuck you." The words only betrayed her own weakness, she knew.

"I don't think you mean it. Too bad. Come on, lunch. *Jamón* and Manchego. I'll even make a deal, I cut it in half, you pick which half you want, I eat the other."

Why not? She'd get to see more of the house, anyway. She nodded.

But he disappointed her. He locked her inside the closet, came back with the sandwich. Sure enough, he'd split it.

"Your choice."

She pointed at his left hand.

"Wise." He handed her the panini, chomped into the half she hadn't chosen.

She couldn't help feeling he was playing with her, somehow he'd known which side she'd pick and had laced it. But she'd picked on the spot. She nibbled at the sandwich. Which was as delicious as it sounded, hot, the cheese slightly salty, the ham rich with fat.

"Still nervous? We can switch."

They traded. She took another nibble. "Thanks." Her manners taking over before she could stop herself.

"I'm sorry about Rodrigo. You're beautiful. But he needs to control himself." Jacques smelled good, a peppery male musk she hadn't expected. Of course Jacques wore the right scent, and of course he wore the right amount. She was suddenly conscious of how terrible she must smell.

"Why don't you get rid of him?"

Jacques laughed, the sound dry, European somehow. "He has his uses. Tell me about yourself, Kira."

She shook her head, *You* cannot *be serious.*

"Come on, just because we're in this position doesn't mean we can't have a conversation."

She snapped to reality.

"Go fuck yourself."

He pushed her backward, stepped out of the closet, locked the door. In the dark she fell back to the wall, the only space in the house that belonged to her.

Only now that he'd left did she realize she hadn't heard Lilly or anyone else downstairs since Rodrigo left. Jacques was alone. She could have waited at the door with the acetone and the lighter. Yet the idea hadn't even occurred to her, he was so completely in control. He'd threatened to kill her family, and *she'd thanked him for making her a sandwich.* She threw the panini across the room. She'd starve before she took another bite.

o   o

Hours passed. The heat in the closet faded. The light leaking under the plywood faded. She didn't relax at all. She'd realized why what Jacques had done bothered her.

Obviously he didn't care about making her feel better. But she didn't think he cared about frightening her either, or proving how

319

smart he was. She wasn't even an animal to him. She was just a *thing* he'd stolen for a while, until he gave it back or passed it on.

He was pure psychopath. She had to assume everything he did was strategic. Even toying with her. He had a reason. A plan. Why had he offered her food? Asked her about herself? To distract her, keep her off balance, as he readied his next move.

The light under the windowsill turned pink. Sunset. Night was coming.

Steps in the hall. She wondered if she should grab the acetone, but the person was moving too fast—

The deadbolt popped back. The light flipped on. Lilly.

"Up."

"Missed you too, Lil." *Come and get me.* Even without the nail or the acetone she was looking forward to getting in a couple of licks. Let them beat her afterward.

But Lilly was ready too. She reached behind her back, pulled out a little pistol with yellow tips. A Taser. No point in arguing. Lilly could brutalize her without even leaving marks. Kira stood.

"Good girl. Now take your clothes off."

Kira raised her twin middle fingers. The gesture reminded her of her father somehow, he'd always liked Eminem, *Put one of those fingers on each hand up . . .*

"I'll count three." Lilly raised the Taser. "Take them off."

"You flirting with me too? It's getting old. And you're not my type."

"What an ego you have. Even now." Lilly stuffed the Taser in the back of her waistband. "You're taking a shower, you dumb bitch. You stink."

o   o

You don't want a shower, Rodrigo had said.

Because a shower meant they would be giving her to someone who wanted her clean.

Don't fight. Don't give her any excuse to come any closer. While the other two were busy flirting or mock-flirting with her, Lilly was canny enough to check the shelf, find Kira's treasures.

Kira stepped out of her skirt and panties, pulled off her blouse and bra. Folded them neatly and piled them in the corner.

"Why do Americans hate your pubic hair so much? Like a child."

Lilly led her into the bathroom, turned on the shower.

"Quick quick." She pointed to a new pink disposable razor still in its package. "And shave your legs."

They were almost insulting her, Kira thought. Did they think she wouldn't understand the reason they wanted her to pretty up?

"If you don't mind, I'll watch. We wouldn't want to lose the razor."

Kira wondered if she could go for the Taser. But Lilly probably had combat training, too.

She showered. The water trickled out, but it was hot. Kira quickly scrubbed herself clean with the pale pink soap. Gave herself a coat of the generic shampoo and a dollop of conditioner. Shaved her legs and her pits. The purity of the hatred she felt surprised her. If someone had given her the chance to toss Lilly into a vat of acid, she would have taken it without a second thought.

"No more."

Lilly wrenched Kira out. She barked her leg against the tub, sending a flare of pain down her shin.

Lilly shoved her into the hallway, water dripping off her, no towel. "Back in the cage, get dressed before you piss me off."

Kira bit back her fury. Don't give her any excuse to look around the closet.

o   o

The heat in the closet dried her quickly. Her leg ached and when she touched it she felt a bruise rising. Lilly would get in trouble for leaving a mark on the merchandise.

She heard the motorcycle rumble back. Voices downstairs, faint, then louder, then abruptly stopping. After another minute, a car engine, fading into the night. Had Jacques left? Lilly? Both of them?

She had to assume the recording for her parents had been a lie, a way to distract her. Jacques was selling her to the highest bidder. Maybe tonight, maybe in the morning. But soon. Either her parents hadn't raised the money or Jacques planned to take it and sell her anyway. To a sheikh, an oligarch, who knew? She wouldn't have believed such a man existed. But then she wouldn't have believed she could be snatched out of a crowded club and made to vanish.

She remembered something Becks had said, years before. *Act like prey, you're prey.*

Time to be a predator.

She reached up to the shelf.

She couldn't find the bag where she'd hidden the nail, the lighter, and the bottle. She bit back her panic, tried again. There.

She brought them down, tucked the nail into the back of her panties. It dug at her. It felt good.

Time for a test. She had to be sure. She flicked the lighter. The flame glowed. She flicked it off, uncapped the bottle, poured a few drops of the precious clear liquid inside into the cap.

She waited. Listened. Heard a voice downstairs. Spanish. Maybe Rodrigo. Maybe the television. No one on the stairs, no one in the hall.

She flicked the lighter again, touched flame to the cap.

Watched as a fireball, tiny and perfect, flared up.

Come on, Rodrigo. You horny bastard. Come to me.

29

Barcelona

At exactly 9:23 p.m., the express to Madrid pulled smoothly away from the platform at Barcelona Sants. It accelerated through a trainyard, swung left, passed through a tunnel whose concrete walls were covered in swoops of red and orange graffiti. Beyond the tunnel, chain-link fences gave a glimpse of busy highways and apartment buildings glowing against the final rays of the sunset. Minute by minute the city fell away.

"She deserves her chance," Rebecca said. She sat by the aisle, Brian on the window, the bag at their feet. Every so often she or he would pat it, their friend and companion. "I'd trade for her."

The only silver lining in this horror, she felt strangely warm toward Brian. He was as torn up as she was. She'd never doubted he wanted the best for the kids. He had taken care of them all those nights when she'd been working late. But over the years she'd wondered if his own broken childhood stopped him from loving anyone properly.

Then again their own relationship had been so messed up for so long. Maybe she hadn't judged him fairly. Maybe she couldn't.

"She's coming back."

He couldn't know. But she didn't argue. She'd always been logical, unafraid to look at the truth. Men liked to think those traits were stereotypically male, as if they had a monopoly on truth. A lie. Women could never forget the core truth that they were physically weaker, that even an average man could kill them with his hands.

Still, right now she wanted nothing more than Brian's unearned male confidence. She leaned against him.

"They won, they'll get the money, that's all they want."

"Two million. Too bad you couldn't just write them an app instead."

"Huh?"

She was surprised he hadn't seen the coincidence too.

"You know, two million, what you got for your app."

He kissed her forehead. "Oh yeah, I guess so."

o   o

CC had sent a plainclothes team along with the officers to the Font de Canaletes. But on summer evenings La Rambla was as crowded as Times Square. Running counter-surveillance was impossible. No one saw anything.

Meanwhile, Rebecca, Brian, and Tony waited in his office, hoping for something from Barraza or the NSA or the FBI. Or anyone.

But despite parsing the recording to the millisecond, the NSA found nothing more. The Mossos didn't find much either. They pulled fingerprints from the Helado fire door, but the prints didn't match anyone in the Spanish or Interpol databases. Still, they could be useful. If an informant led the Mossos to an empty safe house, matching prints could prove that the kidnappers had been there.

Even so, by around eight thirty Rebecca knew they had no choice but to leave the Mossos and take the express to Madrid. But when Brian picked up the bag of money, Tony lost his cool.

"You can't." He stood in front of CC's office door. "Mom please —"

Rebecca tried to hug him. He lifted his arms, shook her off. He was awkward but strong.

"They didn't give us a choice, Tony."

"They just want the money," Brian said.

"They'll take it, they'll kill you—"

"Tony. Listen." The iron in Brian's voice seemed to be what Tony needed. "We have to do this. If it was you we'd do the same."

"Let me come too. *Please.*"

"We will get her, we'll be back, go to Ibiza and party like rock stars. Like it's 1999."

Tony crumpled to the floor, and Rebecca knew the fight was over. "I wasn't even *born* in 1999."

Brian picked Tony up off the floor, sat him on the couch. "These guys will take care of you. Just let us do this, okay?"

o o

Downstairs, an unmarked Mossos sedan. Outside the station, El Raval was the usual tourist carnival. A white kid with Rasta hair drummed on bongos as backpackers danced down the street. Heedless and happy. Rebecca tried not to hate them.

"No plainclothes on the train," she said to CC.

"I promise."

Assuming he was telling the truth—and Rebecca hoped he was—if something happened on the train, they were on their own. But Rebecca didn't see how the kidnappers could make the train work for them. She didn't plan on giving them the money without seeing Kira. Or at least talking to Kira, hearing exactly how the handoff was going to happen. But the kidnappers couldn't have Kira on the train, which meant if they planned to take the bag there they'd have to do it by force.

Then they'd be stuck, too. What would they do with the bag? Toss it out a window and hope it didn't get sucked under the wheels? They'd have an even harder problem getting off the train themselves between stations. The AVE wasn't a freight train where a hobo could jump off and survive with a bruise or two. It ran at two hundred miles an hour.

The Spanish police would be waiting for them in Zaragoza and Madrid. Barraza had talked directly to the police chief in Zaragoza and explained what was happening and why they thought Zaragoza might be their real stop. The chief had promised to have officers on the platform. In Madrid, both the police and Garza's anti-terror units would be on alert.

They had followed the instructions. No trackers in the bag, no dye bombs. But they were each wearing GPS-equipped ankle monitors that provided real-time tracking. The recording hadn't said anything about those.

More than anything Rebecca wished for a pistol. But the recording had said no, and she knew CC wouldn't give her one, and she had no way to get one on her own quickly in this foreign city. She hated losing the initiative this way, waiting for a call that might not come, with instructions that she might not be able to follow.

They'd given her no choice.

CC closed the door of the unmarked. *"Vaya con Dios."* They rolled toward Barcelona Sants.

o   o

"Thank you for figuring Tony out," she said now, as the train sped west, the dusk outside turning to darkness. "In CC's office."

"He just needed to vent."

She heard a helicopter's distant thrum. East and north. She waited for it to fade but it seemed to be pacing the train. She wondered if the Mossos had put up a copter without telling them.

A man walked down the aisle. Middle-aged, a long-sleeved shirt and jeans. Gray-tan skin and almond eyes. North African. His eyes scanning the cabin. *"Buenos noches."*

"Buenos noches."

The man looked at her. She wondered if he'd noticed the bag. She wondered if he was looking for it. But he didn't seem like a kidnapper. He seemed sunbaked and slow. Maybe.

"Do you know which way is the bathroom?"

Rebecca raised a thumb behind her, realizing as she did that she'd let slip she understood English. She waited for him to pass a note, drop a phone in her lap, lean over and whisper, *You will leave the train at the next stop—*

"*Gracias.*" He walked on.

Rebecca craned her neck to watch him go. He didn't look back or acknowledge her.

"What was that," Brian said.

"Maybe he just needed to go."

Brian didn't say anything.

"You have no idea how much I hate this, Bri. Being at their mercy."

They were silent for a while. Rebecca checked her watch. They were a little more than a half hour from Zaragoza. Assuming the Dropbox clue was right, the kidnappers should be contacting them soon.

She sighed. Almost groaned.

"What, Becks? Beyond the obvious."

"I wish we knew whether this is about my job. I mean, Europe has some powerful gangs, the 'Ndrangheta especially—"

"What's that?"

"Sorry. Fancy name for the Mafia. Basically run southern Italy. But why grab an American in Barcelona, what's the point? They make billions of euros a year on drugs, graft. This is more trouble than it's worth. And the care these people have taken, the resources, this feels like a government-level operation. But they haven't asked me for anything."

"Maybe some Eastern European is getting into high-end trafficking."

She squeezed his arm. "I wondered, maybe it's you they want."

"An NSA drone? I doubt it." Brian shook his head as if he hadn't even considered the idea.

He was probably right, she thought. How would the Russians even know who he was?

"Becks?"

"Yeah?"

"Think there's any chance she gets out on her own?"

Oddly enough she'd barely considered the possibility. These people had proven how good they were. The only mistakes they'd made — Dropbox and a couple of fingerprints — were too small to count.

Kira was smart and reasonably well-disciplined. But Becks had never seen any evidence she had a killer instinct. Why would she? She was a nice girl from a nice middle-class family. It wasn't like they'd been teaching her to pick locks or shuck handcuffs.

Anyone who would kidnap you and threaten to kill you in public wouldn't be much nicer once he had you to himself. Take any chance that came your way. But for most people, the natural instinct was to wait, appeal to the kidnapper's humanity. Until too late.

"Anything's possible." She wondered if she sounded as discouraged about the prospect as she felt.

Then their phones vibrated.

30

Somewhere in Spain

Thump. Thump.

The footsteps came up the stairs, a heavy male tread. Rodrigo.

Kira pushed herself up against the wall. The tip of the nail dug into her waist. The bag with the acetone and lighter waited beside her hip. Not much of an arsenal, but it would have to do.

At the top of the stairs the steps stopped—

Turned around. Halfway down, a heavier *thump* as he stumbled. A muffled Spanish curse.

No. Kira could read Rodrigo's drug-addled mind. Torn between his idiot lust and Jacques's warnings.

A few minutes later she heard him on the steps again. More slowly this time. Again he stopped at the top.

Was she ready? If she failed he'd kill her. Even if she succeeded . . . if the others came home too soon . . . if they hadn't left a car . . . if she couldn't start it . . .

No.

She had to try. No excuses.

"Rodrigo! That you?"

"*Sí.*" The door muffled his voice.

"Come on then."

The steps turned down the hall. Toward the closet. Toward *her*.

She reached for the lighter, flicked the little metal wheel—

Nothing. *No.* She tried again. This time the flame came up, bright and strong.

She slipped the lighter back in the plastic bag, next to the nail polish remover. The bottle cap was loose but still on. She didn't think he'd notice the smell if she uncapped it, but she couldn't risk it.

The deadbolt clapped back. Rodrigo stood in the doorway.

She had to stay in control. Make him listen. If he just jumped her, she'd lose both ways.

"Lilly made me take a shower. They're selling me."

He shrugged. She didn't have to fake her shiver. "Do you have any coke?"

He nodded.

"Then come on, let's do it. Time to party."

He looked less enthusiastic than she'd expected. She feared he might leave. He ran his tongue over his upper lip nervously, came to her, offered her the bag of white powder. He'd showered too at some point but still stank of sweat. Was he so terrified of Jacques?

But then Jacques *was* terrifying.

"You first."

He reached in with a dirty fingernail, snorted a bump, a big one. She followed. She kept the hit small. Still, she felt the drug's power. Her heart chopped into another gear. A dry metal taste filled her mouth. Her blood sparkled. The world was brighter. Clearer. Even in here.

"That's good."

He did another hit. The coke seemed to give him courage. He leaned in to kiss her. *No.* She put a finger to his lips.

"Stand."

Am I really doing this?

"Sí?"

"Stand."

He stood. She pulled off the belt, unbuttoned his jeans, pushed them down halfway. His penis was half-hard. And uncircumcised. And thick but not very big. And smelled terrible. *God no.* She'd have to take antibiotics like her dumb suitemate Janice who'd gotten frisky in New Orleans—

Focus.

She took him in her mouth. His erection was fading. He was more flaccid than hard now and stank of stale sweat and something worse. She wanted to gag. But if she couldn't make this happen—

"Coke dick," he said.

Coke dick? Was that a thing? She spat on her hand, tugged at him. Looked up and gave him big good-girl doe eyes, *I love giving head, being on my knees in front of a stranger, it's soooo great, I wish I could do it 24/7,* and she felt him respond immediately. Men. She used every trick she knew or had seen on YouPorn—

And finally got him as close to fully erect as he was going to get.

He wound his fingers into her hair and groaned. *"Madre de Dios."* He tugged her hair, trying to get her into the rhythm that would send him to orgasm.

She pulled her head away. Wiped the back of her mouth with her hand. Retched a little. He didn't notice.

He was still reaching for her head. She grabbed his hands, pulled him down.

"Lie down. On your back. I want to see you. I want to see your face when you come."

I so don't.

But he lay on his back as she'd asked. He had the placid look of a man having the best dream of his life. She straddled him, pushed up her skirt, but left her panties on. He reached for them.

"Wait. I want to play a little."

She rubbed herself against him. She was still sore from the polish bottle, and each time she touched him through her panties a wave of pain ran through her. But she didn't stop.

He grunted with pleasure, reached up for her. She pushed his arms down.

Time.

"Close your eyes."

"What?"

"Close them."

"Be good, okay." He closed his eyes.

She rubbed her hips against him, *Keep the rhythm, keep him entertained.* She pulled the bottle and lighter from the bag, shifted the bottle to her left hand, held the lighter in her right. *Keep moving, keep moving.*

He groaned happily.

She flicked off the bottle cap and it skittered down.

Now, now, if he sees he'll kill you—

He opened his eyes.

Grunted in surprise.

She felt his orgasm begin beneath her—

As he began to sit up she dumped the liquid in the bottle onto his face and flicked the lighter and

The flame at the tip of the lighter caught the acetone and—

Up it went.

Onto Rodrigo's face. And his *eyes.*

The flame danced. And his eyes burned.

He screamed, high, frightened. He clapped his hands to his face, slapping at the flame, but too late. In sitting up he had made himself a perfect target. His eyes were black in their sockets, retinas gone, the eyelids burned, only bloody pulp left. For a moment he sat back against the wall.

The horror of what she'd done stunned her. She didn't move.

His scream deepened into rage. He sat up, knocking her backward, and swiped blindly for her.

She dodged, turned, stood. Before her the door, the hallway, freedom. She ran.

He swept his legs sideways. They tangled hers. She went down, landed hard on her left elbow. A flash of pain shot up her arm into her shoulder. He grabbed her ankle, pulled her in. She kicked at him but he was so strong.

She found the nail in her waistband. It nearly slipped through her fingers but she held it tight.

He reeled her in, clamping his hands to her calf knee thigh. His fingernails tore her skin. She jabbed at his legs with the nail, but he didn't notice.

He put an arm around her waist and squeezed. She tried to scream but only gurgled. If he could reach her throat he could choke her out even blind.

Live or die.

His erection had withered, his cock lay flaccid, semen dripping—

And she knew what she had to do.

She made a fist around the nail. As his fingers touched her shoulders, reached for her throat, she jammed it through his soft sac and into the meat inside—

He screamed.

She flattened her palm, drove the nail deep into his testicle.

His scream rose and he let go of her to reach for the nail.

She scrambled away on hands and knees.

Stood, ran out. He crawled for her, blind, groaning, blundering for the door. She slammed it shut and leaned against it. She heard him stand as she snapped the deadbolt into place.

The door shook as he ran against it, fierce, helpless.

The lock held. He stopped. He slumped against the door, sobbing now.

"*Por favor, por favor,* please, it hurts, it hurts—"

Coke-adrenalized rage rose in her, at herself for hurting him, what she'd done, at him for giving her no choice, his poisoned semen sticky on her legs.

"How do you like it, Rodrigo? How do you like it, how do you like it—" She heard a car in the distance, the engine rumbling, revving.

She was wasting time, she needed to run.

She ran.

31

Near Zaragoza, Spain

This time both phones had the same message, from a Spanish number.

Row 26, last cabin.

"I'll go," Rebecca said.

She walked down the aisle. The automatic door at the back of the car hissed and opened, and she was gone.

This ride was his very last chance to tell her the truth, Brian realized.

Whatever was hidden back there, a note, a phone, a picture with directions scribbled on the back, he could help her find it. Maybe he'd find a way to tell her, too.

As he was considering the possibility, his phone buzzed. A blocked number.

He looked around. No one within three rows. He sagged against the window, cupped hand over mouth. "Yes?"

Irlov. Brian was surprised the Russian would risk calling him on this phone, but Irlov probably figured Brian knew enough not to answer if the NSA were up on it or if Rebecca were close enough to hear.

"Who is this?"

Irlov ignored the feint. "How's your lovely wife? Tragedies can bring families closer."

The Russian's cleverness never ended. Sure enough, Rebecca had been nicer to him, even after the stupid joke he'd made about betting the money. Brian wasn't sure her feelings would outlast the kidnapping, but this wasn't the time to argue.

"This can't be a tragedy, Feodor. It needs a happy ending."

"You have the two million?"

Irlov not even pretending anymore he wasn't in charge.

"We do."

"Then I'm sure everything will be fine."

"Promise."

"Promise?" Irlov made the word sound absurd.

Brian heard the door behind him open. He looked up, wondering if Rebecca could have come back so fast. No. Just the conductor.

"If you don't set her free, Becks will be useless to you. She'll quit the bureau, spend her life trying to find her."

"Best to follow instructions, then. No heroes."

And Irlov was gone. Once again, he hadn't promised the kidnappers would free Kira. But Brian had to assume he wouldn't have called otherwise.

Maybe after Kira came back Brian could tell Rebecca, suggest they team up for revenge?

Funny story, Becks, the real reason our daughter got kidnapped—

Yeah, maybe not.

o   o

The train sped on. Zaragoza was no longer just a faint blur. The outlines of shopping centers and apartment complexes glowed in the night. The air coming through the train's vents was cool and stale. Brian felt like an astronaut returning to Earth, no idea what he'd see when he touched down.

The first Zaragoza announcement came, in Spanish and then English. Fifteen minutes. Where was Becks?

There.

She slid in beside him. Held up a phone, an old-school Nokia.

"Sorry, took me a while, it was under the seat by the window. This was taped to the back."

She held up a battered Toyota key.

"Wonder if it's the same Camry?" Brian flashed a nightmare vision: Kira's body in the trunk.

"Guess we'll find out. As for the phone, we can see if there's video of who left it. But I doubt we'll find anything. That cabin is practically empty. They probably planted it before the train left Barcelona." She was talking fast, amped.

"The phone's locked?"

"No. I already checked for messages, the phone book, everything. Clean. I looked up the number, it's a thirty-four country code, Spanish. I texted Jake the number." Jake Broadnik, her NSA friend, who was waiting at his desk to run numbers for them. Typical Becks, she even pulled strings at his agency.

"I doubt it'll mean much, but anything's possible."

His last chance to come clean with her.

He knew he wouldn't.

o   o

The train ran alongside a highway now. They would pull in soon enough. Maybe he'd been wrong about Zaragoza.

The phone in Rebecca's hands buzzed.

A text. The number not blocked. *Are you there*

Rebecca thumbed an answer. *Yes*

You have car key

Yes

Zaragoza Police on platform

Yes

Get off Send them away Wait there

Yes

Leave phones on the train

Rebecca shook her head. "No," she said. As if the phone could hear. "I'm gonna try a question."

She thumbed in: *What is the key for?*

No response.

With her phone Rebecca took a picture of the phone number attached to the incoming messages. She texted the picture to Broadnik, along with a single word: *Trace.*

She shook her head. "I don't get why they're giving us their number. They have to know the NSA is going to be up on it in a hurry."

"Unless they want us to know. Maybe their way of leading us to Kira."

She nodded. "Maybe. But also they're making mistakes with their English. They're sloppy all of a sudden. I don't like them being sloppy. This is the trickiest part of a kidnapping, handing back a hostage and getting the money without getting caught. Makes me wonder if that's what they're planning to do at all."

She was right.

Her phone and the Kira phone buzzed at the same time. She handed hers to Brian. A 410 number, the NSA trunk line.

"Jake."

"Brian. Okay, we got that phone. Tower's about fifty kilometers northwest of Zaragoza, rural area so it's a wide coverage zone, maybe thirty-five square KM."

"Big."

"Yeah. I'm sending the map with the tower location to this phone. The number moves, I'll let you know. I'll send the map to your phone and Rob Wilkerson and the Spanish Special Ops guy and the Mossos too."

"Thanks, Jake." He hung up. "What'd the text say?"

She showed him: *No questions no Kira*

"Jake says they have the mobile already," Brian said. "Northwest of Zaragoza. He's letting everyone know."

"Everyone except the cops here, the ones we need," Rebecca said. "Barraza will call them but it's an extra minute, two, five. Try to pretend this jurisdictional stuff doesn't matter and then this happens. Guys like Fernandes—"

She broke off.

Both their phones buzzed again, the map from Jake.

"It looks like there's a big highway that runs from Zaragoza northwest to Pamplona in that coverage area," Rebecca said. "Good place to keep her, rural but easy to get away."

"You think she's up there?"

Rebecca hesitated. "It's possible."

"Then we should go up there."

"I'm not being cute, but where? Probably they're moving her right now. They going north or south? North, they can go to France, San Sebastián, Bilbao, wherever. South, Madrid. Nobody's putting up roadblocks. It's eleven at night, what are we looking for? A car with a sign that says, KIDNAPPED AMERICAN GIRL INSIDE THIS TRUNK? We don't know what kind of vehicle they might be using—"

"A Toyota."

"Bri, the only thing we know is that it's *not* a Toyota." She held up the key. "Why give us this? Here, take the key to our getaway car, we'll just walk."

She was right. And cutting and dismissive. Couldn't help herself. Even here. Even now.

"So we just sit with our thumbs in our asses, wait for this guy to give us orders?"

She exhaled heavily. "You think I *like* this? But if we get up there and they text us again and tell us the car's parked around the station and we need to be there in five minutes and we tell them we can't, who knows what they'll do? Waiting is our only real option."

Maybe the most infuriating thing about arguing with Becks, she was usually right.

"I'll kill him," Brian said. "If we don't get her back I'll kill him. Hunt him down and kill him myself."

"You'll have to beat me to it."

She didn't know he was talking about Irlov.

32

Northwest of Zaragoza

Kira skidded down the stairs, bare feet slipping on the slick wood steps. She couldn't turn her head. She felt Rodrigo behind her, his fingers grasping, the reek of his burnt flesh filling her nose.

Halfway down she heard low Spanish voices in the living room. Waiting. Her heart beat so fast it seemed about to explode. They were waiting for her. Then the voices turned to a jingle, happy women singing—

A commercial.

She reached the bottom step, grabbed the handrail to stay upright. *Breathe.* Panic wouldn't save her. She looked up the stairs. Which were empty. Of course. Rodrigo wasn't a shape-shifter from Tony's first-person shooters. She'd locked him away and he wouldn't be getting out. She heard him now, pounding the door, as if sheer fury could free him.

But she'd learned for herself, the deadbolt didn't care about the desperation of the person it held.

She put a hand to her cheek, felt her own ragged breath. Made her heartbeat slow. She listened for dogs barking, horns honking. Nothing. The car in the distance had turned around. Or turned off. Or maybe she hadn't heard it at all, maybe it had been part of her freak-out.

She feared what might be waiting outside. But the house was a trap disguised as safety.

She made a deal with herself. She would look for a pistol. Quickly. If Jacques and Lilly weren't close, she had a little time. And if they were, a gun was her only chance. A gun or a phone. Rodrigo had probably had his stuffed in his jeans, she realized now. Maybe he had already blindly thumbed in his password and called Jacques to come for him.

A few seconds. A minute. No more. She ran to the kitchen, putting aside the nightmare thought of Jacques and Lilly sipping sangria, *Come, Kira, have a drink, join us, we never liked that guy anyway, he's just the muscle—*

No Jacques. No Lilly. Kira found herself alone in a barely furnished room: a toaster, a mini fridge. A card table with three folding chairs and two empty wine glasses, the world's most boring still life. No phone. A closed laptop sat on the counter. She wanted to take it, but it would only slow her.

Dishes and glasses were stacked beside the sink. Might as well be graffiti, *Jacques was here.* By his obsessive neatness shall ye know him. A space for a microwave over the countertop, but no microwave. A space for a full-size refrigerator, but no fridge. The house was incomplete, unfinished.

The air was nearly as hot here as in the closet. No air-conditioning. The smell of gasoline from the garage tickled her nose. She didn't mind. Better than Rodrigo's burned skin.

She pulled open the cabinets. No pistols. But a knife block with a half dozen black-handled knives. She grabbed the second-biggest steak knife and ran.

Into the garage. No cars. No vans. The gas smell was stronger here, stronger than it had been two days ago. A different life. A different girl.

She saw why now. One of the tanks was uncapped. She stepped toward it, thinking of setting fire to the house. Burning Rodrigo alive while he was locked in a closet.

Maybe a different girl but not that one.

Not yet.

Even in here his screams penetrated, faint, desperate.

She turned away from the gasoline. By the garage door, a motorcycle and a bicycle, a mountain bike, nice fat wheels. She didn't know how to ride a motorcycle. The bike it would be. She didn't want to hold the knife while she rode, but she couldn't bear leaving it.

She tugged at the door handle. It stuck. She pulled harder. Harder.

Up it went, rattling its rails. The night air swept into the garage, a steady warm breeze. *Free.*

She hopped on the bike, felt the seat dig into her. She didn't have shoes, but the pedals were flat, rubber. She stepped on them —

The handlebars twisted and she fell. Dropped the knife. It bounced off the concrete floor, nearly sliced open her face.

A Kryptonite lock ran through the bicycle's front wheel and around the frame. She'd missed it.

Maybe they'd taped the key to the wall or something. She looked. Nope.

She screamed in frustration. No bike.

She picked up the knife, ran into the night . . .

Found herself at the end of a cul-de-sac. *What?* The road and neighborhood looked weirdly American, suburban. She didn't see how they could have held her here, all these people, why there hadn't been any noise —

But who cared, the neighbors could call the police. She sprinted for the next house —

And put her left foot in a hole. Her ankle gave, twisted sideways. Her bad ankle, the one she'd hurt playing soccer. She screamed as she landed awkwardly on the pavement. Which wasn't pavement at all. But dirt.

Her ankle. It *hurt.* Why hadn't she found her shoes, why hadn't she looked for them? Why hadn't she looked at the ground instead of running blindly like a four-year-old?

She picked up the knife, stood carefully, leaned on her right leg. Slowly she eased her weight to her left. It was wobbly, loose, but it held. Sprained. Badly. But not broken. She could hobble. For a while.

She limped toward the neighboring house, wondering why her scream hadn't brought anyone outside.

Then raised her head to the sky, brilliant with stars. A country sky. The houses, dark. The yards, dirt. The driveways, empty.

How many more clues do you want?

A real estate development gone bad. She thought that only happened back home, that movie *The Big Short*, Margot Robbie in the tub, rose skin and perfect, Christian Bale in a suit, weird and fat.

A ghost neighborhood. For a ghost girl.

The dirt street ran up a low hill, houses on either side. Kira saw no electric glow, no evidence of anyone within shouting distance. She shouted anyway. "Help!"

"HELP HELP HELP!"

Her voice fell into the night. No answer. Not even a cat meowing or a dog barking. This place was empty.

Okay, move.

She limped up the street, keeping the weight off her left leg as best she could, dragging the foot behind her. She looked for a stick, a metal rod, anything to use as a cane. Nothing. She wanted to run but made herself go easy. She had no idea how far she needed to go. If she pushed too hard she might tear ligaments in the ankle and wind up crawling.

Maybe a dozen houses on either side, empty, windows boarded up. Where was everyone? She was in *Europe*. Had to be a town somewhere. A highway, a farm, a gas station, whatever, somewhere with a phone. Keep moving. Not too much weight on the leg.

She hoped at the top of the hill she'd see lights. She hoped she hadn't wasted too much time, hoped Jacques and Lilly were out for a nice long dinner or doing whatever kidnappers did when they weren't kidnapping. The bike seat had made her ache where she'd stuffed herself with the bottle, and remembering the bottle made her think of Rodrigo and—

No more thinking.

She had never felt so lonely.

At the crest of the hill, she mopped the sweat from her eyes, bit her hand against the pain in her leg. She wondered if the ankle was broken. It was swelling for sure, the bone disappearing under a glove of stretched-out skin. She touched it lightly, wished she hadn't.

A thick black chain blocked the road ahead, metal signs attached to the posts, facing out. Warning against trespassing, probably. Beyond the chain, the road was paved, cracked but paved. They'd kept her at the end of the line, the outer edge of this failed development. Did they own it, or had Jacques just found it somehow, the Lonely Planet kidnapping boards?

More unfinished houses lay to the right. Beyond them, the land sloped down and she saw a cluster of lights. She couldn't judge how far. Didn't matter, she couldn't possibly navigate open ground on one leg. Stick to the road.

She hobbled around the chain. Ahead the road dipped slightly, then rose. The next crest was maybe five hundred feet away.

Move. Move, Kira, move. Her mother's voice.

The flatland wasn't too bad. But when she had to climb, the steps sent fire up her leg, her ligaments giving more with each step. Sooner or later she would tear them off the bone and her pain tolerance wouldn't matter, she'd be on her hands and knees no matter what.

Ten minutes to the top of the second hill? More? She didn't know. At the top, she went to a knee. Wiped her face. Sweat and tears mixed. She'd been crying and hadn't even known.

She pushed herself up. The land ahead was nearly flat, just a few low hills. The road cut straight across it. East, west, north, south? She didn't know. She was a child of GPS and turn-by-turn directions. No one had ever taught her to read the stars.

Anyway, the road was empty on either side, no more houses. No wonder the development had failed. Why had they stuck it out here? Four widely separated clusters of lights glowed in the distance. Villages, she guessed. Closer, two miles ahead, maybe, red and white lights blurred through the night.

Taillights. Headlights. A *highway.* The one she'd heard before when the wind was right.

345

With the bike, she could have ridden to it in ten minutes. Less. Even without the bike if she hadn't sprained her ankle she could have covered the distance in half an hour at most.

If, if, if. If she had an Uber waiting for her she'd be back in Barcelona already, hanging out on La Rambla with Becks and Bri and Tony, telling kidnapping stories. *Then I shoved the polish remover bottle up my twat, ouchie, hilarious, right?*

o   o

You want help? Get to the highway. Stop whining and move. Brian's voice this time.

She walked again, faster now, putting the pain in a corner, *loving* the pain —

And saw a white blur pull off the highway. Headlights. The blur swung right. Onto *this* road.

Yes, someone was coming, help —

No.

Nobody good was driving down this road at this hour. Nobody was coming home to see the fam, hang out in the man cave. Jacques and Lilly had finished the night's errands, setting up the auction or whatever — *one tall American not-quite-virgin, do I hear eight million euros?* — and were coming home to check on the merch.

She was in the worst possible place. She had to get off the road.

The land around her was barren, low scrub. Maybe seventy-five feet away, down a slope, there was a strand of bushes. Not heavy enough to hide her if they searched, but if they just drove by —

She hop-hobbled across the road, down the hill, moving as fast as she dared. If she tore her ankle she'd have to crawl and wouldn't have a chance.

She kept her eyes on the bush, not the road, she didn't want to know how fast they were coming —

Sixty feet, fifty —

Forty, thirty, twenty—

Ten—

The hill steepened a few extra degrees. Enough to throw her off. Her ruined left foot slid in the soft soil. The ligaments popped, she heard them go. The pain in her leg rose like someone had pushed the volume button on the remote and forgot to let go.

She screamed and dropped the knife and fell forward. Landed hard, flat on her face.

Crawl.

She grabbed the knife and crawled. She didn't know what the bush was, but it had spiky green leaves and thorns. The branches hung low. She crawled around it, pulled her knees up, made herself small, tried not to think about the pain in her leg. She could see the road through it, which meant they could see her if they looked hard enough. But would they look at all?

She ran her hands through the crumbly dirt, smeared it across her face. Camouflage. No one had to teach her that one. The soil smelled faintly of sage. Surprise. Now she heard the car, saw its headlights tearing open the night. Closing fast. Not a car at all, a high-sided van, white, maybe the one they'd used to bring her here. It bounced along the rutted pavement.

Had she ditched the road fast enough?

She tucked the knife by her side. She couldn't run anymore, but if Jacques came for her she still had a chance at putting the knife in him. If he killed her so be it, she'd die before she went back in that closet.

She tucked her head—

The van sped by, disappeared. She heard it stop at the chain. A door opened. Seconds later it slammed shut, and the van began to move again.

Okay, they were on their way to the house. In a minute or two they would find Rodrigo.

What then?

Would they take him to a hospital? Kira didn't think so. Maybe they had a doctor they could call. But he wouldn't be their priority. They'd have their eyes on the prize. Once they saw the bike and motorcycle were still in the garage they would know she had gone on foot.

But they couldn't know she'd hurt herself, or how long she'd been gone. Even she couldn't be sure. She thought no more than twenty minutes had passed since she'd trapped Rodrigo, but time had turned blurry, elastic. Rodrigo would be even more confused. Being newly blinded and all.

Jacques would have to worry maybe she'd already found a phone, called the cops. Maybe he'd just grab Rodrigo and run.

But she didn't know who his bosses were. Maybe someone would be angry at him for losing her. Someone who could hurt him even more than the Spanish police. Then he'd have to look for her. And Mr. Magoo could follow the tracks she'd left.

What would he do if he found her?

Probably give her a prize for being so clever and resourceful, ha-ha.

Nothing she could do about it now. This bush was the best hiding spot within crawling distance. She smeared more dirt on her hands and face. In a way she was lucky, if she'd moved faster and been closer to the highway they might have seen her when they turned off.

They had to be at the house now.

She felt her heart fluttering, skipping beats. How did soldiers live with this fear every day? How did they not lose their minds? Her hand ached from gripping the knife.

She made herself count to twenty. Thought of her brother's goofy smile. How her mom's eyes had lit up when she'd seen the piano in the apartment in Barcelona. Of—

A scream from the house, carrying through the night. Rodrigo.

An engine backfired in the night. The scream ended as abruptly as a light going out.

Not an engine. A shot.

Guess Jacques had decided not to find a doctor for Rodrigo.

Nothing for a couple of minutes.

Then the van's engine. It roared up the first hill, stopped at the chain, roared again as it came up the second rise.

Kira pushed herself into the dirt as the van appeared. It was speeding, bouncing hard on the broken road, no way they could see her.

It swerved and slowed as it approached the bush. Kira saw Lilly in the passenger seat, jaw set in fury. Lilly looked down the hill. Kira could swear they'd made eye contact.

Don't stop—

The van sped off, its taillights streaking the night.

o   o

She stayed still until the red lights faded to pinpricks, then nothing.

They were gone. She'd done it. She'd escaped. She was *free*. Truly free this time.

Euphoria.

But it didn't last.

Because now what?

Wait for the morning and then crawl for the highway on her hands and knees. How many feet could she cover in an hour? How many hours without water could she survive?

Cops or the locals must drive on this road sometimes, it wasn't the middle of the desert. Someone would spot her—

She smelled smoke.

From the house.

She couldn't see the fire directly, but the night was aglow. Jacques had decided to put all that gasoline to good use, burn the evidence.

The smoke thickened. She wondered if she should pull herself up to the road right away, but if she did and Jacques came back, she'd be stuck. Anyway, she could wait now, she didn't have to get to the highway, the firefighters would come sooner or later to check on this burning house and when they did she could climb to the road and they'd see her. She could even wait for daylight.

She waited. Curled in on herself in the dirt like a brown leaf. Let herself imagine seeing her parents and her brother. What would she

349

say to them? How quickly would they go back to normal? What would she tell them about what had happened, what she'd done?

From the outside they'd think she was brave. She'd beaten her captors. But she felt monstrous, felt like she'd found the weak link, tricked him, made him suffer in a way she couldn't even dream.

No, she couldn't imagine telling anyone the details about Rodrigo, not even her mother. Even when she slept he'd be with her. She was glad she'd won, glad she'd escaped, but she'd paid her own price, hadn't she?

She closed her eyes.

And only then did she feel the warmth on her leg. The wet.

Blood. From her left calf, the wound a couple of inches long. Deep, too. She hadn't noticed, she'd assumed the pain in her leg was just the ankle. *How?* The last time she fell she must have rolled across the knife. The knife. The useless knife. But she'd been so amped up in her desperation to reach the bush, hide behind it, that she hadn't felt it.

Now—

Her leg was slick with it. The wound hurt, not terribly, an ache inside the muscle almost like she'd pulled it. Not bad compared to the ankle, to be honest. But the blood kept coming, a steady trickle. She pushed her palm against it, the pressure ratcheting the pain higher. Pushed as hard as she could, but the blood seeped between her fingers.

She didn't know anything about veins and arteries in the leg. Didn't know what she'd cut. Didn't know how much blood she'd lose in the next minute, the next hour. But she knew she couldn't survive until sunrise, much less crawl two miles to the highway with this.

What, then? Up to the road and hope that someone would find her. The firefighters had to be coming, right?

She pushed herself back from the bush and felt the wound open wider. She stopped. Looked down. The blood was coming faster now. More than a trickle.

Kira breathed in deep. Not fair, this wasn't *fair*. Crawl up, tear open your leg, die in a few minutes. Wait right here and bleed out nice and slow. There was a name for this problem, but she couldn't remember it right now. Yeah, she was a little distracted.

She wasn't ready to give up. Truly. She ought to crawl while she still had some strength, she shouldn't close her eyes. But right now she couldn't fight. Maybe in a few minutes the cut would clot and she'd have a chance. Maybe. Meantime she would gather her strength.

She ignored the voice in her head, screaming, *Don't quit, come on, Kira.*

But she had nothing left.

She closed her eyes.

Fucking hell. And she'd been so close.

33

Outside Zaragoza

The train took forever to stop at the platform, the doors even longer to open. The phone from the kidnappers remained stubbornly dead. They had no more messages from the NSA or anyone else. Frustration and fear pounded Rebecca. She had to have had a better play, another move, but she couldn't figure it out.

Finally the door slid back. Brian followed her out, holding the green two-million-euro bag, its weight tugging his arm. Two men in blue uniforms waited. A third man in civilian clothes stood a step behind, a phone against his ear. The station was modern and handsome, big triangular ceiling windows alternating with slabs of alabaster. 22:55, the digital clocks above the platform told them. Almost exactly two days since Kira had disappeared. The two longest days of Rebecca's life. Whatever happened next would be easier.

Unless—

She wouldn't even let herself think it.

The handful of travelers who had left the train at Zaragoza walked past, stealing looks at the drama.

"Mr. Unsworth? Mrs. Unsworth?" The man in the suit held up a single finger, *Hold on, please.* A minute ticked by on the digital clock.

Behind them, the train's doors closed. A moment later it pulled out of the station, accelerating, leaving the platform behind. Rebecca felt strangely sorry to see it go. Maybe someone on there had been watching them. Maybe they'd missed a clue.

The clocks ticked to 22:57. If this cop was talking about anything other than Kira, Rebecca would kill him.

"*Sí. Sí.*" Finally he pocketed the phone, turned to them.

"I'm Lieutenant Suarez. I'm sorry, but that call was about your daughter. Come with me, *por favor.*"

"We were told to wait here for instructions."

Suarez shook his head. "It's possible we may have found where they held her."

"How?" Rebecca said.

"A fire, a ghost town in the area where the CIA"—he meant NSA, Rebecca assumed—"found the phone. Come, please."

"Ghost town?" Nothing was making much sense.

"A housing development that was never finished. Because of the financial crisis. Spain has many—" He walked down the platform, giving them no choice but to follow.

"We sent a patrol to the area northwest of Zaragoza as soon as we received the information about the phone. Now the officers say they've seen a fire in one of those developments. They're going to the house. But it's kilometers off the highway."

"Hold on." Brian grabbed Suarez's shoulder.

"*Señor*—"

"No one knows if this fire is connected to any of this. If Kira was there, much less if she still is."

"The timing is strange. To say the least."

Rebecca reached for Brian, found herself looking at pure male rage, his eyes slits. If he couldn't calm down he would deck Suarez and then the cops would have no choice but to arrest him.

And Suarez was right, coincidences were rarely coincidences at moments like these.

"Bri, listen—"

"You're the one who said we should wait here."

"No, this is good news, I promise." Maybe better to keep him away just in case. She handed him the phone and the Toyota key. "I'll go. Stay here if they call."

She saw him gather himself, nod. "If they do, I'm doing what they say. Whatever it is."

"Yes, but call me—"

"Go, then." He turned away, stalked down the platform. Toward the west, open end of the station. Toward nothing.

o   o

She understood. Wasn't even upset with him. Suarez led her through the station, outside. Two police cars waited in front, their lights flashing. He walked her past those, across a wide boulevard, into an empty parking lot.

"Where are we going?"

He pointed east into the night sky. She heard the thrum of a helicopter, distant but closing fast. A minute later she saw its spotlight, following the train tracks toward the station, just a couple hundred feet off the ground. She couldn't see the bird itself, though. Must have been black.

The engine noise picked up and the spotlight pinned them. She shielded her eyes against the glare as the bird leveled out and then landed in the lot. A Bell 407, a standard long-range seven-seater. The FBI used them too. The door swung open. Garza, the special ops colonel, waved to her. She ducked her head, ran through the wash, glad to see him despite everything. Two men dressed in black were in the back, along with an empty seat. For Brian, presumably. Rebecca buckled herself into the harness and pulled on her headphones. The Bell rose into the night and turned north over the center of Zaragoza.

"You followed us?"

"Yes." Garza's voice was raspy in the headphones.

"Thank you."

"Your husband?"

"Waiting at the train station for instructions. He has the money." Though she wondered now, what if this were some ruse to divide them, isolate the cash, take the bag from Brian with no cops around? Could the kidnappers have guessed they'd split up?

"They told you about the fire? They're sending firefighters but it will be a bit. The nearest station is twenty kilometers and they say the road to the development is not good. We may get there first. The police just reached it but the house is burning too fast, they can't go inside."

"Have they seen anyone?"

"No."

Good news, bad news? She didn't know.

o   o

The Bell topped out at one hundred sixty miles an hour. They left downtown Zaragoza behind and sliced through the night, roughly paralleling a four-lane highway. Houses and stores blurred beneath them.

"This road we're following goes to Pamplona," Garza said. "Probably another six, seven minutes to the house."

The land looked surprisingly open beyond the strip of homes and stores that paralleled the highway. Villages were scattered in the night, islands in a sea of darkness. Rebecca understood better now how the kidnappers could have moved Kira here without being noticed.

Soon enough, the helicopter banked right. She saw the fire now, the orange glow in the night. Blue lights flashed near it, tiny in comparison.

Below and ahead, off the highway, more blue lights, taller, no doubt belonging to the fire trucks. They moved weirdly slowly through the darkness, reminding her of Garza's warning about the road.

The helicopter turned off the highway, quickly passing the trucks. As they closed in the power of the blaze became apparent. It was uncontrolled, shooting into the night. If Kira had been inside the house—

Nothing from Brian, but then she hadn't texted either. What could she say? *Yeah, it's burning.*

Now they were only a few hundred yards away. The helicopter's spotlight swept over the scrubby ground, past a single strand of bushes that shook in the rotor wash, a row of skeletal houses.

The burning house stood at the end of a cul-de-sac. The flames reached hungry into the night. The police sedan was parked well back, nothing the cops could do. The helicopter slowed abruptly now, the pilot hesitating, looking for the right spot. It moved forward and set down fast. Rebecca's head bobbed as its skids bounced and settled on the hardpack dirt road.

She unbuckled herself even before the helicopter stopped moving. Garza reached for her but she shook off his hand, jumped out, ran toward the house. The cops on the ground watched her, and one stepped toward her, in case she wanted to try a heroic and pointless rescue. But even twenty feet away the heat was huge, painful. Even if Rebecca had known Kira was inside, she couldn't have forced herself through it.

The house would collapse soon; it was tilting, sending embers through the night. Some had already settled on other roofs.

The fire trucks were close enough now for her to hear sirens.

Until someone proved otherwise, she had to assume Kira was not in there. The kidnappers had moved her, set fire to the place, a plan to distract the cops while they collected the ransom.

Or Kira had escaped somehow, beaten them, and they'd burned the house to destroy the evidence.

Think.

If she'd escaped, she was close.

She would have run for the highway. She was too much of a city girl to head to open ground. She would want to find a phone as soon as she could.

But she hadn't been on the road. Why not?

Rebecca walked away from the house, up the road, trotting now. Garza called to her. She ignored him. Maybe she was wasting time, but she couldn't wait here and watch. Kira was out there. Not inside that house-sized barbeque. Not stuffed in some trunk. Out there. And close. Rebecca had to believe.

Then why hadn't she called? Why hadn't she come out when the police showed up?

Think.

Because she was injured, wounded. Even seeing the cops couldn't get her to move —

The bushes she'd seen, the movement. Not rotor wash. The helicopter had been too far away.

An animal. A *person.*

Rebecca ran now. She topped the hill, nearly tripped on a chain the cops had knocked aside, kept running. The fire engines were only a few hundred feet away. Their headlights appeared, coming faster than she expected. They bounced down the hill toward her and honked ferociously. She angled aside and kept running, feeling the rush of air as they passed. And then she had the night to herself, none of the cops chasing her, *Let her go, she's emotional.*

She ran.

To the top of the second low hill. Where had the bush been? On the downslope.

There.

The leaves shaking. Behind them —

Something, someone, moving.

Rebecca ran down, cutting toward the bush, skidding in the soft dirt, screaming for her daughter.

The bush twisted.

And the voice, weak and thin across the night, just one word: "Mom?"

A *question.* As if Kira couldn't believe her mother had found her. As if she might ever have doubted.

VI

KIRA AND BRIAN

(SIX MONTHS LATER)

34

Chevy Chase, Maryland

The cliché was true. Three inches of snow and D.C. shut down. Like no one had ever driven on a wet road. Waze almost made matters worse; it sent everyone skidding down the same side streets through Columbia Heights. Seven a.m. and Brian had already left, trying to beat the traffic to Fort Meade.

Rebecca was in the kitchen, making coffee and thinking about working from home, when her phone trilled behind her. Kira.

"Kira. You okay?" *Why are you calling so early?*

"Mom." Her daughter's tone was almost aggressively blasé. "Fine. It's five degrees up here. Who thought *Boston* was a good idea?"

"Global warming."

"Funny, Mom. We're the ones who have to live with it."

"Yeah, I'll be dead. Thanks for the reminder."

"And—" Kira broke off. "Ayla's in trouble." Ayla, the girl with leukemia at Boston Children's. Kira had been visiting her for more than a year. "Like going-to-die-this-week trouble."

Rebecca exhaled. She hadn't even realized she was holding her breath. Just a dying eight-year-old. Nothing. "I'm sorry."

"Yeah, but it's connected to the you know what somehow." Kira had the habit of calling her kidnapping *the you know what.* As well as not talking about *the you know what* at all.

A fact that made this call a teachable moment, Rebecca figured. If she could teach Kira anything. She wasn't the one who had fought her way out.

"She's trapped, helpless. Only unlike you she can't win."

More silence.

"Guess," Kira finally said. "All right, gotta go."

"Kira—"

"Yes Mom—"

"I love you."

"Love you too bye."

o   o

Six months since the worst vacation ever, and Rebecca still found herself close to panic whenever Kira called. Or didn't. She was supposed to check in twice a day, 11 a.m. and 11 p.m., one of the compromises they'd made for allowing her to stay at Tufts and not transfer somewhere in D.C. Kira had desperately wanted to go back, resume her life, no bodyguard, no special treatment, not even telling the university or campus police.

Rebecca had tried to persuade her to take the fall off. Jacques and Lilly were still in the wind. Despite massive help from the FBI and NSA, the Spanish cops had struck out on figuring out who they were or if they were working for someone and who that someone might be. Much less finding them.

Of course, the cops didn't have much to work with. The kidnap house had burned to the foundation, obliterating whatever forensic evidence there might have been. Clothes? Gone. DNA? Gone. Photos, computers, phones? Gone, gone, gone.

The housing development itself had been financed in part by a Russian bank called ZAM Muscovy, which was rumored to have connections to the SVR. Interesting, but hardly proof of anything. ZAM Muscovy had lost money on lots of other Spanish developments too. The Zaragoza contractor who built the units had gone broke four years before. The security company that watched the houses was based in Madrid and looked clean, no known ties to organized crime. Looters had ransacked many ghost developments, especially in southern Spain. This one had survived untouched, maybe because it was among the last to be finished, maybe because the houses were far enough from the highway to be basically invisible.

In any case, no one could figure out if Jacques had a connection to the development or if he'd just found it and realized it would be a perfect place to hide someone.

The white van never turned up. But cops did find the Toyota, legally parked on a busy residential street north of Zaragoza's city center. Clean of prints and DNA. Reported stolen from Madrid four years before. An entirely anonymous car. No one who lived on the street remembered who had left it. None of the nearby houses had security cameras. Whether Jacques had planned to tell the Unsworths to leave the ransom money in it or drive it somewhere else was anyone's guess.

Kira had given police artists detailed descriptions of Jacques, Lilly, and Rodrigo. The police matched the sketches to surveillance photos from The Mansion and Helado. But though the Mossos showed the photos to every bouncer and hotel clerk in Barcelona, no one admitted to recognizing them.

And though the Interior Ministry and FBI ran the photos against driver's license and border-crossing databases in Europe and the United States, they never came up with a match. The dirty secret of facial recognition programs was that they were very good at finding known fugitives, not as good at putting names to faces. Maybe Jacques and Lilly had spent their lives in Europe and avoided airports. Maybe they'd come from somewhere else and crossed into the European Union illegally. Maybe they'd subtly changed their features. Regardless, they didn't show up.

Rodrigo was gone too. Without going into details, Kira had made it clear that he would have needed a hospital for his wounds. But no one matching Rodrigo's injuries had been treated at any Spanish hospital in the days following the kidnapping. The Spanish even checked with the Portuguese, French, and Italians, came up blank.

She'd told them about Rodrigo's screams and the shot that ended them, too. But the cops never found a corpse matching his description. Of course, Jacques could have weighed the body down and dumped it in the Atlantic for the sharks. The house was barely a two-hour drive from the coast.

So many unknowns.

Rebecca had detected a slight skepticism from some of the detectives who talked to her: *Maybe this guy Rodrigo isn't dead. Maybe the escape didn't exactly go the way your daughter says.* Underneath that, a question: *If Jacques was such a pro, could she have gotten away if he didn't want her to?*

Which in turn maybe led to two other questions: *Did he let her go? And if he did, why?*

Questions that ended with the ultimate taboo thought: *Was she working with them all along?*

But the Spanish cops were too polite to say any of that out loud, or even hint at it. The Interior Ministry had its two million euros back. The Queen—the old lady who lived across the back alley from Helado—confirmed Kira hadn't been conscious when she left the bar. And Kira had clearly endured two days of *something*. Under the circumstances, pushing too hard on Kira made no sense.

The Spanish had been wise not to ask, Rebecca knew. Because on the nine-hour plane ride from Madrid to D.C., Kira had told Becks more about how she'd escaped Rodrigo. Not much but enough. Rebecca had encouraged her to "talk to someone."

But Kira just shook her head in a way that suggested she didn't plan to talk to anyone at all, and Rebecca decided not to press.

The NSA's tricks had failed too. The phones the kidnappers had used were dead. Their metadata chains went nowhere. The ransom recording revealed nothing more on its hundredth play than its first. And Jacques and Lilly had both been smart enough to make sure their voices hadn't been caught anywhere. They must have known the NSA was even better at matching voices than faces.

Rebecca had even taken advantage of the thin possibility that the case was terror-related to push the CIA and European agencies to look at their raw intel on kidnappings, the semi-legal or illegal stuff the police never heard. But no one came up with anything that looked remotely similar to this case.

So.

Nobody knew nothing. Nobody had answers.

Especially to the question that gnawed the most, the one that wouldn't go away: *Why Kira?*

Until they knew whether Jacques had taken Kira at random or targeted her, they couldn't know if she was safe. If she'd been specifically chosen, then Rebecca had to know *why*, what message Jacques had meant to send, whether he or his bosses were satisfied with what had happened.

Because money didn't make sense as a motive. Anyone who had researched Kira would have known she didn't have enough to matter. Even the two million that Jacques had demanded was far more than the Unsworths could have raised. If the Spanish hadn't come through they would have had no way to pay.

But other parents could have. Every summer, plenty of American college students whose families had ten or twenty million dollars visited Paris. They would have been no harder to target than Kira. They didn't have bodyguards. Only billionaires had personal security for their children, certainly on trips somewhere as safe as France.

If Jacques had taken Kira specifically, he'd done so for some other reason. Try as she might, Rebecca couldn't see what it might be. Nothing in the ransom demand had been political. And Kira insisted Jacques had seemed genuinely surprised to learn of Rebecca's FBI connection.

What then? If Jacques hadn't *targeted* Kira, he'd just happened on her, and—what? Meticulously orchestrated the cross-border kidnapping of an American citizen without knowing if the American's family had millions of euros to pay him off?

One other possibility lurked.

Rebecca didn't like to think about it, but it did fit the facts. Even the strangely messy way the kidnappers had handled the ransom demand. Maybe Jacques hadn't cared about the ransom. He had considered it a diversion. Let the Unsworths bring the money somewhere and the Spanish police watch the pickup site for a day or a week. Meanwhile, he'd go with his original plan: selling Kira. The act might seem impossibly cruel. But men tortured and raped and killed. Men were impossibly cruel. Not always, but often enough.

And for the wealthy psychopath who had everything, the chance to *buy* a pretty teenager might be tough to turn down. An *American* teenager. Not some poor Russian girl selling herself because she had no other options. An American who couldn't imagine being treated this way, who would truly fight and truly break.

Use Kira until she had nothing left. Drug her and dump her in the middle of Istanbul, some giant city, no memory of how'd she'd gotten there, no idea where she'd been.

Or just kill her.

Another reason Rebecca thought this scenario made sense was that Kira said Jacques's group had been relatively small. She had seen and heard Jacques, Lilly, Rodrigo, and the two drivers, the one who'd picked them up from Helado and the one waiting at the van when they'd transferred her. Never anyone else. Throughout, Jacques had relied more on speed, stealth, and cleverness than money. An intelligence service, if one had been crazy enough to be involved, would have put Kira on a plane and flown her to parts unknown — extraordinary rendition, as the CIA liked to say.

So.

So.

o   o

If the kidnapping had been random, Kira was safe.

No matter what, Kira would never forget those two days. But the sooner she could return to classes and friends, parties and volunteering, the better. *Her first goal is normal*, the FBI shrink had told Rebecca.

And in one important way, Kira had been supremely lucky. The Spanish media hadn't picked up on the kidnapping. A travel blogger raised questions about the "Missing" posters on La Rambla, but the Mossos brushed him aside, saying the woman in them had been found unharmed. The fire had received little attention even in Zaragoza. Even the fact that Jacques and Lilly hadn't been identified paradoxically worked for Kira on the publicity front. With no one to hunt for, there was no hunt, no Wanted posters.

Thus Kira could choose what to tell her friends. She didn't tell them much. She insisted she wanted to go back to school as soon as she could.

Brian took her side.

"Let her live," he told Rebecca in early August, weeks before sophomore year was set to begin. Kira and Tony had gone to a movie, the first time she'd left the house without Rebecca or Brian since they'd come back to the United States. Brian had plowed through a six-pack of the eight percent alcohol IPAs he favored. Which made a six-pack more like ten beers. Though he insisted he wasn't rattled.

"Have you forgotten what happened?"

"That what you think?"

She shook her head.

"Then don't say it. They're not coming after her here. It's over, Becks. Whether they wanted her for some reason we'll never know or they just went after her randomly, it's *over*."

"You can't be sure."

"Who is she? Who are *we*?"

Probably the best argument in favor of a random kidnapping. None of them mattered enough to be worthy of targeting. "Say you're right—"

"I'm right."

"Don't you want to make sure they don't do this to someone else?"

"I want our daughter to be happy and I don't think locking her in our house helps. Nor you chasing this, reminding her of it every time she sees you."

So Rebecca gave in. Tufts it would be. On three conditions. Kira had to agree to wear an alarm that the FBI and the Unsworths would monitor 24/7/365. She had to call twice a day. And she had to let them know if she dated anyone who wasn't a student.

Kira agreed to all three rules. And stuck to them.

Even so Rebecca woke up two, three, four times a night throughout the fall. Her days were fine. The Russians were more active than ever. The rumors that they had a new source high in either the NSA or CIA were only picking up.

But the nights were no fun at all, usually starting around midnight, no coincidence. Her dreams sent her to bus stations and airports. Blurred faces on rainy afternoons. Eighteen-wheelers pulling out with license plates she couldn't see. She woke up certain each time that she'd just missed Kira.

She woke desperate to call Kira, sure something was wrong. Brian talked her down every time. As the days grew shorter and the fall wore on she felt closer to him. Like for the first time in their marriage they were truly partners. Like she could *depend* on him.

He was good with Tony, too. Sometimes she focused so much on Kira that she almost forgot Tony. She knew he blamed himself for not telling them about Jacques right away. But trying to make him talk only upset him, and Brian was far better than Rebecca at distracting him. They went to Capitals games, or sat in the basement playing *Fortnite*, while Rebecca stared at her laptop trying to make sense of the case.

She didn't tell Brian how much time she spent on it. She talked to Barraza and Rob Wilkerson, tracked every kidnapping of a woman anywhere in Western Europe. She'd even fallen into the rathole that was the Russian financial system as she looked at ZAM Muscovy.

o   o

Fall turned into the winter. Kira took her finals, came home. Her grades were fine. In fact, they were better. *Not going out much,* she said. *Figure I got my partying in over the summer.* They stayed close to home for New Year's. Kira went back to school.

Now she was trying to be good to a little girl who was dying. In the middle of a Boston winter. Maybe it was all too much. Maybe Becks ought to go see her.

Yes.

She'd find a flight to Logan, surprise Kira. They'd visit Ayla together. Have dinner at one of those overpriced Italian places on the North End. If Kira told her she was making a big deal, she'd insist, no, she just wanted to hang out for a day, she'd missed the misery of single-digit weather.

o   o

By 1 p.m. she stood in front of her daughter's dorm, Harleston Hall, brick and four stories. Like a lot of Tufts, it looked not-quite Harvard. God. What a snob she was deep down. Anyway, she hadn't told Kira she was coming. Now she wasn't so sure of what she'd done. What if Kira wanted to spend the afternoon hanging out with her roommate? Or studying? Or—

Too late for regrets. And too cold. She reached for her phone.

"Kira. I'm downstairs."

"You're *where?*"

"You weren't kidding. It's freezing."

The day went fine. Kira seemed excited she'd come up, a chance to play hooky in a city that somehow belonged to them both, neutral ground. As they finished up dinner at Carmelina's—a no-white-table-cloths North End place that hadn't been here when she was growing up—Rebecca felt relaxed in a way she hadn't since that first night in Barcelona. The bottle of wine they'd shared had helped.

"Let's check out the Encore," Kira said.

"What's that?"

"Casino."

"Boston has a casino? Along with modern Italian food and the Patriots being great? Ohh Tom Brady—" Maybe they hadn't exactly shared the bottle.

"Please don't, Mom."

"Don't what?"

"Don't slobber over Tom Brady like every other middle-aged woman."

"Middle-aged."

"Sorry."

"No it's true. So. Encore. Casino."

"Yeah, it opened like last year."

"Please don't tell me you've been spending lots of time there, K."

"Never been. It's close though. Like up by Logan. Not sure exactly where."

"Hold on. I'll check—"

Rebecca pulled up Bri's app.

But she couldn't find the Encore. Weird.

"You sure about this?"

"No, I just made it up."

She checked again. Nothing. As far as the app was concerned, the Encore didn't exist. In fact, nothing on Twenty-One seemed to have been updated in a while.

Rebecca had the feeling she sometimes did when her phone wouldn't do what she wanted, *I'm so old*. She tapped at it a little more. Nope.

What was wrong with her husband's two-million-dollar app?

"The Encore, right?"

"I think so, yeah."

Rebecca went to Google: *Encore Boston Harbor is a luxury resort and casino located in Everett, Massachusetts . . .*

A hundred pieces that hadn't fit suddenly locked together.

She had the strange sensation she was falling down a well, or maybe more accurately falling *up*, falling away from the darkness that she hadn't even realized was all around her—

"Mom," Kira said. "You okay?"

Not a word to her, not a breath.

Not now. Not ever.

"Never better." She turned the phone to Kira. "It's in Everett, super-close."

"Can we?"

"Girls' night." Rebecca made herself smile. "I think we both deserve it."

35

Gaithersburg, Maryland

Room 310 of the Holiday Inn Gaithersburg had a not-quite-new wooden desk in the corner, a not-quite-ugly blue-patterned comforter on the bed. Brian sat on it, jiggling his legs. His blue North Face puffer beside him. He patted at its pockets like they held a pistol or a knife. But they didn't.

He'd figured Irlov might pat him down when they started meeting again, maybe bring a bodyguard. Nope. They'd gone back to work like Brian had never left. Like Barcelona had never happened.

Like Irlov figured Brian was fully domesticated, would never try anything.

Problem was, Irlov was right. Brian couldn't imagine going at the Russian. Dude had made his point. Had he ever.

The door swung open. Irlov stepped inside. He wore a wool knit cap and a short peacoat, a strangely stylish combination. All dressed up. Maybe he had a date with Eve coming up. The trouble that one had caused, and Brian's mouth still went dry when he thought about her.

Brian didn't ask how Irlov had gotten the key, how he could be sure they hadn't been followed. At this point if Irlov said he had chips implanted in every FBI agent in D.C., Brian would have believed him.

"Comrade." Since Brian's return to the SVR fold, Irlov had taken to using the word. Another way to remind Brian he was owned, now and forever.

"Colonel."

"I hope you don't mind if we begin right away."

The false, mincing courtesy was another affectation that irritated Brian. "Question. If I may."

Irlov turned his hands outward, the gesture of a lord tolerating an uppity serf.

"You know the bureau is chasing this great new Russian asset."

"Naturally. Enough operations fail, even the FBI notices."

"Any reason they would think he's inside the CIA?"

"Why do you ask this, Brian?" Now the hint of an accent slipped into Irlov's voice, proof the question had surprised him.

"Just that my wife has had more meetings than usual at Langley recently."

A lie. The reason he asked, the week before Becks had—more or less out of nowhere— mentioned the mole again. *Looks like Ames the sequel*, she'd said. Meaning Aldrich Ames, the CIA officer now locked in a federal penitentiary for betraying the agency to the Russians.

How is Ames these days? Brian said.

Oh, lots of time to regret his choices.

The way she'd said it bugged Brian. Even though he should have felt better hearing it. More accurately, *because* he should have felt better hearing it. It was so . . . convenient. Nothing for him to worry about, the bureau wasn't even looking at the NSA.

Plus, last week Becks had flown to Los Angeles, a quick thirty-six-hour work trip, out one morning, back the next night. She'd never had a case in Southern California before. And she'd been more than typically cryptic about it. And yeah, she'd been in the SoCal office. At one point she'd called him from there. Which was weird too, nobody used landlines anymore, almost like she was trying to prove where she was.

But why would Rebecca lie to him?

Only one reason, as far as he could see.

Funny, the *other* reason, the one that would have bugged most guys, that Becks was spending quality time with a special friend in the Los Angeles bureau, hadn't even occurred to him. And even now that he'd thought of it he couldn't worry about it. Because, really, if that's what she was doing, at this point good for her.

On the other hand, if Rebecca had somehow gotten onto him—

But he didn't want to tell Irlov he was worried about Becks. So he was lying to Irlov, too. Lying to his case officer about his wife possibly lying to him . . . he could see why people got caught. After a while you needed a spreadsheet just to keep the stories straight.

"Brian. Do you have any concerns about Rebecca?"

"None."

"Certain?"

"We're getting along great." True enough. All through the fall and winter they'd been hanging out a lot, and not just for sex. They even had a favorite show, *Stranger Things*.

"All right. Because, yes, we appreciate her information, but the NSA—you are the Tsar's heir."

"The what now?"

"I believe Americans say 'golden boy.' "

Brian laughed. Was Irlov suggesting the Russians would *kill* Rebecca if he asked? Brian didn't want to find out. Whatever was going on, whatever might be going on, lay between him and his wife.

"I understand. Colonel. Another question." He'd held off on asking too long. Now he wanted to know.

"You think my time is worthless." Irlov smiled, but his eyes didn't. *Ask quick.*

"At the end, with Kira—"

"Oh, Jacques had a buyer for her. We were going to sell her."

Brian rose half from the bed.

"Sit, please."

Brian sat, the voice in his head: *Good dog.*

"Did she ever tell you the full story? What she did, how she got out? We have a saying, you learn from those you live with. She learned fast.

She realized Rodrigo was weak, that if she could get him alone . . . maybe she'll tell you one day."

"But what if she hadn't?"

"The truth? Jacques would have fought with Rodrigo, shot him. Come on, Brian, we aren't monsters." Irlov smiled, a smile that said, *Or are we? You'll never know.* He looked at his watch, the gesture ostentatious, playtime is over. "So. BONITAS"—a new NSA effort to crack Russian naval communications—"How is that one?"

o   o

Fifteen minutes later Irlov walked out. Brian stayed still. Rooted to the bed.

He was stuck with Irlov. He couldn't kill Irlov.

But he could kill *someone*, couldn't he?

36

First stop, Las Vegas.

Rebecca caught the early-morning United nonstop from Dulles to LAX, walked through Terminal 7 looking for a flight to McCarran. By ten thirty she was in a cab on Tropicana Avenue, headed for Silver State Gaming Consultants, the company that had bought Brian's app.

Her ride stopped beside a two-story office building. Just down the block was the Pinball Hall of Fame. Only fitting. She was on tilt for sure. She handed the driver a twenty, stepped out. A check of state corporate records showed that Silver State Gaming had been in business for thirty years. Still, she wanted to see its offices for herself. Both to make sure it wasn't a shell and see if she could pick up what the bureau liked to call "soft intel."

○   ○

In retrospect maybe she should have asked more questions when Brian sold the app. But the deal had come together fast, and the idea someone would pay Brian seven figures for a successful application hardly seemed crazy. She'd read about Candy Crush, how the company that made it was worth billions.

When Brian showed her the app, she could see why people would want to use it and casinos would advertise on it. It had lots of tips about games and even directed users to the quote-unquote hottest slot machines. The play games it offered could easily be turned into real-money versions if the federal government legalized Internet gambling. *Like Hollywood*, Brian said. *Millions of scripts, but most of 'em suck. Write a good one, people notice.*

Plus the download numbers, twenty-one thousand, had seemed solid to her at the time. Brian said even more important was how quickly they were going up, how much people used the app after they downloaded it, was it what developers called "sticky"? *Truth is maybe I'd be better off waiting, but I don't want this thing to take over my life,* he said. *Two million, not bad.*

Even the fact the offer had come out of nowhere hadn't bothered her as much as maybe it should have. She knew Brian had gone to that casino industry conference. And her focus had been elsewhere. She'd been investigating two congressional aides for helping a Russian bank evade sanctions—not exactly espionage, but close. An important case.

Later, she'd wondered once or twice when he'd found the time to write it. When she wandered down to the basement at night, he was usually watching ESPN or Hong Kong martial arts movies. Then again he'd won that NSA challenge. He was smarter than he liked to admit. Maybe smarter than *she* liked to admit. His problem had always been his attitude.

She could see now she'd felt ashamed for doubting him in so many ways. She assumed his secrecy about the app only proved how lousy their marriage had become. She dropped her usual skepticism, played cheerleader instead. Soon enough the deal was done. Brian hired a lawyer in Vegas to review the contract, flew out two more times. Then they were rich. Rich enough, anyway. A million, with another million the next year. She never even met anyone at Silver State Gaming. *You can if you like but they're pretty boring*, Brian had said. *Not worth the flight.*

The contract did have one condition she found odd: A non-disclosure agreement. They weren't supposed to tell anyone that Brian had written Twenty-One. Brian said Silver State Gaming didn't want anyone to know that it hadn't created the app itself.

But don't you want credit, Rebecca said. *Maybe you'd get more business.*

Credit's fine. Two million dollars is better.

Okay, but you'll have to tell the NSA, and I have to tell the bureau. They'll want to know where the money's coming from.

I'll make sure the non-disclosure section has an exemption for our jobs, Brian said. And he had. They disclosed the deal on their financial disclosures, and neither the bureau nor the NSA seemed to care much. She'd only had one lie detector test since the sale—the polygraph examiners were notoriously overbooked. The examiner hadn't even asked about the money.

Otherwise, Rebecca had stuck to the non-disclosure agreement, which looked to her now like a way to help her forget the app. As in fact she had. She hadn't checked it in years. She had no idea if she ever would have again, had Kira not happened to mention the Encore.

Of course, the fact that the app had fallen into a state of quasi-disrepair didn't prove anything, not by itself. Maybe other companies had made their own, better versions. Maybe now that gamblers could bet online for real money in states like New Jersey, they had decided they trusted the big casino companies more.

But there were other clues. The size of the ransom demand, which now seemed less like coincidence than a coded message to Brian. The way he had frozen when she mentioned that fact to him on the train. His nervousness the first night before they knew anything was wrong, so unlike his personality. The way he'd insisted since the kidnapping that they shouldn't push the investigation.

Most of all, she'd always believed Jacques had targeted Kira, that the kidnapping wasn't random. But she'd never understood why, never really convinced herself Jacques planned to sell Kira. That version of the story was too tabloid. And the kidnappers had been so much better trained than a typical gang. Even their response to Kira's escape had been professional. They'd shut the operation down and vanished. No hard feelings, no grudges. Game over.

o　　　o

So. Her husband had pissed off the Russians, and they'd used Kira to send him a message. Why? She could guess.

One thing she knew about Brian, the man always wanted something for nothing, always thought he was better than the bargain he'd made.

Yeah, she had an inside line on this case.

She'd learned over the years to trust her gut on complicated investigations, the moment the answer came into focus. Sometimes intuition outran evidence. But she knew the danger of relying on intuition, too. When it was wrong, innocent people wound up in prison.

She needed proof. So here she was.

o　　　o

The office building on Tropicana Avenue was dated, seventies-style, white cladding and black glass. Silver State Gaming Consultants was in Suite 212. Rebecca marched up the stairs. *Just another investigation.* Lock down the facts, then move forward.

The office behind the wooden door of Suite 212 looked real enough. A secretary out front, a corridor that led to half a dozen offices. Voices on phones, *Okay, lunch, then,* the chatter of business. On the wall behind the secretary, framed photos from industry journals. *Silver State Gaming picked to market Henderson's first casino-brewery!* They mostly featured pictures of a ruddy, chubby guy in his sixties who wore a cowboy hat and an *I'd never cheat ya* grin. Rebecca had to be honest with herself: he couldn't have looked less like a Russian operative.

"Can I help you?" The secretary was in her fifties, bottle-blond hair and electric-blue fingernails.

Rebecca handed over a résumé, *Tracy McDaniel*, a freelance web designer looking for full-time work.

"Too bad you weren't here last month. We just hired somebody."

Rebecca smiled. "That is too bad. I'm Tracy. I mean, obviously."

"Linda."

"Nice to meet you. Just moved here from Buffalo, papering the walls. I know everybody says Indeed and LinkedIn are all you need, but I feel better getting out."

"Buffalo? Like New York?"

"Yeah, done with those winters. Mind if I ask, do your Web work in-house?"

Linda nodded. "Our specialty. We help independent casinos with marketing. The places the locals go, not the Strip."

Rebecca pointed at the framed photos.

"That's the man in charge? Carl James?"

Linda lowered her voice. "To be honest, we keep the photos up, but Mr. James had a stroke a few years back. He's in a wheelchair, doesn't come in much anymore. His daughter and son-in-law run the company. Joanna and Fred."

"Oh. Sorry to hear that. Anyway, if you could please pass along my résumé—"

"Will do."

o   o

She started with real estate records. Carl James turned out to be that rarest of birds, a Las Vegas lifer. He lived in a house valued at a million-five in a gated community in Summerlin, west of downtown. He was long divorced and had two kids, Joanna and Michael.

Michael's last known address was in Eugene, Oregon. He had cycled through jails since his early twenties, arrests for vandalism and petty theft and narcotics possession, the sad litany of a wasted life. Joanna had a marketing degree from the University of Southern California and three kids. She lived close to her father in a nine-hundred-thousand-dollar house. Silver State Gaming Consultants must make pretty good money. Its corporate records listed her as the company's treasurer.

Rebecca had a hard time seeing either Joanna or Michael as a Russian agent. As for Joanna's husband, she couldn't find much about him on the Internet. His name, Frank Brown, was all too common. Nothing popped. No arrests, no convictions. No LinkedIn, Facebook, or Instagram pages. No record of where he'd gone to college, no family members listed. And he stayed in the background at Silver State Gaming.

Frank was so boring he was interesting. For him she needed some law enforcement databases.

o   o

Back to Los Angeles. Lucky her, working counterintel meant she could show up at any bureau office and not face turf battles or sticky questions. She flashed her identification, asked for an empty office, a secure one.

Ten minutes later she was looking at Brown's driver's license records to find his date of birth—May 31, 1975—and make sure he shared Joanna's address.

Turned out he'd had a New York license before Nevada.

That fast she struck gold. 287 Brighton 4th Street, Apt 5G, Brooklyn, New York—

Brighton 4th Street?

As in Brighton Beach, also known as Little Odessa because so many Russians lived there? What exactly had Frank Brown been doing in Brighton Beach?

Then again, maybe he hadn't always been Frank Brown.

Name change records were public. In fact, New York State required them to be published. And there it was, in the *New York Law Journal*, the words dry and bureaucratic, hiding their secret in plain sight:

"Notice is hereby given that an order entered by the Civil Court, Kings County . . . grants me the right to assume the name of Frank Brown, the date of my birth is May 31, 1975, the place of my birth is Moscow, Russia, my present name is Fyodor Borodiev."

The place of my birth is Moscow, Russia . . .

o   o

How could he?

She was glad she had an office to herself. She found herself shaking her head at the absurdity of it. Follow that pronoun, Officer! Not Fyodor, she knew exactly how *Fyodor* could have done what he did. He'd gone to the courthouse, filled out the forms, just as someone in Moscow had told him to do, *We don't know when we'll need you, but one day we will, and when we do you'll be more useful to us if your name isn't Fyodor—*

Forget Fyodor.

He was Brian Unsworth, her lawfully wedded husband.

How could he have let Kira suffer? Knowing they'd taken her to punish him. Because he'd told them he wouldn't spy for them anymore unless they gave him more money, or more respect, or more women, whatever it was that his desperate insecurities demanded.

But he had. He'd let them steal his daughter. And if she hadn't freed herself—

Time to close the loop. Rebecca logged into the bank account she and Brian shared, scrolled until she found what she was looking for. The great advantage of investigating your spouse, so much less paperwork.

She reached for the phone, then stopped herself. She needed to have this conversation in person, which meant another trip to Las Vegas. It would have to wait for the morning.

Instead she called Brian. Let him see she really was in Los Angeles.

"Miss me?"

"The pain is unimaginable, Becks. You've been gone a full fifteen hours."

He sounded the same as ever.

How could he?

"I think we should move to California. It's seventy-eight degrees here."

"Trip good?"

"Yeah, I'm finding what I came for." *You have no idea.* "Anyway, see you tomorrow night, if you need me I'll be at the Hampton Inn in Hollywood, I'll text the number."

"Classy."

"Government rate. Kiss Tony for me."

"I will not."

"Love you."

"Love you too, babe."

Since the kidnapping, he called her *babe*. Since the kidnapping, they said they loved each other. They were closer than they'd been in years. Maybe she was wrong. Maybe this was just a bizarre coincidence.

Yeah right.

o   o

The next morning, 8:30 a.m., she stood outside the Bank of Nevada on South Durango Drive. The wire transfer to the bank account she shared with Brian had come from this branch. She carried a national security letter asking for the financial records of Silver State Gaming Consultants.

Now she *was* breaking the law, no way around it. She had never before abused her power as an agent this way, never come close to crossing a legal line like this. The letter was simple enough, no different from a dozen others she'd written. It ordered the bank to provide her with access to Silver State Gaming's accounts: *"I certify that the information sought is relevant to an authorized investigation to protect against international terrorism or clandestine intelligence operations . . ."*

Honestly, she didn't love using national security letters. The FBI really should come up with a warrant before poking around in financial or email records that belonged to Americans. But the Justice Department had argued that because the records related to internationally focused investigations, they didn't deserve full constitutional protection. In legalese, national security letters were known as "administrative subpoenas." Just like a regular subpoena, without the pesky need to convince an independent federal judge that it was necessary.

Even better—or worse, from the point of view of constitutional protections and privacy—the letters forbade the company that had received them *from disclosing their existence* to the target. In other words, the person being investigated didn't even have a chance to respond.

Of course, real warrants worked the same way—telling a criminal target his house or business was about to be searched obviously didn't make sense. *Again, though, a judge had signed those warrants*, after a law enforcement agency presented probable cause of a crime. That standard didn't apply here. The FBI simply had to "certify" that what it was looking for might be "relevant."

Regardless, the letters were constitutional, or so friendly federal judges had agreed. The bureau used them all the time. In truth, Rebecca could have persuaded the FBI lawyers who oversaw them to sign off on this one. By the standards of national security letters, the fact that a guy born in Russia had changed his name and funneled two million dollars to a National Security Agency employee was plenty.

Only problem was that Rebecca couldn't ask. For the first time in her career, she was running an off-the-books investigation. Thus every word in the letter was correct, except one: *authorized.*

Still, she should be safe. The letter specifically prohibited anyone at Bank of Nevada from disclosing its existence. No one would ever find out. And as long as no one ever found out . . .

She wondered how many people she'd arrested had told themselves the same story.

○   ○

The big blue Bank of Nevada logo gave the branch a slightly glitzy look. Maybe people here subconsciously associated money with casinos, needed a reason to stick cash in the bank.

Inside, though, the branch looked like any other. Rebecca flashed her identification to the woman behind the counter. "The manager, please." The teller picked up her phone. An FBI badge carried even more weight in a bank than most places.

The manager was in her early thirties. She wore a trim gray suit, a less fancy version of Rebecca's Theory set. Light makeup. A no-nonsense haircut. A bit younger than Rebecca expected. Rebecca didn't know if her age would make her easier to impress or more likely to push back.

"Rebecca Unsworth." She flashed her badge.

"Liz Crandall." The manager looked around. "Is your partner outside?"

Smart question. Crandall knew FBI agents usually worked in pairs. Her willingness to question Rebecca from the first suggested she might not accept the letter on faith. Rebecca would need to take control of this conversation quickly.

"No partner. I'm here from D.C. Can we speak in private, Ms. Crandall?"

Crandall's office was next to the entrance to the vault. No personal pictures, not even a motivational poster. All business.

Rebecca closed the door as they entered, pulled the letter from her briefcase. Making Crandall feel like a partner would be the play. "Don't know if you've seen anything like this before. Most people haven't. It's called a national security letter. We use them when we're investigating terrorism or espionage, targets with a non-US focus."

"This is about terrorism?" Crandall's voice rose slightly on the last word.

"I can't tell you more than what's in the letter. I will say if you call D.C., they'll tell you I run the Russia counterintelligence desk."

"Counterintelligence. Like spying?"

"Espionage, yes."

Finally, Crandall seemed impressed. She took the letter, read it slowly. When she was done, Rebecca reached for it. Crandall hesitated.

"Shouldn't I hold on to it?"

"Ms. Crandall, there are two ways to do this. You have every right to keep it, and in that case I expect you'll want to send a copy to your headquarters, lawyers, et cetera. And Bank of Nevada has every right to contest this letter on behalf of Silver State. Though they'd probably want to hire outside counsel, as these are specialized cases. To be honest, I'm not even sure there's a lawyer in Las Vegas who's handled one. It's an expensive process. Also slow. And this investigation is developing rapidly" — true enough — "which is why I'm here."

"I'm sorry, I don't follow."

"A delay could harm the investigation. The other possibility, we simply look right now."

"You mean I—"

Crandall broke off.

"Yes, just pull up the file. I will tell you this, I am looking for something specific, and it shouldn't take long to find if it's there."

"Can I see your ID again?"

The room seemed hotter and colder at once. Was this how the folks Rebecca went after felt when they knew they'd screwed up? But she could hardly take off, the branch had cameras in every corner. She handed over her identification.

"Mind if I ask the main number? For the FBI in Washington?"

"202-324-3000."

Crandall punched it in.

"Yes, I'm looking for the counterintelligence division— Sure, I can hold."

What are you doing?

The silence must have lasted only a few seconds, but it felt far longer.

"Yes, I'd like to talk to someone who works there, Rebecca Unsworth." Pause. "She's not? I don't suppose you can tell me— No, I understand." A long pause. "No, no, it has to be her. Does she have voice mail? Thanks."

Crandall hit the speaker button, and after a few seconds of silence Rebecca heard her own voice: *You've reached Rebecca Unsworth, please leave a message—*

Crandall hung up.

"Wanted to be sure I wasn't an imposter?"

Crandall shrugged, *Better safe than sorry.*

"Bold. What if I had been?" Rebecca smiled. "You should come work for us."

"Come on, I'll pull the records, give you some privacy so you can check what you need."

o   o

An hour later Rebecca was back at McCarran, flashing her badge to skip the endless security line. Working for the bureau had a few privileges.

What she'd found wasn't exactly what she'd expected, but it was enough.

In the months leading up to the two million-dollar transfers, the Silver State Gaming account received dozens of cash deposits between twenty and seventy thousand dollars each. In all, they had totaled $2.9 million.

Are cash deposits unusual? she'd asked Crandall afterward.

Not really. It's Vegas. Might be as simple as the guy plays a high-stakes poker game. I mean, we tell them we're going to report the deposits, and we do. But they aren't illegal. After that, it's between them and the IRS.

Which explained the extra nine hundred thousand. The Russians had wanted the payment to be odorless start to finish. They could hardly expect Frank Brown to be stuck paying taxes on money he was just passing along.

Two-point-nine million dollars. Far more than Rebecca had ever heard of the Russians paying anyone else. But then Bri was uniquely well-positioned, wasn't he? Not only did he work for the most secretive, highest-value unit at the NSA, his wife ran counterintel against them.

She found an empty chair and watched the tourists waddle by, muttering about craps and the slots and blackjack. How they should have quit when they were ahead.

You have no idea.

No wonder the Russians had gone to such lengths to punish Brian, to force him back to work. But once Kira was kidnapped . . .

He could have saved her. As soon as he told Rebecca, the FBI would have told the SVR, *Let her go or reap the whirlwind.* They would have meant it, too. And the SVR would have blamed a rogue team and let Kira walk in five minutes. No way would they have wanted that fight.

But Brian would have paid the price. He'd be sharing a cellblock with Aldrich Ames the rest of his life.

Instead he'd kept his mouth shut. Probably he'd gone to the Russians instead, promised to go back to work if they cut her loose. Which might explain how Kira had gotten out of that closet. Though Rebecca still wasn't sure, maybe Kira had taken Rodrigo down all by herself—

What mattered, all that mattered: Brian had let Kira swing when he could have saved her.

The Russians must have figured he would, too. Figured when the chips were down he would look out for himself first.

She could almost forgive her husband for betraying his country. And her. Because she knew now, every question he asked her about her work was strategic, information for his paymasters. Maybe every touch and kiss and smile too. All to take her secrets.

She could almost forgive him everything he'd done.

Not really, but she could pretend she might.

But she could never forgive him for betraying their daughter.

He had to pay. She *wanted* him to pay.

o   o

So what now?

Option A: Go to the director and the general counsel this very day, tell them what she knew. Let the bureau take over. The legally correct choice. The morally correct choice. What she'd been trained to do.

Only her career would be over. Not just because she'd forever be famous as the counterintel officer too dumb to have known her husband was a Russian spy. But because of what she'd done today. Any investigation would go straight through Silver State Gaming and the Bank of Nevada, and Liz Crandall was not likely to forget this morning's chat.

Ahh but if Crandall disappeared—Rebecca laughed loudly enough that a guy wearing a Bellagio T-shirt stared at her. She really was thinking like a perp. Witness in the way? Just get rid of her. No problem that another crime couldn't fix.

So yeah, telling the FBI would be an instant career-ender.

Maybe she could live with that humiliation. Maybe she even deserved it. But she couldn't live with what the truth would do to Kira. Because Kira would put the pieces together too, the fact that she'd been taken to punish Brian.

Even worse, Kira wouldn't think of herself anymore as a survivor who had escaped on her own. She would assume Brian had cut some deal to get her out. Rebecca was almost sure the main reason Kira had put her life back together so fast was because her escape had given her back her *agency*, made her the hero of the story, not a victim. Instead, she'd just be the daughter of a traitor.

Option A: not so great.

Option B: Keep her mouth shut for now. In a year or two, tip the NSA anonymously. Her career would still be over, of course. And in the meantime Brian would keep doing damage. And after he was arrested Kira would probably still put the pieces together.

Option B, maybe even worse than Option A.

Option C: Keep her mouth shut. Forever. Which would be fine. Except that Brian would keep on selling out his country to the Russians. Worse, Rebecca would be complicit. Worse—*worser*, was worser even a *word?*—if he ever did get caught, and the investigators talked to Liz Crandall, they'd realize Rebecca had known. Hey, maybe she and Bri wind up sharing a cell.

Option C, a new low.

Which left Option D. Which was so foreign to her she could think of it only in flashes, not words, much less complete sentences, much less a plan.

The father of her children. Her husband. The only man she'd been with for more than twenty years.

Kill him.

The thought went against everything she knew.

And she couldn't imagine murdering anyone in cold blood. Self-defense, him or me, okay, maybe. But premeditated murder?

Not even Brian, not even now.

Yeah, put a pin in Option D.

There had to be another way. An Option E. But she couldn't think of one.

o   o

She flew back to Los Angeles, and then she flew home, and she spent the next ten days in a haze.

She told Brian the FBI was looking for the Russian mole at the CIA, just to see what he'd say. Probably a mistake. Though he didn't seem to care much. She thought about putting a tracker on his car.

Snooping software on his phone or computer was definitely out, he'd find it before she even finished installing it.

Mainly she waited, hoping another alternative would suggest itself. None did. Paralysis by analysis. For the first time in her life she understood why people did *nothing* at all in the face of bad news, how they ignored the foreclosure letter from the bank, the glassine envelope in their kid's backpack, the call from the doctor, *We really need to talk about those biopsy results.*

How about not, how about we just hope they go away?

Then Brian suggested the trip.

37

Chevy Chase

Winter was almost over now. Days longer, sun chasing away the cold. Spring coming.

In Brian's mind, a seed taking purchase. Laying down roots.

A wooden box riding a conveyor belt into a crematorium. Hot enough to burn any sin.

The body of his wife inside.

He didn't know what Becks knew. Or if she knew anything. They hadn't talked much the last couple of weeks. She'd been busy. Working three big cases, she said. Awfully coincidental. Then again anyone with a pulse knew the Russians were making trouble these days.

If he had to bet, he'd bet she had no idea. Mainly because he didn't think she could act well enough to fool him. Could she still talk to him? Sleep next to him? *Fuck* him? Back in Houston, he'd sniffed out her little quasi-fling with the ranger right quick.

Though in Birmingham, she'd played the fat real estate guy, Draymond, played him all the way to the federal penitentiary. Becks was a straight shooter. Until she wasn't. So yeah, he'd bet she didn't know. But the bet wasn't a lock. More of a coin flip. He couldn't risk his life on a coin flip.

And he was flat-out tired of not knowing, having no way to find out. If she was on to him, anything he asked her might help her. He'd gone over his car, his phone, his laptop. All clean. Then again Becks must know better than to try to track his phone or laptop.

It wasn't fair, what she'd done to him.

He didn't feel guilty. No way, no how. He hadn't done anything all that bad. Kira had gone through a couple of hard days, sure, but she'd come out the other side. Maybe it had even done her some good. Toughened her up, given her an edge over the average twenty-year-old snowflake at Tufts.

Nah, he didn't feel guilty. He just wanted to be rid of his wife.

But he had to make sure he did it clean. Not much point to beating an espionage rap and getting stung for murder. The cell would look the same either way.

And a clean murder wasn't so easy. Especially with Becks. The bureau would look hard at anything like a mugging. Poison was super high-risk. What if the cops talked to the FBI and decided they wanted an autopsy?

Maybe a fire? A fire had worked out for Jacques in Spain. Tough to get evidence from charcoal. Kill Becks, set fire to the house. But Chevy Chase wasn't the middle of nowhere. Probably a fire would get put out too quick. He couldn't take the chance.

He needed something better. Something he could count on.

No witnesses.

No cops stumbling onto the scene.

No physical evidence.

No body, or a body in such terrible shape that it had no secrets to give.

No murder for hire, that idea never ever worked. *I'm gonna give you money to kill my wife. Promise you're not a cop, mmmkay?*

No chance for Becks to draw on him. A problem, considering that she carried her nine on her hip most of the time they weren't home. He could ask her to take it off, sure, but he'd need a decent reason.

An accident.

Yeah, an accident would be best. Plus, Kira and Tony had been through enough. Especially Kira. For her sake, he needed to be sure she accepted what had happened. *Poor Becks, poor poor Becks.* The story couldn't just satisfy the cops. It had to be airtight.

A plausible accident. A story that made sense. Not, Becks was wandering around East Baltimore at 2 a.m. Not, Becks and I went for a cliffside walk in Glacier National Park. Even though it was raining. Not, Becks decided she'd take her BMW up to 120 on the Beltway last night, hey, why not?

Yeah, killing your wife clean wasn't as easy as it looked.

But it was just a puzzle, after all. And he was good at puzzles. It had to have a solution.

Sure enough he found it.

He had the perfect excuse, too. Their twenty-first anniversary. A chance to get away. Put the kidnapping behind them. Go back to an island they hadn't visited since she was in law school and he was a guy with a rusted pickup truck and a two-minute refractory period.

o   o

"Let's go to St. Barts," he said. "A second honeymoon. Decompress. Rent a boat for a couple of nights. No crew, just you and me. We can hang out—"

"Hang out," Becks said.

"Mmm-hmm, hang out. We're still pretty good at that."

"You're not scared to leave Kira?"

"The opposite. It proves we trust her, we're okay with not talking to her for a couple of days."

"I don't know."

"Think about it this way. It'll be a way to wash off what happened in Spain. We deserve a happy anniversary. Twenty-one years together. Practically half our lives."

"Twenty-one years," Becks said. "Can't believe it."

"Neither can I, babe. Neither can I."

38

St. Barts

The hotel was perfect. The food was perfect. The weather was perfect.

The sex was . . . weirdly enough . . . perfect.

The Fleur de Lis, where they'd stayed twenty-one years before for their honeymoon, had closed. But early April wasn't peak season, and Brian found them a deal at one of the island's fanciest resorts. Their villa had a private terrace overlooking the white sand and blue-green sea of St. Jean Bay. The most beautiful place Rebecca had ever seen. If water could be soft, this water was.

o   o

For two days they hardly left their room.

When he reached for her on the third morning, she shook her head. "I can't. I haven't been this sore in a really long time."

In the bathroom she stared herself down, her frown lines, gray roots, the little stress chip in her top right front tooth. But their sex had made her young. Temporarily.

How many orgasms had she had with him over the years? Thousands, surely. Do the math. Ten thousand? Couldn't be that many.

That would be more than one a day. Two thousand, three, four? So many bursts of pleasure, so many little deaths. Adding up to nothing at all. Even his were more useful. For him they carried his seed.

Yet these two days reminded her of the power of sex. Especially good sex. It might not mean anything in the long run. But in the moment it was *everything*. They'd been tender to each other. They'd cuddled and spooned. They'd watched the sky turn pink from their terrace. Not saying a word, just being present. The afterglow was real. The halo.

Sex had bound them. Then children, its fruit.

What bound them now?

Lies. Did he know that she knew? He couldn't; she'd covered her tracks, hadn't written anything down. But he could suspect. He *would* suspect. He'd be a fool not to suspect, and he wasn't a fool.

o   o

He opened the bathroom door. He looked *good*. His arms were big. Like he'd been working out.

Getting ready for something.

Lucky for her, she'd been working out too.

She ran her hands over his biceps.

"Babe. I'm going to rent the boat. I'm thinking maybe get one with a decent-sized cabin. So if we spend the night on the water it won't be a problem."

"Stay out for the night? Considering what we're paying for this room."

"Might be fun. Blast from the past."

o   o

A few minutes later she was showered, dressed, alone on the terrace. A warm subtropical breeze tickled her wet hair.

A boat ride, then.

Rebecca had never actually been involved in a water case. The local cops or state police handled those, sometimes with the Coast Guard. The FBI involved itself only in exceptional situations. Still, she knew investigating accidents at sea was notoriously difficult. No witnesses except fish. Not much physical evidence. Bodies disappeared. When they didn't, they were waterlogged, in bad shape. Even fires left more evidence. At least arson investigators could usually tell if they'd been set on purpose.

Still. Twenty-one years ago they had rented a cruiser, spent a night on the water. Slow, passionate sex as the stars swam slowly overhead. No one to hear her, so she could give full voice to her pleasure. It was possible she'd never felt more connected to Brian than she had on that boat. She thought she'd gotten pregnant with Kira that night. Her body had felt different even the next morning. Richer. Fuller. Something new in her. How could she know? And yet she *had*. She'd told Brian but he'd always seemed skeptical. Pointless to try to explain to a man, pregnancy was something you had to live.

Maybe Brian remembered too. Maybe he wanted to bring them together. Maybe he thought he could survive forever as a Russian spy and as a husband and father, that now that they had Kira back equilibrium had been restored.

Maybe.

Back inside the room. This was the first time he'd left her alone, the first time either had left the room without the other. She went to his suitcase, which wasn't a suitcase at all. He still traveled with the battered soft-sided blue bag he had used for a decade or more. Brian wasn't a clotheshorse and he wasn't a snob. When he found something that worked for him—a pair of sneakers, a haircut, a bag—he stuck with it.

Maybe his loyalty to his possessions substituted for love of other human beings.

The bag was in the closet along with her Tumi suitcase. She felt through it. Mostly empty. A couple of novels—John Sandford, the hard-boiled thrillers he liked these days—and a navigational guide to St. Barts and the eastern Caribbean. No knife, no Taser, no pistol, no handcuffs or gloves. Really, what had she expected? Then, tucked in the corner, she felt a plastic bag, something thick and flat inside.

She pulled it out.

A black bag, taped to conceal a bundle. She pushed at it. No give. But when she twisted the ends they flexed. She wondered if she needed to tear it open to be sure about what was inside, decided not to bother.

What object with these physical characteristics could this bag be hiding? Could it be . . . a bundle of US currency?

She turned the bag over in her hands, feeling its heft. How much money? If the bills were hundreds, maybe twenty or thirty thousand in all. She had to assume they were. Otherwise why go to such lengths to hide them? And where had he come up with them? They had a joint bank account. No way could he have taken out that much money without her knowing.

Even more important, *why* so much? He couldn't need it to pay for the trip. The resort preferred credit cards, and paying in advance. They'd talked about going to the casinos on St. Martin. But if he planned to pay thousand-dollar-a-hand blackjack, or whatever, he'd have to do it when she wasn't watching.

Yet thirty thousand dollars wasn't thirty million. It wasn't like Brian could buy a new life with it. Maybe . . . an insurance policy? A way to make unexpected problems disappear? And give him a head start if he had to run.

Whatever the money was for, it wasn't reassuring.

She tossed the bundle in the bag, stuffed the bag in the closet, went to his dresser. Underwear and socks in the top drawer, the hipster T-shirts and raggedy shorts he preferred in the second. He took care folding his clothes. A subtle rebuke to her; her suits and skirts were expensive and she had to admit she didn't always take the best care of them, didn't always hang them when she came home. Then again he hadn't been the one working twelve-hour days, was he?

She sorted through the undies and socks. Nothing. She ran her hands through his T-shirts, his shorts.

Felt plastic.

She pulled it out. A tiny orange bottle, no label. When she unscrewed the cap and flipped its contents into her palm, she saw the pills weren't pills at all. They were tiny white bars, sectioned in halves. Xanax bars. Xanax was a prescription benzodiazepine, a cousin of Valium.

She counted the bars in her hand, six . . . seven . . . eight.

Benzodiazepines were powerful drugs. Two two-milligram Xanax bars would get an average adult seriously high. In combination with an opioid or alcohol, benzos could kill. By themselves, they didn't depress breathing enough to be lethal except with a massive overdose. Rebecca didn't think eight bars would be enough to kill her. But they would knock her out for sure.

Thirty K in cash and sixteen milligrams of Xanax. Curiouser and curiouser.

How long could she wait? How clear would the signals have to be? For now she was still paralyzed. She was operating under strict rules of engagement. Until she *knew* he planned to hurt her, she couldn't do anything except watch and wait.

She wondered if her rules would get her killed.

So be it. She had never thought of herself as a martyr, but she couldn't make herself move first.

She heard steps on the path that led to the villa, Brian whistling tunelessly. She tilted the bars from her palm back into the bottle. One slipped onto the floor, visible against the polished wood. She nudged it under the dresser, stuffed the bottle back in the drawer. Hoping she hadn't ruffled dear hubby's T-shirts too much, hoping he hadn't counted his benzos.

She popped open the privacy lock just as he reached it, realizing how stupid she'd been to lock it in place. The door swung open and there he stood. His eyebrows rose when he saw her.

"I thought maybe I'd get a massage." She kissed him. "Since I'm so sore."

"I got us a boat. For tomorrow."

"I can't wait."

39

Caribbean Sea, east of St. Barts

The islands of the Caribbean take a hard right turn just east of Saint
Barthélemy. Puerto Rico, Cuba, and Jamaica lay to the west, nearer
Florida. To the south, a chain of smaller islands runs to Trinidad, just
off the coast of South America.

So as Brian steered the Chris-Craft east, he was moving them
toward the hinge of the turn, away from the calmer waters of the
Caribbean and toward the Atlantic Ocean. The change was gradual.
Even in early spring the Atlantic was fairly calm. They were still a
couple of months from hurricane season.

Still, mile by mile, the waters were slowly becoming choppier, less
blue. Cooler. Less friendly.

Brian wondered if Becks had noticed.

Then again, the boat they were on was distracting. Brian had
splurged to rent a Chris-Craft Launch 36, four years old but still a
beautiful ride, teak and leather and chrome, all the creature comforts
four hundred thousand dollars could buy. Plus a super-modern navi-
gation system. The Chris-Craft had been built more for comfort than
hard-core open-water cruising. Its sun pad—a pair of recliners between
windshield and prow—didn't exactly scream North Atlantic in January.

Still, the boat was more than capable of handling the Caribbean, especially on a sunny April afternoon, the biggest obstacle a light westerly breeze. The cruiser had a kitchen too, so they could boil the lobsters Becks had picked up in Gustavia. And a small stateroom. In case they decided to stay out overnight.

Brian was sure he would. Becks, not so much.

Maybe when she was gone he'd come back here and give the Chris-Craft another spin. Maybe Irlov would even give him another weekend with Eve if he was a good boy.

Eve wouldn't mind. Eve did what Irlov said. So did Brian.

When Becks was gone.

Funny. He was in such a good mood. He already missed his wife, though she wasn't even gone. The last few days had reminded him what he liked about her. Her confidence. Her appetites, sexual and otherwise. For the first time in years, maybe since Charlottesville, work wasn't consuming her.

He realized now, maybe Becks should never have had kids. Maybe she'd never been able to balance being a mom with being an FBI agent. Maybe she'd been jealous of the time he spent with Kira and Tony when they were little. Anyway, she'd taken her frustration out on him.

But being here had freed her, at least for a few days.

Good for her. Her last memories would be happy ones. He'd make sure to tell the kids how much fun she'd had.

The kids were really the only reason he'd considered hesitating. But they were old enough now to know their parents wouldn't live forever. He'd always been more important to them than Becks anyway. They'd bounce back. Plus, after what Kira had gone through last year . . .

No. This was the right choice, he was sure.

o   o

Three p.m. and they were thirty miles east of St. Barts, heading east at about nine knots. Nice and easy. With GPS, radar, sonar, and electronic depth charts, these high-end cruisers could practically steer themselves. In fact, drop the *practically*. They could. When Brian decided to take the boat back to Gustavia, he could simply find it on the nav. The Chris-Craft would do the rest, directing him where to go and how to get there. He could even put the boat on autopilot and let it steer.

The calm spring water and the security the cruiser's automated systems offered were the real reason he'd been able to rent it so easily, after taking only a four-hour training class the day before. Basically, he promised he wouldn't take it into the Atlantic and that he'd let the autopilot handle the harbor water, the only dangerous part. Like cars, ships these days only pretended the human beings at their helms were in charge. The fact he was paying three thousand dollars to rent it for a day, and another twenty-five hundred if he kept it overnight, probably helped too.

Naturally he hadn't told Becks how much he'd paid. She would have wondered why he was spending so much. She might even have insisted on a smaller cruiser. And he wanted the biggest one he could find, the one that would handle the chop the best.

The rougher the waves, the browner the water, the better.

They'd seen plenty of other boats around St. Barts. But in the last hour the waters around them had emptied out. No surprise. Cruisers here hopped island to island, heading southeast from St. Barts to Antigua, avoiding these rougher seas. The big cargo ships ran well to the north, in the deep waters of the Atlantic. Now they could see only a couple of other ships. The closest was a massive yacht maybe a mile south. But it was moving fast, twenty-five knots, running west, away from them. Brian had hoped they'd achieve complete solitude, no other boats in sight, just them and the fish. He saw now that he wouldn't necessarily be able to count on that level of privacy. No matter. As long as no other ships were within a couple of miles, he'd be fine.

o ・ o

Becks had gone downstairs to change. She came back wearing a simple black one-piece whose high-cut waist flattered her. Her legs were long and lean and strong. She looked pretty good for a woman well into her forties. She looked pretty good period. At the mall, wherever, he sometimes caught guys his age checking her out. He could almost read their minds, *How come my wife can't keep it together like yours?*

She stood behind him, wrapped her arms around him, rested her head against his shoulder. She still fit him nicely.

Don't get mushy now, Bri.

"How much farther, Papa Smurf? Is it much farther?"

"Not far now."

"We going anywhere in particular?"

He shook his head. "I just feel like being alone. Having the whole world to ourselves."

"Just you and me and a bottle of Viagra."

"You say that like it's a bad thing."

She nuzzled his neck.

He felt himself stirring, pulled away. "I think it's time for the you-know-what."

"I'm not sure I do."

"Watch the helm." Not that there was much to do, cruising at this speed in open water.

He went downstairs, came back with a bottle of Dom Pérignon he'd hidden in the back of the fridge, waved her out onto the deck.

She raised her eyebrows, *Really?*

"Planning to sell another app?"

"Who knows when we'll get to do something like this again. You say I don't spend money, don't know how to live . . ." She'd said this more than once during the lean years, when he'd complained about her spending.

"Just an excuse for all the junk I bought."

He felt a little flash of something. Not guilt, but *something*. Funny that she'd finally admitted the truth. She never would have said that even a couple of years ago. Maybe Kira's kidnapping had changed her more than he realized.

Too late now.

"Anyway, I wanted to go all out this week. Why not? We have good jobs, it's not like your shop or mine is ever going to run out of cash, the almighty United States gummit—"

"Okay, okay. Open sesame."

He twisted the cork, sent it flying into the sea. Took a swig, pure liquid joy, gold and cold and sharp. Handed her the bottle. She drank deep too.

"Oh, good stuff." She wiped her mouth with the back of her hand. Lusty. "Shouldn't we have glasses?"

"Why?"

"To toast."

"Then toast. We don't need glasses."

"Amen." She raised the bottle. "To our incredible children, Bri. And especially to Kira. Who got herself out of that rathole. All by herself."

Maybe. "Nice toast. Let's get intoxicated."

"Big word for drunk."

"Drunkish. Nobody's getting seasick as long as I'm captain." She took another swig. "Would you still fuck me drunk?"

"I might get the spins." He took the bottle. "Oh, if *you're* drunk. If you ask nicely, maybe." He raised it over his mouth, tilted it nearly sideways and let the liquid spill. Into his mouth and down his chin.

"Careful with that."

"Don't worry, we've got another." Brian was enjoying himself now.

o   o

Brian's plan: They'd finish this bottle, pop the second. He wouldn't push too hard. He didn't have to. He had seventy, eighty pounds on her. And Becks wasn't much of a drinker. Rarely did she have more than a glass of wine at dinner. Even if they split the bottles evenly she'd be far drunker than he was. And he wasn't planning to split them evenly. He'd just poured a lot of his second drink on the deck with a grin on his face. He probably wouldn't even need the Xanax, but if he saw a chance he'd crush a couple of pills and get them into the second bottle near the end. Just to be sure. They were slightly bitter, but they were tiny too. The champagne would hide the taste. And she'd be good and lit by then. Even if she noticed she wouldn't care.

So, good. They'd get drunk. They'd probably screw. One last roll, for old time's sake. *Should old acquaintance be forgot* . . . He wasn't going to force that either, but he didn't think he'd have to. Ideally on the front deck, the sexy sun pad, under the stars, no one to see.

All this done by eight thirty. Maybe nine. Then he'd let her get sleepy for a few minutes. A postcoital cuddle. Then he'd get up, look around, make sure no boats or planes were close. And he'd pick her up and toss her overboard.

If the water had been a little cooler, he could simply have cruised off, let nature take its course. But the Caribbean was around eighty degrees, high enough that hypothermia wouldn't kill Becks. She was in pretty good shape, too. She would last at least a day, maybe two, until exhaustion and thirst or an unlucky encounter with a shark took care of her. He couldn't risk that, not with boats close enough for her to see them, swim for their lights.

A problem with an easy solution. He'd jump down after her, take care of business himself.

Becks had been a decent swimmer back in the day. But like most adults she hadn't swum much since she was a kid. Not Brian. He'd been practicing the last month, going every day. Unfortunately the Planet Fitness didn't have a pool, so he'd had to join a new gym. Maybe the cops would wonder about it if they bothered to look that hard. But they probably wouldn't. And if they did he had a solid excuse, he'd known they were coming down here and wanted to practice swimming.

Anyway. In they'd go. He didn't have to strangle her, didn't have to hurt her. He just had to grab her shoulders and hold her down. She'd be drunk, confused, panicked. Begging for breath. Wondering why he wasn't helping. It wouldn't take long. Those stunts where magicians lasted five minutes underwater happened in perfect conditions. And the guys barely moved. Becks would be fighting, tearing through the oxygen in her lungs. After thirty seconds she would barely have any struggle left. After a minute she'd already be fading to black. He just needed to make sure he remembered to breathe himself.

The best part, he knew she didn't have a gun on her. She didn't even have pepper spray. Why would she? She was completely defenseless.

Not such a bad way to die. After the panic passed the end would be painless. The urge to breathe would overcome her, she'd open her mouth, her lungs would fill with water. Down she'd go. He doubted she would even lay a bruise on him. If she did he had an excuse; he'd banged himself up jumping off the boat during the day. Who could tell? The open ocean was about the last camera-free place left. The Chris-Craft didn't have any cameras, either. He'd checked.

o   o

She took another long drink from the bottle, handed it back.

"Let me go boil the lobsters, Captain."

"Sure you can handle it?" All these years, she'd never learned to cook. Cooking was beneath her.

"Boiling water? And dumping in pathetic crustaceans with rubber bands around their claws?"

She disappeared downstairs.

o   o

Down she'd sink. Bye-bye, sweetheart. Back to the boat for him. He'd putter south-southwest for an hour or so. Stop again. Take a nap. A couple of hours.

When he woke up, after midnight, a little drunk, a little confused, *Where's Rebecca?*

He'd search the boat. *Rebecca! Becks!*

They stopped here, they were drunk, decided to take a break before heading south for Antigua. Sex on the deck. He wanted to go inside. She wanted to lie under the stars. Maybe a night swim. He argued with her, *No way, we're wasted, let's go to bed.*

But once Becks has an idea in her head, well—

Oh God, she's gone. Just gone.

He grabbed a life jacket and jumped off the boat to swim for her. But he couldn't see anything, and he didn't even know how long it'd been, he was asleep for hours . . .

Out went the distress call.

As long as he stuck to the story they couldn't beat him. They could wonder, but they couldn't beat him. Her body might not turn up at all. Plenty of hungry sharks in these waters. And even if it did, what would the physical evidence show? That she drowned? Big shock. The nav system would back the story.

He'd be overcome with grief, blaming himself, he should have made sure Becks came downstairs. But he was too drunk, and he wanted to sleep, and he figured she'd come to bed. *This was supposed to be the fun trip, the safe trip, make up for last year, the close call. We escaped, we thought we were free, now this—*

Don't lay it on too thick. Just thick enough.

Yeah, he can see it. Start to finish. Ending with him walking out of the interview room and into the subtropical sun. Guilt his only punishment.

But then guilt's never been a problem for him.

o   o

The sun was already west, behind them. Five p.m. now. In four hours, less, he'd be free. A quarter-turn of the Earth. Not even one-one-thousandth of a year.

He could hardly wait.

From the kitchen he heard a curse, a yelp. Almost a scream.

"You okay, babe?"

"First-aid kit in the stateroom, right?"

"You don't sound okay."

A few minutes later she limped out, a big bandage around her thigh.

"I literally cannot even boil water."

"Oh Becks."

"Stupid lobsters." She poked at the bandage, winced a little.

"Should we head back?" As soon as he said it he regretted the words. What if she said yes?

But she shook her head. "It's fine. I put ointment on it. It's big but not deep."

"Long as you can still drink."

She nodded.

"You are almost too good to be true."

"You finally noticed."

"Let me cook. Can you handle it up here? Maybe a half hour more this heading and then we can either turn south or just cut the engine and drift a bit, get ready for the sunset."

"Of course."

He stepped aside. "The helm is yours."

"Bri?"

"Yeah?"

"I love you."

"Love you too."

40

Caribbean Sea

The boat was at rest.

The sky rich with stars, the whole galaxy unfolding.

Whatever happened tonight, she needed to remember just how unimportant she was. How unimportant her life was, in the grand scheme. As long as the kids were safe.

Not that she wanted to die. She didn't. She had no intention of dying. But she knew she might. She wasn't sure what Brian was planning. But she saw the position he had put her in. The slow, steady moves he'd made. Separating her from her gun. From witnesses. From police. Anyone who could help, anyone at all. Getting her drunk.

Though she wasn't quite as drunk as she seemed. She'd had her share of the first bottle, but since he opened the second she'd only nursed a glass. She was afraid of getting dehydrated because of her leg, she told him. He joked a couple of times about her not keeping up, but he didn't push.

He stopped the Chris-Craft in time for them to watch the sun disappear over the horizon, the sky above turning from blue to black. Somehow, without talking it over, they decided to stay out for the night. He finished making dinner, cracked the lobsters, tossed a salad.

413

She set the table, poured them water and champagne. The low companionable work of marriage. Maybe if she'd been home for more dinners. Maybe they would have been stronger together, loved each other more. Maybe Brian wouldn't have grown so lost.

Or maybe not. Maybe he was who he was. Maybe they would just have bored each other sooner. Nothing more useless than trying to guess how a mythical past might change an impossible future. Becks knew she wasn't much of a romantic. Even before she joined the FBI, she'd never been a unicorns-and-flowers girl. Brian wasn't particularly romantic either, though he could fake it.

Seemed he could fake almost anything.

o   o

She was standing near the front of the Chris-Craft now, looking into the blackness, the boat rocking on the chop of the waves. She didn't have to be an oceanographer to know that they'd headed into open, rougher water. Maybe it wasn't the Atlantic, exactly, but it wasn't the Caribbean either.

Brian was still in the kitchen, washing the last dishes.

Only he wasn't. He was behind her. His hands on her shoulders. "Gorgeous, huh?"

"Gorgeous."

"I'd forgotten what it's like to be so far from anything."

"It feels good."

"Becks. You ever wonder what our life would have been like if we'd had kids later? If we'd traveled more?"

"Not really. No do-overs, right? Only one ride on the coaster. Anyway, soon Tony will be in college and we can start again. Have all those things."

"Yeah." He sounded unconvinced.

She turned to him, looked into those blue eyes of his. Thought of the first time they'd said *I love you*, how she'd wanted the world to stop forever in that moment.

But the world didn't stop, did it? It whirled like a centrifuge until it revealed every truth. Back then she'd thought his eyes were perfect. Flawless. Now they just looked cold.

If it's going to happen it's going to be now.

Still she had to be sure. She would rather die than not be sure.

He kissed her.

"Can you play through the pain?"

"I'm sorry, Bri. But—"

She dropped to her knees.

o   o

The sad truth: Kira had given her the idea when she'd told Rebecca about what had happened with Rodrigo. *I knew the best way to distract him was putting his cock in my mouth. Works every time. Men, right?*

Jesus, Kira.

Yeah, that's pretty much what he said. She'd laughed, a cold laugh that reminded Rebecca of no one so much as Brian. But then Kira was half Brian, wasn't she? She'd make a great FBI agent. Or a great criminal.

o   o

Brian responded immediately. And vigorously. And he didn't need long.

"Oh God. That was. Wow."

She wiped her mouth, looked up at him. "Where's the champagne."

He handed over the bottle.

She took a pull. Felt it hit her right away.

He looked her over. A gleam in his eyes. Hard. Unsettling.

Her leg itched.

Wait. Wait.

She handed him the bottle.

Tried to, anyway. But he didn't take it.

He picked her up and threw her over the side.

She rolled through the air, landed hard, stung her shoulder and head against the water. The water was warmer than she expected, none of the shock of diving into the Atlantic. She found her bearings, lifted her head, took a breath. Had a moment to wonder whether he would run for the helm, speed off—but no—

He jumped down. Grabbed her shoulders. Pushed her under.

So he planned to finish the job himself.

o   o

She closed her eyes against the blackness. The water churning over her, clammy, enveloping, pushing at her from every side like it wanted to take her in. Which, of course, it did. Brian's hands helping, heavy and firm, squeezing her shoulders. Pushing her down.

She let him. She didn't fight. She didn't panic. All those years as an FBI agent had drained the panic out of her. She'd been working on her swimming too. Every day. As soon as Brian brought up the trip. She knew just how much time she had. Ninety seconds at least, if she didn't thrash around. Probably two minutes.

Everything had brought her here.

Now she knew who he was. What he was.

Now she knew.

She knew, and she could act. He was stronger, he was bigger, but she had one great edge, the one that beat all the others.

She reached down. The bandage had already come off. She'd used tape that wasn't waterproof.

Underneath, her leg was unburned.

And a single spring-loaded syringe was taped tightly to her thigh, halfway down.

The trickiest part. But she'd practiced this too. Practiced in the dark. Practiced wearing goggles and weights. She wished she could have practiced with someone attacking her, but that would have raised too many questions.

Two hands now. No mistakes. She'd decided not to wear two syringes, she was worried about hiding two. Which meant she had one chance. If she dropped it, if it slipped from her hands into the deep, she'd die. She could already feel the pressure building in her lungs.

She peeled off the tape with her left hand, took the syringe in her right. Made sure she had a firm grip.

The syringe was medium-gauge, surgical grade, spring-loaded.

Inside, five milliliters of 50 mg/ml epinephrine solution. Two hundred fifty milligrams of epinephrine.

She could feel his legs brushing her ribs. He was hardly moving. He might be wondering why she wasn't fighting. Maybe he thought she was too stunned to struggle, that she was saving her breath hoping to last as long as he could.

She'd never know. No matter. As long as he didn't start thrashing himself.

He was pushing straight down on her shoulders. So her arms were free, a full range of motion forward and back. Measure twice, cut once. She made sure she could feel his leg.

She jabbed her arm up, putting the needle into the meat of his left thigh. Felt the spring release.

Felt the syringe surge into him.

Epinephrine is adrenaline. A typical adult dose, an EpiPen dose, runs one-third of a milligram. A lethal dose is eight milligrams. This shot was thirty times that.

Brian's heart attack started moments after the needle delivered the dose.

His grip on her shoulders tightened so powerfully that she bit her lip not to scream. His fingers tore at her collarbones. Then his hands came loose and he thrashed, kicking wild and helpless, catching her in the ribs, the back. She swam now, swam toward the boat, away from him. The water no longer her enemy.

She surfaced. Opened her eyes. Watched him as he moaned, grabbed at himself. Tried to swim but his motions were rough and disconnected and she knew he had only a few seconds before he sank. His eyes wild and feral. Opened his mouth, to speak maybe. But water sloshed in. The water took him.

Until he disappeared beneath it. The end he'd meant for her.

Epilogue

Till death do us part . . .

I watched him die, yes. My husband. Watched *Brian* become *him* become *it*. And felt nothing at all. I plotted his death just as he'd plotted mine.

We had that much in common.

I swam around the Chris-Craft. Climbed aboard. Stood at the prow. I could still taste his seed in my mouth. Our last connection. After a minute his corpse bobbed up in the dark water. It frightened me, and then it didn't. I watched the currents take him.

In a minute or two, or ten, I would have to make the distress call. *My husband fell overboard, I think he had a heart attack, he's not moving anymore, he's floating away. I tried to get him back in the boat but I'm not strong enough.*

But still I waited. Alone.

Truly alone, I saw, for this secret I could never share with anyone, not even Kira, especially not Kira.

The night air on me, the smell of the ocean in my hair.

And I wished I could stand there forever.

FIN